Taken to Sasor
Xiveri Mates Book 3

Elizabeth Stephens

Contents

Pronunciation Guide & Glossary

Akimari (*ah-kee-mahr-ee*)
Bed slave to a tasmaran First, though the practice is officially banned.

Dolsk (*doll-sk*)
A form of tent resembling a yurt with rounded walls and a pitched roof, often with only one smoke shaft and a leather entrance consisting of a rolled mat or leather strips.

Naxem (*nacks-em*)
A fabled beast of legend that can shift from between a true form state and into a creature resembling a massive snake. Naxem can grow to over one hundred feet long and weigh over one ton. The largest of the naxem are the mates of Sasorena and are tasked with her protection. Only a Sasorena can free a naxem. No known naxem in Sasor's history have ever been documented.

Manerak (*mann-err-ack*)
The dominant species of Sasor. Those with manerak forms can shape shift, becoming larger, taller, and stronger. Facial features transform to include elongated black eyes, fangs and slitted nostrils. Manerak generally form the warrior class of any tasmaran.

Oeban (*oy-bahn*)
A horse-like beast with six legs, shaggy fur, a long, curved neck and twin horns.

Sasor *(saa-sohr)*
Earth-like planet with moderate temperatures and high-plains landscapes characterized by grasslands, arid deserts, and occasionally, sparse woodlands.

Sasorana *(saa-sohr-ahn-uh)*
The goddess of sky and stars and Sasor's namesake.

Sasorena *(saa-sohr-enn-uh)*
The mortal incarnation of Sasorana.

Tasmaran *(taass-ma-ran)*
Manerak tribe, often formed in permanent villages. A small number of tasmaran are nomadic and typically not affiliated with the United Manerak Tribes.

United Manerak Tribes
The seventeen tribes that form the manerak population of Sasor.

To my friends in Berlin who, the moment I started this writing business full-time, made me feel like a rockstar – or even a star goddess – when I'm really just a goofy nerd a tip-tap-typing.

elizabeth

1
Mian

My breath is hot against my fingers as I sit huddled, muscles straining, body clenched. My head is bowed over my knees. I try to block out the sounds of the other slaves panicking around me, but it slaps onto my skin like the sticky stain I spent all morning applying to the alehouse fence. Flimsy, weak little posts fixed together with braided reed stalks. It hadn't looked like much to begin with and the dark, oily stain hadn't helped. Now the fence is gone and all that's left of it is the black-brown ink still clinging to my arms and the fumes caught in my hair, smelling of chicory and fear.

A huge crash in the front room makes me wince. I'm dizzy with fear and hunger and thirst. *When was the last time I ate?* The fact that I can't remember does nothing but drive an agonized pang through my stomach. *Breathe. It won't matter soon. Maybe it will help. Maybe they won't want to eat skin and bones without the flesh.*

Cold seeps in through the packed dirt under my bottom. I inhale shallow breaths through my mouth, but I can still smell the other two dozen slaves' unwashed bodies beside me, even more powerful and cloying than the smell of the wood stain. More revolting. My fingers curl into the shirt sheathing me from neck to knees, the rough-spun fabric still scratchy despite having all but disintegrated. It clings to my shoulders with threads more than fabric and makes me wonder what they will take from us when they realize we have nothing to give.

Deep baritone laughter follows jests flung back and forth in a language I don't speak. The sounds, though distant *for now*, crash through my focus and behind me, one of the other slaves stifles a sob. I freeze, wondering if *they* heard it. From where I sit near the front of the group, that one little sob rings louder than the huge reed horns that trumpeted when they arrived at our gates. Gates that didn't even stand a full solar. They carved through those gates like knives through milk.

A mutinous thud slowly separates itself from the commotion in the front room. I jump, and then I jump again when it gets louder. *Footsteps? Or the panicked tattoo of my own heart?* I know what they do to the ones they find. Everyone knows the stories. *They eat humans. Flay us alive, then boil the flesh off our bones. They make great big soups out of us.*

"They're going to find us...they're going to find us!" The panicked voice at my back makes my heart clench in my throat. I glance over my shoulder and spot Sorsha over the tops of many crouched bodies trying to stand. Her brother Mika yanks her back down, but she's fighting him. Others are trying to shush them both now, and Sorsha's face is ghostly white, even in the dark. I try to swallow but my mouth is too dry and when my lips part, I inhale dust. I clap my hand over my lips, trying not to choke on it.

Mika's hand slips when Sorsha yanks again. She careens into one of the ceramic casks we stowed away in the hopes that if we did survive, one barrel of vinegar-preserved meat, a ceramic cask of bread flour, two satchels of dried fruit and three casks of water would be enough to keep us alive until we found another human settlement, or rebuilt this one. But now I see no chance of that.

As if in slow motion, Sorsha flails, hip bumping into the cask, hand flinging out to knock off the lid. It hits the packed earth with a dull clunk that rings like shattering glass.

My gaze connects with Mirabelle's, beside me. We were both sold in the last trade to this settlement. At our old settlement, we worked the grain mills together. She was really too old for that kind of work so I took on some of her chores. In exchange, she told me fantastic stories about satellites and ships and cities and great, big bodies of water from a planet once called *Earth*. Stories she says she inherited from her mother, and her mother's mother and her mother's mother's mother's mother who actually lived on the satellite that brought us to this planet.

I don't know how much of what she says is real or not, but I always liked her. A kind woman, she doesn't deserve to die here. *Do any of us?* She reaches out and takes my hand, holding it so tight I can feel the bones through her thin skin like twigs aflame, right before they turn to dust. She smiles, her half-moon lids drooping over bright blue eyes. They frighten me, those eyes. They see everything.

Mika curses, "They heard us…"

"Can we escape?"

"Where would we go?"

"Does it matter?"

"*Is* there even a way out?"

"No, the only way out is through the alehouse."

Sweet silence settles over us. It tastes like death. My vision gets fuzzy. *Fear or hunger? Have I eaten in the last solar? The last two?* I can't remember and remind myself that it doesn't matter. *Skinny humans make for crappy stew.*

Footsteps have entered the distilling room. The weight of my own breath is heavy in my lungs. It's hard to breathe. They're going to find us and skin us and boil us. Even the kids. But maybe, just *maybe*, they won't eat any of us if the offering is poor enough, and there's no offering here more abysmal than my own...

I inhale. Exhale shakily. I squeeze Mirabelle's hand just once before letting it slip from mine. Cool air brushes against my damp rear as I rise to a crouch. My head spins. *Hunger or fear? Doesn't matter. Soon it'll all be over.*

"Mian, what are you doing?" Mirabelle rasps in a voice that's barely audible.

I don't have an answer for her as I step around the bodies in my path and reach the curtain, drawing just one little corner back. I don't look behind me as I step past it into the storage room, letting the only safety I had fall shut at my back.

Silence. No one tries to pull me back in. No one comes out to sacrifice themselves at my side. *Thud.* The quiet is punctuated by the boot. It has to be a boot because it's too heavy, too forceful, to be anything else. I've never seen one of the Sasor in real life, but I've heard stories of their size. People likening them to boulders and houses and hilltops.

The storeroom is ringed in ceramic casks. I take a seat between two grain tuns, press my forehead to the gritty, bowled ceramic surface in front of me and wait for the world to settle. Then I hold my breath as the storage room door is forced open with a short, contained crack. There's a precipitous hush at my spine, but the leaden gait of a Sasori barbarian ruins it. I clench. I focus. My head spins. I nearly pass out. *Fear or hunger?* He's right on me now.

The little hope I had, more delicate than a flower, slimmer than a knife's blade, recently whetted, is filched away from me when the heavy barrel in front of me is lifted and set to the side with surprising gentleness. Goosebumps break out over my arms as I look up into his face.

He blinks and when he does, his already dark irises darken further, becoming the shadowed side of a fray leaf, glittering mahogany, but sticky and thorned. I shudder as I quickly take in the rest of him.

He wears a leather cuirass over his right side only and has similar leather plating covering his legs, but beneath that, he is all corded muscle heaped onto an enormous frame. His skin is a lighter bronze than mine is, but his hair…his hair is shocking. It's *gold*. It drapes almost to his waist on the right side, while the left is cropped close to his scalp. Against the honey of his skin, it looks…it looks like he's a male fashioned by the sun in its own image. Pretty, even if nothing else about him is. He's far too brutal-looking for that.

He's got a scar that twists away from his cheekbone, disrupting his hairline to follow the serrated line of his ear. He doesn't have an earlobe. His jaw is hard. His eyes are mean.

Without warning, he bends down and slides a massive hand through my hair. A shocking surge of laughter rises in my chest that I do my best to choke down. He's a breath away from me now, completely bent over so that I can't see anything behind him. We're face-to-face, nearly nose-to-nose.

He smells like fresh cut grass and sweat. He smells like blood above all else. Human blood. *How many has he already eaten?* A very terrible part of me I haven't met before is pleased he smells like blood. After all, maybe that mean's he's full.

His hands comb across my scalp in a way that's nearly intimate, until the gesture changes, becoming feral as he yanks me to my feet by the hair. My boneless limbs wobble like a newborn's when he sets me down. Fear and hunger war with the adrenaline, which wins out. I plant my feet and inhale blood, wood, metal and leather and I don't exhale. Can't exhale. Not when I take in the size of the alien in front of me.

His shoulders span mine three times over and his chest is as deep as my shoulders are broad. He's three heads higher than I am, maybe more. All I know is that I have to crane my neck way back to hold his gaze. And I do hold his gaze. I hold his gaze like my life depends on it, watching as the color shifts again, darkening until it's so black I can see through it to the depths of the universe.

What a funny way to go. Shipped from settlement to settlement, never staying in one long enough to find friends or family or roots. About to be killed by an alien barbarian with the universe in his eyes because a woman was nice to me once and told me funny stories about the universe. I exhale, ready, and smile.

But when his face-sized palm charges towards me again, it isn't to reach out and snap my neck or sever my spine. The brute is reaching straight for…straight for my breast! Instincts kick in and I give the back of his hand a decisive swat.

Shock.

I jump three feet out of my skin. *I just swatted him. The cannibal barbarian alien.* I meet his gaze, hold fast and watch as the most terrifying thing of all happens. His lips…they curl up, parting to reveal a flash of perfectly white, square teeth. This cannibal barbarian alien is smiling at me.

I jerk back, stumbling into the tun. I reach out to catch it, but he's already there, one hand on its smooth side, the other holding the lid in place. He rights the ceramic slowly, without releasing me from his gaze. It tracks my hand when I touch my chest. My heart seems to be trying to make a break for it, despite the fact that the rest of me is rooted in place.

Cask settled, he reaches for my palm and, catching it, tosses it aside so forcefully, I stumble again. *What's he doing?* He's looking at my…buttons. They're giant mismatched buttons that look like the buttons on doll clothes — some that I think actually did come from the dolls' clothes of the highborn mistresses — and he's *inspecting* them with an expression that suggests they just insulted his dead mother. And then he lifts a single finger and I watch in fascination and horror as a sharp, serrated point *grows* from the tip of his nail.

A finger-long at its longest, he brings that freshly formed claw down in one swift motion and slices through the loose thread anchoring my top button. My shirt falls open to the navel, exposing my bony ribcage and small breasts. I tell my body to grab it and hold it closed — *for comets' sake!* — but my body does something else.

I slap him. *Again.*

I rocket four feet into the air instead of the puny three I shot up the first time. When I land, I forget about the shirt. My arms are frozen away from my body, waiting for him to slice me open as quickly and easily as he did that piece of thread.

I wait. And I'm left waiting.

Because he touches his cheek where I hit him, blinks many times in that strange alien way, then his lips peel back and he laughs. He laughs so full and from the belly it makes razorblades appear in mine. *I can't remember ever hearing anybody laugh like that.* And he's a barbarian cannibal alien.

I jump again, shocked, when his laughter dies and he fixes me with brown eyes that are both condescending and indulgent. He shakes his head, grabs my arm and starts dragging me towards the door.

He says something to me. It sounds playful, but he could just as easily be telling me that it's time to be disemboweled now.

"Okay," I answer, knowing that whatever he means, I don't exactly have a choice in it.

He grunts out another laughter-like snort, but just as we reach the door, I hear a light cough behind me. I freeze. He freezes. He looks over his shoulder and his eyes meet mine and when he shakes his head so slow like that, the long tresses of his wavy hair tickle my bare arm.

"Tokan, ya reesa, teka annak," he says, and though I don't know the words, all I can think in response is, *human stew, here we come…*

2
Neheyuu

"Tokan, ya reesa, teka annak," I tell her. *Close, but not enough.* I call her *ya reesa* — a title of honor when intended and, when sneered, a title of disrespect. Perhaps I use a little of both here when I call her brave. *Little brave one.* She *is* to defy me as she's done. I just didn't realize how brave until this moment.

How clever too.

She nearly succeeded in distracting me, and if not for the clumsiness of the humans behind the curtain, she would have.

I look upon the gaunt human faces in hiding. They are each as poorly clothed as she is, and so thin as to be considered starved by Sasor standards. Slaves. Reesa is certainly one, even if her coloring would be considered rare among the United Manerak Tribes.

Like raw bronze, she is both red and gold at the same time. She shines, even in this dim, dusky cellar, illuminated only by the outside light filtering in through uneven slats in the walls. Similar though our colors may be, that is where our likeness ends. She is a puny, runty little thing with bones like dried reeds and strange eyes that are dark and expressive. *Human.*

They are a species I have encountered before, though never as First of my tribe, and I feel a renewed rush of adrenaline and pleasure that my warriors and I have finally found and taken such a substantial number of them. It's considered a great success to come across a human tribe and decimate it.

Their females are compatible with our species and their males weak. I don't know if I've seen a human that was this pretty though, funny mannerisms and all. She hit me several times — a strange defense as she is without claws and likely a small fraction of my weight, with no warrior training at all — and now she just watches me, as if waiting for something.

Typically, I would have rutted her by now and there is no question — I *will* rut this little reesa. I reach out and touch her hair. I have never seen such a color before. As if it were stolen from the depths of an ocean, or stripped away from the stars. So black it's nearly blue. And even in filth, so *sviking* soft. I pull my hand back, wanting to touch it again — knowing that I *will* touch it again — but I allow her the chance to give to me what I seek. Because not even her matted hair, the stench of her unwashed and threadbare clothing, and the smudges of dirt and ash on her skin are enough to deter me.

"You want them to live, ya reesa?" I know she does not understand my words, so I show her what I mean. I lift a hand again for her breast but she angles away from me, shielding herself with that filthy rag I mean to tear from her body.

She says a word in a language she knows I do not speak. She shakes her head for added meaning.

"Tszk," I say, though why I tell her the word she needs to deny me, I have no idea.

Irritated with myself, I flit away her hand when she tries to block mine, and mold my palm to her chest, admiring the weight of her small tit as I hold it. It's larger than it should be given that I can see the bones of her chest through her skin, and the bones of her ribs. Her hip bones are likely to be just as prominent, and it doesn't matter. I want to see them too.

Her jaw sets, pupils contract. She pries my fingers away from her tunic and shakes her head just once, firmly. She says her strange alien word again.

"Yena," I answer. This is a better word. One she will get accustomed to saying to me, once she realizes who I am.

She does not break. I do not move. We stare one another down, silence stretched like a tanning line between us. I think it surprises her as much as me that I am the one to cede first. Irritated, I am ready to return to my warriors and enjoy the celebrations from battles easily won. I glance meaningfully at her people, huddling against one another, trying not to meet my gaze at all costs. Funny, that they cower when she does not.

Reaching among the mass of their bodies, I grab the first human I see. A female. I assume she is older given the shriveled way her skin clings to her frame. She has thick grey hair tied away from her face. Her lower lip quivers and she says something to the reesa that makes her wince.

Reesa looks from the woman to me. An expression of pain crosses her face. She takes a half-step towards me that surprises me again, then holds her wrists out between us, revealing their slightly paler insides. She is covered in black markings, sketches drawn all over her skin that will not fade.

We don't have this tradition in my tasmaran — no manerak tasmaran does — but on this little reesa, I find the markings beautiful. Though dozens of small patterns are scattered over her arms and shoulders, for now she focuses on thin, black rings just below her palms. The lines are straight, but incomplete. A small gap of clear skin tantalizes me, making me want to rub my thickest finger over it.

She speaks to me then in sentences. When I don't answer, she repeats what she has said, shaking her wrists slightly for emphasis. I don't understand her. Holding the older human by the upper arm, I again feel the front of reesa's chest, making it clear what I want. What is at stake should she refuse.

Her mouth turns down. She breaks my gaze and looks to the female. She is weighing her options. Deciding her price. And when, with the slight lowering of her chin, she agrees to pay it, I don't feel the satisfaction I thought I might. Her shoulders cave, making this already slight female seem almost insignificant. Swirling shadows, where before she was pure light.

I catch her wrist as she turns from me, my gaze roaming over the markings there and wondering about their significance. So many mysteries, beginning with why this little reesa denies me.

"Tszk," I tell her finally.

She blinks at me, her expression hollow. Lost. A deep chasm opens up at the sight of it, and I feel, for the span of a heartbeat, her mirrored emotions even though I have never felt them myself before. She is utterly transparent and through her, I can see and feel and experience everything. Beneath my true form skin, my manerak stirs slowly, as if waking up from a deep sleep.

I squeeze her breast roughly and say, "Tszk." I let her go immediately, dropping the other human female's arm as well. I push the older female slightly back and snap the curtain shut between us so that I can no longer see the human slaves, the alien barbarians.

Understanding flits across her face and she smiles at me just a little bit. Her teeth are white and straight in her small mouth, except for two on the bottom row which overlap. She doesn't have any fangs to speak of. Just reeds for bones and smiles in her eyes. Why does she smile at me when I have taken her kingdom? Mysteries. Interest. She has mine. And she has all of it.

Dangerous. My manerak is fully awake now, needling the underside of my skin. But I ignore it, just like I ignore any thoughts of danger in her presence. She's just a puny little human to be taken, rutted and forgotten. There's no danger here.

"Strena," I tell her. *Come.*

Her head tilts to the side, unwashed hair falling around her shoulders in matted locks. Her thin fingers still clutch her tunic together, but they no longer tremble. She glances to the heavy mud cloth hiding her humans from view.

"Tszk." I snatch up her wrist, which is thinner than the hilt of my sword and far easier to break, and lay her palm against my chest, where the leather does not bind it.

She shakes her head. I nod. Her eyes grow large in her face, making her look like she will soon transform. But humans do not have such an ability. Tszk, my little reesa is utterly transparent, totally defenseless, and mine for the taking.

I pull her roughly out of the smallest room, through the next room and finally into the main area of this shack. There, Dandena and Mor are busy brawling over a golden crown they found hidden in an ale cask. They tower over me in their manerak skins until, seeing me, they shed them and return to their true forms.

The human in my grip tugs pitifully on my arm, trying to free herself. I wonder if she's ever seen manerak before and if she hasn't, what level of terror she's currently feeling. I snort out a laugh at the thought and when I tug her forward, her heat crashes into me. *Warm. Feels nice.* I'd think her feverish if she showed any other signs of it.

She stands frozen on her feet, one hand locked in mine, the other clenched at the V of her throat. She's staring straight ahead and I follow her gaze to Mor. He licks his lips and takes a step towards us, his focus locked on her in a way that makes my skin prickle. My gaze narrows on him, sharpening, becoming lethal. *Becoming manerak.*

"What do you have there?" He says with a cocky sway of his hips. The crown forgotten, he takes a step forward. His gold hair, stained red, flutters in his wake.

"Found her hiding," I answer with a grin. Anticipation rears its restless head. My manerak opens up inside of me like a mouth.

"Was she alone?"

"Yena," I lie for reasons unknown. My fingers twitch.

"Then there is only one to be had."

"Yena."

He wipes the back of his hand across his mouth, smearing the blood of dead humans across his face. "I'd like to have her."

I laugh. "Come on then."

Mor's thick eyebrows fade back into his skin the moment the challenge is accepted. The corners of his mouth stretch back towards his hairline and I feel my pulse hammer, manerak unreasonably thrilled as it expands and elongates in response.

The little reesa jolts beside me when my shoulders begin to swell and my thighs thicken and lengthen. Already hunched over her, soon I tower. The uncomfortable wooden roof is no match for my manerak's size. It brushes the top of my head and then my shoulders, forcing me to either stoop or tear straight through it. *Do it.* But then the roof might cave, crushing her beneath it. The thought nags, and then disappears like vapor.

My manerak sizzles beneath my skin, aching with a tension that feels distinct from the way it usually does, though I'm damned to put my finger on it. *Eager.* I feel my brow bone flatten, my eyes expand, my pupils slit. My fangs come down to shield my teeth and I only release reesa when I feel claws claim my all ten of my fingertips. From between my forked tongues, I issue a hiss.

Mor charges and though he is one of my better fighters, he is still no match for me. I am First of my tribe for a reason. I wonder if his heightened bloodlust is the reason that he issues this challenge — one we both know he's going to lose — or if it has something to do with the slave beside me. Can he also see her radiance? The thought grates. My manerak seethes and spits.

She jerks wildly now, back slamming into the nearest wall. My forked tongues loll out of my mouth, tasting the air she creates. Something sour and sticky, like the tart rathra leaves used by our woodsmiths, and beneath it something sweet that makes the first wave of bitterness possible to overcome. *Blossoms. The nectar of the carnivorous egra flowers. Beautiful. Dangerous.* I release her fully and with a gentle push against her thin chest, guide her behind me so that I can have both hands free when I meet Mor in a clash of thunder.

There are no weapons in a challenge, so he swipes for me with his claws. He is a smaller male, both in his true form and in his manerak, but his strength lies in his speed. He spins away from me as I block and comes in below my arm, attempting to switch around me and bring himself closer to reesa.

My manerak call reverberates deep in my chest, causing my whole body to tremble with its might. I bring my foot down on his thigh, stopping his path. I swing my fist around to meet his cheek, drawing blood. He rises with a hiss, claw raking my ribs as he spins out of my grasp.

My manerak skin stretches, becoming broader with the tangy scent of his blood — and mine. The other warriors back to the very edges of the room, dragging casks — mostly ale — that they want to preserve with them. I attack first this time, moving straight through a flimsy piece of wood these humans once used for a table.

My shoulder connects with Mor's sternum. He tries to absorb the blow, which is his second mistake — after issuing challenge in the first place. I take him down and together we fly through the nearest wall. We land on the sand outside and before he has a chance to blink, I score his chest twice more.

"That's three times to blood, brother," I rattle, my voice distorted as I am still manerak. I push myself off of him with a grin.

He punches the packed sand angrily but still takes my hand when offered. "Challenge is to you, warrior," he says.

I yank him to his feet and feel my manerak begin to settle — at least, until I return to the shattered shed and see Dandena, Rehet and Ock closing in on my prize. I open my mouth and my manerak hiss is so deafening that I can't speak through it.

They turn, surprise etched onto their true form faces. Dandena breaks the quiet. "One blooding to three, in favor of First?"

I nod once. Dandena applauds and holds out her hand to take her winnings from the other two, who curse. I don't care for their bets, and break through the semi-circle they've made surrounding reesa. She stands with her spine still welded to one of the flimsy wooden walls. She's managed to find a knife and holds it out in front of her with two hands. She clearly has no idea how to use it, but it does look sharp. Very sharp. And it has an emerald jewel in the hilt.

"That isn't *your* blade is it, Rehet?" I balk, laughing hard enough to make my belly ache.

The others laugh too, while Rehet at least has the decency to grumble softly in shame, "She is quicker than she looks."

I inhale pride, and exhale relief when I push the males and Dandena away and see that reesa is unharmed. Her wide eyes turn up at me and I glance at the blade in her fist, shaking my head. Misunderstanding my reaction, she jumps in the air, unfurls her fingers and holds the knife out to me. She is shaking. Afraid. *She is unused to manerak.* I hiss as I feel the bones in my body contract and scale, my fangs retracting, my face slimming, my rattle dying, my shoulders narrowing, until I am finally in my true form once again.

Settled, I reach for her hand, hesitating a breath away from her fingers when she jumps, this time half a head into the air. I grin and she seems to like this because half of her mouth quirks. She still offers the knife between us but I wrap my fingers around her fingers.

"Tszk," I tell her. She won it off of Rehet. She has earned this. I press the blade back to the center of her chest and turn to the others, eager to get out of here — eager to get *her* out of here, away from the males and into my own private dolsk. "We ride now."

3

Neheyuu

I call a halt well before the second sun has set even though it is not uncommon that we ride well past the setting of the third sun, or even through the lunar. But after our victory, my warriors deserve an easy ride, to crack open one of the many barrels of ale we took from the human hive and celebrate a successful raid. Of course.

It has nothing at all to do with the fact that even though she has ridden well, I can tell that she is struggling and I am worried. Tszk, it has nothing to do with that. Nothing at all.

Most warriors will sleep out underneath the stars, except for the injured, couples, and some female warriors who prefer to have dolsks as a sign to the males that they are not interested in being bothered. Other females and most males are content to couple with one another in plain view.

As First, I always have a dolsk erected for myself for war council, to receive messengers, and to store the prizes from my conquests, however it's rare that I use it to sleep. I prefer to sleep under the stars, to rut and revel, and this lunar is no different than those.

I pack away my looted gold, debrief with Preena and Dandena — my Second and Third — give the order to have reesa and the other stolen humans fed, and leave her behind in my hastily constructed, dome-shaped dolsk with the rest of my belongings and treasures. Now, I sit within sight of it on a reed mat before an open flame. Dandena twirls the forgotten crown Mor relinquished on the tip of her finger while Xi and Xena — well, Xena at least — laughs loudly at the spectacle.

A short ways away, Rehet prowls the pen where we keep the human females we've taken. Ock and several of the others look on as well. Preena barks orders at the guards to remain vigilant and for the rest of the warriors to remain calm. It will be difficult to keep them contained. A number of them already marked females.

Erkan, even now, sits crouched outside of the pen, staring in at a female with dark skin and wavy hair that falls to her hips in an expansive cloud. An interpreter from our tribe will need to explain to her that though the three-day sessemara — the joining ceremony — has not yet taken place, Erkan has marked her already as a warning to other males. He plans to claim her for himself and, even if another male does show his interest during the sessemara, I know Erkan's fighting abilities. He will not lose. But will that be enough?

She cowers away from him, holding her skirt together. It was likely torn when Erkan marked her. These humans are very fragile and I cannot forget my human's frightened — *disappointed* — display when I suggested to rut her. Part of me had been *offended* that she had been unwilling — as First of my tribe, females have always been available to me — but now, looking upon Erkan's female, I wonder if they are not *all* conditioned to fear sex. I wonder distantly what could have caused such fear when their males are all insignificant, shriveled things without even manerak skins to wear in defense of their families.

"I don't think I've ever seen our First think so hard," Dandena laughs.

Mor glances meaningfully at my tent. "His mind is in that human's cunt. I know that's where mine is." My manerak hiss echoes loudly across the fire and tension bleeds across my chest. A grin splits Mor's face then and laughter picks up. "You're acting like a manerak in rutting heat."

"Better a manerak in rutting heat than a manerak licking his wounds. How many was that again today? Three from me alone?"

Mor snorts. "I'd have won in a fair fight and you know it."

"A fair fight?" I balk. "What wasn't fair about it?"

"Her scent. You had more time to let it fuel your manerak rage than I did. Give me a few more moments in her presence and I'd have met you in size. It was simple…weight distribution that was off."

"Weight distribution?" Xena laughs. "First is three times your manerak size. Get lost."

"And what is this about her scent fueling his manerak, hey?" Ock butts in, taking a seat to Dandena's right. "That's not a thing and you know it."

"You didn't see what I did. He was larger than his usual form, faster and more aggressive. Like the Naxem of old." A reverent sort of silence falls as we think of the Naxem and the stories we were told as children. Said to be warriors born of the stars, the Naxem were the first beings of the Sasor. They walked the cosmos only in their manerak skins before Sasorana — the goddess of the stars — chased them down from the heavens and gave them their true forms. Every warrior fights now in tribute to the Naxem and their creator. Sasorana rules and guides us all.

I grunt my disbelief and roll my eyes, ignoring the incessant pull plaguing me to look at my tent, hoping for a glimpse of her shadow against the light within. "Psh. Don't fuel tall tales. I took the female as a prize. That's all. I didn't want to see you pawing all over her." I gulp down ale from the wooden chalice clasped in my fist. I've had several and though this human swill isn't anywhere near as strong as Sasori spirits, several cups in and I feel my muscles relaxed, my eyelids heavy.

The others laugh, all except for Dandena who watches me with an eerie, knowing quiet. "What?" I bark at her. She is one of a select, elite few female manerak warriors. I trained with her since we were both kits uncovering our manerak skins for the first time.

She gives me a wry grin and leans back onto her elbows. She is not an attractive female, but she has still bedded most of the males here and has received offers of interest from neighboring tribes. I can see the appeal, but to me she has only ever been one of my warriors, my Third, and one of the prides of my tasmaran.

"He's not wrong. You *were* larger than your usual size. And even now you disgrace yourself. You know we don't take prizes. We stopped taking prizes long ago. And you males with your tiny cocks and even tinier brains can't seem to remember that we aren't supposed to be marking the females anymore either. Not until we return and they've been taught our language. You remember how that's backfired.

"Females of these…*softer* tribes don't like the marking. Some don't even see that the males have demonstrated to them superior combat by defeating their clansmen," she says in disbelief — a disbelief we share. But she isn't wrong.

I remember the fear and the water that surfaced in my female's eyes when I wanted to rut her. Even though she has seen me compete for her in combat, I doubt very much that makes any difference to her. Strange.

"Remember, Neheyuu, or have you forgotten what your time was like as Third of the Nevay tasmaran?" Tszk, I haven't. And I take it Dandena has not forgotten her time there either. It was the tasmaran that made and shaped us. That trained us as warriors. "In our time there, we raided three human settlements and the females that were marked almost all viewed it as a violation."

The thought makes me uneasy and I squirm in my seat as Dandena continues, "And those females that could not understand even *after* assimilation into our tribe left for new tribes at the first sessemara that they could. We lost valuable females to the Hox, Sessena, and Pikora tribes because of you stupid men and your cocks. The Neheyuu tasmaran, as small as we are, can't lose any. Not least of all because of what it does to the males who lose their marked females." Unease turns to dread.

She's right and the other males around the fire know it. I know it too. And yet, the accusation in her gaze still remains. Because I am accused. "I am First. And I have not marked her."

"Then you plan to assimilate her?" Dandena raises an eyebrow in challenge. The flames of the fire flicker harshly over the square lines of her face, and the stern set of her chin and jaw. Her half-shaved hair spills onto the reed mat below her and glimmers like rippling water in sunlight.

"Yena."

"Then why not keep her with the rest of the slaves in the pen?"

I hesitate to answer. When I do, the words come out stretched. *Because they are lies. Because she is ours.* Ours? I shake my head quickly and stutter, "Because we aren't yet returned to the tasmaran and she isn't yet assimilated. As of right now, she's still a slave."

"And what will she be when we return to the tasmaran?"

I groan, "What is with the questions, Dandena?"

"We all saw the way you looked at her. All of us in the shed."

I don't know what to say, so I just shake my head. "Unless you question my judgment and would like to issue challenge, then I suggest we end this conversation."

"I question all males' judgment when it comes to females," she says and the others laugh. She smiles at me from across the low flames. "But tzsk, I do not issue challenge."

I smile in return. "Speaking of cocks, you'll be happy to know then that when we return, she'll be my akimari." An akimari was a *gentle* term for a bed slave. They were banned in name many turns before, but in practice it is still common for the First to keep an akimari to warm his pallet, and in my case, for females to vie for positions as my akimari in the hopes of being selected as my Sasorena, my mate.

"And aren't you forgetting Tekevanki?"

In truth, I had. She is my current akimari, or at least that's how she sees herself. The daughter of a revered warrior in our tribe, and one of the first who joined my tasmaran, she sees herself far above the status of many. Not wishing for my irritation to play across my face, I only smile. "Tzsk, of course not. I plan to entertain them both."

She rolls her eyes. "Males disgust me."

"I don't remember you saying that last lunar," Ock says, nudging her hip with his foot. The warriors around us roar with laughter and I feel weight lifted from me as the conversation flows away from the human female I've hoarded away in my tent to keep all for my own.

The lunar thickens and I feel the effects of the ale sinking in. Unlike the Sasori spirits, which kick the unsuspecting hard and fast in the skull, this human ale is a dangerous drug. It creeps upon me slowly, keeping me lucid until I realize I'm wavering where I stand. My warriors all point up at me, rocking with a laughter that is undeserved because I can tell in their slurs and their squinting, bloodshot eyes that they feel it as well.

I stagger off to the outer edges of our camp and take a piss among the tall grasses. On my way back, I weave among thickets of thorny bushes. Dried, crackling grass stalks crunch beneath my feet. I walk carefully and with purpose, not bothering to lace up the leather bindings. I've drunk too much and my skin feels hot from the day's ride. I long for a bath, knowing the best I'll get is a soggy towel in a bowl of water. But maybe I can have her wash me…

The thought makes me salivate and my feet fly forward with renewed purpose. My cock is lengthening and by the time I arrive at my dolsk, not bothering to wish my warriors a hearty sleep, it's as stiff as a leather rod, my sack weighted below it.

Aching. Ready. *Mark her*. I shake off the intrusive thought and take a few steps forward into my dolsk until I spot the mound of her hair swirling around her shoulders like a brush bush. She's got her meal spread out next to the reed mat she's lying on, a smear of food on her cheek and another on her nose, and she's got a piece of purple grain loaf trapped in her fist. She holds it tight, like she's afraid to let it go.

I shake my head, but my smile wavers a little. She looks so small and vulnerable in her threadbare clothing against the bare mat on the floor. And I packed so... negligently, all I have here are the linen sheets I stole from the human camp to warm her with. I frown a little deeper as I fan one of those linens over her, then crouch at her side and begin extricating the bread from her hands and clearing away the place beside her.

The instant I've got all her food scraps gathered into a little bowl, which I set aside, she jerks up, still gripping the knife she'd won earlier. Sleepily, she lists back and forth and blinks several times until she focuses on my face, my hands, her food bowl. Her whole face falls.

She says something and points at the food scraps with the tip of her knife. I don't understand what she wants until she drops the blade and reaches for the mashed bit of grain loaf I took from her. I block her hand and she makes a terrible little mewling sound. I meet her gaze. Watch her cheeks flame with emotion her eyes do not betray. Embarrassed, she looks away, and in her embarrassment, I am ashamed.

Another tray of food had been set on the opposite side of the domed structure for me, but I already feasted with my warriors. Even if I hadn't, I would have given it to her anyways. She can't look at me like that. *So dangerously.*

The dazzling array of foods are piled high on the board and her lips part at the sight of them. The choice slices of meat, the softest breads, the richest cheeses and smears, fruits from her fallen village, and even a decadent sweet from a village we once raided in a land far, far from this one.

A smile stretches her face and when she wipes the back of her hand across her cheek, she only smears more dirt across it. She reaches for a piece of meat, but then hesitates. She meets my gaze and retracts her hand. She grabs her breast and gives me a questioning look that, combined with Dandena's words looming so large in my mind, make me feel as if I deserve to be flayed.

"Tzsk," I say.

Her smile returns. Surprised by her trust, I watch the eager way she chews and swallows, moaning on every third bite in a way that makes my blood flow harder and faster. I coerce her into drinking from my skin of water and when she finishes that, she belches and drops back down onto the mat on her back, utterly exhausted.

But just before she closes her eyes, she does two things: she gives me a soft, sad little smile, and she takes a piece of bread from the tray, balls it into her fist and crushes it to her chest. She curls around it like a child might a toy and returns to sleep. It makes my bones ache watching her like this, knowing that I have never known a hunger like hers.

My manerak fangs start to protract and score the insides of my true form lips before I catch them. When I do, I also realize a deep rattling fills the entire dome and I can't seem to quell it. I lift my hand to my chest and bore my fingers into my skin, hoping that the pain will distract from the crazy feeling in my chest and the mirrored madness in my groin. Nothing has ever hurt so much as seeing her eat. Nothing has ever felt so good as seeing her eat.

I meant to check on her and leave, but I find myself going to the bowl of water set aside for me and lifting the rag from it. Water drips through my fingers as I wring out the cloth, cool but not cold. I wonder if the fabric is too rough for her skin as I return to her and drag it gently over her cheek. It reveals a strip of skin that glitters. It shocks me. I thought I'd never seen her *exact* color before, but now I'm sure of it.

My breathing comes harder. For a number of reasons. The first — I want to see the rest of her. The second — I can't believe she's hidden from me by filth. The third — How'd she get like this? I want to know who failed so miserably in caring for her. *Maybe there was no one. She was a slave.* But even then, how was she left unclaimed? Who would not want her?

She sleeps so soundly that when I roll her onto her back, she doesn't wake. Her shirt is split down to her ribs and I don't have the decency not to look. In fact, I pull the sheet further down. Her breasts are fallen to the side. I like the shape of them. Little and round, studded by dark tips the perfect size to lave with my tongue. *Tongues…*

I take the rag to them as a surrogate. *Take her…mark her…* I shake my head, dispelling these strange, alien thoughts encroaching on my own. I won't take her when she's this tired. I'll wait until the morning. For now, I content myself with watching color roll out across her flesh, bright and beaming. And even though my cock is fully erect and the pressure on the underside of my leather armor is uncomfortable, I am not desperate to do more than this. At least not yet. For now, it is enough to watch her glow.

By the time I've finished, the water in the bowl is so thick with grey I can't see the wooden basin below. Her skin, on the other hand, shines like liquid gold. Her face, free of dirt, is unblemished perfection. The color glides down, equally uninterrupted, over her neck, her chest, her breasts, her ribs. Too thin, those ribs. But it doesn't seem to matter to my body. I still want to kiss each of them. *Now.* The coming solar. As soon as the day breaks and she is rested.

Tearing my gaze away from the clean strips of her skin, I set the bowl aside, extinguish the last of the lamps and slide onto the mat beside her. Tossing the linen blanket over us both, I tuck her into my side. Her head rests on my chest, her arms spread out to either side. Complete vulnerability. One that could be mistaken for trust.

I snort at that. Not gutting me with that knife she stole off Rehet had nothing to do with trust and everything to do with her own sense of survival. At solarbreak, when she wakes, we will see what she thinks. All females soften after a good rutting. I inhale deeply, smiling at the thought. And at our stink.

Between her unwashed odor and mine we make for a ripe pairing, yet it doesn't matter, because her skin is soft where I touch her outer arm. *So sviking soft.* I work my fingers down to her hand and, reaching it, gently open her fist and extract the bread, crumbs now. I dust them off of her hand and twine her fingers with my own. I exhale and let her heat wash over me.

Against the tiny shell of her perfectly rounded ear, I whisper words I know she cannot understand, but that echo through me like a vow I know I will never forget, and never be able to undo, as Sasorana is my witness. "You will never go hungry again, little reesa," I tell her in the quiet dark.

Even though she is lost from me in Sasorana's realm of dreams, she sighs just a little deeper and releases a light moan that sounds like pure happiness. Even in sleep. Such deep satisfaction is dangerous, but what is more dangerous is what it does to me. It makes my chest expand, my hearts thump hard, my cock thump even harder.

My manerak feels dangerous too, swirling so close to the underside of my true skin, as if it wants her too. *I do.* Not now. Not yet. Patience, I tell it all the while knowing that with such imminent danger, I should shove this little reesa from my tent and put her in the pen with the other slaves. *Tszk. Never.* But I don't want to and I don't move.

My manerak quiets now with the promise I've given him. Sleep eventually settles over me, and as it does, all thoughts of danger fade away, forgotten as quickly as they'd come. They are replaced instead by the tickle of her unwashed hair against my chin and throat, and the weight of her callused hand in mine.

4

Mian

I wake to the sensation of being completely warm
— maybe for the first time in my life — cocooned in
bliss. It feels so good my whole body tries to recoil from
the world because this dream state is too fantastic. But
reality is persistent and sleep loses its teeth.

I wake with a frown, my forehead wrinkled, my
nose too. My eyes are squeezed shut tight. My ears cock
forward at a strange sound filtering in through the
muted haze of sleep. Laughter. *Someone is laughing at me.*
And they are close.

"Dogo de gamo rek, reesa," the voice says against
my cheek. Distinctly male, I don't know what he said but
that I should probably be offended by it.

"Mmph," I grunt and slump back down against the
heat. It's not as soft as it should be, that heat, but rather
firm and smooth in some places and in others, hard and
scratchy. I'm all tangled up in the warm sensation. It
wraps its steely arms around me, tangles with my legs. I
don't mind. Not one bit.

"Dogo de gamo rek."

"Shh," I answer back.

There's more laughter but luckily, the heat resettles itself, growing stiller and calmer and closer too. It's pressed up against my back and I can feel it snuggling even more deeply against me, shifting, sliding, gliding… gyrating.

My eyelids fly open. There's something *huge* at the seam of my behind, burrowing between my cheeks and prodding at my tight rear entrance. In a panic, my hands fly down past my waist, finding fabric. I'm still wearing clothes but the voice is rumbling something foreign in my ear and when I gasp, the warm weight at my side shifts on top of me. I'm pressed onto my stomach and a massive hands appear on my waist, pulling up on my shift. Searing hot flesh flops against my lower back and I know the weight for what it is. It's a *cock*. And it's a huge, straining erect one.

"No! No, no, no, no, no, no." I'm totally awake now and I start to flop on the floor like a fish, hoping to dislodge him.

A little space comes between us and the cock slows its descent over my rounded rear, coming to settle itself just in the crack of my behind. The softest thing I've ever felt stretched over the hardest thing I've ever felt. And though I've never been *had* before in that way, I'm still no stranger to cocks.

He says something again, but I shout over him, "No, no no nonononono!"

That does nothing at all because in the next breath, he lowers even more of his weight onto me and arches over my shoulders and head. His cool breath fans my ear and I'm shocked by the sensation of hot, sensual kisses to my earlobe and jaw but when he draws near my lips, I manage to free my hand from under my own weight, reach up and slap him. He jerks. So I slap him again.

The back of my hand connects with his face awkwardly, palm against chin, his teeth clacking against my knuckles. He curses and draws back so I know I've caused him at least a little discomfort and I feel great about it. At least until a low rattle starts up behind me and I remember what happened the solar before in living color.

By stars, he's a snakeman! I watched him turn into a snake creature — thing! How was that even possible? I have no idea, all I know is that, like snakes, his member is very long and that, like snakes, I want it far away from me.

I try to hit him again, but he grabs my wrist and forces it to the ground. His weight intensifies on top of me and I choke, starting to feel panicked and in my panicked state I shout the only word I know in his tongue. "Tszk!"

He freezes. "Tszk?" He says, as if daring me to repeat it.

"Tszk."

The rattling grows louder, deafening. I can't hear myself think over it! But then I know I've won when a gust of cool air claims my back and a curse fills the quiet. Furious to have been woken up — like *that*, no less — I scramble upright. I spin around, tucking my legs beneath me, and see him kneeling at my side. I start at the sight of his eyes, which are terrifying because they're big and bulbous and stretching towards his hairline, and in my panic, I slap him a third time.

What is wrong *with me?* Whatever it is, seems to be a permanent affliction because even though his face is transforming in front of me — widening and lengthening to make room for his mouth full of fresh fangs — and I'm fully prepared to be devoured alive, I still don't break his gaze.

"Tszk." The voice is strong. *Is it mine?* I can't believe it.

His huge snake head suddenly snaps back into focus, his eyes narrowing and his fangs retracting into his mouth. He lurches away from me and issues a harsh command to no one because there's no one here but me and he knows I don't understand him.

He paces back and forth between the many items crammed into this dome. There's a table but no chairs. It's made out of a heavy dark wood that I don't recognize, but it matches the wood of the chests stacked around the curved walls. Huge wicker baskets and ceramic casks that I *do* recognize take whatever places the chests don't so that he's left pacing in a space barely more than his own height.

He's also completely naked.

I flush, heat ravaging my cheeks. I can count the males I've seen naked before on one hand — all of them in situations just as precarious as this one. *But I wiled my way out of those just like I'll wile my way out of this one.*

I concentrate on looking anywhere but him — he doesn't need the encouragement — and instead, focus on the chests around the room…and the baskets…and his broad shoulders streaked with dried dirt, the muscles in his back flexing, the mirrored indents just above his high, taut rear. The length of his hair flutters over his left shoulder down to his sculpted pectoral in glittering tangles. His ribbed abdomen flows out below that. His thighs are so thick…as thick as my waist but it's the *thing* between them that's got my attention and won't let it go.

Hard, huge and jutting up into the air, it's the length of my forearm and twice as thick around and right now, it's straining towards his abdomen, curving up so that the gigantic mushroomed head almost meets his belly button. Horror follows swiftly on the heels of dread. *He means to use that thing on me.* Me, *who's never had a man* like that *before in my life.* Covered in veins that seem to be straining, I wonder if it has its own pulse.

"Tekana xiva ged," he says, seemingly to me since there's no one else present.

My gaze jerks up to meet his. Essences of snake person ripple over his body, never fully settling. He rumbles out a rattle and repeats the command he shouted before, this time with even greater urgency.

Forcing myself to be bold, I lift my chin. "Shout all you like, I still don't understand you and I'm still not having you near me with that…thing."

I cross my arms over my chest and don't dare look at *it* again, forcing myself instead to meet his gaze, the color of black river stones and just as slippery. Right now he's focused entirely on my mouth, to the point that I feel self-conscious. I don't touch my lips though. I don't want him to know how affected by him I am. *So what if I've got dried drool on my chin? He can just deal with it.*

"And why don't you put on some pants?" When he just stares at me blankly, I gesture to my legs and emulate putting some pants on. "Pants," I repeat. "Put some on."

"Dima kena andono kan." He reaches down and fists his member ferociously, like it's the enemy — or I am, and that thing is what he'll use to do battle against me.

I throw my hands in the air. "For the sake of the comets! I'm leaving and don't you dare try to stop me."

He issues his fearsome command at the same time that I turn towards the tent flaps, which is incidentally, the same moment that they slash open and a female steps inside.

She's got medium brown skin, a shade darker than mine and a few shades darker than his. Her hair is almost as dark as mine, but surprisingly, her tight, frizzy curls are coiffed in the same style as his long, golden locks. The hair on the left side of her head is shaved close to her scalp to reveal a scar identical to his, while on the right side, her hair falls in shoulder-length braids that brush against her light, leather armor every time she moves. Several weapons are attached to a sling she wears around her back, the most impressive of them being a dark wooden staff that's nearly the same height she is.

She stops and, following his fixed stare — the one trained on me like a throwing axe to its target — she tosses a dismissive glance my way before asking him question. He answers. They do this back and forth a few times before the female shocks me completely and approaches him. She has one hand on the shoulder of her armor and with her other, she reaches for his…thing!

Does she intend to pleasure him right here? Now? At his command? And in front of me? A stranger? I may be a slave, but I still have my dignity and I don't want to be a part of this in any way shape or form. I have only just started to turn away when the snake male snatches her hand from the air and flings it to the side, sending her whole body cantering into one of the casks, a light grunt punching out of her. She rights herself and mutters curses as she closes the distance between them. Instead of reaching for his cock again though, she shoves her face right up to his and they shout back and forth at each other.

Startled enough to make me jump, I force myself not to cower. *I never did at the slave auctions and it helped. I never got sent to the bad settlements. I never got the very bad owners. Except for the ones who thought my determination would be something fun to break. But I didn't. And they couldn't. No matter how many times they laid hand to me or how many meals I was forced to skip.* So I hold fixed, planted where I am with my arms crossed over my chest even though I'd rather be out of here and with the other human slaves I saw them round up. Out under the sun among the high grasses. Anywhere else.

The female warrior turns to me and says, "He wants me to ask you why you don't want to rut him."

I jump back, spine connecting with one of the baskets stacked up against the curved edge of the tent. Goosebumps tickle the backs of my forearms. *Did she just speak my language?* "Did you just speak my language?"

"I just spoke your language, yes." She squares her shoulders to face me and when she speaks, does so in an accent I can't identify even if the language is one we share. She also sounds annoyed. "I'm half-human. My mother was taken in a raid and her human tribe spoke a similar dialect. Now, I'm asking you why you don't want to rut him."

I want to ask her more — Where did her mother come from? How many settlements have been taken? What will happen to us? — but the male grabs her roughly above the elbow and jostles her a bit. He says more to her and she fires back, just as roughly. I like her. Comets, if he isn't terrifying, but she doesn't take any of his shit.

Instead, she takes a step towards me and I tense, remembering quite suddenly the dagger he let me keep. *Where is it?* I glance around and find it next to the reed mat, in between some scattered crumbs of bread. I dive for it and clutch it in a fist.

She glances at it as if it were a cup of hot, sour milk I've offered her and repeats, "He wants to rut you."

I huff, exasperated, "Yes, I know that."

An expression crosses her face, something akin to surprise. Slowly, like she's speaking to a child, she says, "So then rut him."

Has she lost her mind? I want to ask her, but then remember she was the female who just offered herself to the snake male so crassly. "*No*," I repeat with emphasis, my shoulders clenched up by my ears. "Absolutely not. Never in a thousand eons."

He must know that word — he's heard it enough by now — because his skin rattles and shivers and he grows another three heads taller. It would be kind of funny, him stooping over, his gargantuan hands planted on narrow hips, but I'm too rattled by this interaction to laugh. His voice comes out more hiss than vocabulary, but the female still nods when he's finished speaking and says, "He says that if you don't rut him now, he'll throw you out into the pen with the other slaves."

"*Finally*. That's where I've wanted to be this entire time. I'd like to see the other humans."

She hesitates, mouth twitching, but never quite realizing its smile. She speaks to him and with every word, the bones beneath his limbs bend and shift. He's like a lidded kettle on a stove, screaming out its warning second before it bursts.

"He says you stink. That if he puts you out there, none of the males will want to mark you."

A wound successfully delivered. *Unwanted. Disgusting. Slave. Shame. Hunger. Thirst.* He cannot know how deep the well goes, but he's added another droplet to it all the same. I fumble, flustered, and hope he doesn't see it.

I take a steeling breath and say, "Well you should tell him *he* stinks. None of the females will want to mark him either."

A sharp clack of laughter fires out of the female's mouth that blunts some of the sting of his words. The male shakes her by the shoulder with hands the size of plates and tipped by rough black shards. She jerks out from under his hold and continues speaking to him, gesturing more wildly now with her hands. And when she finishes, he surges up even higher. He nearly has to bend at the hips, so as not to rip the dome clear off its foundations.

He opens his mouth and a rattling roar comes out of him from some place deep. So loud, I drop my dagger and slap both hands over my ears and close my eyes and when I open them, the female is suddenly standing between me and the snake male.

She releases her fighting staff, spinning it in a fluid motion so that it rests horizontal to the ground, suspended between her two hands. She looks so strong, but the snake male is...well, *whatever he is*, and I've seen him fight another snake male before his same size and win. She's no match for him.

I dive to the ground at the same time the snakeman barrels forward. She swats him several times, delivering blows that would have wrecked me, but they barely glance off of him and serve to make him even angrier. Releasing another charged roar, he grabs her staff and shoves her whole body back, sending her crashing into the same chest he threw her into before, only this time, she topples it. The chest opens, spilling pieces of black glass and white pearls and other fine treasures all over the ground. Once the wealth of the human settlement, now scattered among blankets and linens, they look like the discarded toys of children.

The male charges towards the female, but she rolls out of his path. He doesn't stop though, and reaches straight for me. I have almost no experience with a blade, but I grab it and score a diagonal line across the center of his palm. His blood bleeds blue, but that doesn't surprise me. Through my skin, my blood appears blue too.

He knocks my hand with the back of his and sends the blade flying. He grabs my upper arm and drags me into the cavern of his chest. His other hand grabs my shirt and pulls hard enough to scatter the remaining two buttons. I close my eyes, brace my palms on his chest.

"Tszk!" I shout.

The rattling coming from his chest is stronger now. Thickening the air. He looms over me like a shadow at sunset, comically large, distended and not true to form. *He can't possibly be real. None of this can possibly be real. I can't possibly be here right now.* But he is and it is and I am and there's nothing else I can do but stand my ground and repeat, "Tszk." Barely more than a whisper, it's a word whispered with meaning.

His snake self shudders and expands, then shrinks and then, becoming large again — the largest I've seen it — he thrusts back from me and charges the dome's only opening, shattering it as he exits.

The whole front half of the dome collapses inward and I quickly scramble to the woman, stuck akimbo underneath the fallen chest. I heave it off of her and grab her under the arm and together, we manage to make it to the back of the tent where she cuts an opening for us in the hide. Scrambling out, we plop ungainly onto a pile of dried, dead grasses in a tangle of human linens and limbs.

"Are you alright?" I say first, but the female slaps the ground, throws her head back and laughs instead of answering. She rocks back and forth on her bottom, gripping her knees, slapping her thighs with loud thwacks, and I'm easily infected. I start to laugh too, and I don't even know why. All I know is that it feels good.

Her chestnut cheeks are high, making her eyes appear as slits on her face. She wipes water from below them. "May Sasor help me," she finally wheezes, "I never thought I'd see the day."

"The day?"

She shakes her head and ambles to her feet, checking her leather bindings as well as all of her weapons. She slaps a leather buckle back into place on her shoulder with force and the sound makes me jump. My laughter dies, but I'm still grinning in response to her smile as she stares down at me for longer than a moment.

Finally, she offers me her palm. I take it and as she pulls me to my feet like I weigh nothing, she says, "Reesa, I think we're going to be friends."

5

Neheyuu

They come at me in waves. Hard, fast, hungry. I'm hardly conscious of them. My manerak form is dangerously pure, the haze sharpening my sight, even as it casts the world in a green-grey hue. When I cut, I don't feel their flesh. When I bleed, I don't feel it either. But the cut on my hand. I feel that as if it were a fatal wound.

Ordinarily, I wouldn't work my warriors this hard a day after a raid. Ordinarily, I'd let my warriors rut themselves into oblivion, sating the manerak among us in the way our manerak forms like most to be sated, and ordinarily, I'd be among them, cock deep in the female I'd chosen. Whatever female appealed to me best. Rutting and humping and moaning until my manerak form went quiet. Until everything went quiet. Until I found that sweet calm in between wakefulness and dreams.

But today is not an ordinary sviking day.

She said tszk. To me. What was she thinking? And what has she done to me? My manerak is out of control, raging against my warriors, raging against my true form. It doesn't want to sleep. There is no peace. There are no dreams. There is only a cutting need. Which means that for my warriors, there is no playing this lunar. No rutting. No reveling. The dolsks will not be broken down. We will not move on this lunar. We will stay and stand and fight so that they can be reminded that I am their First and I am in control. I am in control. *I am in control.*

I deposit my twin swords in the weapons dolsk. Glancing around, a sour taste fills my mouth. What is a tasmaran without its weaponry? Ever since our previous weapons keeper joined with a high-ranking Sessena warrior, our weapons have been in this cruddy state. Gilded in rust, rather than blood or gold, they dishonor me and my entire tribe.

I will need to pick a new weapons keeper as soon as we return. I roll my eyes and snap the dolsk flaps shut behind me with enough force to startle the warriors nearby. Just one in a thousand and one things required of me upon our return. Part of me doesn't want to return and leave the thrill of battle behind. The bloodlust. Fighting savages with even greater savagery. Decimating villages. It is the way of the Sasor. How it has always been and how I was raised.

My mother and father were fearsome warriors. They trained me day in and day out. It is because of them that I became the youngest First in Sasor history, and because of them that my tribe will be the biggest and strongest to have ever honored Sasorana. *Our place in her realm will be eternal.* I frown. No manerak has ever entered Sasorana's realm with rust-covered swords. With a flick of my forked tongue, my manerak issues a hiss between my true form's teeth.

I stamp my way between the mats and notice that the warriors avoid my gaze as I walk to the river. *Good.*

Part of me feels guilty. *Don't.* My manerak doesn't care. My manerak…my sviking manerak. More talkative than usual, I can hear what he wants but I have no interest in giving in to his demands. He is sated. He *should* be sated. I fought for him the entire solar and now it is time to wash, eat and to rest so, come solarbreak, I can lead my warriors on the six-solar journey back to our tasmaran village.

I feel confident as I bathe, rubbing cold river water roughly over my skin. The brush of the air is warm and dry against my cheeks, far more arid here than it is back home. I straighten against the stiffness of my limbs. There is no akimari here to rub them, no helpers to bring me a bath of steaming water, so this river bath will have to do. In the same river where Chimara took the slaves to wash earlier. *She washed in that water…*

I hiss, silencing my manerak as I return finally to my dolsk, shoddily repaired. It is still warm inside, despite the slit in the rear of the tent Chimara made that lets in the cool air, colored twilight. I wade towards the mat and the tray of food that has been laid out for me, but when I reach the center of the dome, I don't walk any farther. *Can't.*

My manerak whispers through me, causing the air around my body to vibrate. I can feel it, like an extension of me. I can feel *everything,* and yet I feel everything through the filter of *her.* It's her scent. It clings to the air. Sweat and dirt, an unwashed body, but even as tarnished and muddied as it is, I can't escape the underlying notes of vanthia seed and palm, the spicy nectar of a begua blossom desperate for its next kill. *Dangerous.*

Where is she? My manerak form demands me to know. I take another step forward, against his will, and glance down when I step on something hard and cold. Her knife. Well, Rehet's knife. Scattered lazily amid purple crumbs.

An image flashes in my mind. Her body curled around the bread. Her eating every piece of food I offered. And then an image that didn't happen, but that I want to see happen with every burning fiber in my body. Her eating directly from my fingers. Like a mate would. I balk at the thought, take another step towards the platter of food on my mat, but I can't sit. I can't reach for it.

She will never go hungry again. That was the promise I made her.

I bark out a laugh that eases the pain in my chest as I arrive at a decision. Tszk — an acceptance. "Alright," I shout to no one but myself. Myself and my manerak. As I stand, I feel a warm current rush through me at his approval. The air stops vibrating. All is settled.

"Sviking female," I curse, and when I realize I'm still naked and that she does not like to see me naked, I curse again, grab a linen sheet, and head off to find her. Sviking female… *Our sviking female.* The thought stumps me for a moment. Whose? My manerak laughs quietly without giving an answer.

Fires spark the freshly fallen lunar. Though I pressed them hard this solar, only half of my warriors are asleep. The rest sit gathered around fresh fires, speaking and laughing quietly among one another. Dandena catches my gaze as I walk. Seated between Ock and several other warriors, she glances in the direction of the slave pen, at me, then back to the pen and laughs so hard she topples over backwards. I can't keep the answering grin from my own expression. I pull my manerak forth and grin at her with all my fangs. Her gaze genuflects, but she still laughs softly and shakes her golden mane which twinkles in the firelight.

The slave pen sits on the edge of our camp and I frown as I arrive before it. Though none of the males *except* for ranked warriors — myself, Preena and Dandena — are allowed to touch the slaves, the other males still swarm. A muscle ticks in my cheek. Erkan I expected to be hovering over his female, but there are *six* males here now, circling like carrion. And then it hits me. Her scent. Just a touch of it twining its spindly fingers with the breeze. The begua blossom spice is a drug and I fall face first into the delirium.

My feet miss their next step. My manerak shimmers beneath my true form. My fingers flex around the tray in my grip, the tips of claws already visible shooting out of my fingers. *Shred. Them.* The grey-green haze flickers at the sight of Mor and Rehet. I want to take the heavy nolla wood platter and rip it in half, then take the shards and impale their skulls with them. *But the platter is for her. Protect it.*

I pass by Erkan kneeling on the ground and staring into the pen as if his mind is inside, and he's somehow lost it. *Not his mind. His hearts.* I frown harder. But what is strange is that his female seems to be the only one whose expression doesn't scream terror. Even though he marked his female, *against* Dandena's advice, his female is sitting a little closer to the wooden fence posts than the others.

"First," Rehet barks, "what are you doing here?"

"What are *you* doing here?" I counter, trying to be civil. *Eat them. Tear them to pieces. Feed them to her.*

My manerak snarls and Xi, Xena, Rehet and Mor share an uneasy glance between them. Mor's eyebrows bunch together. His gaze is on the platter balanced in my left hand. "Scoping the females, obviously. I heard you discarded the little reesa already. I'm trying to decide how you managed to get her onto your mats and what I'll have to do to get her onto mine. She's glaring at me something fierce."

He called her reesa. That name is ours. The only thing that helps me suppress the urge to kill is the platter in my hand. *Her platter. Hers. I'll kill anyone who says otherwise.* The rattle of my manerak is audible to anyone near the pen.

I swallow hard, forcing down the threat of my manerak and choke, "The female won't be sharing your mats this lunar or any other." A surge of vicious protectiveness rises up within me, eclipsing every other sensation. Every other sound. Thought. Scrap of reason. This isn't me. *This* isn't *you.* But why? I've never felt protective over a female before, let alone a *human.* She isn't even of Sasor. *She is borne of the stars. She is better than you.*

Thoughts fall away as I arrive at the fencepost. My gaze snares on her form. She's curled on her side, legs tucked, propped up on one arm. And Mor was right. She *is* glaring. Lances bolt from her expression. Her lips are twisted in defiance of her face's perfect symmetry. What in the svik has Mor said to her?

The spell of my anger lifts like the wings of a bird and I bark out a laugh. It can't be helped. Her gaze snaps to mine and I can't stop grinning as her expression changes, becoming even *more* hostile, though I hadn't thought it possible.

I forget about the males at my back. The anger and rage and desire to hurt and to kill has all but faded. My manerak is almost satisfied, switching back and forth in my chest like a lazy cat.

I crouch down against the fence and lower the platter beneath the bottom rail. "The food is for you," I tell her.

"Food?" She says, in *my own tongue.*

I reel. "You speak manerak?"

She pulls up on the collar of her shift. It's the same shift all of the slaves wear and it's clearly too big on her. It gapes around the neck, giving me a clear view of her collar bones and the long lines of her neck. *Dangerous.* She's bathed. The darkness does nothing to repress her glow.

"Learn manerak," she says, and her heavy accent causes our hard, guttural language to lose so much of its bite. It's damn near *cute.*

"Chimara is teaching you?"

She considers, then nods. "Chimara, yena. Chimara human," she tells me, as if I might not know.

I grin. "Yena. Chimara is half-human, half-manerak." But cursed. She has no manerak form. She will never amount to anything in our tribes, even if she is an exceptional warrior.

Reesa doesn't say more. Her gaze is fixed on the food, but she still doesn't take it. Annoying girl. I take the grain loaf in my hand and extend it towards her under the bottom rung of the fence, feeling like a sviking idiot as the wood from the enclosure brushes my cheek.

I am First of my tribe and here I am, begging at the door of slaves. I should just jump the posts and go in, gather my female and take her back to my dolsk. But somehow, all I really want is for her to come to me.

"Food," I tell her again. "It's for you. Come here and eat."

After several long, grueling moments, my stubbornness is rewarded. She edges closer to me, off of the mat she's been given. I notice the humans don't have blankets and my reesa cowers against the next gust of wind. Is she cold?

I bark an order to Rehet and Mor to find spare linens to cover the females. It doesn't escape my notice that Erkan's female already has one. Shame washes through me that Erkan is treating his female better than I am treating mine. She *isn't* mine. She's just a slave, and will soon be just another faceless member of our tribe. *You know nothing.*

I shake my head, annoyed at how the conflicting thoughts enter my mind, finding no resolution.

"Food." She's reached the pen wall and is holding onto the wooden beams. Her gaze is pinned to the board of food at her feet and she licks her lips.

"Food." I push the tray even further towards her. "Eat."

She glances over her shoulder, points to her eyes, then points to the others and I understand. She feels shame to eat in front of the others. And I put her in such a position. I snatch back the wooden board and as she looks at me with grief in her big, brown eyes, I stand, reach over the top of the pen and grab her under the arms. I lift her up and when I set her down at my side, I take the platter and her hand and begin dragging her away from the pen, towards my dolsk.

I'm surprised when I meet no resistance — at first. But when she misses a step, I look over my shoulder and see her watching Erkan kneeling there, looking so very lost. And then my reesa says to me, "Rita, Erkan. Erkan, Rita." I don't know exactly what she means but I can guess when she lifts her hand — and mine — and gives it a little shake. I didn't realize, but our fingers are laced together.

I don't even hesitate. I know what she wants, and I give it to her. She can have whatever she wants. Whatever she needs to get me to the point that I'm feeding her. I *need* to feed her. "Erkan," I bark hastily. "Take your female. Find a dolsk. She is yours for the lunar."

Erkan doesn't blink. He doesn't move. He doesn't hear me at all with how fixed his gaze is on the female in the pen.

"Erkan," I bark.

He flinches, face tilting my direction after a moment. Shadows do nothing to make him look less lethal. His upper lip is curled away from his teeth in a snarl and the muscles in his neck and shoulders are straining.

"Did you hear what I said?"

"Tszk." His gaze then jerks to the female in my grip. His growl grows louder. My little reesa pulls away from him, recognizing the danger he presents. Does she think I can't protect her? I humph at the thought. She has seen me fight for her against a warrior equal to Erkan's size. *Or perhaps, she does not trust you to. Does not trust* us.

I jerk her forward and coil my long arm around her frame, securing her to my side. Erkan's growl intensifies. I feel my own manerak rattle in response. "I said go to your female. Take her for this lunar. And every other. And do not dare make threatening gestures towards my female ever again." *My* female? Svik! Why did I say that to him? Luckily, he does not comment on it.

Instead, he stiffens. His manerak shifts and shudders, threatening to break forth. "But I...it's never been allowed, not in any of the other tribes."

He is new to my tribe and more apt to question my authority. I don't like it. "Well, I'm allowing it and I am your First. Do you issue challenge over this?"

"Tszk. Tszk, I do not. Thank you." He rises to stand and lurches towards the pen, but I call out to him, remembering Dandena in that moment.

"Erkan," I say, "Dandena reminded me that tribes have lost females before because of our aggression. They are not manerak and do not understand our ways. Be careful. And when you have finished securing your female, tell the other males who marked their females they may do the same, so long as the females are *willing*."

Understanding flits across his features before his chin jerks down in a short bow, and then jerks again a little deeper. I watch a moment longer as he leaps the fence in one lithe movement and advances on his female. She stiffens, but does not edge back as many of the other squawking females do.

Erkan drops to one knee and bows his head deeply, forehead nearly grazing the sands at his female's feet. He speaks to her reverently, making her oaths she cannot understand. Yet the little female surprises me, because when he offers her his hand, she offers her own and lets him close his fingers over hers and drag her to her feet.

Beside me, my reesa grins. She watches the pair with water in her eyes that alarms me, but she does not seem to be unhappy as she watches Erkan guide his female to the enclosure's only exit.

She asks me a question in her language. I shake my head, failing to understand. She mimes an angry expression and beats on my chest with one of her fists in a gesture that means nothing to me. Frustrated, I make my way back the way I came, weaving between the fires and the mats and the warriors until I find Chimara. She is lying on her side, speaking with one of the males when she sees me approaching.

"First," she says with a start.

I wave my hand when she starts to stand and instead, gesture to reesa. "Ask her to repeat to me what she was saying about Erkan."

A short communication takes place, then Chimara says, "She explained that before we took their village, Rita was joined with a repulsive human male. He beat her often. Rita was terrified and hurt after Erkan marked her, but apparently the human females view it as a good thing that Erkan fought Rita's previous male and killed him brutally. Apparently, he tore off one of the bastard's arms and then speared him in the throat with the bones."

She laughs at the imagery. I can't deny it makes me smile too. Erkan. An otherwise uninspiring male — who knew he had it in him? "Reesa says it brings the females satisfaction — I heard them talking about it earlier as well. And it brings Rita satisfaction. What concerns your reesa now is that Erkan will be violent with Rita."

My voice is all snarls when it shoots out of my throat. I have to remind myself to loosen my grip on my reesa's waist so as not to crush her. "Did you explain to her that no male here would ever beat his female?"

Chimara does and I hear reesa exhale at my side. She looks up at me, a little doubtful, but hopeful. As if daring me to challenge such a truth. I can't control the direction of my hand. It lifts and sweeps her cheek in the most tender gesture I've ever managed. Just softly enough to feel her heat, but light enough not to chafe her skin with my calluses.

She inhales sharply, and then she smiles, seemingly satisfied.

"Tell her that Erkan has specific interest in this Rita female, and will do whatever he can to win her affection. He wants her for his Sasorena, his mate." Chimara translates and I feel a surge of hostility rise at my next question, though I try to suppress it against my manerak's better judgement. Down. *Tszk.* "Ask her now if she ever had males who beat on her."

I grind my teeth as I await the translated response. "She says that she's a slave. That it's common practice to beat slaves."

I close my eyes and hallucinate returning to that human village, resurrecting each of those males and killing them all one more time. A dozen more times. Instead, I peel my eyes open, drinking in the sight of her. I sweep her face with my hand, searching for bruises or more serious damage. She says something to Chimara and when I reach her neck, she captures my wrist, halting my progress. She shows me the insides of her wrists.

Chimara says, "She says she was beaten, but never violated sexually."

I blink, surprise tamping my anger. It only lasts a moment. A small thought has triggered in my mind and it grows larger and larger as I drag my thumb across the gap in the black band tattooed across her wrist. I can feel her pulse beating frenetically beneath her bronze skin. *Gorgeous.* As are all of her marks. *I want to devour each of them, lave my tongue across their smooth surfaces, see if I can read their disparate histories through taste alone.*

I lick my lips. "This mark. What does it mean?"

Chimara's face echoes a shock that I feel as she says, "She…the human females with complete tattoos — bands that go all the way around their flesh — they are the ones who have had sex before. If the tattoo is broken then they are…untried. My mother's settlement didn't have this custom, or a ritual of tattoos. Apparently, each of hers tells a story of the master who owned her. The fewer the tattoos, the higher the rank within the tribe. She…reesa was a slave so she has many, but she says she never let any male complete her bands."

My head spins. Untried females are unheard of, not at this age. Manerak need sexual release. Sex is natural. Common. We grow up with it as a facet of life, and many couplings happen even before the twelfth turn of the second sun. Adolescents discovering one another as they discover their manerak forms. That is what happened to me.

The female I took after my first shift had been my sparring partner then, now joined off to the Wenna tasmaran's Fourth. We lusted after one another like dogs in rut, but only for that brief period of time. At least, on my side. When the joining ceremonies happened, I never thought to vie for her. I wonder if she thought I would.

"Reesa is asking that you allow her to keep her band broken. She is deeply fearful of being taken."

My body stiffens and I yank reesa closer to my chest. She stumbles. "How many males tried to take from you?" I snarl, arching down towards her face, lips separated by a gasp from her lips.

She shrugs. Chimara says, "She says she didn't count."

I ripple again and am about to ask Chimara more — *I want details* — when reesa licks her lips. "Tszk," she says, but there is meaning beyond the word. She takes my free hand — the one that is not still balancing the tray of her foods with a pendulum's precision — and places it on her chest.

My cock bucks, but I do not betray any other motion. No movement at all. I don't even breathe. Everything hangs on this moment and what I do next. I should put her back in the pen. I *really* should put her back in the pen. She is untried *and the others know it* and she doesn't want to be tried, not by me. *Make her.* I should push her away and keep her at a distance. If she doesn't want to be rutted madly like an animal, then I have no use for her. *Fool.* Her body is all I'm interested in. *Lies.*

My hand squeezes around her breast. Small. *And perfect.* I rattle though I don't mean to. My manerak is full of surprises and part of me knows I should worry that I've lost control over it — the first sign of a strong leader's doom — but I can't seem to muster any concern for anything but the worried, wounded look on her face that she tries to cover up with scorn and hostility. Such a tough little thing, my reesa. So brave.

I drop my hand from her breast. "Tszk." I brush my thumb over her wrist and though it pains me in a way I can feel acutely in my loins, I repeat the word again.

I can see the disbelief in her eyes, but I want to end this discussion before she shames me in front of my warriors. I swivel the tray of food between us. "Food," I tell her.

"Food." She smiles. Her fingers dart forward furtively and she takes the grain loaf, as I suspected she would. She bites into it immediately and takes a seat on the ground. She crowds onto Chimara's mat and glances up at me, then pats the place beside her.

She has no idea that the warriors in this circle — all of whom are awake now and watching me — are well below my rank and would be honored by my presence here. But it doesn't matter. Reesa asked me to sit, so I will sit. *Whatever she wants, reesa can have.*

The warriors stare at me with wide, shocked eyes as I laugh and drop down beside her. I cross my legs and sidle up close enough that the outside of her thigh and mine press together firmly. *Svik, her skin is so smooth.*

"Food," she says to me and she slides the tray closer to my legs. Her gaze glances to the erection tenting my linen covering and I feel her entire body flush with renewed warmth. It stirs my erection even more.

The platter is heavy, laden with enough food to feed me twice over. Spiced nuts, thick cut battar beast, a flank of endrea steak, dried fruits and even fresh berries that remind me of the ones I saw growing wild near the river outside of the human settlement, soft curd and salted fish, and of course, grain loaf.

She holds a piece of battar towards me and I fight the urge to coil my forked tongues around her fingers and pull the meat free with my lips and teeth. My cock bobs once more at the thought. I take the food from her fingers with my own and pop it in my mouth. I wonder if her scent has infected the meat because it tastes better than usual.

"Food," I say proudly.

She giggles and hands me another piece of meat. *It does taste better.* It tastes so good I'm going to choke on it and die and when I die, I'll be satisfied. I clear my throat, unsurprised to find that the warriors around us are all seated upright now and that they've brought out a cask of Sasori spirits and are passing cups around.

Reesa chokes on her first sip and the gathered warriors laugh. Concern flickers through me until I hear reesa laugh too. Her head falls back and she exclaims, *in our language,* "What is that?"

She turns to Chimara, but I get there first. I want to be the one to teach her everything. *We will be. She is ours.* My thoughts flicker dangerously to her sexual inexperience and then veer quickly away from it. My manerak is somehow both seething and yet, grateful just to be near her at all. *Dangerous.*

"Hibi. It's for warriors. For manerak. Not for you." I reach for her wooden cup, but she quickly brings it to her lips and gulps down some more of it.

Coughing. Choking. Laughter. Hibi. Those in our circle number near nine now, more than twice their original number. Someone stokes the nearest fire, sending embers up to meet the stars. Smoke is pulled away from us by Sasorana's grace. I plant my arm behind reesa's back so that her heat falls under my shadow.

The male across from her, Ofrat, asks her if the humans have fermented drink. "Ale," she answers in her own tongue, before saying, "No strong. Water." She makes hand gestures and we understand her meaning. "Hibi strong."

"Yena," Ofrat says and I bristle at the indulgent smile he gives her. He's just being friendly, I tell myself, but it doesn't help. *I hate it.* What I hate more is the smile she gives him. Shy and cute. Does her temperature rise? *It better sviking not.* My manerak is eager to challenge, but before I can, she turns her gaze my way.

"Water?" She asks in between bites of grain loaf and I feel my chest puff out with pride that she seeks sustenance from me. She knows I can provide for her.

I nod, hailing one of the warriors for a fresh water skin. When he returns, I take it from him, rather than let him hand it to her. "Thank you," she says to me. She also thanks him. I don't like that either, but I am pleased to see her drink and then immediately continue in on the food.

Chimara says something to reesa in her human tongue that I ask her to repeat. "I told her she'd make herself sick eating like that. She's finished over half the tray *and* the females have already been fed."

I frown. "Reesa, eat slowly," I tell her.

"Slow?"

She stares at the tray longingly and for a moment my manerak and I war. He wants to give her the tray to do whatever she wants with, but I know better. I hand her the hibi drink and pull the tray farther from her.

"No food," I tell her. Her eyes widen and my manerak seethes, furious with me. I suppress him. Down! *Tszk!* "You'll get sick."

Chimara explains and Reesa's hand goes to her stomach. Chimara nods. "Reesa doesn't believe me. She doesn't think you can get sick from eating too much."

Across the circle, one of the warriors pretends to vomit all over the warrior seated next to him. Reesa gasps. Several warriors laugh, me among them.

Chimara speaks to her more and she gasps and clutches at her stomach again. "Food make sick?" She says, unapologetic in the way she speaks up, butchering our language. It's cute. It's brave.

I nod at her. "Food make sick," I repeat.

Reesa bites her bottom lip and adjusts the shoulder of her shift. It's fallen down again, revealing the smooth curve of one shoulder. A few small black tattoos decorate it. They're beautiful, square shapes and swirling lines. But I don't like that she has been branded by other males. Other masters and their marks. I want her to be branded only by mine. *Tszk, it is we who should be branded.* I balk at the notion. I am First. My manerak is absurd. *Fool.*

"Food…solar?"

I shake my head, returning from wherever place the hibi had taken me, and ask Chimara to translate. "She wants to know if she'll get food on tomorrow's solar."

I speak through clenched teeth. "You insult me. I am First of this tribe and I do not allow my people to go hungry."

Reesa and Chimara speak at length, but I cut in, cupping reesa's chin to claim her attention. *So smooth.* My manerak purrs. I lift her folded legs and drape them over my lap. She tenses but doesn't pull away. I don't let her.

"Reesa, you will never go hungry again. You will eat every solar until you are a fat woman."

Chimara translates with a smile. Reesa listens to the end before barking out a laugh. She laughs so hard, she doesn't notice me lift her up and reposition her in my lap until it's too late. Her back is to my front now, my legs spread around her. I lay my arm across her chest when she tries to rise and anchor her against me, taking her weight. I feel her heat flare and bend down to whisper in her ear.

"Reesa," is all I manage to say. I don't even remember what else I was going to say…

She looks at me over her shoulder, blinking very quickly when I don't back away. Our faces are very close together. I touch my forehead to hers, stroke her cheek with my cheek. She doesn't know what to do with her hands and keeps them folded softly in her lap. But I see how they fidget. I reach around her and smother one hand beneath my palm, bringing my palm against her thigh on the outside of her tunic. I want it off.

"Reesa?" She says, and I wonder if she's trying to distract me.

"Yena. Reesa."

"Tszk. Mian." She points to her own chest and I almost explode right then and there. Who knew hearing a foreign name could make me feel like a boy? My cock is rock hard against the warmth of her ass.

"Mian," I whisper and the word sounds reverent, even to me. I stroke her cheek. "Mian, ya reesa."

"Reesa?" She points to my chest.

"Tszk." I grin. "I am Neheyuu."

"Neheyuu." She smiles. Sasorana help me. My name. On her tongue…it does something to me. Something dark and pure. Like a single drop of ink against bleached sands. Perfect and wrong.

"Say it again," I huff, barely contained.

She just smiles at me, confused. "Again. Dena. Mian, Mian." I point to her, then I point to me. "Dena."

Realization dawns on her. "Neheyuu," she says. "Neheyuu reesa?"

I laugh and shake my head. "Tszk. Mian is you, you are my reesa. Chimara tell her what reesa means."

She does and immediately after, Mian glances away from me and bites her bottom lip, managing to look five turns younger. It takes every ounce of self-restraint I have not to kiss her, and it's because of that self-restraint that I decide not to return with her to my dolsk that lunar. My manerak can't handle the proximity it so desperately craves. Or maybe I can't.

So instead, I wait for her eyelids to droop and her body to grow heavy in my arms. Then I lay us down on the mat one of the warriors provides me. I unwrap the linen from my waist and throw it over us both, and even though my warriors talk on through the lunar, their low voices and laughter chiming close, I close my eyes. I am sucked into the smell of her skin, vanthia and starlight. Darkness swirls around us as I clutch her too soft, too thin body in my arms, and my manerak's contented, rattling purr soon drowns everything else out.

6
Mian

I've had it.

It's been four solars. Four solars practically welded to the infuriating male's side. While he *has* kept his promises to keep me fed — I've never been full like this before, or rather, I've never experienced fullness before of *any kind* and I'm not sure what to do with myself because of it! Not to hunger? Not to thirst? What is this new existence? Is this living? — as well as not to mount me, he has been doing his best to convince *me* to mount *him.*

A not-so-accidental caress on the outside of my thigh while we sit wedged together atop his beast — a six-footed creature with shaggy fur and great big horns that I've learned is called an oeban — holding my hand when leading me around the camp, little nibbles and kisses along the back of my neck when I sleep…

It's infuriating. *But only because it's working.*

I feel flushed and a little frantic as I explain all this to Chimara as we approach the entrance of the pen where the human females are kept. "Don't worry. I know you don't want to be taken by any male but your future mate." She rolls her eyes at that. She may be half-human, but her views towards sex are all manerak. "I'll do my best to help keep him away from you, though I can't make any promises." The solar is bright and she uses her forearm to wipe the sweat beading along her hairline.

"Thank you," I say, a little more irritably than intended. I glance around at the females gathered around large, dark wooden trays laden with foodstuffs. Half shoot me friendly smiles and as I return their uncertain enthusiasm, my belly growls. So determined to get away from Neheyuu this solar after waking up to find his hand on my behind, *and my body wrapped around his willingly,* I forgot to take from the tray he provided me. I forgot to eat. *What in the comets is happening to me? How long will I be able to resist him?*

Chimara brings two fingers to her lips and whistles loudly, "Hivet! Togo dogo bai kath!"

A few moments later, another female warrior jogs up to us carrying a tray, this one even fuller than those the other females eat from. *You will never go hungry again,* I think, and I can't help but wonder if this is his doing. Even though I left him at solarbreak with no promises to return. With promises *not* to return. He'd just laughed and told me that I'd be back.

Chimara and I take a seat and in between bites of the squishy bread I like so much, I say, "Do you have to ride with the warriors?" I'm starting to really like Chimara. She feels…almost…like a friend. I've never really had a friend.

She shakes her head, sucking out the innards of a yellow fruit in one magnificent slurp. I giggle at the lascivious sound it makes — and the even more carnal sigh she issues afterwards. I reach for the other one on the tray, eager to try it.

"I'm all yours," Chimara says, taking the fruit from my fingers and turning it around so that I see the correct opening. I peel it back and lift it to my lips. Sweet, but also bitter, Chimara laughs when I put the gourd back onto the tray unfinished. "First wants me to watch you."

"Watch me?" I mutter, incensed. "For what?"

"No idea. He just said — and I quote — keep an eye on reesa." She shrugs. "But whatever. I'm happy to do it."

"You are?"

"Are you kidding?" She raises an eyebrow. "You have got to be the most entertaining female I've ever come across. First is behaving all kinds of erratic because of you. He says he won't rut you, but then follows you around like a manerak in rutting madness. He says he won't mark you or join with you, but treats you like a spoiled little Sasorena."

I nod, blushing a little at the thought. Neheyuu's mate? I cast the notion aside. Males of worth don't walk with skinny slaves at their side. Males of worth rut skinny slaves behind closed doors. I wince at the direction of my own thoughts even though they're nothing new. Nothing I haven't heard from other masters before.

"But I will tell you now," Chimara says, pointing the yellow fruit at me as she picks up the husk I discarded. She slurps out the rest of it greedily and only when she's finished, tosses the shell over her shoulder. "I'm no match for First. Not even close. So, your best defense is going to be you. Now let's keep working on that vocabulary. You're making progress, but let's focus for a moment on the things you *really* need to know."

"I thought I learned the things I really need to know." Thanks to Chimara, I'd been getting around alright in the short communication between myself and the other manerak I'd met so far, including First. Single word sentences, lots of hand gestures, and a few basic verbs like "want" "have" and "go" are mastered, as well as a plethora of vocab. I can't quite string them all together though. At least not coherently.

"True. You are learning like a fish. Or whatever that human expression is. But we need to get some of the other basics down. The good stuff. Like *begda na*."

"Begda na," I repeat.

Chimara laughs and nods. "Good. You're a natural."

"What's it mean?"

"It means fuck off."

I'm momentarily surprised, until I realize the importance of this phrase and it's utility. "Begda na," I repeat.

"Perfect." She pops something small and round and red into her mouth and bites down with a grin. "This is going to be fun."

I return her grin happily. "It already is."

My mind is swirling with all the new words and grammar I've learned by the time we break. Chimara and I eat with the other human females beside the river, apart from the males. Several of the human women are already stripped down and wading into the water. The rest are soon to join them.

It was Rita's suggestion to bathe and when she removes her shift, I see why. She has evidence from her previous solars with Erkan still staining the insides of her thighs and the thatch of pubic hair between her legs.

And it's *gold*. The same gold as their hair. The sight of it makes me blush. Quickly, I turn away.

Dusting off her hands, Chimara laughs and tosses her spear to the riverbank where it lands among the high reeds with a swish. "You truly are a virgin." She sheds her outer armor and splashes into the water. I shove one last loaf of that purple bread into my mouth and am still chewing as I follow after her.

"Ooph," I cry as I wade into the river up to the knees.

It's cool against my baking skin and I cup my hands, flinging water into the air as I shower in it. Several of the women laugh and repeat the action until the entire sky is full of water droplets, like raining diamonds.

Moments later and we're joined by more females — manerak this time. They undress down to their skins and looking at them, I can't see any noticeable differences between their true and our human ones, short of their above-average height.

Varying shades of brown skin, all the way from cream to onyx. Deep-set eyes. High cheeks. Flat foreheads. Most boast the same glittering golden strands that the males do, but some have hair on their heads and between their thighs in darker strands of copper and mahogany. None so dark as mine though. *I wonder if this makes me unappealing? I mean* more *unappealing…* I frown at the thought, then dismiss it. Even if it is the case, I can't do anything about it.

One of the women approaches us and starts making conversation with Chimara that I struggle to follow. Something about their warrior training and another tasmaran called Nevay — a name Neheyuu and some of the others have mentioned. Turning her attention to me, she says something to Chimara about my size and I frown, self-consciously covering my belly, which is far gaunter than her muscular shape.

Chimara grips my shoulder in a way that's firm and confident and speaks slowly enough that I'm able to understand the salient bits. "She was a slave. Human slaves are treated poorly. She is a warrior already for having survived at all."

My heart does a little dance. *Kindness. I'm not used to it after so many human settlements.* The female nods many times and somehow the cutting lines of her face manage to soften. "You...strong soon. I am Dandena."

"I am Mian." I thrust out my hand. She only stares at it until Chimara explains that it's a human tradition. At this point, Dandena grasps my hand firmly in her own and gives my palm a strong shake that jolts my whole body. "I'm honored to meet you."

She grins and speaks rapidly before Chimara hushes her by lifting both palms. "...too quickly. She knows our language...only these solars..."

Dandena huffs out a breath, clearly irked, but diligently, she begins again. "You are welcome here." She places her hand on her chest, and then another on my own in a way that fills me with renewed warmth. *Affection. Like kindness, this is an entirely new word.* "We... no slaves. You will...find place and...work hard...like everyone else. No more. No less."

"She searches for a mate," Chimara says teasingly.

Dandena shudders and rolls her eyes. "A *male* mate?" She says, aghast at the notion. I nod and she groans, "Why? ...large, stupid creatures..."

I laugh so hard I choke and Chimara responds by pounding me on the back, which only makes me laugh harder. I straighten up and am just about to agree with her sordid opinion of males, given those I've met so far — well, the one — when shouting draws my attention up the hill to the handful of males standing there slack-jawed.

"You see?" Dandena shouts, exasperated. She turns and cups her hands around her mouth as she shouts up at them, "Go back to…" From there, the meaning eludes me though I can only assume she's shouting insults. The males are undeterred and eventually, the one called Mor crunches through the bright purple and green reeds and starts down the knoll towards us.

"Ugh. Xena, Reffa, on me." She bursts forward, but Chimara grabs her arm.

Grinning, she shuffles through the water, taking long, awkward steps. "You stay…I…"

"…not manerak," Dandena retorts.

Chimara frowns and I begin to understand the conversation. I feel my heart pinch on her behalf. *She's not manerak. And she never will be.* "I…fight…manerak."

Dandena bows slightly, having recognized the insult. "Yena…" She says, "no dishonor." Shock. Even though Dandena is a ranked warrior and Chimara isn't manerak, she still apologized? Humans would not do this. Not in the settlements.

With a nod, Chimara makes it to the river bank and grabs her staff from her pile of armor. She and two other manerak females start up the hill, weapons in hand, totally nude and dripping with water. Several of the males retreat, but Mor stands his ground and the females don't hesitate to take their staffs to him.

His skin shimmers and he starts to transform, but doesn't, except for his enlarged hands. It leaves him swatting at the females and their staffs like a belligerent oaf and I can't help but laugh.

"Such idiots," Dandena crows, throwing her hands in the air before planting them on her narrow hips. "Look…them standing there…" She mutters more under her breath that I don't even try to follow.

I lower down onto the river floor and let the cool water glide up over my shoulders. My knees sink into the muddy sand below. It's soft against my skin. Little pebbles and rocks and shells clatter against my thighs. I think I feel the fluttering tail of a fish or two, and tilt my head up towards the sky. I drop my hair into the water, wishing I had a wide-toothed comb or some oils or ideally both. It will take more than water to detangle it, but I still try.

The trees that line the riverbank make gentle creaking sounds as they sway, and their sparse foliage casts shadows over some of the women as they splash and speak in warm tones among one another.

I lie fully on my back and let the current carry me into slightly deeper waters, wondering about the strange turn of events that brought us here to what feels, if only in this moment, like some shard of paradise. Where masters, hunger and thirst don't exist. Where friends do, and where a mate might. *Where desire* does.

I swallow hard, thinking of Neheyuu and the way his face looks in the depths of the lunar, where light cannot touch him. Chimara is right. He *does* treat me like I'm something worth treasuring. I just wonder how long all of this will last… And then a startled shout wrenches me back upright.

A scream flares to my right and the human women bathing together disperse. Thrashing as they are, I don't immediately see what's wrong until, mid-cry, one of the women disappears under the water's surface. Sunken like a stone in fresh water. *Or grabbed by its depths.*

"There's something in the water!" A woman shouts in our human tongue. An instant later, she's gone too. In the blink of an eye, the clustered women are half their original number.

"Mian! Strena!" Dandena shouts at me in between the orders she relays to the other warriors present. I can hear Chimara also say my name, but the moment I kick towards the shoreline, something grabs me by the ankle.

I gasp, breath wrenching from my lungs, as the thing pulls me under. Water sloshes over my head, taking the warm air and sunlight with it. I thrash and claw and bite and pull as charring heat hits my spine and a mirrored heat fills my lungs. I can't breathe, but the pressure of arms circling my body kicks my adrenaline up.

I fight back ravenously and when I open my eyes, I see his murky outline. Deep brown skin. Hair spun of gold and sunlight. *Neheyuu? The lascivious brute!* Momentary hope, crushed, when I realize it isn't him. There's no laughter in this male's eyes.

As he tries to reposition me, his fingers slip over my calf and I manage to wedge my knee up to my chest and extend my leg fully between us, thrusting him against the riverbed and me, to its surface. Breaking through, I shout for help, but mine is just one voice among many.

Bodies are shooting up and down while water sprays and froths. The female manerak warriors are now armed, fighting nude on the banks of the river, while equally naked human females scramble up behind them. A few of the males that I do recognize, like Mor, sprint down the hillside while the golden heads of other males — ones I don't recognize — surface from the water all around me.

A scream to my right tears my attention to a female trapped in the arms of one of the males. *Stars…it's Rita.* She screams for Erkan as the male who holds her carries her and another human woman away. Though they are both fighting, his hold is fixed and his jewel-colored eyes blaze. With a grunt and a splash, he kicks off of his feet towards the center of the river where the current is at its strongest and in no time, he's too far for me — or anyone — to reach him.

All of the males are employing the same tactic — grabbing females and letting the river do the rest. A few of the intruders are armed and are giving chase to human females scrambling towards the shoreline, but the manerak females are a formidable force and hold them back. I know that I'll be safe too, if only I can get to them.

"Mian!" Chimara's voice rings in my ears.

I swim until I'm close enough to the shoreline to stand. Dandena closes in on me. I throw myself forward when she reaches for me, but our fingers glance and slip. We miss each other by a hair and then the heavy cage of the foreign male's arm snares my waist and lifts my whole body into the air. Hauled up against his enormous frame, I can feel him shudder and shimmer behind and around me and I can feel as the human-esque skin begins to take on a harder, rougher hue. *Another snake male. Another manerak.*

"Dandena!" Chimara tosses Dandena her staff and Dandena does not hesitate, but darts forward, her own mouth distended and her eyes, enormous black diamonds atop her elongated face.

"Release…one of ours," Dandena hisses. Pitter patter goes my heartstrings. *I've never been claimed before. Not by anyone. At least not by someone who didn't also claim to own me.*

The male answers in words I don't know yet, but the fact that he wrenches me higher up his body, crushing my ribcage in the process, speaks volumes. Dandena snarls even louder, "…won't let you…ours!"

She charges, but he takes a step backwards towards the center of the river and I notice that most of the other males are gone. One of them seems to have been trapped at the riverbank by the warriors there, while two others are engaged in battle with Mor and another nude, fighting female.

Dandena opens her mouth, but a low, terrible sound pulls her attention — and mine — around, past the warriors that have formed a protective circle around the human females, to the hill's crest.

Neheyuu.

A rattling, like war drums, makes the air and earth tremble. Or maybe I'm just trembling. Because Neheyuu is watching me with unveiled hostility, with need. With something greater and more terrible than both.

"Neheyuu," I whisper and even though he's so far away, his body spasms, then breaks. As if I were watching him through the heat above a flame, his whole body shimmers, unbecoming until the world shrinks around him and the trees spear the ground at his feet like the staffs of giants, ready for battle. His face is no longer one I recognize as human, but is almost entirely serpentine, nose flattening until it's just two slits in a broad expanse of brown, characterized by fangs and rough scales.

I flinch, frightened — but not of him. No, somehow the fact that his shoulders have become boulders, his legs the trunks of trees, and his hands, little more than skin stretched over knives, doesn't scare me at all. What scares me is that the male above me is shaking and rattling himself and that he's pushing further into the river. That I'm about to be taken again. And maybe even more frightening is the realization that I don't want to be.

"Neheyuu!" Why I call for him, I don't know. I'm just a slave. Something to be stolen. A prize to be claimed among other wares. Probably the same value as a tun of ale. Probably less.

A wall of water crashes over my head, thickening my thoughts, melting my senses and invading my ears as it sucks me down, deep, under. It pulls into my mouth, taking away whatever words I might have shouted next. For the best, I think glumly as the male and the river carry me so insouciantly away.

7

Neheyuu

My manerak is misbehaving. I have never felt like this before and I have to keep my hand clutched over my hearts because it's the only thing I can do to keep my manerak from exploding over my true form and decimating everything in its path. Dangerous. *You have no idea.*

I stare across the ring of warriors to Erkan, whose eyes are as black as mine. They took his female, but she was marked and had shared his mats and could already be carrying his young. I have no such claims towards Mian, and yet there is no denying the color of my eyes or the violent surge of my manerak. He has taken my claws and I fight a losing battle to keep him from claiming everything else.

"It's an insult…they think we're weak," Preena says, manerak claws flashing silver in the light.

Creyu, the most senior warrior I have and sire to Tekevanki, shakes his head. "It was only a loss of six females. We still gained fourteen others. To go after the few in favor of the many puts them all at risk."

"He's right. There could be a second attack. This could only be the first of several," says another.

"Do you think they intend to unseat us, and come after the rest? It would be too bold a strategy…"

"The first was bold enough! To take our females by water, counting on their manerak forms to allow them to hold their breath for the length of time it took to approach undetected…"

"It was smart was what it was," Creyu huffs, "meanwhile, we let the females bathe like we are invincible. Like there are not desert dogs, hungry for fresh meat, lurking in this region. Like there are not sandstorms that would tear apart their delicate skins. They are weak and our actions were pure arrogance. We should have pushed through the lunars and ridden like oeban. Even though they may not be manerak, with so great a prize, it was no surprise that another dolsk sent warriors after us. What's more surprising is that only *one* did."

Creyu meets my gaze boldly. An older male, and a formidable fighter. But he is too bold now to challenge me here like this. *But he's right. You are a sviking fool to think that we could hold onto pure starlight without another daring to rip it from our grasp. Tatana.* Tatana. Tatana has the female my manerak and I coveted. Our female. Ours. *Mine.*

Silence descends. They wait for my word, as they have been waiting for the past few moments. As I have been waiting for the past few moments for my manerak to settle. He does not. He defies me. He wants to run. He wants to be unleashed. To blood-let and to kill.

My gaze flicks to Erkan. He is watching me and when our gazes connect, his skin ripples. Perhaps he blames me. He would not be wrong. Perhaps he blames himself. He would not be wrong in this either. And I am his First. I failed him. *And now they have her. I want her back. I want her back* now.

My manerak surges and I issue a terrible hiss. At the same time, Erkan's manerak rises to the call. His face bends and distends in disgusting proportions. My shoulders arch back and my knee joints snap apart and stitch themselves together at new angles. I tower over the others, no longer in control. *Get her back.* I've never felt so vulnerable before. Or so strong. Like I could decimate villages all on my own. *I can. I will.* Tszk. We will not go in unprepared and unarmed. *Want her back.* We will not risk the warriors we have. *Need her back.* We will not risk our position. *Get. her. back.* Tszk!

We will not risk her. Charge in unarmed and unprepared and risk that they close ranks around her, risk that they form a protective barrier keeping me from her. Risk that we don't get her back. Risk that Tatana recognizes her value to me and harms her as retribution for the dolsk I stole from him. He could *kill* her.

My manerak is silent. Still present, stirring, but he does not rebel against me or offer contradiction. Not this time.

"First?" Dandena's voice is wary. They are all watching me as if I am someone they have never seen before. *You are. They haven't.* "We are *your* tasmaran's warriors. Whatever you want to do, we're behind you."

Creyu makes a spitting sound in the back of his throat and though I would ordinarily bite back my irritation — Creyu is a male who commands influence — my manerak digs its claws into my throat and works my mouth like a puppet. *"You dare!"* I pound one heavy, clawed fist against my breastplate. "You dare voice such disrespect here? Now? In the face of your First? I would take your hands for that if I did not have need of them. We will go after the females. Should you so much as attempt to dissuade me, I will take this for a challenge and I assure you, Creyu, my bite is much worse than my bark."

The male narrows his gaze. He is not accustomed to being spoken to like this, and for once, I don't care. I don't care about anything but the pounding in my chest — my manerak's fists telling me we're wasting precious moments standing here arguing like this.

"I meant no disrespect First," he says through clenched teeth.

I hiss and though I'd like nothing more than to throttle him, I restrain my manerak, which longs for blood. Any blood. *But especially Tatana's.* He had his bare arms wrapped around her glowing, golden body. She'd been pure firelight. Something exquisite. *Incandescent.* I'd never seen her naked before. Over the past few solars, I'd pictured it. Oh yena, I'd pictured it.

From her thin ribs and luminescent skin to her dark nipples and the even darker toile of her hair. The way she'd looked with water droplets clinging to her. She'd looked ethereal. The way she'd looked reaching for me, calling my name, needing me. *Needing* me. *And we weren't there. And it is all your fault. Fool!*

I exhale, shoulders twitching as I step back from Creyu, addressing the six warriors gathered around me. "As you stand by me, know that you are not wrong. None of you. I was arrogant in thinking that another tasmaran would not come for the humans. And now humans have been taken from us, Erkan's chosen female among them." *My female. Mine.* My manerak rattles. The darkening skies betray my turmoil. They are streaked through with blazing orange and bitter red.

"This I cannot allow. My own pride and that of my dolsk is secondary. We will go for them now. No delays. I will take nine warriors. The remaining twenty-eight will take the females still in our charge and ride with sviking wings to the tasmaran. Abandon all carts. Each warrior takes one to two females with them on an oeban. Abandon the river route. We ride inland. Take the shortest possible path and stop for nothing. No one eats. No one sleeps. No one rests until you are back safely within the tasmaran. Preena and Dandena, I need you to lead this charge and watch after the tasmaran in my absence."

"Yena." My Second and Third say in unison.

I turn to the others and call out, "Xi, Xena, Rea, Mor, Rehet, Chimara, Reffa, Issa and Erkan." I see the slight relaxing of Erkan's shoulders. As if he thought for even one moment that I would deny him this. "They think of me nothing more than an impetuous youth, a fool quick to temper. And we will let them."

8

Neheyuu

"This is the way they took the females?" Issa says.

Rea sweeps his fingers through a patch of mud, sniffs them and tilts his face up towards the twilight. "Yena." His head swivels on his thick neck. His manerak form rises. He breathes in through his slitted nostrils and when he blinks his serpentine eyes open, he hisses, "Erkan's female's mark is strong. She is still with them."

"They should have ditched her by now," Mor seethes.

I snap my jaws at him, though I am thinking the same thing. As I'm sure they all are. Marked females carry a strong scent to ward away other manerak males. Any other carrion and they would have left her the moment they realized she was marked. But they didn't. *They do this to taunt us. To dishonor us.*

A splinter of pain shoots through my neck at the thought. And then a second follows in its wake at the thought of what they're doing to her. What *he's* doing to her. Is he marking her now? *Marking my female? My female. Mine!*

My oeban — a beast called Danon — beats his forward hooves upon the hard ground. He and my manerak know one another well and often feed off of each other's emotions. This lunar, the bond feels even stronger. "Rea. The way."

My strongest tracker, he rises from the riverbank, now in his true form, and turns to his oeban. Before he mounts the beast in one single stride, he says to me, "We are not far behind. Less than moments. The females will have slowed them down. Especially if they were fighting." He pauses, eyes flashing to Erkan. "And they *were* fighting."

I nod at him once, my core flooding with an unfamiliar pride, and then I press my knees into Danon's flank and we ride.

We reach the camp before darkness claims the sky. I can see it shimmering in the distance, glowing torches taunting me like they were put there explicitly for Sasorana to know my shame. I grit my teeth and snarl, "Bring them back to me. All of them. *Unharmed.*"

My warriors peel off and when I'm sure they've been given enough time to position themselves, I goad Danon forward.

The lunar glistens and glitters. Torches from their camp create stars against the earth. *I loathe them all.* My manerak is swollen, absconding with my true form. I press this to my advantage in drawing them out, and roar, "I am Neheyuu and I come for what has been taken from me!"

Danon stomps closer to the perimeter. Tatana would be leading them, since their First no longer needs to raid — the Nevay tasmaran is too large and too successful for that. And Tatana has them organized… well. Two dozen triangular tents form a large circle while rolled furs and the warriors that occupy them spread out in the center. As I approach, Nevay warriors step up between gaps in the tents, forming a shield wall. One I cannot alone penetrate.

The treasures inside of their roving tasmaran are well protected. Much better protected and better organized than mine. I am reminded brutally that I am still the youngest First warrior of our tribes. *You put her at risk with your naivety and arrogance.*

My subsequent roar is fueled with rage — mostly self-directed — and I shout louder, "Come out here with the human females and I will not decimate your roving tasmaran!"

There is no response. I see shuffling among the warriors I can see, several of them shifting to manerak. An act of defiance. I wonder what has been said of me. I wonder what they think. That I am nothing. *Let them think. I am not here for you or your foolish pride. I am here for her only.*

My manerak grows larger and more belligerent. My teeth sound like knives clattering together when I mash them. "Bring me Tatana!" Danon growls out his consent. He wants to fight and to feast.

The warriors stand fixed to their posts, silent and unmoving. The crackling of the fires and my own oeban's heavy breathing are the only things to disrupt the lunar. I shout a few more insults, cursing them to the ends of the cosmos. More warriors appear, drawn forward by my rants. *It is working.*

"Only cowards or carrion steal from a successful tasmaran's raid. Do you not know what a female looks like, Tatana? Is that why you could not find and claim your own? Where are you, Tatana? Why do you not come out to face me? Or do you fear me, knowing the tasmaran I have taken from you?"

My manerak hisses his rage to the sky, becoming ravenous. Danon bucks. There is a stirring among the warriors, who number fifty, at least. This is nothing for the Nevay. They have over two hundred warriors and the second largest tasmaran after the Sessena. Meanwhile, my tasmaran numbers less than two hundred, and I have only sixty warriors total. If Nevay truly wanted to, he could use the full force of his tasmaran to keep her from me. If Tatana wanted, he could lead that attack. *Their numbers do not matter. She is ours. I will recover her alone.*

"Tatana! After your boldness, do not disgrace yourself here. After all you did to steal a few females and shame me, do not let shame be your undoing now."

I think of him. I think of why he does not come. *What is he doing to her?* I think of his hands on her body, roaming over her flesh and I want to scream. Not because of my jealousy — no, not *only* because of my jealousy — but because I know that she does not want this.

She wishes to keep her wrist bands intact. They are precious to her. And she needs food. *He will take her in the way humans view as a violation and she will go hungry. Two things we promised her would never happen to her.*

My manerak releases a battle cry and I surge up into the lunar and it's only as Danon shrieks that I realize I've grown too great for his size. I leap from his back and my feet hit the ground and seem to…sink into it. They turn to sludge while the sound they create is a booming thunder, grass reeds billowing back from my body as if pushed by the invisible hands of our god. It echoes all around and I notice that the tasmaran standing against their dolsks are shifting agitatedly now. What is happening?

A darker voice, one unfamiliar, bleeds into my thoughts. *You have hidden me away for too long. And for too long have I sat by. Now you risk what is mine.* At the same time, my legs fuse, becoming one. A sudden, delirious haze parts my thoughts and when I glance forward everything burns in even brighter clarity.

The lights from the torches blaze against my skin. *Not skin…scales.* My skin has sloughed away entirely and when I glance down at my body, I see that it shines like oil. My arms fuse with my sides, becoming immobile. I can't reach my sword. *Who needs a sword, when I am me?* I surge forward.

The Nevay tasmaran who had stood by so stoically moments ago, canter back. They are panicked now, shouting at each other. Manerak forms surge forward, but they are all moving, rushing…and then they part. Tripping and stepping over one another as they move aside, Tatana appears in the gap they create.

My hearts skip. My head swivels on a neck…or, *not* neck, feeling heavy and mighty. What am I? *Fool. You know nothing of me.* Danon stomps at my side and when I glance to him, he bends his large head down, exposing the soft underside of his throat. An oeban sign of submission to a greater alpha. No oeban has ever made such a sign to another beast of Sasor before. Not even a manerak. My skipping hearts begin to pound. What am I, if *not* manerak? *What she has made you. What you have always been.*

As the last of my armor falls from my new, reptilian form, I am propelled forward across the high grasses by a will that is not my own. As I draw closer, Tatana's form becomes more indistinct against the bright fires circling his camp. But I can *sense* him, down to the weight of his steps and the vibrations they create through the sand. The faintest brush of the wind he stirs. The scent it carries. Vanthia and palm. My scales ripple. My rage tears itself apart in order to begin again. *He carries her scent.* He carries her scent! *I will rip his skin from his flesh and swallow it whole. Her scent is mine, and mine alone.*

"Neheyuu?" The sound comes from a distance, somewhere in the back of their camp where not even my heightened senses can reach. "Neheyuu, is that you?" Voice as soft as petals and full of disbelief. As if she does not think we are here, or does not believe I would come for her.

The beast that I have become reaches its curved hood towards the stars until I can see the full stretch of their camp, so puny now that it's laid out before me. *She's in the back. I will retrieve her.* But this was not the plan. *I will eviscerate everything in my path.* My warriors were meant to retrieve her while I distracted Tatana and the other Nevay warriors present. I am not to take on the entire roving tasmaran single handedly. I'm not foolish enough to think I could win that battle. *You're right. You won't. But* I *will.*

I see the tasmaran surging into their manerak forms, grabbing weapons, creating a wall between me and the one I've come for. *They try, but they are nothing.* Wait. My warriors will go for her. My tasmaran will retrieve her. *I will retrieve her.* Wait. *Tszk. And do not ever again attempt to command me.*

The hiss comes from deep within me. In response, the warriors crowd tighter around their Second, like chicks seeking shelter from a storm under the wings of their mother. *Decimate them all.* Tatana takes a step forward and the last of my control slips away, like crumbs of grain loaf through her tightly clenched fist. A dark laughter fills me. *Manerak is nothing. Not against the naxem we have become.*

9

Mian

Not again. That's all I can think as the male who took me kneels on the edge of the furs. They have fur here. I didn't expect that after sleeping under the stars on woven reed mats with the infuriating Neheyuu *with his body wrapped around mine like a coiled snake.* I didn't mind it, now that I think on it. I didn't like waking up and having to fight him off, but the sleeping part, being cocooned like that, his heat, his whispered promises in the dark…that I liked. Very much.

And now with this new male towering over me, I don't know what to think. He hasn't been mean to me since he pulled me roughly into and then out of the river. He hasn't hurt me. He hasn't violated me. *Yet.* I swallow hard, managing to shift out from under his touch when he reaches for my shoulder. I'm too depleted to do much more. He jerks back, then approaches me again with more surety. His hand falls onto my skin, hot and heavy as he strokes a downward path toward my elbow.

Quickly, I grab the loose furs by my hip and drag them up over my breasts and waist. He doesn't stop me and it takes me until that moment to realize his attention isn't on my breasts or my sex.

"…wound…" he says to me and I'm shocked, surprised to hear him speaking the same language I've heard over the past few solars, though I don't know why I should be. He *is* one of those crazy snake people, after all.

I follow his gaze to a shallow strip of red marring my right forearm and jump. "Oh! Yena. Wound."

I expect a smirk at my clumsy word-choice, but then remember I'm not with Neheyuu anymore. This male doesn't laugh, but gives me a sharp "tut" before climbing off of the furs and retrieving a small bronze chest. It reeks of medicines and, when he opens the box, the smell of herbs and antiseptic grows stronger.

I cough a little at the overpowering smells and mask my revulsion with a small smile. I try to hold it, for his benefit, because he's staring at me now. He says something.

I shake my head. "Wound?" I ask him.

He blinks several times, like he's trying to clear his vision or his thoughts or both, before returning his attention to the cut on my forearm. It's deep in its center and requires stitching, which he does in tight, elegant sutures. I bite my bottom lip, but I don't complain. I just watch in horrified fascination as little red droplets wind like rivers down the smooth curve of my skin. They drip onto the furs beneath, but he doesn't seem to mind.

"Are you okay?" He asks when I wince.

Elated that I can understand him, and that he asked, I force a smile through my pain. I nod, but he presses on my arm with his thumb, drawing a hiss from me. He responds with another tut of his own and retrieves a bronze cup from a basket against one hide wall.

"What is this?" I ask, taking the cup when he hands it to me. His fingers are warm against mine. Not as rough as Neheyuu's, but just as hot.

"Drink," he tells me.

"What is it?"

"Pain…less…"

"Oh, I…" I lick my lips. Thirst washes over me. But I still shake my head down at the cup even instinct compels me to do just the opposite. *You don't know when you'll get fed next. Drink and let it fill your stomach.* On the other hand, it could be poisoned. *Why would he bother stitching you up if he planned to poison you? Drink. Feel full. Don't feel hunger. Do anything not to feel hunger…*

My hand shakes as I lift the cup to my mouth and take a sip. Cool. Clean. Fresh. Water hits my tongue and slides down the back of my throat like some fine ale. I almost choke on it, and before I know what's happened, the cup is empty and droplets are slipping from the corners of my mouth and my tongue is darting out to lick each little droplet away.

I hold the cup towards the male who watches me with an intensity and severity that succeeds in making me feel self-conscious. "More?"

He tuts at me again and takes the cup away only to hand it back a moment later, full. I stare down at the liquid for a moment as I feel my torso gently sway. A fuzzy warmth starting in my belly radiates outwards, everywhere. Must be the effects of the pain…less… "Pain…less?" I ask.

He scowls. "Tszk. Water only."

Relieved, I exhale. "Good. Thank you."

"You…relax…" He says much more that I don't grasp, but that little bit is enough.

I grin at him and I can feel that it's a loopy, confused kind of thing. "Yena." I am relaxed. Very relaxed, without being sleepy. Suddenly the low lighting from the ensconced torches make the atmosphere feel quite nearly cozy and I quite nearly forget that I've been kidnapped twice in a small handful of solars.

"...you join...Neheyuu?" He says abruptly.

"Tszk," I answer and I answer too quickly because the moment I've spoken he rocks forward onto his knees, straddling one of mine. His large hand reaches for the blanket bunched at my chest and he starts to pull, while the material on the front of his pants starts to tent and bulge.

"Tszk tszk tszk!" I rasp harshly and when I speak, I do so in full, well constructed sentences — sentences I've memorized. "I am not joined. I am untouched by a male. I will only lay with the male I am joined to."

The male before me with his glittering hair and wet, shimmering eyes tilts his head to the side. He tuts and his hand firms around the blanket. I lift my arm to block his. "Dishonor," I shout. "Dishonor."

"Tut." He rises and for a second I have a complete déjà vu. Though he may be taller than Neheyuu and less bulky in the shoulders, the frustration Neheyuu had when I wouldn't rut him that first time is succinctly echoed by this new male.

He paces in the small space the tent allows and runs his fingers back through his hair that is more silver than blonde. Not like Neheyuu's wheat-colored locks. Surprising me, a small pang nicks the edge of my conscience just then, daring me to miss the cocky, grinning brute. I have no idea why. I shouldn't feel any differently about my new master than the last one, or the one before, or any of the others. There have been dozens. *And knowing my luck, there will be dozens more…*

Depressed at the thought, I don't pay close enough attention when this new master speaks. "What?" I ask him.

"Join…with you…"

"What?" I say again, surprise warring with the fresh lethargy settling over me.

"I…join…with you…" He says other words but those are the ones that have me at attention, seeking to find alternate meanings for what he's just said. *Is this male attempting to propose marriage to me?* The thought makes me giggle. I *do* giggle. He furrows his brow and his lips turn down at the corners.

"Why…" he says so much else but I know he's asking me about my reaction and I can hardly explain it away. All I know is that I feel sleepy and content, like the tide has come upon me suddenly and I present no resistance when it threatens to take me back to the ocean's depths. None whatsoever.

He stares at me severely and I don't realize I've dropped fully back against the furs until he falls on top of me. "Tszk!" I squeal. I press my hands to his shoulders and repeat, "Tszk."

He grunts in my ear, "I will join with you." The words I understand well enough, but I don't know how to tell him that we have to join first *then* couple as couples do. And not …like this! High on pain less and in my panicked state.

His hands reach for the laces along the front of his pants, and I flinch. "Tszk!"

He must finally understand me because he freezes. My own frenetic breathing quiets. Then I hear it. A distant murmuring on the breeze filters in through the tent's parted curtains. *It sounds like rain.* The male hisses and I don't miss the way his muscles bunch and shift beneath his skin. They swell, becoming larger and more imposing. His mouth distends towards his hairline. His hairline recedes. His skin shimmers as he rises to stand in his manerak form.

He waits another moment before disappearing so quickly, one blink and I nearly miss it. The wind flutters in his wake. I sit up higher and paw through the blankets to find something more suitable to wrap around myself, without succeeding. The furs are heavy and getting harder to lift. Even though they're more luxurious than the linens, I liked sleeping under them much better. *Like sleeping under Neheyuu, I could free myself anytime I liked.*

I frown again, conscious that I'm thinking about Neheyuu again and worse, I can almost *smell* him. The breeze wafts into the tent once more and I look up, a thimble of clarity threatening the delirium of my exhaustion.

"Neheyuu?" I say his name out loud and the moment it's spoken, I feel the hairs on the back of my neck and arms lift.

The tent is empty but the breeze that passes through it is weighted, as if in expectation of a coming storm. My mind must be playing tricks on me, and if not my mind, then certainly the pain less because right then, as I breathe in, I breathe in *him*.

I look around, feeling foolish as I say, "Neheyuu? Is that you?"

A sound, not too far away, reverberates its own response. And I *know* it's a response because it's not a natural sound and it's *mine*. It's a sound made for me. *The pain less must really be working if that's what I think.*

I shake my head, trying to center and orient myself, but the effect is bizarre. Because as I shake my head, trying to clear it, everything in the entire world around me *lifts.*

The wind. The tent. The sensation of danger. The pulse in my wrists. The beat in my chest. The drums. There were drums outside in the camp somewhere but now they're stopped. There was shouting before, too. Clear, crisp voices. But they're all gone.

In their stead is just the sudden, brutal rush of wind. The dance of lightning across my lips and the tops of my legs. I feel fire brew deep within my core and then whoosh… Thunder.

It barrels down on me at the same time the tent collapses into pieces. Fabric falls inwards and then is ripped back up. The plugs bearing its weight are no more. They're just *gone* in the time it takes to blink, and in their place stands a giant. A snake.

And I know him.

So I smile, my breath and pulse both accelerating. The feeling of being discarded is a distant memory. *He came. He grew into a snake and he came for me.* Okay, perhaps the pain less is really having an effect then because this actual animal creature can't possibly be…

"Neheyuu, is that you?"

The snake shifts its giant head to peer at me closely. It's the size of a thousand year old Valwood and slick like oil with copper scales and a great yellow underbelly. With a wide, flaring head whose width is the diameter of a body laid flat, I'd say he is quite perfectly formed. For a snake.

Without fear — or perhaps sanity — I reach forward. The huge, scalloped head twists sinuously as the eyes take me in. He's inspecting me with those eyes, each the size of an oeban's head. I can see myself in their blackness. I can also see the fires.

The camp has been decimated. Brought to the ground in tattered ruins. Not a single structure stands and the stones caging the fire pits have all been disrupted. Pieces of fur and the hides that once made up so many tents are alight and no one seems eager to put them out. Why aren't they putting them out?

They have plenty of water stored in huge sealed barrels alongside bins of dried meat, fruits, nuts and oats. They came so well prepared compared to Neheyuu's warriors. But now so much work seems to have been rendered meaningless as they let their tents and stores burn. Almost everything has caught flame and a fierce sort of panic presses its ugly face in on me, making me cough. It's either that or the smoke. The whole world has become a crucible.

The mammoth snake that is Neheyuu hisses and suddenly something comes up behind me. *More snake.* Smooth like stone and just as hard, it's cool against the surrounding heat and makes me feel as if those flames can't touch me. That against him, nothing stands a chance. Not even fire. *How long is he?*

The tail end disappears in coiled ropes of Neheyuu's body while the head bends low and two forked tongues, the color of ash, slip through the thin line of his mouth.

I shudder all over as that cool moisture presses against my shoulder. "Neheyuu…"

Through the flickering firelight that's sizzling and sputtering as it catches and claims new things, I can see the other males who came and took us from the river. They all stand so far away, staring in at me and Neheyuu. Staring at the snake. Their faces are blurred apparitions that still convey shock. I don't understand. They all can shift, can't they?

The snake hisses. I press one hand to the space between the slitted nostrils while the world burns around us. "I'm alright." I offer in answer to a question that was never asked.

The snake eyes blink slowly, the mouth widens and parts. Fangs as thick as my arm drip with what I can only assume to be venom, thick and viscus, but I feel no fear. None at all. As if I know this snake. As if it knows me. I grin and the snake shimmers again.

"Neheyuu!" Comes a rabid cry and my attention is torn. The flames are waist high now, eating up everything around us.

The snake's body squeezes around my middle while the head twists to face the male being restrained by three of his warriors. He is in his snake skin — or he's in his snake-man skin, because unlike Neheyuu, he still has legs and arms.

His face is distended, eyes two pools of pitch, hands clawed daggers, and bigger than any male I've ever seen but he's still only a fraction of Neheyuu's total size and from this angle, appears far less menacing. Especially when Neheyuu's bottom jaw unhinges, his twin tongues loll out, his fangs drip thick liquid that douses whatever fire it touches, and he releases a terrible screeching hiss that has me clapping my hands over my ears.

I scream as Neheyuu lurches forward, the force of the motion giving me whiplash as I'm dragged in the cage of his thick coil. My feet don't touch the ground, I'm just cocooned from the waist to my toes.

"Neheyuu!" He jolts to a sharp stop and his head swivels around. "Home," I tell him, first in my language then in his. Ironic that this is the word I've chosen to say when I don't understand its meaning. In any tongue.

The snake bows its great head as if it's been given a command and me, its sovereign. Without warning, it changes direction and we shoot left. Fires rage up and ash falls down and warriors jump right and left as we barrel towards them. The world passes in a symphony of color and all I can do is hold onto the snake's sliding scales as I'm dragged away, out of the fire and out of the camp.

The front of the snake ahead of me is sliding smooth, rippling over the tall grasses like a wave seeking the shoreline, but I'm the unnatural knot at its center. Each jolt is pure agony. His body is a heavy, coiled rope wrenched tight around my ribs and his scales chafe the skin of my lower half while my torso and face are completely exposed to lunar's harsh wind and the cutting pellets of sand Neheyuu's body kicks up. And he doesn't stop.

He doesn't stop as the smoke from the campsite clears, revealing a sky full of stars. He doesn't stop as an oeban beast whinnies its arrival and its hooves pound out a beat to measure our pace. And it's a brutal pace. He doesn't stop, not even as we reach the river.

Crossing it in one enormous rush, I'm not ready for the gush of water that follows. I gulp in air convulsively as a sheet of ice crashes over my head. He doesn't stop as my bare skin flares in a rash of goosebumps so painful my whole body seizes. My breath hitches and my teeth start to chatter audibly.

Then Neheyuu stops all at once.

The snake head stops its forward momentum while the tail slingshots out behind it, unraveling from around me as it moves until I plop on top of a pile of furs and shattered pieces of wood.

I waver where I sit, the contrasting effects of the pain less and the adrenaline crashing and the cold coalescing to create a dreadful sensation in the pit of my stomach. *Don't be sick, don't be sick, don't be sick.* My stomach heaves but I clap my hand over my mouth and swallow repeatedly. *Don't give up any of the food or water. Keep it in. You need the nutrients.* The mantra helps. Taking deep breaths helps even more.

Pawing through the tattered remains of the tent, I find a large swatch of fur and yank it over my shoulders. But even as I finally stop shivering, Neheyuu still doesn't move. He just watches me and flicks his tongues near my cheeks.

"What is it? What's wrong?" I say in my own human language before stuttering out a weak, "Sevebeya?" The word for what, or explain in the manerak tongue. He hisses out a response, but I shake my head. "I don't understand sssisss ssis," I say in wry imitation of his snake speak.

Neheyuu growls up at the stars, shakes his head, spits several times...and then his scales begin flaking like sugar in water. He shrinks, tail jerking inward, head slimming and shortening, arms and legs taking shape. His shoulders seem to catch for a moment, remaining these hulking wings that jut up and over his head. Then he spasms, head whipping back and forth and as it whips, tendrils of familiar golden hair fly free. He swipes the back of one arm across his face and the last of his scales tear free from his cheek.

I grin as a familiar face pops into view, but when I open my mouth to speak, I find that I...I can't. The air is still, heavy with something. I clutch my throat. I'm suddenly having trouble breathing. "Ne...Neheyuu?" I croak.

His face — his *humanish* face — twists with rage. *And fear.* He charges forward, grabs the edge of the fur I just tucked around my body and rips it free. "Neheyuu!" My adrenaline spikes and I hold up both hands. *Is this it? Is it now, after everything, that he'll finally violate the promise he made me?* I start to stutter out some semblance of protest, but Neheyuu speaks over me, issuing an order to his oeban.

The creature kneels just beside me and as it drops to the ground, Neheyuu blankets the beast in the fur he stole from me. He grabs a second, thinner swatch of hide from the pile and as he falls on top of me, he whips it over the both of us. Beneath the fur it's so dark I can't see. I can barely breathe. The little hole he rips open hardly helps.

He keeps his weight off of me, but his head is bowed. His shoulders are trembling just a little bit. I pat his shoulder, hoping to get his attention as his heat and fear penetrate deep. "Neheyuu, sevebeya..."

"Kogoyo," he grumbles.

"What?"

"Kogoyo."

And then I release a second scream, sharper and louder than the first, as the sky above punches down. A sandstorm is upon us.

10

Neheyuu

Nothing about this is sexual, and yet everything is. Our bare bodies meld together, sweat acting as the adhesive between us. Her small breasts press against my abdomen. She's completely tucked beneath me so that the hammering from above can't touch her. I cover her legs with my legs, her hips with my hips, and fit the entirety of her torso beneath the curve of my chest. I try to keep my thoughts focused and my cock from rubbing against her belly, but that's difficult when I'm naked and she's naked and every fiber of my sviking soul is acutely, *painfully* aware of it.

Her soft fingers clutch the sides of my rib cage and even through exhaustion, the scrape of her nails against my skin sends pulses of lightning shuddering through me. My hips shift in small thrusts and fire scrambles my thoughts. It's an inferno under the hide covering us. The first sun has risen and even though its light is blotted out by the storm, its heat is immune.

The muscles in my arms, chest, ribs and back shake with the effort it takes to hold my body off of hers so she's not crushed beneath the sand or my weight. She's so much smaller than me…bones like reeds…I hold like this for the eternity it takes for the sand storm to pass.

Near to us, Danon whinnies in pain. I have nothing to offer him. I should have stuck to the plan. I should have rejoined the others. I shouldn't be here. I shouldn't have lost control of my manerak. *What makes you think you were ever in control here?*

I growl and I brace and I hallucinate. She smells like oils and sweat. *Tatana's oils.* I hiss. *She should smell like me.* Like us. *Mark her.* The thought flashes along with an image of me mounting her. All I'd have to do is slide forward. It would take almost no effort at all. Just shift to the right and let my hips be cradled by her soft thighs. Spread them wider around me. Find her heat and bury myself deep inside. Palm her breasts, flick her nipples. See what she likes. Lick the sweet flavor from the side of her throat.

I'm startled by the sound around me. The lack thereof. How long has it been quiet? How long since the storm passed? How long has she been sipping in air like a female drowned beneath me? I collapse to the side and even though I topple off of her, I keep her sweat-soaked body lined with mine.

I rip the fur back, tossing it off of us and Danon both. Her ragged inhale hurts my soul, even as I take one of my own. My chest rises and falls in waves. The sky is dimmer now, streaked with ash and orange-colored vestiges of the sand that just came and went and now seeks new territories to conquer. Beside us, the once bright purple and green grass has been flattened while a few tough, dry stalks too stubborn to die jut askew beneath a new layer of sand. The landscape is entirely changed, but I know better. Again, they will rise.

I close my eyes and focus on calming myself. I'm shaking with the exertion of my transformation. All young manerak learn the pain of shifting early — before their third or fourth turn, for some. We learn to control our transformation, learn to lessen such a pain so that eventually, a manerak shift feels like a mild itch or light burn. But becoming whatever that thing was — *you know what I am* — that *hurt*. And unbecoming? That's a new agony built just for me.

And it's still not enough to stop the desire coursing through me. It has scales and claws and fangs. She's hurt. *She's ours. Mark her now.* I clench my teeth and, to keep from looking at her, throw an arm absently across my face.

Her breaths are shallow after the first, her heartbeats quick. I wonder if she can hear the desert dogs in the distance. Unlikely. We will need to move quickly to outrun them. Dogs ride the heels of sandstorms. Scavengers, they feed from the wounded and weakened creatures the storm leaves behind. We will not be among them. But I'm too weak to fight. *I'm not.* But can I ensure her safety while I fend off an entire pack? My manerak is silent.

My oeban is weak and meanwhile, my reesa can hardly breathe, let alone stand, let alone walk, let alone run — and we will need to run. I will have to carry her. Her body pressed to mine for spans. Her naked flesh melting against me, our two colors looking so similar underneath the suns…

I roll onto my side with a growl, and then keep revolving. I plant both forearms in the sand on either side of her head. I stroke her bottom lip with my thumb. Dry, but so soft. Too soft. She licks her lips, throat working against her thirst. Still, that small act sends blood firing into my cock.

I stiffen as it brushes against her outer hip and try to push more of myself away from her. Not for her benefit but for mine. I made her a promise and keeping it in this moment is agony. But what was that promise? I said I'd let her leave her broken tattoos as they were. I never promised more than that. *And I promised nothing at all.* I cage a groan looking at her mouth. Her sviking mouth…

I lean in to kiss her but she flinches back. I slide my fingers along the side of her face, the grit of the sand between her skin and mine. Her cheek is just a little rounder than it was when I first found her.

Just a little.

I doubt anyone would notice that wasn't wholly fixated on her every waking breath like I am, but the sight of it is cool against my boiling insides. Her skin still smells like begua beneath Tatana's musk. The first traces of a marking. Does she even know? *It doesn't matter. She'll never see him again in this life.*

I lean in again, my manerak pushing…and I'm too weak to pull him back. "Just to taste," I exhale against her skin, voice half-growl, half-plea.

She flinches again and this time her eyelids flutter. She watches me with that same look I cannot place and I do not break her gaze even as every nerve in my body screams in unison to take her. Have I ever wanted anything so badly?

"Tszk," I tell her, sweeping my hand down the length of her arm and circling her wrist with my hand. "I will not take you. I just want to taste."

I think back to when I was Third within the Nevay tasmaran, a green warrior desperate to stand out, to ravage, to claim a tasmaran for my own. I thought I knew need then, but this…this is an entirely new form of desperation. Because when her chin jerks down in agreement, my entire body breaks out in goosebumps. I tremble. I *tremble*. And all I feel is sviking relief.

I don't wait for her to change her mind but sweep a hand back through her sand-swamped hair and crush her lips with mine. It occurs to me that I should go slow with her and that I should be gentle — she's small and she isn't manerak and she's beneath me and I could and should ignore this strange obsession my manerak has with her — but there is reason and there is madness and I crossed the line into the latter solars ago. The moment she was taken.

The moment I met her.

So there is nothing delicate or gentle about this kiss. My larger mouth claims hers punishingly, teeth nipping and biting, tongue spearing her wet heat. She tastes so sviking good I can't stand it. My bones loosen. My mind disintegrates. Her lips are a nirvana I never thought I'd reach.

"Mian," I pant in the small space between us. A whispered gasp leaves her lips and I groan loud, hard, deep. I hold her face still with one hand, wrapping it around her jaw and neck, then I tilt her chin up so I can take control of her completely, and kiss her how I like.

And it's as I deepen the kiss that the unthinkable happens… Little delicate Mian starts kissing me back.

She shoves her tongue into my mouth and arches her back, pressing herself closer to me. A shocked guffaw escapes my lips. Her subtle eagerness heightens my intensity and I nearly black out when she circles one arm behind my back and cups the nape of my neck. Her callused fingers are smooth against my skin. They twine with my hair and pull.

"Svik," I curse between us. Her soft lips suckle my lower one and my mouth goes slack. Pure euphoria blasts through me and I'm left stunned as Mian then sidles slightly to her right, pushing her chest up to meet my chest. Her little dark brown nipples form tight peaks. She rolls her hips. She scratches me. I drop further forward onto her with a strangled cry.

My cock is cradled now in the valley of her hollow stomach. *Too thin. We will feed her every solar for the rest of our lives.* Yena, I agree madly. I pump my hips and the engorged head of my cock glides lower, finding the juncture of her thighs. I freeze. I freeze because it's all I can do not to pry her thighs apart and slam forward. No female has ever felt as good as this beneath me. *Tszk. Never.* And I'm not even rutting her yet.

I moan into her mouth. "Who sviking taught you to kiss like this?" *We'll use his bones to pick our teeth.* I'm thankfully spared from having to hear her answer when her fingers snake down the length of my body. She grabs me.

A strangled sound leaves me as her fingers circle my cock. "Mian," I gasp, hips plunging forward, wishing I was sheathed by her body but happy to use her fist as surrogate. "Svik. You don't…I said taste only…you don't have to do this…"

But she isn't listening and her expression doesn't *seem* to be one of someone who's been forced. But I can't be sure. I reach for her breast, then snatch my hand back.

I said just a taste. I promised. But if she wants to use me for more…she can use me for more.

She starts to stroke me up and down, and I don't even care that there's sand between her skin and mine. The grains are soft and I'm too hard, too sviking desperate besides. I pump and she spreads her legs a little wider.

"Will come," she says and I have no idea what the svik she's talking about, but her fist tightens and she's guiding my cock somewhere…oh sviking stars, is she… does she mean to…

She takes the head of my cock to her entrance, and glides it through the folds without allowing me entry. *Not yet.* I groan out loud, both in disappointment but also in relief. I will svik her, I guarantee it, but I don't want to rut her for the first time like this. Wrecked from the sandstorm, desert dogs howling in the distance.

We have time. *We have all the time she needs.* I growl into her hair as she starts to swivel the head of my cock back and forth over her softest skin. She's wet. She's wet *for me*. Knowing that is nearly enough to make me blow right there.

I hold fast, letting her fingers glide up and down my shaft at the same time that she switches my cock over her own steaming, wet flesh. Her core pulses in time with a heartbeat and every time she strokes my cock over that most dangerous little nub, she releases a whimper, and a gasp.

"Svik, Mian. Use me," I growl against her ear. I fist her hair harder than I mean to and tilt her head back, then clamp down onto her neck. *Break the skin,* a dark voice whispers softly, but I don't understand what he means and I don't give in.

"Umf," she cries, then more softly, "Neheyuu."

"Come for me, reesa." My loose lips almost whisper words too precious to take back, but I hold them firm behind the cage of my teeth. *Fool. Ravage her. Mark her. Take her for everything. In return, give her all of you. All of us. All three.*

She grunts again, her hand around my cock picking up speed. I could have exploded all over her a dozen times already, but I want to wait for her. Her release is more important. *We are her servant.* The thoughts come faster and harder now, and so does her hand and so do my thrusts.

"Mian," I snarl.

Her head falls back, the cascade of her hair looking startling against the light sands below. Her mouth opens wide, revealing the flash of her teeth. She's smiling as she comes for me. She's smiling. She's always smiling. Because she's a perfect thing.

I explode, seed thrusting out of me and over her curls, over her clitoris, over her full, brown lips. Her fist holds me tight, angling my cock away from her entrance. She knows…she knows she doesn't want to get pregnant by me. Svik!

I hate that. I *hate* that.

But I love this. I *love* this.

As my seed pours over her skin, I force my eyes to remain open so that I can sink further into her gaze, sink further under her spell.

"Mian," I grunt, thrusting against her fist one last time before dropping my weight onto her. "Svik!"

My female breathes out a light laugh and I lift my head with great difficulty. I ravage her mouth one last time. I'm breathing hard as I pull back, committing her flavor to memory. Sweet and salty, both, she is the nut of a canyon tree and its syrup at the same time.

It hits me then — *my* female? Tszk, she is just a prize. I will not mark her. I must mark and claim a female from another tribe, one from an ancient line. Mian is not mine. She can never be. She's just a slave for rutting.

Foolish boy... Short, dark laughter echoes through me.

I open my mouth to speak, to say something. To ask her why the svik she did this and when we can do it again, but I'm silenced by the howl of a dog. Closer. *Close enough to pick up our scent.* It's time to go. And even my manerak — and perhaps even that other darker being living within me — agree.

Without a word spoken between us, I take both of her wrists in mine and haul her up. I wrap her hastily in one of the discarded furs, using it to create a buffer around her body, and toss her over my shoulder. I turn away from the distant thrash of the dogs tearing into some animal and the sounds it makes as it dies, and when Danon stamps his heavy feet, shakes out his sandy mane and bullets towards the distant horizon, I sprint at his side.

//
Neheyuu

I want her again. I want her again a thousand times. *And we will have her. We will have her forever*. I wince, hating the voices singing triumphantly through my skull. Since I spilled my seed over her bare thighs, they haven't stopped singing. But now is not the time.

The lights of my tasmaran look like stars as we crest the next rise, but the serenity of the vision does nothing to compliment the sounds of chaos beyond the perimeter. *What perimeter?* I clench my back teeth and order my manerak to quiet. I'm too exhausted to fight. Too exhausted for the voices. And way too sviking exhausted for the sounds of discord emanating from voices that I recognize.

In my absence, there is no leadership within my tasmaran. No transition of power. People do not have clear roles. It would be so easy for another warrior seeking to claim my tasmaran to just do it. Kill me and it is won. There would be no rebellion by those who follow me when there is already bedlam among them.

Disappointment shreds me and I miss my next step. The lights of my tasmaran shift out of focus. The slowly swaying grass stalks surrounding me up to the hip make it difficult to discern where the ground actually is. I stagger but I do not fall. Cannot. She is dragging herself after me, clutching my upper arm in a locked, death grip as she tries to walk for herself. A quarter solar ago, she refused to let me carry her any father.

Even though the dogs were out of range and had long since shifted south in pursuit of the sandstorm and fresh targets, she didn't know that and that's not what I told her. She'd let me carry her a little longer before she said that her ribs couldn't take any more and that she might vomit. Strangely, Mian seemed more upset about the latter than the former.

Mian whispers something in her tongue. It sounds like, "Tank-ses-tars." I want to know what she's saying but when I ask her to repeat herself, she just smiles up at me. It's an exhausted smile. Past exhaustion. Her shoulders hunch forward and, in Sasorana's light, shimmer like elstone, that unassuming pearlescence.

Her eyes are swollen and so painfully slitted it doesn't look like she can even see. Her mouth is swollen too. Her lips are dry and cracked. She doesn't look good. Svik, she really doesn't look good. And instead of caring for her, all I could think about was tasting…

I'm about to call Danon to see if he can take her the rest of the way, but when I look back, I see that Danon trails over a dozen paces behind us. Svik. He's suffering. They both are. *And it's because of you.* It's because of you! There was a plan! *There* was *a plan. Retrieve her. We are not the reason she was stolen.*

My tasmaran draws near and I know that scouts have spotted us when I see the small contingent of my warriors peeling away from the lights and thundering towards us. Preena reaches us first and starts issuing orders, sending for healers, ordering a bath, food, and water to be brought to my dolsk and for Trekor, the oeban's lead handler, to be roused.

While warriors rush past me to secure Danon, Dandena arrives at my side, face riddled in shock. We must make quite a sight, the two of us. "You look like a desert dog chewed you up and spit you back out, First."

"Almost did. The others make it back?" My throat feels raw, like I swallowed a star.

"Dusk. Not too long ago, but they looked better than you sviking did. A lot better. What happened to you?"

"Sandstorm," I grit.

Dandena curses again and loops my arm across the back of her neck, trying to take some of my weight. Ock storms towards us and reaches to do the same for Mian but my manerak surges and spits, *"No one touches her."* Lurching forward, my manerak's strength pulls me, Mian and Dandena forward and sends Ock stumbling back onto his ass.

From his position on the ground, Ock blusters, "I was going to take her to the other humans we brought in."

"No one touches her." My chest heaves. I grip her tighter to me and feel her release more of her weight onto my arm. "She stays with me. Bring food and water to my dolsk. Lots of it. A second bath for Mian. I want Verena to take a look at her first, before anything."

"Verena is tending to one of the females brought in last solar. She was pregnant when taken from her village and seems to be facing complications. They aren't sure if the child will live."

My mouth goes slack. One of the females was pregnant? And I didn't even know? And now the kit's death might be on me? Shaken, I stammer, "I..."

"I'm okay," Mian says beside me. I glance down at her. She's hanging off of my arm and her face is bright red and her skin is dry and speckled with my seed and her hair is full of long grass stems and sand and the comets only know what else. But she smiles. Because she is always smiling. *Did she smile like this at Tatana?*

My gaze drops to the blood staining the bandage on her right arm. I noticed it before, when I first grabbed her, but back then the bandage was white. Now, it's brown and yellow and clinging to her skin by little more than sweat. Tatana healed her. What have I done for her but drag her through a sandstorm and nearly get her killed?

"Send Reepal then," I clear my throat and trudge further forward, letting Dandena take most of my weight.

As we near my dolsk, she whispers low in my ear, "You're acting a fool, First."

"Settle the dolsk for the lunar. Then at solar's first light, I want you to gather Preena and the most senior warriors. We need to make some changes." The writhing manerak within me reels. *We?* "I...I need to make some changes. A lot of them."

Dandena looks at me as I step away from her with a healthy dose of skepticism on her face and on her breath. "Changes?"

"This place is a sviking chaos," I grit.

"It's always been a chaos. You've never cared before." She plants a hand on one hip and her gaze flashes to the female I've got clutched in my grip. I hold onto her like I'm holding a beating heart. *Mine*. I grip her tighter.

"Just call the others to meet at solarbreak," I spit.

Dandena's mouth quirks, her mismatched lips making her face look squished, yet pleased. "Good." Good? As she turns from me, I realize she hasn't responded to my command and I have no idea what she means.

And I don't care.

I usher Mian into my dolsk and release the flaps so that we are finally inside and finally alone. I pull her across the carpeted floor and snatch back the entrance to my sleeping section. It is little more than a large, square mattress raised off of the wooden floor but when I pull Mian onto it beside me, she sighs like she has fallen straight into a pile of the most luxurious furs and pillows. *And she will get them. For her, we will get them all.*

Her eyes close and her shallow breathing deepens, but I'm still worried about her alarming red coloring and the dry, ashen skin around her lips and fingers. *Dehydrated.* She needs to drink something. Where is the healer? I curse Reepal and whatever is delaying him. *Bring him.*

With a will I did not know I possessed, I heave myself out of the dolsk to locate the healer and supplies Mian needs myself. It takes me a little time to organize both and when I return to my dolsk once more, arms laden with supplies and Reepal jogging to keep up, I frown.

It is a wide, squat structure up on a raised wooden platform. Round, it has a slanted roof that comes together at a point, but the walls are made of hide and the wooden support beams look crudely cobbled together. I think of the magnificent dolsks of the Nevay tribe, of Tatana's in particular. He is only Second, yet he could do better for her.

I step into my dolsk to the sound of a high-pitched screech accompanied by a muted thud as Mian's body hits the floor. Tekevanki stands over her, holding one of Mian's ankles, leaving Mian sprawled naked on her back. She tries to prop herself up, but it's clear that each move she makes pains her.

"Tekevanki!" I roar, thrusting all of the materials in my arms onto the sideboard to my right. "Release her!"

Tekevanki drops Mian's ankle like a hot stone and rounds on me. "I found a slave in your bed and I plan to return her to the stable with the other breeding mares. That is, of course, after I teach her her place in this tasmaran." Tekevanki raises one arm and I watch, slowed by my exhaustion and frozen in my horror, as she whips the back of her hand across Mian's cheek.

Mian grunts very softly, even as her head rips to the side with violence. I reach Tekevanki in a blur, moving faster than I can ever recall moving in my true form. I move as fast in my true form as if I were manerak. *As if you were more.* I grab the offending arm and my manerak screams at me to break it. And not just that bone, but every bone in her body.

I realize some control and fling Tekevanki towards the entrance to my dolsk where Dandena appears at Reepal's shoulder. Dandena catches her and both females stumble into the wall. Tekevanki rises in a whirl and when I blink, I notice for the first time what she's wearing. A sheer, nearly transparent gown. Its many layers do little to disguise the body underneath.

It's a body I know well and I'm certain that Tekevanki specifically prepared herself this way for me and ordinarily, I would be eager to meet her on my bed and tear through that gown, layer by layer but for the very first time since I accepted Tekevanki as my akimari, the sight of her like this has no effect on me at all. It's the quick breaths and the murmured curses coming from behind me that threaten my sviking sanity and when I speak, that insanity shows.

"The next being who tries to take Mian from me will lose life or limb, I swear it on the sviking stars! Now get out!"

Dandena tries to pull Tekevanki towards the exit by her arms, but despite what Tekevanki would have others believe, she once trained as a warrior. She manages to evade Dandena's grip and plants herself in the center of my dolsk, right below the skylight. Anger does nothing to denude her beauty and again, I am shocked. That beauty slides off of me like water off of an oiled shield.

Meanwhile, I am undone by the shallow, "Ooph," uttered behind me.

Mian is struggling to stand and when I turn to face her, the sight of her tattered skin makes me feel like my whole body is one giant scab, picked raw. And then in contrast, the sight of her nakedness, marred only by the matted curls between her legs, some of which still glitter gold…well, I don't try to cage my reaction. My cock hardens abruptly at the thought of spending the full length of the lunar dressing every inch of her in gold.

Behind me, Tekevanki balks, making me wonder if she noticed. I grin at the thought, and reach down for Mian to help her to her feet, but when she swats my hand away, I laugh outright, my cock bobbing between us with glee.

My laugh must come unexpected — svik, it feels unexpected to me — because Mian jumps. On her feet, I reach for her again and she winces away from me. I don't like that. I hold up both hands and approach her more cautiously.

"I didn't mean it, Mian," I say again more softly. "I'll be careful." *Like Tatana was.* My hands twitch at the thought, claws elongating before settling again to nails with rounded tips. Svik! I'm tired — *svik* tired, I'm a bruise with legs — I have to be careful. Need to be careful with her. But I don't sviking know how. *Tatana knew how.*

"Reepal!" I glance over my shoulder to see that my dolsk is still full of people. "The svik are you all doing here? Get out!"

Tekevanki flips her long, golden hair over her shoulder and takes a step forward, rather than back. I black out. Rage is all I can see for a breath. Sparing Tekevanki from an untimely beheading, Dandena slides her hand around Tekevanki's arm and pulls the female towards the exit.

"Leave him with her this lunar. Our First has found a new toy." Dandena meets my gaze with intent, as if she's trying to communicate something — a new toy, or anything but? Either way, her words seem to have the desired effect because Tekevanki's shoulder blades slide down her back and a sanguine smile reveals a mouth full of white, straight teeth.

She pulls a hand back through her long, golden hair and says, "A new toy. This is a first for our First. I suppose I can be...accommodating." Her large, aqua-colored eyes shift from my bare chest to Mian. Dismissing her. Like she thinks Mian is worthless. I shouldn't care. I should let it slide. Accept the out that Dandena has given me.

But I don't.

"Mian is not a toy." I don't know what she is, but she's not that.

Tekevanki's cheek twitches and I can't stand the penetrating way she watches Mian. It feels like a threat. So, I shove my body between the two females and after a moment, Tekevanki says, "I am your akimari. I expect to…"

"Get out." My voice is low this time. Deep. Guttural. Full of threat. "I will not repeat myself again."

Tekevanki's face twists as she turns. She glances over her shoulder, meeting my gaze, but when I say nothing, she disappears into the lunar before I am forced to further disgrace myself and toss her out by the neck. *Or break it.*

Reepal starts to follow her and I damn near gut the male. I shout, "Not you, you sviking…get over here. Tell me how to heal her. Dandena!" I whirl around, but Dandena hasn't moved. She's standing in the doorway trying to smother her laughter with her hand.

Glowering at her, I demand, "Where the svik are the baths?"

"They're here." She whistles between her front teeth and two steaming copper baths are hefted into my dolsk, carried by helpers — three males, one female. Though of the manerak species, both were cursed with the inability to shift. If they could shift, they'd have been made warriors when they joined with us, or were taken — I don't keep track of my tasmaran's people, so I'm not sure which. Like Mian…she will also be a helper. *She will be my helper*. And then what? *You know what.* I incinerate the thought. *Fool.*

The helpers come and go and I turn to Mian. I say her name and offer her my hands. Her puffy eyes blink quickly and she sniffles several times. She looks down at my palms and very tentatively, lets her fingers fall onto them. I rejoice unnecessarily at the small acceptance.

"Come."

"The…" Reepal stutters. He's never been much of a talker, but now he seems more tongue-tied than usual.

"What?" I snarl.

"The water…it is too hot. Her skin looks badly burned. She needs a cool bath."

Svik. And I was going to put her in that. *Would Tatana have prepared her a hot water bath or would he have known?* "Replace the water. Cool water. Nothing warm."

"*You* may still use the hot water," Reepal tells me but I shake my head.

"Just bring us new water. And Dandena," I say as she turns to follow my order.

"Yena, yena, I'll run damage control with Tekevanki…"

"Tszk. I don't give a svik about Tekevanki. I want Danon to have this water for his bath. Treat him to a feast. Make sure he's well looked after. And keep an eye on the horizon. I want eight warriors posted at the perimeter at all times from this moment on."

Dandena blinks, surprised. Then nods at me once. Her lips do that funny quirking thing again and I want to ask her about it, but just before she disappears into the black backdrop of the open doorway, she says, "Play nice with your new toy. Unlike Tekevanki, I happen to like this one."

I wonder if she means she does not like Tekevanki or that Tekevanki does not like Mian. "Both are true," I grumble under my breath as Dandena disappears and I return to Mian to help lower her into the bath that arrives for me.

I give her the first one that comes. It takes the helpers a while to bring the second, so as I wait, I sit at the edge of her tub and keep her upright. I'm the only thing that does. Mian's head lolls and on her face she wears a smile, even in sleep.

She lets me apply oils to her hair and gently massage her scalp. She winces a lot at first, until I finally adjust and get the pressure just right. When I'm done, I sweep my hands over the rest of her body and she lets me do that too. I wish my calluses were less rough and as the thought comes to me, scales appear on my palms, making them smooth. *Naxem scales.* Very good. Very useful. That strange, low brogue reverberates through my thoughts. He whispers, *I do not do this for you…*

I wash her gently until she's as clean as I think I can get her without hurting her. Then I lift her from the tub. Her swollen eyes are closed now. She's putty in my arms. I dry her and place her in the center of my bed before rinsing off in the same water. When the fresh water appears in time for me to take a towel to myself, I tell them to leave it. She can use it in the coming solar.

"Now what?" I ask Reepal.

He approaches the bed and the skin on the back of my neck prickles. My manerak is active again… *He's approaching* our *female in* our *bed. The svik does he think he is? Dismember him! Devour him. I'm hungry and so is your naxem...*

"What are you doing?" I snap.

Reepal flinches. His hair is pulled into a top knot, but he still strokes imaginary strands behind his ears. "I'm going to apply a cooling salve to her skin. It will help heal the burn and take down the swelling."

"I'll do it. Tell me how."

"It...it can be applied to her entire body, but her face will need a more aggressive treatment around the eyes. Verena has used cooling masks to treat burns on humans, who lack the natural protection we have. I would recom...recommend starting with that..." His voice fades under my stare.

I snatch the equipment from him and make him stand near — but not too near — as I begin the grueling task of applying the ointment to Mian's skin. "When you have finished, you may drape this over her eyes. And if she wakes and is in pain, you can give her these. Just one is enough, but I will leave three here for you and deliver more on the coming solar when I come back to check on...check on you..."

Reepal struggles not to look down when I turn to face him. Kneeling on the bed as I am, he and my cock see eye-to-eye and my cock is sviking livid that he's still here.

"Is that all for this lunar, then?" I say.

"Yena." Reepal swallows and gives my cock a little bow.

"Thank you. You may go now."

Reepal bows twice more as he makes his way to the door, finally stumbling over the raised lip of my dolsk and falling outside. I hear the crash of his supplies, but the curtain of the door falls closed, blocking everything else out and trapping Mian and I in. We are alone and clean and warm. Hurt but healing. I exhale.

"Mian, can you hear me?" I say. I want to hear her voice. *Need. Need to hear it.*

"Mhmm," she moans. *Not enough.*

I tap the center of her forehead with my longest finger. "Say my name."

"Shush, Neheyuu. Sleep."

I smile at the same time that that strange sound fills my dolsk, the one I've only heard a few times before and only in her presence. Like the rattling of chains meets the purring of some great cat. Maybe she hears it too, because she tries to open her eyes.

"Don't," I whisper, "Your eyes are swollen. I'm supposed to put this on you." I lay the green strip of cloth over Mian's eyes and my pulse sviking flutters when she exhales her relief.

"Thank you," she says to me.

I grin down at her though she can't see it and smooth one hand over her hair before picking back up the tin and dipping my fingers into it. I apply a strip of salve to the center of her chest, marking a thick line between her breasts. Her breathing stays even, but I don't miss the slight wiggling of her toes.

I add another stripe next to the first and massage it across her right breast. Her nipple puckers and hardens, begging to be sucked. I try to focus. I'm here to heal, not harass her. Quickly wiping down the rest of her body, I douse the torches mounted in brackets on the walls and crawl up beside her on the bed.

Curse the light that filters in from overhead. Senta, Sasor's seventh moon has a bright blue hue that makes it possible to see her. The halo of damp curls spread out across my bed, her splayed legs and arms, hands slightly curled as if reaching for her forgotten bread. It reminds me that she didn't eat. *We failed to feed her*.

A sensation of loss opens up in the bottom of my stomach, more powerful than grief. And it's made worse by the fact that my cock doesn't seem to give a svik about food or her injuries or anything else. It still juts forward, ever so often bumping against the outside of her thigh or hip.

I want to sviking hump her — at least grab my cock and pump my seed across her body, or better yet, watch her grab it — I want to lick her body clean of the salve I just applied to it. I want to do it while feeding her. I want to do it while feeding her while she sucks my cock into her mouth. I want to wrap my fist into those curls at the same time. I want to bend my limbs into cruel contortions around hers just so I can have her complete submission. I want her. *I want her…*

But first, I want her to eat.

I lean over her and drag just the tip of my tongue over the seam of her lips, wanting entry for one final taste before sleep crushes me between its powerful jaws. I'm rewarded by her light mewl and the press of her tongue to mine. I slant my mouth over hers, but the moment I deepen the kiss, she releases a pained sigh.

"Svik. Did I hurt you?"

"Tszk," she says, but she's not answering my question. Her eyes are covered but her knees are squeezed together. Her hands are clumsily fumbling across her body, trying to block it from my view. Irritation comes first, but guilt makes itself known too.

I fling her wrists back from her skin and spread her legs with my hands. She's too weak to fight against me as I cover her sex with my palm. The heat rips into me, demanding worship, but I hold fast. I hold as gold seed weeps from the tip of my cock, like it's mourning the pleasure it knows it will not feel. Not this lunar. Perhaps not on *any* lunar if she does not agree.

"Tszk," I repeat, cupping her core firmly and letting myself be branded by it. *Ruined.* "Tszk." I bend over and plant a kiss to the center of her forehead, the taste of the salve strong — fire nettles and sweet bray seed — but not strong enough to blot out her sweet syrupy skin.

"Sleep, Mian."

Irritated and pleased in equal measure, I throw myself onto my back and feel as Mian, beside me, settles. Her breathing deepens, her knees unclench, her hand flops out and hits me in the stomach, her face turns in my direction.

I watch the mask start to slide off of her eyes and fix it. I watch the smile on her face eventually fall into something more serene, then twitch. I watch her thin chest rise and fall under the light of the seventh moon. I watch her and know that she is dangerous. And for the moment, I am just fine with that.

12
Mian

Fire and then ice. Fire and then ice. Ice and then fire. Ice. Fire. Fire. Fire. Hurt. Agony. Reprieve. The pattern repeats itself on a loop. The only thing that lets me know that any time is passing at all are Neheyuu's lips.

He's not always gentle when he applies the clear paste to my skin, and he's never gentle when he kisses me on the forehead or the top of my head or my cheek or the tip of my nose, but it feels nice. I like it. And sometimes, after he kisses me, he applies a soothing salve to my skin and other times he feeds me until my stomach rebels and other times he whispers words I don't understand against my flesh but that make me feel like I'm floating.

I know that at some point, the pleasantness has to end though, and as all pleasant things inevitably do, it ends in violence. Almost in the exact same way it began, I feel the rough clasp of fingers around my ankles instances before the world is yanked out from under me like a carpet. I fly.

And then I fall.

"Get up."

Pain lances up my right side as my still raw skin is rubbed rawer still by the hard, textured rug below. "What?" I say, somehow managing manerak words, though they feel forced after so many solars of disuse. All words feel difficult at this stage. How long has it been since the snake that was Neheyuu rushed me through the lunar? How long has it been since I was in the tent with the male who made me an offer? How long has it been since I was snatched from the river? How long has it been since I cowered in a supply room alongside other hungry, gaunt human faces?

"Don't…" More words. I can't make sense of them.

"Slower please," I say, cutting her off.

A shrill shriek greets me and the female grabs my upper arm. With strength, she hauls me up onto my feet. My knees buckle and I fall again, but she just keeps dragging me. "Up. Time for…" She says something else and this time, I don't bother to try to decipher her meaning.

Instead, I let her pull me out of Neheyuu's tent into a violent white light. I hold up my free arm to shield my face. It helps a little, though every place the light touches sends more pain shimmering across my skin. I moan and grunt but the female doesn't seem to hear and if she does, she doesn't much care. I don't blame her. I've had this treatment before. As slave master, she's only performing her role. As am I. I don't try to fight back.

"You are a slave," she says.

I blink many times and eventually am able to see the tall grass stalks that I feel wrapping themselves around my legs, slowing me down with each step. "Yena."

She makes a brutish sound, maybe a curse, before she whips her head around, golden locks spearing me in the face like the points of needles. "You know...what promises for your... That...you akimari? *I am akimari.*" I somehow decipher a bit of what she's trying to tell me. What I don't know, is how to answer.

So I just tell her, "Yena."

She releases a frustrated trill and I notice that people are coming out of their tents now to watch us. I haven't seen the settlement before — the tasmaran — or the many dolsks that make it up. I try to peer through the blindingly bright light to catch a glimpse of where I am, but from the little I gather, it's rather chaotic. Dolsks with rounded walls and pitched roofs seem scattered in no particular order. Some are large, some are small, but none look big enough to be warehouses or workshops, like the many I've worked in for my human masters.

Around another dolsk, I trip over a stick, hissing as its hard edge brands my foot like a lash. The female in front of me seems to delight in this. "You...here! Do not..." She shouts and an instant later, we come upon a river. The sun glints off of it, succeeding in distracting me from the sight of a large tan dolsk resting near its shore, until I'm tossed forward, into its shadows.

The female with the golden hair in the purple and brown robes is shouting down at me, and keeps shouting. I get some words. Akimari. Neheyuu. Slave. Go. Don't. But I struggle to link them together. The tent flaps I was just shoved through open again and a human steps inside. One I recognize.

"Chimara," I exhale.

Chimara looks at me and then at the other female. "You do not belong here," she says to the robed woman, and I find that she's easier to understand. Maybe because she's half-human and speaks with a slight accent. Maybe it's because she's the one who's been teaching me manerak.

"Tell your…no Neheyuu."

"That is not for you to decide. He is First."

I gasp and struggle to try to stand when the golden-haired female tries to strike at Chimara, but Chimara hardly reacts. She lifts one hand and uses it to trap the female's wrist as it flies, then says, "Do not…ever. again. You…are a manerak shifter and your father…Creyu, but I am a warrior of this tasmaran, and these humans… have value…"

When Chimara gestures behind me, I follow the line of her arm, surprised to see that we aren't alone here. This dolsk is full of humans, all female, including members of the party I traveled with to get here. Some were even stolen from the river with me. I'm glad to see that they also made it back. Especially Rita. From across the dolsk, she gives me a little smile and an even smaller wave. She has a cut on her cheek that was not there before, but otherwise, looks unscathed.

"You are no manerak. No warrior. You are nothing," says the golden-haired female, the mean one. I look at her face again and decide then and there that it is truly not so beautiful. Perhaps not at all.

Chimara's jaw clenches. I can see that from here. But she somehow manages to restrain the bulging muscles in her arms. "That is not for you to say. You are not First. You are not Sasorena. You are akimari…"

I don't fully understand the rest that is said, but I do see the female's eyebrows draw together and her shoulders bunch. She isn't happy with the outcome and I can't help but wonder what Neheyuu thinks of all this and if he's the least bit embarrassed that the female he pleasured — me — now finds herself in competition with his other female, who clearly holds some standing within this tasmaran. *Oh my stars — what if she's his wife?*

The thought makes me feel sticky and unwelcome and the sensations remain long after the golden-haired female is gone.

Sighing heavily, Chimara shakes her head, then comes and helps me to my feet. "You're going to have to learn to ignore her."

"Who is she?" I ask, grateful for the chance to switch into my own language.

Chimara barks at one of the human women in the tent to fetch me a shift while we both brush the dirt from my naked flesh. We work carefully, because my skin still aches like a hot bruise, freshly placed.

Chimara rolls her eyes and snatches an errant feather from my hair. "She is Tekevanki, daughter of Creyu. He is one of the dolsk's most senior manerak warriors. That alone commands her respect. She also thinks she's destined to join with First as his wife."

"She's not his wife?" I ask, clenched, fearing her answer. I let Neheyuu kiss me, but if I'd known there was a female waiting for him, I'd never have.

Chimara laughs hollowly and rolls her eyes. "Not for all the wreaths in the world." I don't understand what she means and make a face. She shakes her head. "No. She isn't. She wants to be, but she's not and she never will be. Neheyuu plans to join with a female from another tasmaran to build an alliance." She shakes her head and laughs hollowly. "Personally, I don't ever see him joining with a female."

My insides tighten just a little bit when she says that, but just as quickly, release. I shake my head, feeling foolish. Neheyuu's plans to join have no bearing on me. I'm just glad to hear he isn't *already* joined.

"Is this how one joins another tasmaran? Through a joining or a raid?" I ask.

"Yena."

"And there is no other way?"

Chimara raises an eyebrow and then frowns. "You're not thinking of leaving, are you? Neheyuu isn't a total slob, despite his best efforts."

That wins a smile from me. "No, it's not like that."

"Good," Chimara says, "We'd hate to lose you. At least I would."

Little flutters of warmth fill my chest like spots in my eyes from staring into the sun. Before I can answer, a human voice tugs my attention around. Recognizing the female, I give her a shy smile as she hands over a thin shift and helps Chimara yank it on over my head.

"Thank you," I tell the two of them.

"You're welcome," the female says, "It's good to see you up. We were worried."

The little spots blossom ever brighter, but I'm not given a chance to respond. "Sit, please for today's first lesson." One of the human females who wears no tattoos stands in the center of the dolsk and claps her hands together. When I turn to face her, she smiles generously at me and gestures to the females gathered before her. There must be thirty of us or more, all in different shapes and shades. Some with tattoos, but none so many as I have. I rub my arms, feeling self-conscious of them.

"Lesson?" I whisper.

The red-haired human tugs on the edge of my shift, pulling me forward alongside her. "Yena, we're learning to speak manerak."

"And that's my cue," Chimara says. "I'm going to join warrior training now, but I'll come find you at second meal."

"That sounds great." I wave goodbye to Chimara, who just laughs at me again and shakes her head, then I turn back to the redhead. "I'm Mian, by the way." I offer her my hand, which I'm surprised she takes. She has no tattoos marring her pale skin.

"Nice to meet you. I'm Claire."

"Claire. A name from the old world."

She returns my grin, but her voice lowers as she sits cross-legged at the back of the gathered crowd. "It is. All of the women in my family have been called Claire since my great-great-great-great grandma left the old world on the space station that brought us here."

"Amazing," I say, because it is. "I also can't believe they're actually teaching us." No slaves of any human tribe I ever belonged to ever received such a luxury. I can hardly read our own script, let alone the script of another people.

"Yena. I'm not really making progress, but you've spent more time with them and Tri is very good. She was apparently a teacher before her human village was raided by the Hox. She left them though a few years back when she joined with Gergoro. Now she teaches us."

"Are there other classes?" I ask and Claire nods but our teacher, Tri, gives us a pointed look that serves to quiet us.

From there, Tri dives into her lecture. Beyond sentence structures and the vocabulary that make them up, she describes customs and cultures of the manerak people, detailing how each tasmaran is known for its own speciality — the Nevay, for their spice and grain production while the Hox salt and trade different meats and dairy products; the Sessena produce much of Sasor's fruits and vegetables; the Wren, its swords and weaponry.

The Neheyuu are known to produce and tan hides for dolsks and armor, though many of the human females among this tribe are experimenting with different textiles to make new forms of dress as well as mint metals to make jewelry.

It seems as if Neheyuu's tasmaran is still figuring it out, but Tri maintains that they are respected for what they do produce, and for their warriors' acumen. Apparently Neheyuu himself is one of the most adept warriors Sasor has to offer. After seeing him turn into a hundred-foot long snake, that does not surprise me…

Tri explains that there are seventeen manerak tasmaran on Sasor, all are worshippers of Sasorana, the star goddess, and most have joined together to form the United Manerak Tribes. A few tasmaran remain nomadic and unaffiliated, the largest being the Gevabara, who number near ninety. They are one of the largest threats to the Neheyuu tasmaran, including to us raided females — at least, those of us who do not choose to leave during the next sessemara, the joining ceremony.

Fascinating. She then goes through words needed to describe the different tasmaran and their many functions. I close my eyes and repeat words and phrases as she does, committing them to memory. As we recite, I notice several women looking at me. One of them is Rita. She lifts a few fingers, giving me a tight wave and a sweet smile. She's glowing. Even between the bodies of a dozen other girls, I can see that.

Tri calls on one of the girls in the class — a petite woman with brown hair a few shades lighter than mine. She's also wearing a dress and not a shift, hers in green. Very capably she replies to Tri's question in full manerak sentences. I start to sweat. I'm nowhere near that advanced. What if Tri calls on me next?

"Mian!"

I start, immediately worried that I missed a question directed to me, but the voice isn't Tri's. Loud and hard and distinctly male, I'm surprised to find that the voice is Neheyuu's...*but not* that *surprised*. And secretly, I'm a little bit elated that he's come looking for me.

The class breaks up, everyone shifting and shuffling, faces turning towards the entrance where Neheyuu stands silhouetted in sunshine. He's wearing linen pants and nothing else. His hair hangs in tangles around his shoulders and the muscles in his shoulders and strapped across his chest stand out in relief. He's furious again and I have no idea what could have set him off this time.

"Where is she? Mian!" He surges forward at manerak speed and several of the girls titter, frightened.

I wobble when I stand, the effects of not eating or drinking anything this solar getting to me. Not that they are new sensations. I'm quite adept at fighting them. Swallowing hard and focusing on Neheyuu's outline, I raise my hand. "Neheyuu?"

His head swivels and his eyes turn to pitch black diamonds for just an instant before settling back to golden-brown rings. "What are you doing here?"

He starts forward, but a dozen women sit clustered between us. He tries to lift his knees high and bring his feet down carefully to step over and around them, but it takes some effort. After three steps, he stomps one foot down, looking very much like an overgrown child, and I can't help but stifle laughter.

He glares at me. "Strena, Mian."

I inhale deeply, fully intent on arguing, but not in front of so many eyes. Instead, I edge forward, moving around the women with a little more agility than Neheyuu showed. Already though, the women are clearing out a space around him. And they're all. still. watching.

Heat rushes up the back of my neck, which does nothing to help my burn. I quickly coil my hair around my fist and knot it so that it sits off of my neck. When I meet Neheyuu's gaze again, he's staring at it, fixed.

"Neheyuu," I say quietly. "This is manerak class." What I want to tell him is that we're disturbing said class, but I don't have the words for that quite yet.

"I know that," he snaps and seems to snap out of it. He looks away from my hair to my face and then slightly lower. My throat? He licks his lips. "My question is, why are you in manerak class? You…in bed."

His words aren't difficult to puzzle out, even if I don't understand every single word, and I frown. "Tekevanki."

His eyes slit and he huffs through his nostrils, like a dragon might — the fire-breathing creature from one of Mirabelle's stories. "Did she hurt you?" He grabs my arms and starts a thorough canvas of my body with his fingers. If he's made uncomfortable at all by his dramatics, he shows absolutely no sign of it.

"Tszk, tszk. No pain. I like manerak class. I stay."

His frown becomes nearly comical, the corners of his mouth nearly meeting his severe jawline. "You will come back to my dolsk," he snarls.

"Tszk."

"Tszk?"

"Tszk."

Neheyuu rises up, becoming tall enough to arch over me. The women behind me are shuffling again, and whispering now amongst one another. "You...rest...I am First. You will come back to my dolsk."

He's got fair points, from what I've gathered. On the former, I am exhausted — muscles saggy, bones soup, skin stretched far too tightly over both, caging it all in. On the latter, I'm not even sure I'm *allowed* to say no to him. He *is* First. And I'm just a slave, aren't I? *Kings don't follow slaves around and make fools of themselves. Kings don't recapture slaves they've lost.*

I touch my fingers to the fresh bandage wrapped around my forearm and blink back a half-memory of Neheyuu and another male replacing some of the torn stitching and applying ointment to the wound.

Neheyuu had wanted to do most of the work, getting the male to explain things to him step-by-step. He was very careful. The kind of care I expect he'll show his wife someday, even though I know I can never be her.

I wince at the thought though I wish I wouldn't, and look down at my feet before remembering the challenge he issued me. I open my mouth, but Neheyuu speaks first, this time with a little less hostility, "Did you eat?"

At the mention of food, my stomach rumbles. Neheyuu curses. "Come with me...feed you."

"What?"

"Food." He jabs a finger against my stomach, tickling my bellybutton. "From my hands. I want to." I try to piece together the words he's saying but they don't make sense this time.

"You want to feed me?" I choke out.

"Yena," he answers like it's the most normal request in the world. "Strena."

My stomach flutters, like dry leaves dancing in a wild wind. I shuck the emotion away though. Just because he came for me, dragged me through the desert, we kissed and he's made promises of feeding me that he's kept doesn't mean that he likes me. No, I'm sure he does these things every time he finds a new female on one of his raids…

Maybe he's just angry because he hasn't *had* me yet — at least not in the way that he wants. I'm sure that once he does, his ministrations will end and he'll move on to the next female. I frown at the turbulent direction of my thoughts, not liking any of them.

"Mian," he says, voice bringing me back to the present. He holds out his hand and I notice that his rough palm is streaked with many different lines that my hands don't have. However, it's still lighter than the color of his skin, like mine. A commonality. A commonality with the snake man. I smile and when I look up, Neheyuu blinks brightly at me, looking a little lost.

"Okay," I sigh, placing my palm in his. "I am hungry."

A grin splits his face and the leaves in my belly pick up their pace. *This is bad. Dangerous, even.* "Good." His fingers curl around my hand, engulfing it and he starts to tug me towards the entrance without acknowledging any of the other human females. Like he doesn't even see them.

Neheyuu makes no move to release me, so I have to awkwardly twist around and wave over my shoulder at Tri and Claire and Rita and the rest of them. "Bye! I'll be back for class later, I promise!" Several of the females stare after me in horror, but the majority of them wear smiles.

Claire waves. "Don't worry. I'm happy to provide you with additional instruction," she answers in human and I don't have a chance to even thank her before I'm yanked the rest of the way outside.

Neheyuu moves quickly, hissing up at the sun ever so often as he moves. He glances back at me, ensuring I'm keeping up, maybe. A couple times he opens his mouth, but then snaps it shut. We reach his tent in no time and inside, Neheyuu looks at the bed, eyes narrowing. "Did she…" I don't understand exactly what he means and shake my head.

He takes my arm in both hands and exaggerates the motion as he pulls me forward. "Trekara," he says, and I get what he means. *Pull*. "Did she pull you out of my dolsk?" He repeats.

I nod. "Yena."

He scowls. "She…" I don't know what he says after that, nor do I care when the massive wooden platter piled high with food appears in his hands. My gut rumbles again and when Neheyuu points to his bed, I don't hesitate this time. I perch on its edge, waiting eagerly as Neheyuu seats himself beside me — maybe *too* eagerly because Neheyuu's stiff upper lip cocks and when I suck the first piece of meat out from between his fingers, he laughs.

His laugh is deep and full and from the belly. It makes me smile. And I keep smiling as he keeps feeding me meat and fruit and cheese and nuts and other things I've never heard of, tasted or have the vocabulary to name. I ask him about all of it though, trying to commit my favorites to memory.

He holds up one of the seven purple buns piled onto the plate. "Opikopi," he says and I repeat it.

"Opikopi favorite," I tell him, taking a second bite of the bread directly from his fingers.

He smiles and offers me water and as I drink from the skin he says, "I know." His eyes are soft, jaw lacking its hard edge. His muscles are relaxed and when I burp, he laughs so hard a few berries spill from the edge of the tray. He ignores them, gaze never straying from my face.

Full now, and grateful for it, I smile sheepishly and point at the rest of the food on the tray. It's just less than half full. "Neheyuu hungry?"

Neheyuu looks like he's about to answer, then pauses. He glances down at the tray and nods but he doesn't reach for any of the foods himself. Instead, he's watching me, as if waiting for me to do something. He must expect me to feed him. Since he fed me — *and he has no wife* — I see no harm in returning the favor.

I pick up a fatty piece of flank, likely from a beast they call battar, and hold it to his lips. He opens his mouth and I can't mistake that strange rumbling hiss this time, because it's loud and I'm clearheaded and absolutely certain that sound isn't one a human could make. *He's not a human. He's a snake.*

I giggle at the thought, but rapidly my laughter is silenced when he lunges forward, capturing my fingers between his lips. I wonder if he even chews the meat, because one moment it's there in my hand and in the next, it's gone, but when I try to pull my fingers back, Neheyuu sucks harder.

I had no idea how intimate it could feel to feed someone and flush. I open my mouth — maybe to say something? I'll never know — because Neheyuu shocks me silent when he grabs my wrist and slowly pulls my fingers free of his lips with a loud pop.

He says something, but I'm too distracted to focus on understanding manerak in that moment. I shake my head. "What?"

"Kiss you."

"You want to kiss me?"

"Yena. Only taste. Like before."

Like before. I feel my face burn as I remember being completely delirious on the pain less and under the heat of the charring suns. I let him kiss me. I let him do *more* than kiss me. I cradled his cock in my fingers, stroked it, let him spill his gold seed all over me, used his length to make me come. *And I liked it.* And I liked that he kept his promise. He let me do all the touching, not touching in return except the kisses he traded with me. Maybe…I could let him do a little more? *Dangerous,* I think, but I still nod tentatively.

I gasp, not expecting the voracity of Neheyuu's next move or its suddenness. He's on me right away, the tray settled on the floor, his muscular arm looping my waist and dragging me higher onto the bed. He braces one forearm on either side of my forehead and attacks my lips with his tongues.

Their split and textured surfaces feel strange on my tongue, which so far has only the experience of kissing aggressive human boys that plunder more than caress. And even though Neheyuu is breathing hard and his lips are battling mine furiously, every bit the plunderer, his tongues are pure caress.

They lave my own tongue, skimming the roof of my mouth, twirling past my teeth, sucking on my moans. And I do moan. It doesn't help that the food has made me lazy or that Neheyuu came and found me and fed me from his own hand. Both of those things working in tandem have lowered my defenses. I have to take deep breaths in order to keep my wits about me and make sure I don't let Neheyuu have more than I'm willing to give.

His mouth leaves mine and urgently finds my jaw. He licks and sucks his way across it, reaching my ear, which he bites. I mewl a little and grip with my fingers, only aware in that moment that they're wrapped around his back, pulling on his bare skin. *Clawing at it*. As if I were manerak, marking him. The thought makes me smile and I shiver when Neheyuu looks at me, eyes oscillating between pitch black and his true form's lovely brown irises. I wonder what the colors mean... The brown holds for another second and he grins wolfishly at me.

Worry rises in my belly, sending those fluttering leaves fully scattering. He's making his way down my body, licking and biting my throat, my collar bones, following the line of my shift. "Taste...Mian?" he says.

My thoughts scramble, I nod absently. He squeezes my breasts and I open my mouth to retract the permission I just gave him, but he's massaging them so delightfully, coercing my nipples to harden, which they are more than happy to do.

I look up at the ceiling. Plain hide. The hole teasing me with promises of daylight. It's warm in here. There should be windows. Yes. Windows. Try to think about that. Try to remember that I'm not going to let Neheyuu complete my wrist circles. That only my future husband will do that. It's all I have to offer. And that husband, he'll keep me fed and clothed and will give me shelter. *But Neheyuu does that.* But he doesn't want a wife. I'll have to find someone else and they won't want me if my circles are filled in because one time I forgot myself to the feeling of Neheyuu's warm breath through my shift, pressing against my belly button, wetting it with his tongues in equal parts caress and plunder.

I shouldn't, but I glance down my body at him anyways. The sight of his golden hair and bronze shoulders makes my vision blur, and never more than when I realize his intent. He lowers himself down my legs, which are pinned apart underneath his torso, and then he looks up at me and holds my gaze as he slowly edges my shift up my thighs and over my hips.

"Neheyuu," I exhale.

"Tszk," he answers, though his voice is gravel, "only taste."

I nod, though that hadn't been the question I was going to ask him. I was going to ask him if he knew that I'd never had a man put his mouth down there before, if that's what he was even planning, and if it was, if he'd go gentle. But I don't get anything out besides a strangled yelp before Neheyuu looks down at the thatch of curls between my legs and uses both hands to spread me wider.

He curses and spreads me more, pushing my hip flexors to their points of resistance. He places his palm flat between my hips and pulls up, revealing even more of me to his hungry gaze. Then he leans in close and inhales. His eyes close and he mutters what sound like ritual incantations.

I'm shaking a little now, with nerves but also with anticipation. I didn't realize it was possible to be so aroused, but somewhere between being yelled at and then being fed, my pussy started to melt and now I can see his finger glisten when he swipes just the tip through my wet, slippery center. My hips buck, but he holds them down long enough to lick his finger clean. Just like he licked my fingers with the steak. The parallels are titillating.

My chest rises and falls in rapid bursts. I'm getting lightheaded. Neheyuu looks up at me and says, "I'm hungry now. Are you ready?"

This is okay, I tell myself, this is not going to damage me in the eyes of other males. *But will this damage other males for me?* I'm not sure. I nod quickly before I can think too much harder about it and reach for his shoulders.

He takes my hands and shoves them into his hair. "Tell me what you want…direction." And then he surprises me by winking up at me. "Like I am…slave. Your slave."

I open my mouth, like I'll say something, but there's not a chance for that. I receive no further warning.

He holds me down and buries his nose between my thighs, lips coming down hot on my clit, his twin tongues licking and stroking every crest and every wave.

The shock of it parts to the sound of me screaming. My thighs are trembling and the muscles behind my shins twitch and flare. My toes dance across the sheets. My fingers grip his hair and pull and push, utterly reckless as I use him to find my own release.

He does whatever I nudge him to do, his brutish cockiness forgotten. There is no master here. No slave. There are only my whispered moans and pleas and curses coming to me in my native language as he tortures me with pleasure.

His tongues dip inside of me while his lips pull at my lips. I think I might have tears on my face, rolling out of the corners of my eyes, but I can't be sure. Because it's coming. The heat. The pressure. With all the power of a sandstorm, euphoria strikes.

I start to shake and shudder but Neheyuu is a ruthless male. One hand anchors my hips while the fingers of his free hand stroke my core, finding my lips and edging past them. He pushes one finger inside of me at first, and then adds a second.

He says something, but I don't hear it. All I can feel is the pressure and the wet, wet desire as he pumps them in and out of me, not all the way, but enough to make my chest constrict. It's too much. I want more. I can't breathe. *Who needs breath, anyways?*

While his fingers work themselves in and out of me agonizingly slowly, his lips find my clit and suckle, once, twice, and by the third time, my body gives up and gives out. I spiral into some unknown direction for what feels like forever, surfacing only to realize I'm yanking so hard on Neheyuu's hair, I think I might pull all of it out. He laughs when I let go of him, but he doesn't stop.

142

As I start to come down, he presses harder with his tongues and pumps harder with his hands and even though I *never* thought it was possible for me or for any female — or any male — I shatter apart a second time, this time even harder than the first.

I scream his name for the whole tasmaran to hear and when the storm finally settles, leaving me drenched and broken, my chest is shuddering with escaped breaths. I can't move.

Neheyuu flicks his tongue at my clit one final time and my whole body spasms. "Tszk, tszk," I beg, pushing on his crown and forehead.

Neheyuu laughs and licks me once more, punishingly, before removing his mouth and fingers from my body. He prowls up the bed, the bottom half of his face soaked with my orgasm. I imagine other males would be embarrassed, but he's grinning down at me like he just vanquished an entire tasmaran by himself. Which I suppose is possible, considering I've seen it happen with my own eyes. *And he did it for me. He took down a tasmaran for* me, *a slave.* But then why don't I feel like one?

I feel a breath bubble in my chest and I hold it, expecting him to use my drunken delay to mount me, but he just falls onto one elbow beside me and strokes some of my hair off of my cheek and forehead.

"Rest. I..." I don't know what he says, only that he starts to pull off of me and I can't have that. Not when everything feels so topsy turvy. He called himself slave and worshipped me as if I were a master — no, a queen, a goddess — but he has not been satisfied himself. I can *see* that he hasn't. I'm not sure I've ever seen an erection so...well, erect as he pushes off of me and the front of his linen pants come into view. They are soaked around the crotch, like he already came and for a moment, I wonder if he has. The thought makes me smirk.

I reach out, flailing a little, but manage to catch his wrist before he's too far away. I bring his hand to my mouth and lick a line up his fingers — the wet ones. They taste like me and though I've never done anything like this before, I'm surprised to find the taste so erotic. Or maybe it's the knowing where they've been. The knowing that he just wove magic across and through and against my body. And I'm a slave. I'm not good at being treated — doted on, sated. Not without giving something far greater in return.

"Mian...I must train," he says but before he can finish, his voice strangles. I've got his fingers all the way in my mouth now and am sucking on them hard, like I would a man's...member, though I glance down at the front of Neheyuu's pants and know that I've never sucked on anything so large before. Still, I would like to try.

With great pain, I manage to push myself up onto one elbow as Neheyuu falls back onto his. He collapses onto his back, all while muttering futile words of resistance. "Mian, you don't have to. I enjoy..." blah blah. Manerak manerak.

I'm all syrupy and slow, but Neheyuu doesn't notice my clumsiness or doesn't care as I slowly edge his pants down his muscular legs. I forget how big he is — everywhere — his thighs easily each the size of my waist and his member long enough to choke on. *I'll find out...*

I inhale sharply as I find a seat — sitting is a new kind of pain. The pain of desire. Of wanting more. Of being too swollen to take anymore. Between my thighs is a wondrous prickly explosion.

Focusing on Neheyuu, I wonder if this would be better for him if I were naked and quickly pull my shift off over my head. Neheyuu grunts and opens his mouth, but instead of words, that same rattling claims the air again. It punctuates the rapid tattoo of my heartbeat. I sit up on my heels and let him drink his fill of me, massaging my breasts and unable to help the swell of pride I feel when his eyes slit and his chest shudders, making him look vulnerable.

He mouths my name, but doesn't seem to be able to speak. I know that there are far more beautiful females in Sasor, in this tasmaran, who have shared his dolsk — like Tekevanki — and that I'm too skinny and weak, but right now he looks at me like I am someone else. Like I am his equal.

I slide my hands up his thighs, digging my nails into his hips. He garbles my name along with about a dozen other words as I fan a light breath across the length of his cock. And then lick my way up it. I lap at the seed that's formed in beads along the slit of his cock's bloated head. He smells like some distant woodland and sweat and metal and a little like me. I smile down at his pulsing manhood before unhinging my jaw and filling my mouth with him.

He pounds on the bed with a fist, nearly startling me, but not enough to interrupt the rhythm of my head bobbing up and down — at least for not more than a moment. I can't get more than half of him into my mouth, but when I look up at his face, it doesn't seem to matter. He's staring down at me with huge, round, sometimes-black-sometimes-brown eyes. His chest rises and falls in heavy pants. He mouths my name again and curses when I slow down, and then stop.

I reach up and take his hands, one at a time, and place them on the back of my head. I wink at him. He curses again.

I work him over with my tongue and my hands, moving fast and then more slowly when I feel him tense beneath me, and then I return the torture he gave me by repeating the process again and again. So long that I feel the mattress between my slightly parted thighs get damp…and then wet outright. I want more. I'm *ready* for more. *Ready for him to slide into me up to the hilt and ride me for the rest of my life.* No. I clamp down on that thought and focus on the sensation of his fingers clenched in my hair, showing a restraint I didn't know he possessed as he lifts his hips and pushes my head down just a little bit. Not enough to hurt me.

I choke a couple times and he yanks me back up, checking my face to see if I'm okay. I wink at him both times and he grins at me, once he even laughs, and then lets his head fall back as he gives himself up to the sensation.

He holds out for longer than I'd thought — than I'd hoped. I've only done this a few times and he's larger than the human males I serviced. My jaw starts to ache at the hinge, so I increase my speed and with one hand on his shaft, I snake the other down to cradle his stones. He barks my name loud and hard and without warning, explodes. His seed punches into my throat with surprising force. I jerk, but then hold steady, taking him even deeper and doing my best to swallow repeatedly.

Eventually, I manage to choke down his seed and the second I release him from my lips and roll onto my back, he reaches down, hooks his hands under my arms and drags me up the length of the bed. He rolls on top of me and kisses me hard. He spreads my legs with his knees and before I know what's happened, I feel the hot, velvet length of him pressing at the entrance between my thighs.

I freeze, but he pulls back just long enough to say, "Tszk." He's panting, breathing hard and I'm panting too, sounding like an animal in rut. I feel the strangest sensation come over me as he lines his cock up with my core and begins to glide up and down, moving through my folds without penetrating me — just as I once did to him.

A choked moan bursts out of my throat. A strange smell fills the air. "Mian," he says. He. Who is he again? Where am I? I open my eyes and see his face. *Oh yes, I'm here with the snake man.*

I grin up at him and start to gyrate my hips in time with his thrusts. This is the closest I've ever come to rutting any male and a small, bitter, angry part of me is delirious with want. *Okay, forget about small — a very large part.* He lowers his hips even more, pressing them into me so that now, every time he thrusts, a delicious and wicked spark ignites in my clitoris.

I moan louder. Neheyuu says my name again and again, like the part of his brain responsible for speech has suddenly broken. The scent in the dolsk thickens becoming almost too much to breathe through, but I inhale anyways, like I'm sucking in sand from that storm all over again, only this sand tastes like metal and salt and a little like me and like all things masculine and divine, and also like promises of more grain loaf, whispered against the dirt-covered shell of my ear in the middle of the lunar even though I've only known him a smattering of solars.

My smile breaks as the rupture hits, Neheyuu stiffening above me, but refusing to relinquish the hold he has on my gaze. I'm held captive by him. His fingers lace with my fingers. His hips pick up their pace, bearing down on me with more urgency now as a sudden gush of hot seed soaks my core, my lips, my folds, my clit and everything in between.

He grunts like a savage, but in between the grunting and the moaning, his hand finds my right breasts and flicks my pert nipple and all I can do is grab onto the back of his neck and try to concentrate on his face as the rest of me spirals apart, splitting at the seams, shooting off into a million pieces as I find a mirrored chaos, a mirrored peace.

The spots in my vision clear to the sight of his eyes, looking deep into mine. And as I look up into his gold and brown and black liquid eyes, I know that there's something he's trying to communicate to me in his expression. Something profound. Something that can only exist now and in this moment.

And I have no idea what it is. Pity, because as I grin and he stares at me like he's never seen me before in his life, I think it might be important.

13

Neheyuu

What have I done?

My manerak flicks inside of me, showing off his disappointment — and not because of what I did, but because of what I didn't do. *You're a fool for not rutting her.* He's been repeating himself in my head since I called on two helpers and two warriors to escort Mian to the female bath house. I could have ordered a bath brought to my dolsk, but I needed time to think.

About what I did. About what I didn't do.

I look down at the mayhem of seed and Mian's orgasm smeared across my dick and stomach. I'm still half-erect, like my cock is on standby, just waiting for her return. For svik's sake. *That's right.* The scent of the air in the room is different. *That's right.* My manerak laughs. I try to block it out — the scent, the laughter — but nothing changes when I open my eyes.

I exhale shakily. My whole damn body is shaky when I rise to stand and head to the shallow tub the helpers brought for Mian to use this morning. I tell myself to dunk in quickly, but I hesitate, one foot in, one foot out. The water's cold — as requested, though maybe colder than it needed to be — but that's not what stops me. I don't want to wash her off. I like the smell of her on my skin, the feel of her orgasm drying on my stomach and thighs. My cock hardens fully at the thought, wishing we could bottle her nectar and bathe in it.

I look towards the closed door of the entrance, wondering where she is now — even though I know — and wishing I hadn't sent her away and wanting her back. *Mine.* She's dangerous. *We told you that.* We? That darker, deeper voice surfaces in my thoughts, the one that's distinct from my manerak, the one that's wilder and colder at the same time and infinitely more ancient. Like I'm speaking to some ethereal being. And that being lives inside of me. *We have been waiting for this. For her. For our Xiveri. For the one to release our naxem. Me.*

I shiver as I settle into the water, scrubbing hard at my skin as my thoughts flicker with indecision and doubt. A doubt that my manerak does not feel. Both he and the other guy seem to be immensely happy with the way things have turned out.

"This wasn't the plan," I grumble out loud.

My manerak laughs. *In your life, nothing ever is.*

I'm startled by the sound of the dolsk entrance opening and falling shut. Mian steps through and sees me and blinks rapidly and for all my doubt, I can't help but grin at her. That seems to ease her and I feel pleased that she isn't recoiling from me, or running in terror of what I might do to her next. *Of what we will do to her. All of us. All three.*

Still, she's nervous to hold my gaze in a way I don't like. What I like even less is that I don't know at all what she's thinking. Does she regret it? Being with us? All three of us? My manerak and my naxem are both silent. But they are still present. Yena, I've never felt them like this before, like two separate presences who live right between my two hearts, nestled just under the surface of my chest.

There is no fighting to draw them forth and there is no denying his existence. Not anymore. Not after what I just shared with Mian. Whatever I did by marking her like that seemed to break something inside of me. Or put it together. I can't tell which. All I know is that if I wanted, I could transform into my full naxem form without pain or difficulty, and then back again in less than a moment. We are three separate entities now, each with our own thoughts, but we have also never been more *one* than we are now. I don't understand it. Or anything.

"Are you okay?" I say. My voice catches like a youth in puberty. I cough to clear it.

"Yena. I um…I never…with a male…like that…" She makes a gesture with her hand like something exploding.

A fierce and alarming pride beats through my breast. All I can do is grin.

Her lips tighten, but her cheeks lift. She rolls her eyes and steps forward into the room and I notice she's still wearing the robe I gave her, and not a shift. I grit my teeth a little bit. Only claimed females wear robes. All helpers wear shifts and she is not even that. *Fool. We will give her more. Everything. Anything she wants.*

I swallow hard and say, "Then you should let me finish the job."

She tilts her head, not understanding me. Better, her language skills, not perfect. I stand up from the bath and take my erection in my fist, like a sword. One I mean to slay snakes with. Her bronze skin darkens and I laugh, stepping from the tub.

"I think you should get back on the bed," I gesture to it, "and let me forget about my warrior training for the rest of the solar. Help me forget."

She must understand enough of what I mean, because she looks at the bed and bites her bottom lip like she's considering it and svik, if that just doesn't undo me. I growl — my manerak and my naxem, one of them or both, growl — but she holds up her hands and steps back. "Tszk. I will only be tried by the male I am joined with." This sentence she says perfectly. She must have memorized it.

Join with her then. Easy. The thought crosses my mind and then leaves just as quickly. I must join to unite my tasmaran with another. That is my duty. Select a strong female — a manerak female — to ensure and protect my line. *But what happens to her? We have already marked her.* I wince at that. I did mark her. I shouldn't have. But I did. *She may not be yours, but she is* ours. *Mine,* and then a much darker, more threatening brogue, *mine.*

I shake my head, shaking out the voices. Feeling even more like a madman when she looks at me like I am one. "I'm not joining with any female anytime soon."

At least this much is true. I'll worry about what my tasmaran, manerak and naxem want later. For now, I just want to couple with her again, even if it is still a… weaker imitation of the kinds of activities we could be doing. *The kinds that produce heirs. Naxem heirs,* the dark voice says again, *and manerak.*

She nods. "That's fine. But I can do no more with you. My lines." She points to her wrists. "No break."

"Why?"

She bites her bottom lip in a way that makes my cock kick. She glances at it, and it kicks again, dancing for her before I take a thin linen towel and dry off with it, then wrap it around my waist as if to tell my cock that it requires my submission. *It doesn't. It belongs to us.*

"I have nothing else," she finally says.

I frown and open my mouth — to contradict her — but then shut it just as quickly. Even though manerak don't worship and fear sex in the same way these human tribes evidently do — though perhaps we *should*, considering that after *not* having sex with her, I'm feeling all kinds of unsettled and ripped open and wounded — she has no skills to speak of, can't defend herself, and is scrawny, probably a poor cast to pop out a strong litter.

She doesn't have much else to offer the male that will claim her other than the fact that he will get a few seconds of satisfaction knowing that he is the only male to enter her heat. *A tight heat. A tight, wet heat.* My cock fights with my towel, wanting to be rid of it. *Take her.* Tszk.

I shake my head, trying to imagine what it would be like knowing that another male claimed that sacred space for his own. That he was the one to tattoo that little strip of black to her skin to complete her lines. That he would own her. Forever.

Because she won't mate with a male just once, for pleasure. This one mates for life.

I frown even harder. "Strena," I say.

She tilts her head. "Where?"

"Warrior training."

Her eyes round and she tilts her head in the other direction. "I am no warrior."

"Yena, I know." If she were this would be easier. *This* is *easy, fool. Take her!* "You'll come with me and watch."

She holds out her arms and gestures to her robe. I see her problem, but before I can address it, she says, "I want manerak lesson with humans."

Frustration tickles the nape of my neck. I close the distance between us — or I try — but the instant I come within reaching distance of her, my manerak revolts and tries to grab her. I end up controlling the motion, but gracelessly. To her, it must look like I'm a top gone loose on the spin, arms flailing about.

Pretending I'm in control and not the least bit embarrassed, I jab a finger at her chest with force. Her *thin* chest. *Too many solars she went without food. Did Tatana feed her? Or did he just try to mark our woman?*

"I am First. You have to come with me. It's an order." The words sound weird and wrong as I say them, but I hold firm. Try to hold firm. *You do not order her. She is our master. She owns us.* I swallow hard at my manerak's words, taking them for inflammatory garbage.

"Why?" She throws her hands up into the air in a way that doesn't help my stern disposition. My stoicism cracks and I grin. Then I think hard about what she's asked.

Why? That's a good sviking question. "I'm... because I said..." I growl out my frustration and stomp one foot on the floor. Frustrated herself, she turns to leave. *Stop her.*

I think to grab her, but register that that action might appear threatening and I have no intention of threatening her. Instead my manerak surges — perhaps my naxem — and I shift across the room so quickly water would be jealous. I block her exit. She plants her arms on her hips, lifts her chin and glares at me. Hard.

I think about all the orders and commands I'd like to give her and come to the rapid realization that none of them will work. And besides, after she wrung me out like she did, I'm tired. The thought brings a faint smile to my lips that she clearly doesn't appreciate.

"Why this, when manerak class?" She says, pointing to her lips and miming a smile.

It makes me laugh. Everything she sviking does makes me laugh. She's pleasure incarnate, in all its many forms. I take a step to breach the space between us and take her wrists, gently this time. I bring her hands to my mouth and kiss her knuckles. As I do, I linger. My eyes close. My hearts blunder their rhythm. I taste egra and sand and tall reeds, freshly plucked. *Mian. Sasorena*…

"Neheyuu, I…tszk," she says. Her jaw is working, she's floundering as she gestures back towards the bed. "Pain."

She gestures to the space between her legs and my eyes flare, my senses heighten. I'm just about to scoop her up and throw her onto the bed and examine her myself when she starts waving.

"Tszk, tszk. No pain. I am…too many," she says, shooting me a crooked grin as she brings her hands together — with mine — and makes her symbols for explosions again.

I grin impishly at her, rakishly, and kiss the center of each of her palms. "I cannot take you again. If I tried, I'd have to take you all the way and then you'd kill me and then I'd be apart from you in death. That's why I can't let go of you yet." She blinks at me quickly, trying to make sense of what I've said. I don't know that she does, because she squints at me and bites her lower lip.

"I need you." *That's right.* "Just for now." *False.* "You'll go back to your humans and manerak lessons on the next solar." *Tszk, she will not.*

She looks skeptical. So, she has understood me then. I'm glad that she doesn't respond though, and rolls her eyes instead. "Only this solar," she blurts, snatching her wrists out of my grip and rubbing them, like she didn't enjoy the feel.

I frown and cock my head. "Fine. Come with me now then. We have already wasted too much time." *A waste?* My manerak hisses in disappointment, chilling my bones.

I lead her out into the light that is no longer at its brightest. We weave between the many dolsks and then pass onto the surrounding fields and within them, the packed dirt arena our warriors use for training. Thirty warriors train now and I frown around at them, imagining Tatana leading Nevay warriors, a hundred strong, to come and rip her from my fingers.

My fingers twitch. I need a stronger tasmaran. I need more credibility. I need the respect of senior warriors to join my tasmaran and bring their families within the safety I provide. *What safety?* I need to join with a respected female, one who wields warriors. I glance back at Mian and frown. She is not such a female. I cannot join with her, I know that, but it feels strange knowing that my main motivation would be to ensure the strength of my tasmaran so that I don't have to give her up. So that I can better protect her. *There are other ways, fool. You forget about us…*

I don't understand the musings of my naxem or my manerak and decide to sviking ignore them — and everything — for now.

A large dolsk sits on the far side of the packed sand pitch and I walk Mian to it, drawing the eyes of all warriors not engaged in battle — and several that are. I ignore them too as I wave Mian inside. The entrance is a slim piece of fabric, rolled up, and though I step into the darkness, Mian only pokes her head past the barrier.

She sniffs and makes a face. "Bad…" She waves her hand in front of her nose. "What is this?"

I cross my arms over my chest and frown harder. "Weapons. You will stay here."

"What do I do here?"

A reasonable question. "I don't know." *Do you know anything?* I throw my arms in the air. "Clean something."

She squints into the room behind me. It's big, but because of that, poorly illuminated by the dolsk's solitary smoke shaft. To my manerak's eyes, it isn't a problem, but her human ones are likely weak, just like the rest of her human senses.

She nods slowly and points to the weapons racks nearest to us. "Clean with what?"

I glance around. Heat rushes up the sides of my neck, making the muscles there pulse with tension. How should I know what to clean weapons with? I'm First. This is the job of a weapons keeper. And I'm a First… with no weapons keeper. *And you expect your dolsk to grow? Tsk, tsk…* A dark laughter floods my thoughts and I bark outside for a helper.

A passing female hastens over, carrying a basket full of spices. *Vanthia seed.* The smell reminds me too much of Mian and for a moment I just stare at the female and her basket when she clearly expects me to speak.

"Fetch us polish," I stammer, "leather oil, soap and water, and several rags. Bring it to this female." I gesture to Mian.

Mian smiles at the female who smiles back tentatively. She is another manerak without a manerak skin, as so many helpers are. "Of course. I'll just deliver this to the healers first."

I nod. "Good."

She scuttles off, faster than she was moving before. Mian stares after her. "Helper, her name?"

My lips quirk at that. "Tszk. Helpers perform tasks around the dolsk. Anyone can ask them to do anything. Eventually, they find their specialty and are no longer helpers."

"Again," she says, squinting up at me in a way that's too sviking adorable not to want to reach out and touch her face, so I do. And I repeat for her, much more slowly and in fewer, simpler words.

Her eyes light up when my fingers skim her cheek — because she likes it, or because she understands, or both, I'm not sure. She nods and points to her chest. "I am helper too?"

"Yena. You are *my* helper. You don't help the others. Only me." Somehow, the thought of one of my warriors ordering her to do something — *to bring water for a bath in their tent* — makes me want to stab something.

I jerk my hand back and rub it on my linen pants. Svik. I forgot to change into my armor. Guess I'll go without it... "Now stay here. I'm going to go with my warriors and when I'm done, we'll go back to my dolsk and I'll feed you."

"Tekevanki?"

Irritation shoots up the backs of my legs. My manerak pushes up against my chest, a caged creature demanding release. "I will speak to her. She won't bother you again." *Or get in our way.*

Mian smiles a little uncertainly before tucking her hair behind her ear. It's messy, shooting up in all directions. I grin at her. She grins a little more fully. And I am still grinning when I turn to join my warriors. Judging by their varied expressions, there's not a doubt as to what they think. Dandena is smiling when I approach her fighting circle. Chimara is a part of it and is the only one frowning.

I meet her gaze and her eyes genuflect, and the strange urge to explain myself to her rises within me. "I did not complete her circles, don't worry."

She doesn't look much like she believes me, but who cares, I tell myself. She's just a warrior among my tasmaran, and the only one who's business Mian's is, is mine. *Ours. All of ours. But Chimara? Chimara is a friend. She cares for Mian.*

Dandena steals my attention and says, "So glad you could join us, First. I thought poor Preena was going to quit after you didn't come out of your dolsk that first solar." The other warriors in Dandena's circle chuckle and I smile too.

"I see you successfully scared him away."

"Not at all. I ordered him to rest after he did not do so for the past two solars. Since you returned to the tasmaran."

A flare of guilt surges, then retreats as quickly as a startled oeban. "And you took over?"

"Yena. Just for the solar. I figured someone ought to teach these sad sacks some proper fighting techniques, rather than the brutal chaos you usually enforce."

I wonder if she's teasing me, or telling a truth. I can't ask though without fearing her answer. Instead, I say, "And have you made any progress?"

"Some. Wilen is looking slightly less manic than usual, and Torbara has finally managed to block more than two attacks in a row."

I nod. "Good. Let's see how well you've taught them then. Torbara, Wilen," I call and two younger warriors trots over from two separate training groups, sweat on their brows and small smears of blood on their armored breasts.

"First," Torbara says, bowing slightly. Wilen repeats the gesture. Good warriors though they are, I haven't spent much time practicing with them, preferring to focus on the manerak warriors in my tasmaran. They are only forty of the sixty warriors I have and I do not hide that the manerak warriors get preferential treatment from me. Though perhaps…they shouldn't. What if, one day, it is up to one of my warriors without a manerak form to defend Mian from something or someone?

Wilen's expression belies a surprise that speaks to the fact that I don't often call on him and guilt trickles through me. I clear my throat. "I hear you all are improving. I am coming to test that."

I call on my manerak and he responds in that instant, surging forward, coming to consume me faster than he ever has — so fast, that the warriors nearest me jump back — even Dandena is knocked onto her ass when Torbara elbows her in his haste to withdraw his weapon.

She curses, "Sviking stars, First. Some warning next time would be appreciated."

Even if my true form had wanted to apologize, my manerak just grins down at her as she dusts herself off and ambles to her feet. "I didn't train with them as manerak. It's never been protocol before."

"They need to be able to defend against any opponent. Manerak or not," my manerak says in his grumbling hiss. He is thinking of Mian. What if Wilen were left to defend her and Tatana came? He may be her last defense one solar. *"They may be the tasmaran's last defense one solar. They cannot let her be taken from us."* I stand back from the pair weaponless. As I crouch into a ready position, my linen pants tear up the front around thighs that bulge, preparing to leap.

The two males share a glance. An uneasy one. *As well they should. This is a new beginning.* But before either of them has a chance to strike, Dandena says, "Her?"

I give her a look, a tilt of the head.

"You said *her*, that they can't let *her* be taken from us. Who is her?"

I shake my head, confused by her question. *Isn't it obvious who we mean? If it isn't, it should be.* My manerak, in an act of defiance, glances up towards the weapons dolsk before I can catch him and control the act.

To mask it, I quickly bark out, *"The tasmaran."*

Too late. Dandena is already looking towards the weapons dolsk, a knowing smirk on her face. "Since when is the dolsk female?"

I don't wait for my manerak's reply, but attack all three of them at once.

My naxem sits just on the underside of my breast, high on his pedestal, a spectator watching his sport. He makes no move to intervene — he has not been called on, not yet — and I enjoy his delight at watching my manerak fight these others. What I enjoy more is the control I have over my body. My being. It's something I've never had before, never experienced. And it must show.

When I knock Wilen down for the fourth time, I return to my true form quickly to coach him on how to avoid being mowed down by someone of greater weight — he has no chance to brace and block, as he'd been trying to do, he must rather use my own weight against me, or roll to escape my path and rely on speed to surround me.

Another seamless transition later, Dandena curses. Still in her true form, she crows, "Dammit, how did you do that? Switch back and forth so quickly? You've never done that before. Is there something I'm missing? If I try that, I'm exhausted afterwards for solars."

The solar itself is winding down, the second sun already bowing to the horizon, while the third still hangs above us, too far to be a threat. The first is long gone. I notice that though training goes on well past the setting of the second sun, many of the manerak warriors have started to laze. Or maybe to watch. They're looking away from their groups, eyeing me as I move, maybe wondering the same thing Dandena does.

But I don't have an answer for her. I do, but not one I'm willing to voice. I glance again to the weapons dolsk, though I try not to — of all the things I suddenly can control, I can't control *that*.

"Get back to your groups! Next warrior I see staring gets first lookout this lunar," I shout loud enough to make the warriors of the two groups nearest mine flinch.

In my true form, I ignore Dandena and approach Wilen. I offer him words of advice, showing him where and how to position and plant his feet and when to rotate his hips in order to avoid being trampled and, if successful, flip me over his head and onto my back.

"Getting a manerak on his back is your best — dare I say your *only* — chance to kill him."

"Or her," Dandena chimes.

I grin at her and transform again, winning another startled look from her, before snarling, "*Again*."

He doesn't manage to throw me, but Wilen and Torbara both manage to block me using the techniques I've just taught them — until, in a surprising display of weakness, Torbara collapses onto his ass when I sweep his feet.

"*That was a feint. You should have sviking seen it coming*," I say, advancing on Torbara with every intent of grabbing the whelp by the throat.

He stutters, eyes shifting in their sockets like caged snakes. "First, I…I know. I just got distracted. I shouldn't've, but I…is she supposed to be doing that?" He points, and I follow the direction of his finger to the weapons dolsk. My hearts damn near skip a beat when I see her first.

And then I see what she's doing.

"What in the sviking comets…" I curse, returning to my true form.

Dandena chuckles somewhere behind me because I'm already half way to Mian. She's standing on an overturned crate — one that isn't weight-bearing — and when I shout her name, she turns and topples backwards off of it. She doesn't hit the ground because I'm standing beneath her, her body cradled in my arms.

I don't know how I arrived to her so quickly, certain that it was more than my manerak propelling me across the packed sand. *That's right*. I don't have time to dwell on it. Her scent hits me like a full-frontal attack. A pack of desert dogs eager to tear me apart would be less lethal.

I'm hard instantly and my tattered linen pants don't do svik to hold back the raw need shivering through me. I should put her down right away, but I don't. I take my time just to hold her, feel her weight against my chest, her subtle heat, her vanthia seed, her palm, her otherworldly essence. It would be too easy to let her scent take me away. And beat me to death.

And then I see the knife in her fist. It's a huge dagger — freshly polished. It glints in the light the way the other swords no longer do. The length of her entire arm, it's way too sviking big for her.

"You could cut yourself with this," I snarl, reaching to take the blade away from her. She tries to keep it from me, forcing me to snatch her wrist in one hand and with my other, lower her feet to the ground. "What are you doing?"

She starts explaining something to me, but her manerak is too choppy to understand, especially when she throws human words in to fill the gaps. I don't realize we have company until Chimara steps out from within the dolsk and says, "She told me that this is what you told her to do." I notice she's holding a similar sized blade in her hand. It's also just as clean as Mian's, except Chimara is competent enough to wield it.

I glare at her. "You let her use this weapon? She's going to hurt herself." I whisk it from Mian's grasp while she's looking at Chimara. Her bottom jaw drops open when I refuse to give it back to her.

"You say clean. I clean."

Chimara says, "If I might add, she's unlikely to hurt herself given the state of that blade. Who knows when the last time it was sharpened. If ever."

I refuse to let myself get riled and say, "What the svik does the knife have to do with cleaning — even a dull one? And what are you doing to my dolsk?" My gaze expands its focus to consume more than just her face, but the world around it. That's when I see that she's been cutting huge strips in the outer hide of the dolsk, rolling them up and fixing them with ties so that there are several entrances adjacent to one another. I don't understand what she's doing at all.

She shifts away from me and I don't know why, but I don't like it. Then she throws her hands in the air and when she plants them on her hips, her face twisting up and her eyes squinting in a way that's purely hilarious, my previous irritation is forgotten.

"How to clean when I not seeing?" She glowers.

Chimara laughs and when I glare at her, she looks away quickly and shrugs with one shoulder. "She's got a point. It *is* dark in there. Half the time, I'm not even sure what weapon I'm grabbing."

I don't like that. I don't like that at all. I look back at the dolsk and what's become of it. Worse than when we're traveling, this permanent dolsk looks like all the travel stores were just shucked in here after every raid with no care at all. *Perhaps because they were.* The rounded walls of the dolsk house different racks with various weapons piled onto each one. Each rack is overflowing. Each weapon is in a different state of dilapidation. Some might even be prizes, but they're too far buried and blemished to know for sure.

Only one rack stands out, near the front. All the weapons have been cleared off of it and now only two swords hang side-by-side, clean, hilts oiled, blades polished. The weapons gleam, but only because of the rolled hide that lets in the fading late-solar light. It turns the closest blade to purple.

"You did this?" It's only been a short while. I step forward into the dolsk to inspect the weapons at the same time that Reffa comes around the corner.

"My sword," she says bitterly as she tosses the broken shard of a thing onto the shaded earth beneath the dolsk. It thuds mutely as it falls and as I look down on it, I wonder what it was before. Not a sword, certainly, even though that's her claim.

I hiss between my teeth, "We're busy here."

"I can't fight. I can't train. What am I going to use to defend against Ofrat? My teeth?" She steps all the way under the dolsk and her eyes flare with understanding as she looks up and sees me. "Sasorana strike me down. I didn't see you there, First."

"It's not *that* sviking dark."

Reffa looks at the other two females in the dolsk with me, then sweeps her gaze around. "I mean, it's not as dark as when I grabbed my first weapon, but it's still pretty dark."

"You're *manerak*."

"I mean, it's dark for my true form. I could switch, sure, but that's a lot of work for a weapon." She swallows audibly. "But I will, of course, if that's what you command."

Too frustrated to come up with the right words, I grunt, "Just leave us."

"Wait," Mian chimes, voice light and cute with her heavy accent and slow, clear speech. "For you." She takes one of the two swords she's polished from the rack and hands it to Reffa — clearly, she didn't miss Reffa's complaint. The thought that she heard it makes my face warm. *She is our female and she thinks you a fool. She thinks you weak. Not suited to care for a dolsk, let alone a tasmaran. Not suited to care for her. For her future kits. For anything.*

Reffa looks at Mian skeptically, but still takes the blade from her outstretched hand. Reffa tests its weight. Tilts it left and right. "Sturdy weapon. And it actually shines in the light," she balks. "Not too dull either."

"I make…" she looks to Chimara for help, says something in human.

Chimara explains, "Mian says that she'll sharpen it the next solar." Then to me, "I don't mind taking some time to show her how. She says she didn't do it already because she doesn't know how to work a whet stone."

Lightning shoots up the backs of my legs. I shake my head. "Tszk. I'll teach her." I suddenly don't want anyone teaching her anything but me. Especially after what we shared in my dolsk or on the sandy plains… But wait — no untried female knows how to do the things she did. Who taught her? What males has she been with?

I edge slightly in front of her, suddenly not wanting her near *anyone*, even another female. "The blade will be sharp tomorrow," I mutter by way of dismissal.

Reffa heads to the exit — the very *wide* exit — but just before she leaves, she turns back and says, "Thank you — Mian, is it?"

Mian nods, asks Chimara a question, to which Chimara answers with a smile on her face. "When someone thanks you, you reply, *it's nothing*."

"Trego nogo na," Mian repeats, a smile on her face that not even the shade underneath this dolsk can diminish.

Reffa chuckles and leaves and when she does, I turn to Mian and begrudgingly allow her to continue her work. I leave Chimara with her and send two other warriors to assist. I don't want her using any of the weapons — handling them to polish and clean, is fine, but I don't want her getting cut on any of the shit.

I return to the groups, to Wilen and Torbara, and run them through some exercises before sending them each on staggered runs around the entire tasmaran. As if they weren't worn out already.

Dandena finds me as she returns her weapons to Mian and sets off after the last group to depart. "You know none of them will be able to keep up a lunar shift without nodding off given how you worked them today. You want me to hang back and take the first shift?"

I shake my head. "Tszk. I'm taking the first shift. Chimara and a couple others have been helping Mian with the weapons dolsk. They will take the first shift alongside me. You hang back and command the second shift. I'll send you warriors when it's time. *Rested* warriors."

Dandena gives me one of her smiles that says both too much and too little before disappearing into the lunar. The weapons dolsk is still a hive of activity when I make my way over to it — Mian, trying to wrestle some order into the weapons that have been recently discarded, and the rest attempting to secure the dolsk's many flaps to one another so as not to let the wind carry sand in.

I issue the orders for shift guards and command everyone else to rest. Including Mian. As much as I'd like to keep her with me, I tell Chimara to take her for last meal with the other humans and then return her to my dolsk where she'll sleep this lunar *and every other*. A final command is issued to Chimara — this one to send Tekevanki to me during first watch at the lower rim of the tasmaran in the direction of the third sun and where it sets.

I don't say goodbye to Mian. I don't like the idea of it. So I just leave her with Chimara and her weapons and her arms covered in smudges from polish and oils and take off.

Weaving through the many dolsks, the earth tickles the soles of my hardened feet. Even though the wind is quiet and the sky is decorated in somber shades of slumber, the tasmaran is never more alive than now. Helpers are rushing between the various dolsks, providing food platters to the families living within them, though most will eat around the freshly kindled fires. Already, great orange wreaths float up into the lunar while manerak — and human — sit around them, eating under Sasorana's light.

Small kits are being cradled in the arms of adults while the larger children run around, playing games with sticks and wheels. One smaller kit nearly crashes straight into me. I reach out and grab her shoulders, holding her at arm's distance. She giggles and runs off again, leaving me smiling. Smiling and a little surprised.

This kit is *not* manerak. She is smaller than the others, and a little more delicate, built with thin bones, but she still has the golden hair we share and a pale brown skin tone. If she will uncover her own manerak form remains to be seen, but for now, she's running the camp as if she were born to one day rule it.

And she isn't manerak.

Dangerous. The danger surfaces in my chest like a balloon, that tired hope. I try to quash it, but it remains, distracting me from the scents of roasting rednuts and sugar reed stems, from the sounds of laughter, the distant wail of a babe, of a group of males arguing amongst one another.

I make it to the edge of the tasmaran village, and the pressure in my chest dulls. I blink and feel a little more grounded. I stare out over the dark world, watching the tall grasses bend and sway in the shadows, looking like sinister things. Other tribes could approach quite close without my being certain. It makes me think that I should cut the grasses much further out, and establish a second, more distant perimeter of torches. *Yena, you should have done this turns ago. Even before you had such a prize worth protecting. Fool…*

"Neheyuu," comes the crackle of a voice behind me.

So deep in my thoughts, it takes me a moment to remember who the female is and why she's approaching me in a hazy cloud of brightly colored silks. She smiles when I look up at her, and I cannot deny that the effect is dazzling. It's meant to be, of this I'm sure.

Her hair is silky and her eyes are tilted up at the edges, as if in allusion to her manerak heritage. She would make a strong match to *any* First — and what's more is that she'd take Creyu and the manerak warriors loyal to him with her. Svik — if she had any fighting bones in her body, she'd have made a good *challenger* to *any* First. To me. Perhaps she would have won the fight that Tatana lost. Perhaps the newest dolsk would not then have been given to me, but to her. Perhaps… *But she has no naxem,* the deep voice growls, *because she has no Xiveri.* What is Xiveri?

"Neheyuu," she coos again, voice high and singsong and throaty. All things I once found enticing. As I once found her. Now I can't see it at all.

All I can see is the meat on her bones, the height to her frame and the notes of deception in her gaze — all things letting me know that she isn't the puny human with broken rings around her wrists and the universe in her hair.

"Tekevanki." I clear my throat and straighten, turning away from the darkness beyond the perimeter of my tasmaran, but only just enough to see her. I will not leave my post. "Thank you for coming." The words sound awkward, because I've never said them before.

Tekevanki must notice, because she falters. Her steps come up short. Her face twists and in one sudden motion, she is no longer elegance and grace, but some evil sorceress sent to spew curses. "What is this?"

I glance around, genuinely confused. "What is what?"

"What is the meaning of this? Why are you speaking to me in this way? I am your akimari and you haven't called on me once since you returned from your last raid."

"That is what I wanted to discuss."

Her expression turns cold. The fires shining brightly around us cannot touch her. "There is nothing to discuss except for the human slave who continues to slither back into your bed. I will order guards outside of your dolsk to prevent it."

I laugh, "Tekevanki, I don't know what privileges you think your father's status here allows, but if you think to order my tasmaran around like they're your own, then you'll need to challenge me for that right first. Is that your intention?" I take a step towards her and my manerak flares — no, my naxem. My shoulders broaden, neck and head forming a diamond shape as I loom over her. *She threatens Mian. Strike her down. There is no question.*

She canters back two steps, and then one more. "You…me…I am your akimari…"

"You are my self-appointed akimari, and yena, I will admit that I did enjoy our encounters in the past, but like the past, your status as akimari is now over."

Her eyes narrow. Her shoulder set just beneath her earlobes. "Because of a human?"

"Because of us. Because we were never intended to be anything. I am First of this tribe, and you know it's my intention to take a female from a neighboring tribe to secure an alliance. What you could possibly hope to gain from continuing as my akimari is beyond my reason."

Her jaw clenches. Her eyes blaze. A hint of manerak surfaces in her shoulders and neck. "You would speak to me this way? Have you forgotten who I am…"

My naxem surges up at the threat to Mian, and the thought that she'd ever be taken away from me. *From us.* My naxem doesn't like it. My manerak doesn't like it. *I* don't like it. "Have you forgotten who *I* am? You did not issue challenge, fight and best Tatana to form this dolsk. Your father didn't either. If I choose to name a new akimari, that's my right as First of this tasmaran, and if you don't like it, you can leave. Take your father with you." The words darken as I speak them, deepening until they enter waters too deep to swim out of. Svik. I shouldn't be saying this. Knowing Tekevanki, she *will* leave and knowing her father, he *will* follow her.

Tekevanki's fists curl, and then they uncurl. The tension in her neck remains taut, even though she balks, "All for a human."

She shakes her head and when she pushes her hair back over her shoulder, the purple of her robe comes into view. She isn't wearing anything underneath. I guess she thought this was going to be a very different kind of meeting. Or hoping it would be. Or if it wasn't, hoping she could sway me.

"She is of no concern to you. And if I see you bothering her again, I'll have you join the helpers. See if you can't find another role here."

Her jaw opens and snaps shut with a loud clack. She points a finger at me threateningly. "You are a fool, Neheyuu. And if this girl doesn't see that, then she's a fool too. She's giving you her cunt with the hopes that you'll take her for your Sasorena, but does she know that you have no intention of ever taking a female from this tribe, let alone one who isn't even manerak?"

I return to my true form and take a step back. I look away from her, out towards the horizon.

"Answer me, Neheyuu."

"Go to bed, Tekevanki."

"Does she even know what an akimari is? Does she know that without rank, she's just a whore?"

Rage. It hits like a fist to the jaw. The taste of blood fills my mouth. *Tekevanki's. Bite her head clean off.* I round on her and I know I'm not myself when she stumbles back and falls. Control. I reign it in easily, even if my naxem wants something else. He listens to me and retreats. *For now. Don't get cocky…*

"She is Mian. She is reesa." *She is mine.* "You don't need to know any more than that."

"You don't even know what she is to you. You are *pathetic.*"

Somehow that insult doesn't sting in the way that it should. I shake my head. Let the cool wind sift through my hair, pulling it off of the back of my neck. "Mian is mine. And she stays safe. She's completely under my protection. A hand to her is a hand to me and a hand to your First is a hand that you no longer need."

"You don't…"

"Tekevanki!" My tongues slither out of my mouth to wet my lips. My patience is running thin. "Bed. Now. Don't make me tell you again."

I meet her gaze and hold it and after a long, trembling silence, the accord is signed. She swishes back the way she came, shapely form swaying as sultry as the tall grasses. And it does nothing for me. I smile to myself and shake my head, switching my stare away from Tekevanki and out towards the sky where two bright orange moons float side-by-side, Sasorana's eyes.

She stares down at me and I laugh up at her. For the first time in my life, I've got no idea what she's trying to do to me.

And for the first time in my life, I've never been so happy.

14
Mian

"The sword you polished for Reffa — do you have another one?" A warrior approaches me holding a weapon so rusted I'm not sure what color it was before — or if it can even be salvaged.

I place the spear I'm working on aside, along with the wood oil, and jump to my feet. "Yena, I do." The warrior is male and leaner than Reffa, taller too. He is familiar in face, though I cannot place his name, and the sword he holds looks a little short for him. I quickly pick up the longer of the sword options I've got polished and hold the hilt out towards him.

"Not so sharp, but better," I say, gesturing towards his discarded blade.

He grins when he takes the new sword from me and swings it in a wide loop. With the front half of the dolsk rolled up and opened, he has the space for it. "Much better. Reffa's sword has been so shiny these last solars, it's blinding me. I can barely keep up with her as it is. I need something to level the pitch."

I feel a little warmth bubble in my chest, and pop. I grin back at the male. He hesitates, then extends one hand forward. "I'm Ofrat, one of the warriors. I joined this tasmaran after the last sessemara."

"Oh. You meet a female?" I snatch my hand back quickly, not wanting to be caught doing something I shouldn't be. Judging by Tekevanki's reaction to me, females seem jealous here. Or maybe they're jealous everywhere. *I wonder if, when I finally meet my mate, I will be.* My thoughts flash to Neheyuu, but I know I shouldn't be thinking of him in this way, so I stop.

He laughs lightly. "Tszk. You can choose to join a new tasmaran for any reason. I was part of the Pikora before, but it's too big. Too hard to move up...to train... better here," he says, I think.

I nod along, not quite sure how to answer — even if I could. He thanks me for the sword and offers to join me for final meal. That comes as a surprise. It's been three dozen solars — maybe more — and so far, I've been joining other humans for manerak classes in the first half of each solar, and in the second, joining the warriors here where I clean the weapons and the room that houses them. I eat first meal with the humans and second and last meal with Neheyuu and the other warriors — in the lunar, typically around their roiling bonfires.

I don't know what he means, but I nod anyways, wanting to be polite. He gives me a little bow and a half-salute with his polished sword. I wish I could have sharpened it, but I still don't know how to use the stone. I'm mulling over that fact when Neheyuu appears.

"What did he want?" He snaps.

I point to the rack of polished weapons and raise one eyebrow.

Neheyuu purses his lips and disappears again. He reappears a moment later wearing a grin. "Be less..." I don't understand what he means, but after some explaining I get to the bottom of it.

"I do not pull eyes away from training!"

Neheyuu laughs and comes towards me — prowls towards me — then reverses, as if an invisible hand grabbed him by his armor and yanked him back. "You do. You just don't know it."

I stick my tongue out at him. He sticks out both of his. I laugh and when he abruptly changes course once more and starts creeping towards me again, my stomach flutters and my pulse picks up a second beat. Less than arm's length from me, he freezes and swallows repeatedly.

"I can't." His shoulders slump forward, just a little. He looks starved.

I nod, understanding. He can't because we'd end up kissing for much longer than either of us has time for. I've been late to first meal more than once — *try every solar*. I like sleeping in the bed with him. I like sharing meals with him. I like when we…please each other in the lunar and whisper softly afterwards in the quiet dark. *Dangerous.* Had I thought that once? Now, as Neheyuu backs slowly out of the dolsk, as if retreating from a predatory animal, I'm sure of it.

I laugh and toss a rag at him. He races forward to catch it, moving at a speed my gaze can't quite track, and then he's gone, rejoined one of the seven groups that are formed. Some solars they form in bigger groups, other days smaller, sometimes just pairs. Every solar though, Neheyuu walks among them, spending time correcting and coaching. It's nice to watch him work. He may seem young, but when he speaks to his warriors, he does so with the aplomb and concentration of a much more seasoned male. He also speaks to each of them like he cares.

As the sky falls, my gaze wanders across the training ground, finding Chimara and Dandena, then picking across other humans practicing, eyes widening at the sight of the manerak. They don't always fight in their manerak forms, but when they do, it's a deadly-looking dance.

My gaze hooks on Reffa in her manerak form. She's fighting Ofrat, who either doesn't want to turn to his snake person form, or can't. But his new sword stands out. I smile a little at the sight and when he flashes it in a way that I can't wrap my head around — somehow arcing it, and then pulling, making the blade look liquid — Reffa's sword goes flying. In the next instant, he barrels into her, shoulder first, and when he rises, he's got one foot on her chest and his sword pointed at her throat.

He grins at her and helps her onto her feet after that, but I'm so surprised still that he could defeat a manerak in his human-looking shape, that as soon as the training ends, I set down all the weapons I'm working on unceremoniously and approach him.

"That is amazing! How do you — did you," I correct, "with Reffa?"

Reffa's standing there too and the two of them share a glance. Ofrat's grinning, but I'm pleased that Reffa doesn't look the least bit embarrassed. "Only once…It must have been the sword." She winks at me and I feel my face warm.

I shake my head. "Sword not sharp. I don't know how."

Ofrat says, "Sword and skill work together. And the sword was an integral part." He winks. "I can teach you how to sharpen them at last meal, if you want."

"Yena, thank you," I say, and I don't mention the fact that Neheyuu says I'm not supposed to be using the whet stone. He thinks it's too dangerous.

"Happy to. But do you really want to know how I got her on her back?"

I nod. "Yena. She is so much bigger as manerak. How?"

"It's…" he says, but the words he uses are too advanced.

Reffa smirks. "He just means it's easy. We'll show you."

The two of them spend the next few moments pushing and pulling me around like a large stuffed doll. Eventually, I get my own feet planted beneath me, my shoulder lowered and my arms braced tight to my sides. I'm able to put up some resistance then when Ofrat charges me. Some, but not enough.

He must not expect me to go flying, but that's exactly what I do. I land hard on my bum and get the wind knocked nearly clean out of me. Ofrat rushes over and asks me if I'm alright. I can't help but laugh while I respond.

"Okay." I nod and let him help me up onto my feet. He dusts off my front and back a little too aggressively and I jump out of his grip. "We try again?"

He smiles and Reffa laughs. "We try again," she repeats, in the same bad manerak I'm so often using. I warm a little, knowing that she's teasing me.

We try again two more times, but the second time Ofrat knocks me hard enough I decide to call it. The two of them and Chimara help me tie up the weapons dolsk before we join the others at the bonfires. By the time we arrive, food is already being served. Dandena calls us over. She has a platter waiting for me. Just for me.

"Courtesy of First," she says as I take a seat beside her. She slides the platter onto my lap and reaches past me for the one Chimara hands to her.

"We can eat together," I offer, extending the tray.

She waves me off. "First made it expressly clear that this tray was yours. I'm not going to take first watch this lunar by eating off your tray." She winks at me and when she twists to face the fire, the scar snaking its way across the side of her head shimmers in the light like water.

"Where is Neheyuu?" I ask her.

"Meeting with Preena. A messenger arrived earlier in the solar. They are making plans, leaving me to babysit these sorry sacks." She says that last part loudly, winning her a few scathing remarks from Xi and Xena sitting across from us. Twins, it creeps me out a little how, even though Xena is laughing loudly and Xi is quiet at her side, they both tilt their heads in perfect unison.

Dandena rasps a fiery retort that wins her another round of laughter. Xena opens her mouth, like she'll say something back, but Reffa gives her arm a good thwack. More laughter. Xena jerks her chin towards Ofrat on my other side and when she does, the fire catches the line of her scar too. It also makes the scalloped edge of her ear look like a dagger. She looks lethal. *Like the kind of female to stand down for nothing.* I try not to let my failure today with Ofrat and Reffa bother me. I'm no warrior, and I know I never will be and I've always been okay with that. But just once, I wish I could be…or feel…*powerful.*

"You looked good out there today, Ofrat."

"The difference a polished sword can make." He nudges my arm and winks at me when I look up at him. The outside of his thigh is pressed against mine. I try to shift a little so that there's more space between us — but without making it obvious. He must not notice because he scoots just close enough to bridge the gap.

"Is that all?" Xena's gaze flashes to me and I notice that her irises are a stunning shade of gold. I also don't need to know the rest of what she says to glean her meaning.

I take the cup Dandena offers me and even though it's more of their terrible hibi liquor, I swallow a draught, coughing a little as I do. Chimara, across from me, laughs. I don't so much as fidget, not wanting anyone around the ring of warriors to know that I'm uncomfortable — to prove Xena wrong, or to prove her right.

I'm grateful then for Ofrat, who seems to take the comment in stride. He answers back and several of the others simper and hiss. Chimara leans behind Ofrat and taps me on the shoulder. She whispers, "He asked if she would say the same to Reffa or if she's just trying to cause a little mayhem, like her name implies. Xena means chaos in manerak." She sticks out her tongue and I laugh too.

"Maybe she *should* say the same to Reffa," Dandena adds, "She was fighting better as well. And I saw some of those moves when you were teaching Mian. You're not bad at it."

"At flipping little manerak males? Of course not."

"I meant at teaching. I'm thinking it might be nice to put you in charge of some of the new warriors when we receive them."

I must be imagining things, but when Reffa's bottom jaw falls open, I swear I can also see the rumblings of a blush high in her cheeks. Reffa looks at me and shakes her head. She goes back to eating more of some soup I haven't had the nerve to try yet and grunts noncommittally in my direction.

"She's easy to teach."

"Maybe we can show you a few more moves tomorrow. Help defend against a bigger opponent," Xena offers. Xi nods along.

Their offer surprises me. I take a sip and nod at the same time, spilling a bit. Xena laughs lightly as I stutter, "Yena. That would be fun."

"Fun. She thinks it'll be fun," Xena chides. Talk devolves after that and I'm grateful when the spotlight shifts onto some of the others, then disperses.

That is, until Ofrat whispers my name. "Would you like me to show you now?"

"Show me?"

"How to sharpen a sword."

"I…" I look up at him, senses a little dulled from the drink. I swirl what's left around my wooden cup and shift a little away from him on the bale of scratchy dried reeds beneath me. They poke through my shift, making me itch. The fires against my face are hot. "I am drinking…"

"Are you drunk?"

I shake my head, maybe a little too quickly. My palms feel a little clammy. Ofrat is an…*attractive* male. He has broad shoulders, a little cut on the left one, and I have seen him fight. But then why does speaking with him like this feel a little like a betrayal? I'm just being silly. Neheyuu and I aren't joined. There is no reason not to take him up on his offer when it would be helpful for the entire tasmaran and its warriors.

I set my shoulders and set down my cup. "Yena. I mean, tszk. I am not drunk. That would be kind. Thank you. We learn here?"

His mouth quirks. "Yena. Here is good." He pulls a whetstone from the half-plate of his chest armor and holds it out towards me. In his other hand, he takes away my platter, sets it between my feet and pulls a huge dagger from the belt at his waist. "It's already fairly sharp, but we can practice on this anyways."

He thrusts the hilt of the knife in my slack left fist and then reaches behind my body to take that fist in his own hand, his arm slung across my shoulder. He hugs me against his chest — the bare half — and I glance at the fire, wondering if it's been recently stoked. I might be sweating. I think I *am* sweating. Does Ofrat know about my wrist tattoos? I'm suddenly nervous. I suddenly miss Neheyuu.

"You want to take the whetstone to the blade in firm, even strokes. Apply a good amount of pressure, but not too much — you don't want to slip." He takes my free hand and, placing the whetstone in it, strikes down against the blade.

I jump at the sharp, steely sound it makes. The rock is smooth in my palm, a little groove on the front the only indication it hasn't just been plucked from the river. He repeats the gesture a few more times, really wielding my arm. I'm not doing much, but it still feels wobbly and uneven.

I try to concentrate and focus on the motion, but he's moving too quickly. I shake my head and am just about to tell him that maybe I should practice again in the morning when I'm less exhausted, but before I can, his arms go slack around me. His whole body pitches right, even though he makes no sound. I jump and let out a little yelp when he tips backwards off of the reed bale, leaving me weakly holding both stone and knife on my own.

I jump again at the sound of a second thump, and then at the third. This time, it's a body taking the place of Ofrat's on the bale beside me. Neheyuu's.

"Neheyuu!" I suck in a breath, cheeks feeling like flames themselves. I also feel distinctly like I've been caught doing something wrong. His expression isn't one I can read as he finishes tossing Ofrat's legs over the edge of the bale. I glance back, worried, and see that he's out cold.

"What did you do?"

"What are *you* doing? Give me that." In a move too quickly to track, he filches the objects in my hands and tosses them over his shoulder onto Ofrat's body.

"Did you kill him?" I hiss, panicked.

He balks, even smiles, though it looks like he's trying not to. He rubs his face roughly as he says, "Course not. But maybe I should have. You could hurt yourself with those things. And what was he doing with his arms all around you like that?"

Well, at least my suspicions that Ofrat *was* too close are confirmed. I flex my fingers, glance around the fire. Dandena is staring hard, a wide smile on her face. The others at least have the decency to *pretend* not to look. "I...he...sharpen weapons."

"That's what I was sviking afraid of. Dandena, when he wakes up, tell him he's on shift all lunar."

"He can't stay awake that long," Dandena says, but she doesn't sound that concerned or upset.

"I didn't say I wouldn't send another shift. But Ofrat stays for both."

Dandena grins. She polishes off her cup and tosses it to Mor to refill it. He takes that opportunity to squeeze in next to her on her bale. "Maybe I can teach *you* how to sharpen swords later," he says to her, and the whole crowd crows with laughter.

I don't dare meet anyone's gaze — especially not Neheyuu's. "Did you eat?" He says to me in a low voice, and it's like everyone else has faded away.

I nod. "A little."

The rumbling in Neheyuu's chest that I've gotten so used to picks up, quietly at first, and then when I start eating, louder. Neheyuu doesn't take the platter from me when I offer it, but…when I offer him a piece of fatty flank from my fingers, he bends down and licks the whole length of my hand before sucking the meat free.

I swallow automatically and when I lick my lips, Neheyuu's eyes hover on my mouth for long after. "You really want to learn to sharpen swords?"

It takes me a moment to realize what he's asked me. When I do, I nod quickly and glance over my shoulder. Whatever hold Neheyuu has on me breaks as I look at Ofrat. "Do you…you do not…he does not sleep here…"

"If I make sure he does not sleep here, will you let me teach you to sharpen swords the *right* way?" He picks up a wedge of opikopi from the tray and holds it to my bottom lip.

Something beyond warmth slithers up my spine. Like a snake eating me whole, one vertebrae at a time. I flick my gaze to his and time seems to stand still. I nod, slowly this time, and even more slowly take the bread from his fingers, letting just the edges of my tongue brush his skin.

He shimmers where he sits, the top of his head arching towards the sky. He returns to his true form and before I know what's happened, me *and* my tray are flying. Up in his arms, up in the air. I let out a wild, whooping laugh and the last face I see is Dandena's. She's rolling her eyes.

Back in his dolsk, hunched over in concentration, I ask, "Like this?"

Neheyuu kneels across from me and tilts his head. The warm light of the fire illuminates the oils on his skin. Freshly bathed. His gaze is still feeding that snake from earlier. The one that lives in me and doesn't seem to want to go away. It's distracting. *He* is distracting.

"Don't look at me, look at the blade," he says, but he's grinning.

"Not so difficult when you wear clothes."

"I am wearing clothes."

"That is a towel."

"Huh." He looks down. "You're right. But it's only fair when all you're wearing is a robe."

He's not wrong. The linen robe is a new item, one that appeared in the dolsk when the helpers came in with the water for our baths. I thought they might have made a mistake, but the female who came with my water said that the robe was for me. Neheyuu just shrugged and made no comment, though I don't doubt that he must have had something to do with it... The material is a delicate, pale cream that, unlike the previous robe I wore for a time, actually fits me...but it's also see-through. I glance down and see my nipples creating stiff peaks in the fabric.

"This is not a good idea." I huff and drop the blocks in my hands — in the right, I have a whetstone, in my left, a block of wood. "I cannot..." I don't know the word and stab around it until Neheyuu finally offers, "Concentrate. And you will need to learn to sharpen with distractions if you intend to sharpen at the dolsk while the warriors train. So concentrate." His smile doesn't fade, but he does roll forward and place the block of wood back underneath the tip of the blade.

He extends the file towards me and explains something that I can't make sense of. When I finally do, I understand that I'm meant to shape the blade before I start to sharpen it. Neheyuu coaches me through the motions. It takes a while before I can do it on my own. The sharpening takes even longer. But at least Neheyuu coaches me to keep the whetstone on the ground and pass the blade over it, rather than the other way around, as Ofrat attempted. I have more control this way and after a dozen passes, start to get the hang of it. *More like a hundred.* Lastly, Neheyuu shows me how to very carefully sand the blade with a thin piece of gritty paper to blend the sharpened parts with the rest of the blade.

When I finish, the sword looks magnificent and I beam with pride. I tilt it towards Neheyuu, waiting for his verdict, but he's just looking at my eyes. "It looks good. You did a good job."

"Better than good. It looks...super!" I don't know any other words.

Neheyuu laughs and rocks forward. He pushes my hand aside and presses it to the warm, carpeted floor. His other hand slides through my hair and he wrenches me in to meet his kiss. His lips pull and suckle tenderly. He tastes like smoked meat even though he's as smooth as fresh cream and the smell of him...the earthy, masculine smell of him...it's a dangerous thing. And it's only gotten more dangerous over time.

I'm still recovering when he pulls back less than a moment later. A moment that's over too soon. "You did a *super* job. But you need sleep. We both do." He groans as he rises and the towel falls away from him completely. It surprises me, even though it shouldn't. I've seen him naked many times.

I keep my gaze averted, trying to stave off thoughts of desire and heat for a little while longer. "Why are you tired? How was your day?"

He grins at me over his shoulder, all rugged and clean. "I don't want to talk about my day. I just want to go to sleep beside you."

I try a smile, but I don't feel it reach my eyes. "Of course." *I am his bed slave, after all, why would he want to speak to me?*

Dutiful as ever, I remove my robe and crawl onto his bed. He watches me as I do so and only when I'm settled does he bother to douse the lights. Then he prowls over the dense, padded mattress and falls onto his back. I roll to face away from him. He pulls me back. I let him. *Akimari.* I know the word. I've learned it in manerak class. The lesson where she went over different roles was very embarrassing.

But there will be a joining ceremony and then I can find a male who will not mind that I am akimari for now, especially when my rings are still intact. Not a *true* akimari. At least that's what I tell myself. The male I find will need to be from another tribe, though. I don't want to watch Neheyuu with another female. But then I'll lose all of my friends and this little life here that I've built that I am quite learning to like. I wince.

"What is it? Did I hurt you?" He rumbles, arms uncurling from around my body, where they'd been fixed.

I use the opportunity to extract myself from his grip and pull a blanket over me, leaving a little more space between us. "Tszk. I'm fine. Sleep deeply, Neheyuu."

He doesn't answer right away. Then, "Sleep deeply, reesa."

He tries to turn onto his side to mold himself around me, but I don't make it easy for him, tossing and turning this way and that. I can't get comfortable. Not with these sudden sour thoughts pressing themselves in on me.

As such, I'm only half awake when I hear him exhale heavily at my side. "After training the next solar, I'll be leaving on a raid."

"Mmh?"

He bends over me, warm breath fanning the side of my face. He plants kisses along my earlobe with every second word. He explains something else, but I don't understand. I shake my head.

He grunts, "Food."

I hug the blanket tighter to my chest. "More food?"

"Yena, food for you."

Dangerous. "Dangerous?"

"Sessena territory. But only a little." He pushes the blankets out of the way, and then slides under them beside me. He holds me to his chest, fixed, and this time there is no getting away. "I will miss you," he whispers. He kisses the back of my head.

"I will miss you too," I say back, almost on reflex, but as I say the words, I know they're true. "You be safe. Keep warriors safe."

The rumbling picks up, louder and louder, but instead of being distracting, I find it soothing and am lost to sleep so quickly I almost miss it, the scent. It's back again. Usually it only comes when Neheyuu spills his seed, but I can feel his erection, dry and wedged against my back. Not fully hard this time, and he hasn't spilled. It must not be his seed then. It must be him. Earth and metal and sweat and sweetness. It's a nice smell. Strange, but nice. Smells like home.

"I will. For you."

15
Mian

I watch the tasmaran prepare to leave and remind each of them of the promise they made me the previous solar, at training — to come back in one piece, and to prove that they will, to bring me a stone. I finish making my rounds and finally find myself standing near Ofrat. He has an oeban's reins in each hand and one of them is a creature I recognize.

"Danon!" I approach the beast and pat him in firm, even strokes down the bridge of his long nose. A six-footed creature, he stamps his front two feet while one in the back kicks involuntarily. The two in the middle remain grounded.

I laugh lightly as Danon tilts his head into the pressure of my hand, urging me to scratch him closer to his small, round ears. "I am happy to see you and that you are well. Thank you for helping me cross desert. You are…were very brave."

Danon huffs and shakes his head, his shaggy grey fur tickling my face as he moves. I laugh again. Above me, Ofrat sighs, "Of course he likes you. I shouldn't be surprised given the way you smell."

"Smell?" I say, hands still sunken into Danon's coat, petting the long line of his neck, roped with muscle.

Ofrat blinks down at me. He says something that I don't understand, then ends with, "...like Neheyuu." I understand that much and blush. "I should've known better, but I wanted to talk to you. Then..." He makes a chopping motion to the side of his neck and I grimace, remembering the sound it made when Neheyuu toppled him so unceremoniously.

"Are you okay?"

"My neck is alright, but I'm stuck on oeban duty now. And this one doesn't like me much."

Danon huffs out of his nostrils, baring his big blocky teeth at Ofrat before returning his cheek to my hand. I reward him with a few more scratches before letting Ofrat start the process of leading Danon and the other oeban towards the tasmaran's main entrance. Or exit.

It's crowded now with beings and oeban, but beyond them, Sasor's three suns shine brightly over the tall grasses. Bright green, they appear nearly electric in this light, but at dusk appear near purple. They sway very gently. So calm. Like the promise of a reward. I exhale and feel...strangely...settled. Home. Dangerous, knowing I cannot stay. Not just dangerous. Deadly.

"Mian?"

I look up. "Sorry. Thinking."

"I can see that. I just wanted to let you know I plan to bring back a stone for you. Mine will be the biggest." He winks and I laugh and I'm still smiling when Chimara jogs up to us.

"Ofrat, I think First needs his oeban, or something." She tosses me a sideways glance — one full of meaning

— and I immediately scan the horizon, trying to root out from where Neheyuu is inevitably watching us. He told me on the last solar that he wouldn't tell me goodbye before the raid and that I shouldn't expect it. Grumbled something about not liking goodbyes. I took no offense to it, but thought his explanation was kind of funny anyways. I just didn't expect him to still be watching us…me.

Ofrat rolls his eyes, but I don't miss the slight tensing of his shoulders. He glances to the left, as if Neheyuu might be coming out of the shadow of the nearest dolsk. But that's just where Rita and Erkan stay. Now, she's standing in the open doorway dressed in the same simple shift all of the unclaimed females wear, Erkan standing just behind her. Strange.

I tilt my head and as I wave goodbye to Ofrat, who waves back in the human way, I ask Chimara in human, "Is Erkan staying here?"

Chimara sighs, "Yeah, me too."

That surprises me. "I thought it was a big hunt?"

"Yeah. Ordinarily most of the tasmaran goes on big hunts, but First has been um…behaving differently since the last raid. He wants more of us staying behind than going on the raids. Says that we have more to lose." She lifts an eyebrow as she speaks and I feel that same heat attack my cheeks all over again. "Now about thirty-five are staying behind to defend the dolsk. Only twenty-five will raid."

"Is that a good thing?" I say, unsure of how to phrase the question. On the one hand, I'm sure Chimara isn't pleased about being left behind. On the other, I'm grateful to have her and the others looking after the tasmaran. Stars forbid I'm captured *again*. And unlike last time, I might actually miss these funny folks. Even though I am a slave, I strangely…don't feel like one.

I rather like working in the weapons tent. I like watching the warriors and I sense that they seem to…to *care* about the praise I give them, and they take the time to show me maneuvers when I ask. I get the sense that I am at least, in part, respected by the majority of them. I mean, would they promise to bring me stones if they didn't like me at least a little bit?

Chimara shrugs. "Not sure yet. Just another way First has been shaking up the tasmaran. So far, the improvements like the extended perimeter markers and the new rotation system seem like smart steps. Seem like calculated ones." She grunts out a laugh. "Not anything our First is known for. But maybe it's just random. Who knows."

"Well, I'm happy to have you."

Chimara grins at me crookedly. "I think the tasmaran feels the same way about you. I know I do. Now come on. The others are leaving, but warriors are still training. We need you on those weapons. Maybe you can help a fellow human out today and get me on the short list for one of those sharp spears."

I beam. "I can do that. I'll just get more wood oil from Eoran and meet you there."

Chimara hesitates, then nods. "Be quick!"

We split apart quickly, Chimara at a light jog, me at a skip. I make it to the large supply dolsk where Eoran keeps most of the tools and utensils I need to maintain — strip bare, repair and refurbish — the weapons dolsk and the weapons within it.

In and out with a short greeting to Eoran leaves me with much-needed supplies in hand. The tasmaran village is quieter now, free of the indistinct chatter of those wishing the warriors well in their hunt, and the warriors and oeban readying for said hunt. Like buzzing insects. Now there's just a calm, strangely foreign peace. Strangely alien.

I giggle to myself and go back to skipping, only to run straight into a body. "Oh my stars, I'm so sorry," I hiss in human before quickly making the switch. The words die almost immediately on my tongue when I look up and see the last face in this tasmaran I enjoy seeing. "Oh…Tekevanki. I am sorry. I just go…was just going…"

"To the training grounds. Yena, I know." I struggle to meet her gaze — part of it is guilt, part of it is intimidation. My position here is tenuous, at best, and she walks this dolsk like a queen among peons. I can't imagine anyone who wouldn't be intimidated by her. When I don't say anything right away, she snaps, "You don't have to fear me, girl. I'm not going to bite. Even though I could if I wanted to."

When I look at her face, she flashes a mouthful of distinctly manerak teeth, sharp as blades. I swallow the warm, dry air with difficulty. "Alright."

She shakes her head, strands of her gold hair scattering around her shoulders like they are worth their weight. "Tszk, I am not here to hurt you. But can I give you some advice?"

I nod, wishing I could say no, but still not totally feeling as if I have that right.

"Neheyuu will choose a manerak female from another tribe at the sessemara. You may want to start making space in Neheyuu's dolsk for her now."

I shake my head, confused.

Tekevanki shifts towards me and huffs, "It will be easier on all three of you when she joins this tasmaran. It is clear that you actually like him and that he may even like you in return," she says, but I still don't get it. All I register is the potent, sulfuric sensation chewing away at my insides, leaving nothing in its path.

"Start making space now so it hurts less when she joins with him at the ceremony." She shakes her arms and that's when I notice what she's carrying. A huge series of rings made of — is that *gold?* — hang off of one of her elbows. A pile of silks and strings and fabrics sit jumbled together in a basket she carries in her other hand.

She's trying to impart some knowledge onto me by the shaking of the items, but I'm at a total loss. I shrug and before I can say anything, she barks out a clack of laughter and it is a terrible, wretched sort of sound. One intended to wound. And it does. Even if I have not yet understood its provenance, it hurts everywhere it lands.

"Sasorana, help you. You truly are a pitiful little thing. Why do you think they are going on a hunt so urgently? It is to have an offering for the *sessemara*. Neheyuu did not even tell you, did he? Tszk. If he had, you would be making one of these." She holds up her rings and drapes them over her neck.

"The wreath is necessary to participate in the sessemara. All males and females seeking to be joined must have one. The larger, more ornate the wreath, the higher your status. While those without status don't often participate in the ceremonies, I was sure I'd see you busying yourself with some fabrics at the very least, in the hopes of being selected. Unless you *want* to remain here and watch Neheyuu share his dolsk with a new female. I certainly have no such desire."

Her eyes narrow a little bit, then relax, and when she stands up taller and sighs, I feel a little of her hostility displace itself, revealing a female with very different colored insides. "I do not like Neheyuu. He's selfish, spoiled, and stupid. A warrior. Not a strategist. I wanted only the position of being mated to a First, of being Sasorena, and thought that Neheyuu might be the best way to get it. I've realized that's a mistake. Clearly.

"I'll be leaving at the coming sessemara, taking my father with me and at our count, as many as sixteen of Neheyuu's warriors. That means he will *have* to join with a female at the ceremony. If he does not, his losses will be too many to defend his tasmaran. He may have to merge back into another tasmaran, take the position of Second, or be killed when a competing tasmaran raids. And they *will* raid, given the spoils. That means you have exactly thirteen solars to cleanse your system of all things Neheyuu. Of his dolsk. Of this tasmaran. Of your life here."

"Thirteen solars?"

She nods. "This is when the sessemara will take place. It will be hosted by the Hox. Since only those incapable of travel and the minimum warriors needed to guard them will not attend, it will be a good opportunity to meet other members from other dolsks and determine if joining another dolsk is something you would like. And I hope it is something you will like, because if you really do like Neheyuu, you cannot remain here. It will destroy you both."

I nod. I feel dumb. I feel like crying.

The bottom of my stomach has opened up and its contents mix with the tips of the tall grasses. When I look down, they've totally swallowed my feet. If left to stand here, I'm certain that it won't take long for them to swallow the rest of me.

Tekevanki's hand claps down on my shoulder. Firm. A female who knows who she is and what she wants. *But who am I? What do I want?* I want to join with someone. I thought I didn't care who he was as long as he was kind and gentle. And then I let *him* get under my skin, infect me like a virus. I frown, feeling foolish. Feeling fooled.

"Here. Take this. Make yourself a wreath. At the sessemara, get Neheyuu's attention. Just talk to him, chat him up. The longer the better. He may be a fool but he *is* still First of his tribe, and if he shows you even a little bit of attention in front of the other males, you stand a good chance of being approached by a lesser warrior from a competing tasmaran. Hopefully more than one. When that happens, you will accept their wreaths and on the second solar, they will fight for you and then present you with a gift.

"On the third and final solar of the sessemara, you will return the wreaths back to the males you will not choose, and then give your chosen male your own wreath, keeping his for yourself. Now here. You can have this to make your wreath. I don't need it."

She hands me a beautiful piece of fabric. Pure white. As white as the second sun if you stare directly at it. I take it in between my fingers, immediately smudging it with dark brown wood oil. And somehow that just sends my stomach past the tall grasses, past the sand below them and into the foundations of the earth.

How could I have let this happen? How could I have started to feel for a male way beyond my reach who I knew, from the beginning, I could never have?

I exhale heavily. *I've got no time for pity. Slaves never do.* I shrug my shoulders back, set my chin and meet Tekevanki's gaze directly. She straightens herself, meeting my gaze but seeming surprised by it. "Thank you, Tekevanki. And I am sorry things did not go the way you wanted them to."

She just makes a sound between her teeth. A very human sound. "It doesn't seem like things are going the way you wanted them to either. I only hope that you manage to get chosen by a half-decent male. You are not a bad female. We both made the mistake of walking down a path with no destination. It's time to change course." She closes the distance between us, takes my wrist holding the fabric. Drops her tone. "Find a decent enough male. Join with him. Don't look back. Don't let anyone stop you. Not even Neheyuu. *Especially* not Neheyuu."

Then she's gone. Fluttering away in a whirlwind of pretty dyed fabrics and gold. And all I can think, as I stare down at a swatch of pretty white fabric in my dirty, polish-covered hands, is that Neheyuu knew. He hugged me close and told me about the raid and the hunt, but not the sessemara. And he knew.

I'm in a daze for the rest of the solar and as lunar approaches, I cut myself twice on two different weapons in an effort to sharpen them. Chimara takes the whetstone away from me after the second time. Though it isn't deep, the cut spans the full length of my palm. She takes me to see Reepal who seems nervous as he applies the bandages to my skin. He apologizes many times that Verena is not here to tend to me, but explains that she is with the tasmaran. I tell him that I am glad it is him and he smiles a little brighter.

Quickly patched, I insist on returning to the weapons dolsk to finish polishing the sword I was working on, but we only make it halfway there before the warning reed is sounded. Its low, eerie melody wafts on the air, like wind chimes gently shaken. And yet it precedes the panicked stomping of feet and the hysterical shouting of families rounding up missing kits and orders dispatched across and among the remaining warriors.

"What…what is happening?" I say, finally finding a speech I'd lost since my earlier conversation with Tekevanki.

Chimara grabs my wrist and starts to pull me across the village, following a path whose destination I can't determine. I just flail along behind her. "Desert dogs."

I shudder. I know desert dogs. Huge, carnivorous creatures, on their hind legs they stand much taller than manerak. On all fours, they loom nearly as large as the largest oeban. Two mouths means two sets of teeth, one stacked right on top of the other. Claws built like daggers. Their mangy fur hides scavenger insects that feast on the flesh of the fallen. I watched a swarm of them devour the remains of one of my slave masters who'd been pulled apart by a dog while I hid, forgotten in the rafters.

One of only ten survivors of that attack, we wandered the plains of Sasor for nearly fourteen solars before finally finding another human settlement. In that time, I didn't eat. It was the longest I ever went without eating… And by the time I made it to that camp, I was willing to sell myself for a loaf of bread and a glass of water.

So I did.

"I…are we…can we…where are we going?"

Chimara shakes her head and pulls me inside a dolsk. I'm surprised to find several other humans already inside until Chimara tells me, "This dolsk is Ock's. Somehow his dolsk is the closest to the middle." She shakes her head. "It'll be safer here. I warned the human females to assemble here in case they hear the warning bell. The others should be arriving."

Two more females burst through the entrance and my jaw is left working as I meet Tri's frightened brown eyes. She huddles closer to Chimara. I wonder if we don't all feel a little safer knowing she's with us…

"But should you be here? Don't the warriors need you?" I ask her.

She glances at me over her shoulder and smiles. "I wasn't assigned to protect the dolsk, Mian. I'm assigned to you. But don't worry. We've got the warriors. I shouldn't even see any fighting." She pulls a staff from the sling on her back, and a sword from the belt on her hip. She holds both of them out in front of her just as the sound of rabid, vicious howling takes off in the distance.

16

Neheyuu

As we near, I'm surprised to find my people already out celebrating, even though we are not yet returned. The revelry seems to be in full swing — I can hear the laughter and see the scattered bonfires from the farthest perimeter of torches surrounding my tasmaran as we ride in.

Cheers rise up moments after we are spotted by the watchmen and when I dismount Danon and hand him off to Ofrat, the whelp, I turn towards Erkan, the highest ranking warrior I left behind.

Though I hadn't wanted to, he'd offered. And he'd had good reason. My gaze flashes to the female fixed at his side and my gut pools with heat. My mouth salivates. My mind turns, already envisioning how I will spend my lunar — with my own female welded to my side just as searingly.

I'm envious as I watch him, until a grin splits his face, bringing my focus back to him and not to Mian. Where is she? *Where is she? We want her here.* "First. Good to have you and the tasmaran back. In one piece, I hope."

I nod. "We've never had a better raid. Never fought better."

"And we have the little reesa to thank for it," Mor says, clapping me hard on the back as he swaggers confidently by, tossing a stone in his hand. It's a dazzling blue, a color I've never seen. *What if she likes his more than ours?* I ought to fight it off of him before he can give it to her. *Do it. With her, we take no risks.*

I snap at him with my manerak's teeth and he stumbles, the stone flipping between his hands half a dozen times before landing somewhere in the grasses. He curses but stoops to look for it, like it's some great treasure. *It is, because she asked for it.*

"Stones…Mian?" Erkan's female says, surprising me. Her manerak is difficult to understand and I'm grateful that Mian is progressing faster. But I'm also pleased to hear this female speak. It takes bravery to speak to her First. It must also mean that when the sessemara comes, she will stay with us. With Erkan.

I give Erkan a subtle look, one that I know he sees for his chest puffs. Pride. It is well deserved. He has won a worthy female. "Yena. It made for fun sport. We found a tribe of Sandorn scavengers following the trail of the Hox. They had numbers, but the battle was short. We lost none and have claimed a dozen slaves, plus many treasures."

"And for the feast?"

"Sandorn delicacies, but also a pack of wild Ern."

Erkan looks taken aback. "So much and only with thirty warriors?"

I nod, grinning, feeling the weight of the stone I found for her underneath my leather breastplate. Close to my left heart. "With only thirty warriors."

Erkan laughs. The sound surprises me. I have not heard him laugh often. He claps me on the shoulder as

Preena falls in line beside me and asks Erkan the question I should have asked first.

"What is going on? Why are you celebrating when the tasmaran has not even returned?" His tone is bitter, bordering on dishonorable, and I shoot him a look in warning. This is a victorious day. No need to spoil it. *Nothing can spoil it. Not after our victory. Not knowing that we will have her this lunar in our bed, her naked body pressed against us. We must take her…take her fully…*

Erkan is not fazed by it. He pulls his female tighter to him as we walk further into the camp, passing bonfires raging and many faces grinning in their light. One of those faces — a warrior called Tegra — sports a bloody gash. It splits her forehead and cheek, narrowly missing her eye.

I freeze. "You were attacked?"

Erkan nods. "Yena. We were attacked. A pack of wild desert dogs. They must have seen the tasmaran take off and assumed we had no warriors left." Every bone in my body seizes. Thoughts fire. I cannot hear. I cannot speak. My naxem and manerak both are scanning the crowds and the faces, searching for one. The only one that matters to us.

I grab Erkan by the buckle on his shoulder. There are deep scratches covering the leather armor he wears. From this attack? Or one before? "Casualties," I blurt, "tell me."

Erkan grabs my wrist. He grabs it hard. "None, First. Everyone is okay. There were two near-fatal injuries and minor wounds to several others, but all were warriors and all will recover according to Reepal. He's been earning his keep, I'd say, while the rest of us celebrate. We killed over a dozen dogs today. The keepers have already begun to skin and brine the meat. We're feasting on some of it now. Come, join us."

"I need…I need to find…" I clutch my chest, like I'm trying to rip the stone out through the leather. Or maybe just my skeleton.

But then Erkan's female leans forward and meets my wild, manerak gaze with her calm, steadying one. "Mian…with human females."

"Where?" I don't bother to feel the embarrassment I should that this human female knows exactly what I need even though she does not know me. Am I that transparent? *Yena. Well, except for me. You hide me because you fear me,* that dark, destructive voice says.

The corners of her full, dark brown lips tip up. She points towards the third sun, where it sets. "Ock dolsk."

"Ock? Why the svik is she in Ock's dolsk?"

Erkan frowns and pulls Rita away from me, edging his shoulder in front of hers. "Ock's dolsk is the closest to the center. It was where Chimara told the human females they'd be safest, and where Dandena also ordered the young and the old to congregate in case of trouble. It was a good order. I thought you gave it." He lifts a brow and I shudder inside. Closest to the center. I glance around at the chaos that is my tasmaran, remembering the way the Nevay structured theirs. The way Tatana structured his — and that was only a raiding tasmaran. *Disgusting.*

I shudder again. I don't have anything to say. My tongue is a sviking block in my mouth. I feel feverish and a fool and embarrassed and also a little like laughing. My order to keep some of my warriors behind today proved to be a good one. A successful raid was met with a successful defense of my tasmaran.

This wasn't a decision I would have made a turn ago — svik a turn, how about forty solars? Has it been so little time? *Tszk. You have known her as I have known her. Forever. Xiveri does not know time.* I might be a fool, but I'm learning. And that knowledge makes me feel light. Makes me feel hopeful. There's hope for this tasmaran with me as it's leader. Hope to be good, if not *great*. Hope for it to thrive, more than just survive.

I reach Ock's dolsk and throw back the leathers closing it. It's empty, but the chaos within the dolsk tells me there was a fight here, and the sight of blood on the dolsk floor and the small, human-shaped footprints that appear to have walked through it let me know that at least four different humans left this dolsk alive.

My ears cock towards the sound of laughter. Human laughter. I let the leathers fall closed and make my way around the dolsk. There, at the tasmaran's center, a group of humans sits clustered around a roaring fire. My gaze snaps to Mian instantly.

She's holding a wooden platter in her hand and is laughing at something someone has said — likely Chimara, what with the way her hands are waving wildly. Somehow Mor and Reffa have already found them, despite being slower to return than I. And then I see the small stack of stones at Mian's side.

She's arranged them neatly into a pyramid that, as it currently stands, rises to her hip. She's sitting on the ground and waves as Xi and Xena approach to find seats among the humans. I'm surprised at that. Usually the warriors keep to themselves — and the ranked warriors are even more exclusive — but not here. Not now. Not with Mian widening the circle to include not just them, but Dandena and Ofrat when they make their way over. They hand her stones as well.

Mor is preening over the blue gem he found for reesa, asking her which is the most beautiful. I rub the stone I took for her through my armor and, before she can answer, step into the light.

Dandena's mouth quirks. Ofrat jumps up from his seat beside her and finds a new spot on the opposite side of the fire, as far from her as can be. *That's right.* The human chatter dims slightly. They all look at me. But I'm only looking at her. She's smiling, but when I meet her gaze, she looks away. I pause. Something isn't right. But I move around the circle and take the seat that Ofrat vacated anyways.

Everyone else is speaking about the raid and the attack, but I'm just listening to the sound of her breath, her laughter. I close my eyes. *Touch her. Steal her away. Take her.* The more she laughs, the more she speaks, the more she sviking exists, only serves to heighten my need. My cock is straining against my armor, my hearts are pounding against it. Something is wrong. Different. Changed.

"Mian," I bark, my voice louder than it needs to be given that she's seated close enough to touch.

Everyone is looking at me but I don't give a comet's tail. The weight of the stone feels heavy. My fingers curl in on themselves so that they don't reach out and grab her. Instead, I wait the eternity it takes for her smile to tilt in my direction, so that I can see the orange light of the fire reflected on one half of her face, turning her bronze to amber.

"Yena?" She says.

I swallow. This is strange. She should be teasing me by now. Laughing. Frowning. Reacting in *some* way. For now, she's just being *polite*. Like she doesn't sviking know me. Like I haven't held her dripping cunt in the palm of my hand. "I saw blood in Ock's dolsk. Are you hurt?"

Her eyes widen. She shakes her head. "Tszk. Chimara was incredible. One dog comes in...came inside. She took sword and spear and whoosh." She makes a sweeping motion with her hand, perhaps trying to emulate a feint and jab, but in poor imitation. Tszk, this female is no warrior. Perhaps if she were...I shake my head, hating the thought as it's not the first time I've had it.

"A dog made it all the way to you?" I growl.

She nods. "Scary. But only one. And I trust Chimara. Thank you for...for her." She offers me a half smile and though it takes me a moment, I understand that she knows that I asked Chimara to remain here for her. Chimara must have told her.

I still grimace. "Next time, I'll have four warriors on you. I don't want you to even see blood. I want the world in your eyes to be like you. Beautiful and good," I huff, kicking a stiff, dead reed into the fire.

She tenses. My anger rises. I can't help it. I turn to face her fully, block everyone else out, and hiss, "What is it? What's wrong? Did someone hurt you or bother you? Are you mad that I went raiding? What is it?"

She blinks many times and when she twists to face me, I see what she's got on her lap. My gut plunges to my knees, to my feet, to the reeds and beyond them. There is nothing but sand. Nothing but the hollow shell of the earth. I'm staring at the *thing* so intensely, she's got no choice but to explain herself.

She fingers the stiff loop of her wreath. A skinny, flimsy thing. The warrior females will have thick wreaths that dangle the bones of their kills. The wealthy females will have rings on rings of gems and, if they're very wealthy, gold, bronze and silver.

She's just the newest member of the youngest tribe of Sasor. Her wreath will attract no one. *And we have marked her. She is ours for the claiming. Only ours.* I open my mouth to tell her all of this — that she's wasting her time — but her small, delicate fingers move so gingerly over the fabric, so cautiously. Timidly. Proudly. I wait for her to speak first, even though it hurts.

She licks her lips, turning to face me fully — away from the fire, to give us as much privacy as this tasmaran full of beings will allow — and says, "Why you did not tell me about sessemara?"

The tall grasses tickle the backs of my shins. Her knees nearly brush mine. I can feel their heat. She's so warm. *What will it be like when she lets us in?* And then it hits me with a deafening truth: if I get my way, she will never be ours. *Fool. We will not allow this. We will destroy you first.*

I swallow hard and speak through a mouth full of rage and spittle. "What does it matter?"

"We were together many lunars and solars and you did not tell me."

I feel hot. The lie I have told, or have not told, coils around me like a snake. Like a naxem. *Lie? Which one? The ones you speak to yourself?* "I don't have to tell you. You can't participate. This is a waste of time." I point at the wreath she holds, the one she put so much hard work into, and it cuts me when she covers up the wreath in her lap with her hands. I've never received a wound more brutal.

"All can join. And I *must* join."

Fury bites at my heels, threatening to slice them and topple me. "And why *must* you join?"

"Because you will. Because I do not like to watch you with another female."

Her raw honesty throws me, threatens to undo me. I can't think straight. Her jealousy. It sends a fire to my cock, hardening it to the point of pain. "So what? You want to join with another tribe? You want to leave?" The thought of her leaving makes me want to wrap her entire body in chains and anchor her to me so she can never go away. *She's mine.*

"Tszk. I do not want. But I cannot stay here. Like Tekevanki. Cannot watch…"

"Tekevanki. Did Tekevanki put these sviking ideas in your head?"

She opens her mouth and huffs, looking frustrated, as if there is more that she would say if only she could say it. On the other hand, I'm well past frustrated. I'm going to slaughter Tekevanki. I'm going to slaughter everyone.

"All can join sessemara," she repeats, "Even humans. Even if wreath is small."

"Are you threatening me? Do you think you can pressure me into joining with you?"

Her lips fall open. She even gasps. It would sound fake if the rest of her expression weren't so brutally honest. If I didn't know her. If I didn't know already that she was willfully incapable of deceiving anyone.

"Tszk. I know you join with high female. Warrior. For the dolsk. So it can be bigger. So I must find new dolsk. I must try…"

I issue a dark, sick laughter I have never heard before. One full of spite. One full of impotent rage, misdirected. "You will fail. This wreath isn't going to do anything for the other warrior males."

She frowns and water wells along the rim of her lower eyelids that makes something terrible happen inside of me. Both my manerak and my naxem retreat. Like they're falling backwards off a cliff with nothing to slow them, nothing to stop them. And then Mian stands. She clutches the wreath in her tiny, shaking fist and arches over me, like a shadow. Like a god. And below her, I'm but a lowly king.

"I have more than wreath." Her voice is shaking. It hurts me more than swords can wound.

"What do you have? Your body?" I glance at her arms. Her tattoos. My gut pools with dread. The thought of another male on top of her while she closes her eyes and whispers his name — any name — but mine. Agony replaces the rage raging through me.

"Sex isn't prized here," I try. But the words sound cheap.

She clenches her jaw so hard I think she'll break it and shakes her wreath at me on every word, as if to punctuate them. "Do you think you are first male to lay with me? I learn what to do…learned…from masters who want sex from me. I offer other things instead. Like in sandstorm."

I can't sviking think. My mind is a swirling sea of bitter images that hurt like pulled fingernails. The thought of her perfect fingers wrapped around another male's cock, pumping his seed across her pussy so that he doesn't rape her... And then worse... The thought that she views *me* as just another master among them. Anything she has said to me before is lost. By jealousy, by regret, by grief, it's cleanly erased. I am *nothing* to her. Nothing. My manerak is quiet. My naxem even quieter.

Maybe I am nothing at all.

Rage yields to agony yields to oblivion. I sink in deep and when I wake, I'm on my feet and in her face, speaking in a low, quivering snarl, "So you're a whore then? That's what you'll offer all of the males at the sessemara?"

"I *am* a whore. I am *your* whore. That is what you make me. Akimari, tszk?" I don't answer. I wish I had, because then I might have kept the sword she jammed into both my hearts simultaneously from twisting. "I do what I need to keep rings broken and join with male. If this male is not you, I do not know why you are so angry."

If this male is not you, then there is no reason for me... The dark voice fades to nothing and I feel like I've been struck to the gut with a spear. I step back from her and speak over my shoulder, unsure of whether or not I have the control to look at her face. The strength. "Tszk. I am not this male. I belong with a female whose wreath is more than a strip of dirty reed paper."

17
Mian

I don't know what I expected — if what I had in my head was simpler or grander than this. The sessemara took three solars to journey to. Three tense, difficult solars. The suns were hotter than usual, for one, but Neheyuu was also in a...mood. It permeated the tasmaran, everyone. Everything.

Fights broke out among the males. Fights broke out among the females. I just tried to keep to myself and to keep busy. With no weapons dolsk, I only polished and sharpened the swords that warriors asked me to and when I wasn't working on the weapons, I practiced my manerak with Tri, learning the important phrases and customs I might need for the sessemara from someone who used them effectively.

Arriving, my nerves mount as light from the torches brighten the lunar's sky until finally a wonderful sort of chaos unfolds before us, and then gobbles us up. The different dolsks converging is a fun, yet frightening thing to behold.

Different dialects sound around me, threatening my comprehension. Differently colored robes and people, both manerak and human, draw my attention. So many of them clapping hands and laughing — even dancing — beside bonfires roaring under Sasorana's broad, starry sky. It makes me wonder how it could possibly be that these warriors from so many different tasmarans could be in competition with one another.

I join the human females I know from Neheyuu's dolsk for drinks around one of the fires. It doesn't take me long to worry that we're only speaking amongst ourselves, but Chimara laughs as she explains that the sessemara hasn't started yet.

And when it does? I am inundated in so many ways. *And I miss Neheyuu to guide me through the madness of it.* But I don't think of him now. Instead, the gong rings and I follow Chimara tightly as she leads me away from the fire to a dolsk larger than any I'd ever seen.

Only those looking to join, as well as ranked warriors and their mates, accompany us as we walk until finally, Chimara holds the leather flaps of the dolsk open for me, leaving me utterly speechless. My hand clenches around a palm that isn't there. *Where is he?*

The decadence is overwhelming. Huge, gold and fur carpets are strewn wantonly about, fully covering the floor, while garlands of dried flowers hang from the supports overhead. Fat candles as thick as my thighs and that stand as tall as I do ring the room while smaller candles sit artfully arranged on heavy, wooden tables. Food items flood every available space on the tables that the candles do not and immediately, my stomach lurches, desperate to sample every single delight on offer.

Instinctively, I gravitate towards the nearest table and the nearest dish on that table — some sort of bright green gourd with something mashed and orange in the middle, but the moment I arrive and bring the gourd to my lips, I look up.

Tekevanki is standing with her back to the table, watching me over her shoulder. Her eyes flash and I follow her stare across the room. Seats of all kinds are scattered here and there, but even in the full room, the Firsts stand out. Seventeen tasmaran form Sasor's United Manerak Tribes. And of the Firsts who lead them, six seek to find their mates during this sessemara.

Small crowds have formed around them, bodies jostling for their own time to be seen, to learn, to decide, and I...I understand what Tekevanki is urging me to do, but I don't know...how can I?

Among the other Firsts, the cluster around Neheyuu is not the largest, but there are still eight — maybe ten — near him and most are females. I would need to insert myself quite boldly to gain his attention and he *hates* me. And right now, I'm not sure I feel much different. It would *wound* my pride to ingratiate myself with him now.

I glance back at Tekevanki and shake my head just a little. She sighs and shrugs one shoulder, then turns back to the small court she seems to be holding herself. Three males stand before her and she laughs at something one of them has said. They're all several heads taller than I am — and that includes Tekevanki herself — and around each of their necks they wear wreaths that are utterly magnificent.

I swallow and touch the wreath around my neck. *Dirty reed paper.* I understand now what he meant. Compared to what the others wear, my little wreath *is* dirty reed paper. I added a few of the stones I received from the tasmaran on their return, braiding them into the white fabric Tekevanki gave me. But compared to what so many others wear? My wreath truly does feel like nothing.

On Tekevanki's neck, glittering jewels and precious metals forming intricate shapes have been woven among the gold loops with colorful fabrics that look tough enough to bind wounds and soft enough to cradle kits. At least a dozen rings loop her neck — so large, the entire wreath stands up off of her chest by at least a forearm's length. If she didn't have such a long face, she'd probably struggle to see over it. And the males... while their wreaths tend to lie flatter, they are *huge*.

The loops are as big as my chest and while some are made of fabric, most are made of rough hewn metals and dark wood. The warriors in the crowd are easily identifiable because they wear their kills around their necks like badges of honor. Desert dogs' teeth clatter against the male's chest Tekevanki currently speaks to, while the male beside him boasts a *skull* that looks slightly too small to be manerak. *Human.*

I shake my head. I don't need a heavy wreath. I just need a male who's kind. One who wants me...and even that still might be unattainable. *He was right. No male here will give up their wreath in exchange for this.*

I bring the green gourd to my lips and take a bite, prepared to let the taste take me — big mistake. The thing is tart, sour even. My mouth fills with saliva and I choke. I set the rest of my gourd down and come up to the sound of Mor laughing.

"Deringa. It's a Hox delicacy. Taste like svik though, don't they?"

I nod and examine his wreath. While it isn't as big as those of the males speaking with Tekevanki, it is still impressive. "Yena, they do."

He laughs. "Try the evrol instead." He reaches past me for a puffy pink delight and places it in my hand. Our fingers touch and he immediately flexes his, as if the contact were strange.

"Delicious," I say, even though the evrol really *isn't* delicious. It's sweet, cloyingly so, and tastes like a flower. Like the perfume a female might wear — if she bathed in it.

Mor still smiles and tilts his head, his blonde hair catching the light. His gaze drops to my wreath and I tense momentarily, waiting for his ridicule. Instead, his voice is gentle as he says, "Glad to see I made the cut. You look great."

I realize he's talking about his stone, which has a prominent position in the center of my wreath, and smile. "You look great too," I tell him, the tension in my chest easing just a little. He inhales, puffing his bare chest out in a way that makes me laugh.

"Will you join this sessemara?" I ask.

He shakes his head. Then shrugs. "Tszk. But I'll look. If a female really catches my eye, then I might throw my wreath in the ring for her. But only if she's open to relocating to the Neheyuu dolsk. I like it here."

I look up into Mor's wide face and am reminded that if I am selected this sessemara, I will miss the Neheyuu dolsk and the friends I've made. Sadness twists somewhere in my center as I say, "I like it too."

Mor shifts uncomfortably and his eyes flit away from my face. "Come on, let's go see Neheyuu. I'm sure he's wondering where you are."

I shake my head, tensing, and cross my arms over my plain shift dress. Even though unclaimed females wear simple shifts, some of the wealthier females bend the rules while others break them altogether and stand draped in colorful robes intended to draw the eye. And they do. *I will never find a mate. I don't need Neheyuu to rub it in, or make me feel any worse than I do already.*

"Come on, I'm sure he would like to see you," Mor says again.

I back up a step and shake my head again. "Tszk. I will…"

"Mor," a voice cuts in abruptly. It's Xena's. Xi is just behind her, looking uncomfortable to be here. "Why don't you take a trip to see Neheyuu. He's in need of some rescuing."

"I will see you later then," I offer, stepping back with a wave, but Xena darts forward swiftly and grabs my forearm.

She drops her pitch and says, "I'm not here for Mor." She raises an eyebrow. It's full of meaning.

I cringe a little, but follow her when she carves a path through the dolsk. Before I do, I give Tekevanki one last look. She's watching me too and when our gazes clash, she tips her chin down ever so slightly.

I'm nervous as I pad barefoot across the carpets, but I'm cautious not to show it. I don't want Neheyuu to think that I think that he's right about me. That I'm worth any less just because he says so. So I tilt my chin up and I smile up at the manerak who smile down at me and I'm reassured when all of the ones I know give me glowing looks and even some that I don't offer me subtle, polite nods, as if to say, it's okay for me to be here.

I approach the raised platform where Neheyuu has taken up his seat and receive less-than-welcoming glares from the three females standing before him. I don't recognize any of their faces, but I smile at all of them and ignore the way they look from my face to my shift to my wreath.

I know I don't look as neat as they do, or as fancy, but…this is me, who I am, and what I could manage and I have to be proud of that. At least, I have to try to be. And no matter what happens, I can't let Neheyuu's opinions frighten me away.

Xena and Xi step out of my way and I see him up close for the first time this solar. He's seated up on some pallets piled with plush pillows, his long gold hair falling to his lap in tangles. I nearly smirk at the sight. Unbelievable that, not even for this, he managed to comb it. Then again… I take another step and can smell the harsh fragrance emanating from his cup. *Not just his cup, his* skin. Is he…is he drunk?

His gaze flicks to mine and looks sharp, contradicting the notion that he's wasting away on hibi or something even more toxic. He glances down at the space beside him on the platform, at the one red pillow adjacent to him. I feel a little silly pointing at it, but I don't want to feel sillier taking a seat I haven't been invited to.

He tips his chin down in acknowledgement and I reach forward to shift the pillow a little bit away from him since its fringed edge directly abuts his thigh, but he smacks my hand away and yanks it back into position against him. My lips twist. I meet his stare directly and hold it, even if I have to look up. It surprises me that I break first, but there's something lethal underlying his expression this lunar. The impulsive, playful Neheyuu seems to be absent, leaving behind one that is much more volatile. One I'm not sure I can trust.

"Here, let me help you," Chimara says, appearing at my side. I blush as I use her hand to amble awkwardly up onto the high pallet. Even though Neheyuu's got his feet firmly planted on the floor, the tips of my thin leather sandals dangle by his calves.

"Thank you," I tell her, plopping down on my bottom, practically on top of Neheyuu now. Our legs are pressed together and if he were to lean back, there'd be nowhere for his broad shoulders to go. Luckily, he's leaning forward for the moment, talking to a male warrior I don't recognize.

The male looks at me questioningly, as if to ask what in the comets I'm doing here — I don't know — even as he speaks to Neheyuu about his tasmaran, its size, how often we raid and what our last successes looked like. Our last losses too. *I mean* their *successes*. Their *losses*.

He leaves with a low bow, but no promise to even consider joining Neheyuu's tasmaran, and in his wake, the crowd of three females shoves forward to stand directly before Neheyuu — and with how close we're sitting, in front of me too. The moment the first female opens her mouth to speak, Neheyuu holds up three fingers on his right hand in a manerak gesture meaning *wait* or *hold*.

"I will join with no female at this ceremony," he blurts utterly unceremoniously.

Six eyes widen in surprise. Eight if you include mine. One of the females — a tall female with a dark shade of golden hair I have not seen before — says,

"That wreath looks awfully heavy, Neheyuu. Are you certain you would not like the chance to have another female carry it for you?" Her voice is sultry, seductive, and even without the impressive size of her own gaudy wreath, I know that this is a female of wealth and stature by the way she speaks down to him so easily.

"Not on this solar, Mervene," comes Neheyuu's jerky reply.

Her attention passes rapidly to me. "Is this one of the helpers you stole from my tasmaran?"

Her tasmaran? Neheyuu nods. "Stole back. Yena." His voice is even, cold.

She tilts her head and I try not to squirm under her assessing stare, but when her gaze finally falls to my wreath and lingers, I can't help it. I look away, towards Chimara. She's glaring at the female with her bottom jaw clenched. Her hand flexes towards the sword on her belt that isn't there.

None of the warriors are weaponed in the dolsk during the ceremony. It's a sacred time. Even raids are banned by any member of the United Manerak Tribes. But right now Chimara is looking very much like she wishes that weren't the case. Even Mor, just behind her, is watching the scene unfold with an icy frown clouding his typically warm expression.

"She is…" the female starts.

"*Careful.*" The voice hisses out of Neheyuu's mouth, but it is not Neheyuu's. It is darker, more sibilant. His hand, still raised, makes a quick gesture. A dismissive one.

Mervene's face darkens. "I give you three more turns of the three suns. Three more failed joining

221

ceremonies. Then your tasmaran shall fall and we shall reabsorb it. Along with all of your *helpers*."

A growl booms out of Neheyuu's chest so abruptly and with such force that Mervene jumps back. Her own face transforms, lower jaw distending to form the diamond-shaped manerak mandible before snapping back into place. She pegs Neheyuu with one last glare before grabbing one edge of her airy gown and disappearing into the crowd with a whirl.

I feel hot. I feel unsure.

Neheyuu is breathing hard beside me and though the rumble in his chest is audible, he is otherwise almost completely still. A handful of his most trusted warriors are nearby, but none of them approach or say anything. They all just stare, like they're suddenly unsure...even, *afraid* of him.

The silence is threatening. "I tried Deringa," I say suddenly, breaking it. My voice isn't loud but everyone looks at me. Inadvertently, I start fiddling with some of the stones dangling from my wreath.

As slowly as a rusted bolt in need of oil, Neheyuu twists to look at me. He's very close. I can smell his hibi. I can feel his heat.

"It tastes yucky," I say, making a sound and making a face.

One corner of Neheyuu's mouth twitches. But only for a breath. Then his gaze switches out, like a predatory bird trying to find its next kill.

"I also try evrol. I mean, *tried*." I struggle with the past tense, still. I shake my head and kick my feet a little, heat flaring in my cheeks.

"What did you think of it?" He rumbles so abruptly I almost miss it. His gaze hits mine and is purely black but I don't know what it means. Any of this.

I swallow, unsure. *Afraid*, even. Just like the rest of them. "Too sweet for me." I lick my lips.

He sucks in a breath and his gaze switches past my mouth to my hair, coiled up off of my neck and fixed with small, white flowers. He exhales a little deeper, "For me too. Did you hear what I said to Mervene?"

I nod. "Yena."

"I will not be choosing a female during this sessemara."

"I don't understand," I say, but what I want to say is, I don't understand why he's telling *me*.

He lifts his cup, drains it, and passes it off to a warrior called Petra, beside him. The male scuttles away. "I need more time. Establish myself. Establish this tasmaran. Then I can take on a female."

I want to tell him that this doesn't make any sense. That taking on a female will help him do all of those things he's mentioned — at least, that's what he seemed to think a few lunars earlier. That's what Tekevanki thinks. That's what Chimara thinks. That's what all the members of his tasmaran think. What they gossip about over hot bonfires and cool cups of human ale and manerak spirits. But I don't say that. I don't say anything. Mostly because he doesn't seem quite…right. I want to ask him if he's okay — even if he hates me and even if I'm angry with him, I still care if he's ill or upset — but not here in front of everyone in the middle of the sessemara.

So I nod and bite my tongue and glance out at the crowd, spotting Menerva chatting with Tekevanki and her father, the warrior Creyu. "Which female will you choose when you do choose?"

He grunts like he's been beat. Bad topic? He runs a hand raggedly through his hair, rumpling it even more. "I don't know."

"Menerva? She seems…nice," I say for lack of a better option. "Pretty. Is she a manerak warrior too?"

"*Mervene* and yena. Of one of the oldest lines." Neheyuu grunts again, shakes his hair and passes his hand through it again even more roughly, fingers catching on some tangles. "She only wants a wreath from me so she can leverage it into an offer from a more established First. If rumors have anything right, she should get an offer from both Wren and Gigida, both Firsts of their tribes. She's trying to get as many Firsts to make her offers in the hope that Hox does. The Hox and the Nevay are the two most powerful tasmaran after the Sessena. She wants a better offer." Neheyuu exhales. "She won't get one from Hox though."

"Why not?"

"They say he's in love with a female taken in a raid."

That surprises me. Neheyuu doesn't look at me, but I know he can feel my gaze on his face, because he turns away from me entirely. "A human," he finishes.

Stitches around the fresh wound that covers my chest are picked apart. I inhale cleanly and as I exhale, say, "It will be easier for Hox. They are big dolsk, as you say. He can join with any female he likes."

Neheyuu nods, but his shoulders are slumped forward. He looks…broken. "Yena."

"So, for your female, you do not want Mervene or Tekevanki," I say quickly, hoping to bring the conversation back to something else. Something light. Something that doesn't drag down our entire tasmaran like a weighted stone. *His* tasmaran… "Then what about her? She is a warrior. She wears warrior armor."

I point through the crowd at a female that stands a little shorter than the others. Still, she does not look like the kind of female I'd choose to fight, but one I'd like fighting by my side. Her armor hugs her chest and hips and ends in brown leather boots that match those of the males. Gaps along her belt show places where weapons go. Many weapons.

"She's with the Nevay. She'd make any male a good match, but she's only half-manerak. Her mother was a human."

I perk up, noticing that her hair is brown. "Like Chimara."

"Yena."

"She has many things on her wreath," I offer. A small skull, large teeth, a clattering of rusted bits of things I don't want to know about. *Not rusted, bloody.*

"But she has no manerak form."

"Ah." Sadness pulls me down a little bit deeper, but I straighten taller, pushing up and kicking against it.

"Well, what about her? She has biggest wreath I have seen." I point randomly to a female with so many different gold and silver and gem-addled hoops stacked over her neck, she actually *can't* see over the top of them.

Neheyuu barks out a laugh. The sound surprises me and I turn to catch the corners of his eyes crinkling. He shakes his head and drinks from his cup when Petra returns with it. Petra also hands one to me and I sip from it gratefully.

"That is Egretha. She is daughter of the Sessena's Second, a pure-blooded manerak and completely insane."

"She will be perfect for you then."

Neheyuu laughs again, even harder. He shifts so that his knees are pointed in my direction and stretches a muscled arm past my face to point across the dolsk. "That is her father."

The male he points out has a wreath so big around that when he turns, it smacks directly into a passing male, completely scattering the platter in his hand and its contents. I cover my mouth as I laugh quietly. "Oh stars," I say in human, then in manerak, "I see. Lucky I have a small wreath then. I will not be afraid to attract males like him."

Neheyuu is quiet, but he's very close to me now. I can feel his heat swamping my entire left side. I don't dare look up into his eyes. I don't want to see myself in them. Don't want to see my blush or the way my lips pucker. *I've missed him.*

"I missed you," he whispers against my hair. "These past seventeen solars without you in my dolsk have been a sviking torment." Lightning shoots up my spine before zinging back down it. My toes curl. "And I should never have said any of the sviking nonsense I said to you."

A chill brings goosebumps to the surface of my skin. *Do I dare?* I hold my breath and turn to meet his gaze, but his eyes are closed, his nostrils flare and his forehead wrinkles in concentration, like every word causes him great pain. I relieve him of the burden.

"I don't need these words from you," I say, flushed. "I…you speak truths. Spoke truths. My wreath is small. I will not find mate."

He grabs the back of my neck in a move so startling, I jump. He grabs me without fumbling even though his eyes haven't opened. He squeezes me harder than I wish he would, but I don't ask him to stop. Instead, I cross my ankles and clench my thighs and pray that he cannot smell the surge of heat pooling at their juncture. *Damn him.*

"Any male would be honored to wear your wreath. *I* would be honored." Shock. It numbs me, but not enough to dull the fresh scent of earth and grass and metal blooming out of his skin. "I *will* be honored. But I just need…time. I need to figure out my sviking tasmaran and what to do with the lost warriors. Creyu and Tekevanki are taking twelve warriors with them. I need to make that up. After I do and after I make our tasmaran safe, I'll come for you. I'll join with you. Until then, I just need you to stay by me. Back in my dolsk. In my bed. Helping my tasmaran. Can you do that?"

I'm so stunned by the direction of this whispered conversation that I don't respond. I don't know how. I suck in a breath. I don't want to tell him that it's a bad idea. That there's a chance that the *only* way he can strengthen his tasmaran is through a union and that even if there is another way, it will take him so much time that I'll be an old maid when it happens.

I also know that I can't chance spending more time with him in his bed without eventually giving in to what his body wants — because it's also what *my* body wants. I'll be a well-used old human helper with no skills to speak of by the time he figures it out — or *doesn't*. And when he doesn't, he can still form a union. Meanwhile, I'll be left with no options. Nothing. And no one.

And yet...it's a sweet offer. I might not get any others. And I *like* Neheyuu when he isn't being a spoiled brat. Maybe more than like. Though I don't even know what color that elusive L word is, because I've never seen it. Never even dreamed it. All I ever wanted was something solid. A mate. A roof. Food on my table every single solar. Perhaps little kits to feed every solar too. *Neheyuu would make a good father.* I close my eyes.

"Mian," Neheyuu says. The pressure of his hand on my neck intensifies, but I gently pry his fingers off of my skin. I slip down from the pallet onto the floor and shake my head, mouth working wordlessly.

Neheyuu's eyes fly open and his brows draw together. His fists clench. Everything about him tenses. "Are you rejecting me?" His voice is a low, cruel whip that burns as it shreds.

"Tszk. Tszk," I say quickly, "I just...must think. It is...very much *if*. It is hard to know what it will mean for the future," I blabber, aware that my manerak isn't making much sense.

Neheyuu's face darkens. Fear washes over me — not that he will harm me in any way — but that he will cause a scene, embarrassing me and himself and our entire tasmaran. *His*...his tasmaran... "If you walk away now, this offer no longer remains and I will select another female *this sessemara* to take home with me."

Anger. Shock. Betrayal. I want to spit at him. I want to claw and hit and scream and curse. I stamp my foot, trying to rein in the onslaught of my emotions, but struggling. My hands tremble. My face flushes. My mouth is totally dry.

"How can you be like this?" I heave. My voice breaks.

His lips part, but he says nothing. His eyes flash and pass over my shoulder. And then all at once, he growls, shifts off of the pallet, steps out in front of me and extends his right arm across my chest, as if to shield me from an approaching enemy.

"Tatana," he snarls. "I'm busy. We can discuss your joining my tasmaran as a helper later." The insult slashes through the air, bringing the temperature down several degrees and silencing those in the near vicinity.

I'm still riled, amped, ready to lash out and fight Neheyuu with everything I have, but all those thoughts still when Tatana's black eyes blink to me. "I am not here for you, Neheyuu. I am here to speak with Mian." His voice is total calm, a complete contrast to the way I feel now and everything that is Neheyuu.

Neheyuu seethes, "She's busy too."

Hushed whispers spring up around us and the chatter across the entire dolsk seems suddenly dimmer. I flush. Tatana clicks his tongue against his teeth in that way that I got to know in our short time together.

He says, "You would attempt to block a male from speaking to an unmated female during a sessemara? You will be banned from all future ceremonies, if this is the case. How will you grow your dolsk then?" He tuts again, this time with a bit of dark laughter. "I would reconsider."

Preena suddenly bursts into the small clearing around the two males and slaps one hand down onto Neheyuu's shoulder. I can see the way he tries to urge Neheyuu back, but Neheyuu doesn't budge. Preena's eyes slit. He glances at Tatana and bows from the waist.

"Our First is just a little drunk. He doesn't mean anything by this slight."

"I thought so."

"You *dare*."

Both males speak at the same time. Tatana's lips are flat. His eyes are empty, but that's when I see what he's holding in his hands. The same thing he's not wearing around his neck. His wreath. My heart starts to pound. My full belly suddenly feels as empty as a cloud.

"Mian," Tatana says, looking directly past Neheyuu, as if he isn't even there. The word *dishonor* rings in my mind. "Strena."

I swallow hard, feeling unsure and *definitely* afraid as my feet carry me forward, past Neheyuu. Neheyuu breaks towards me but Preena grabs his arm and Mor shoves his way into the circle, meeting Neheyuu in time to place both hands on Neheyuu's chest and help hold him back.

My upper lip is clammy and so are my palms. I'm standing in the center of the small space now. Tatana is right in front of me and all I can think about is the narrow miss I had with him in his dolsk, moments after he told me he'd join with me.

He smells spicy and clean and says, "I apologize for allowing you to be taken from my dolsk."

I like that he doesn't apologize for kidnapping me and nearly drowning me in the river to do it or for ignoring my wishes when I didn't want his naked body near mine, but instead of remarking on that, I just nod. "Thank you for your apology."

His mouth doesn't quirk. It stays flat. But his nostrils flare. He leans forward onto the balls of his feet and a vein pulses across his forehead. "You've been marked?"

Behind me Chimara rasps, "He did *what?* Neheyuu, you sviking…"

"Yena," Neheyuu snarls, shouting over the whispered curses all around me, "I marked her. She's *my* akimari. Too used to be taken by a Second. Even if that Second is only a failed First."

"Tut." Comes the sound, sounding involuntary. Tatana's neck twitches. He lowers the wreath in his hands just a little bit.

Panic flares in me. Anger. Betrayal. "Marked?" I look over my shoulder at Neheyuu, but he refuses to meet my gaze. I look at Mor instead. "It's true," Mor says, "All the manerak males can smell him on you. Neheyuu marked you." He nods solemnly and licks his lips. His expression belies a pain and regret that should have been Neheyuu's, but that Neheyuu would never betray. Because Neheyuu isn't the male I thought he was. He isn't good. Not even a little.

It isn't just the size of my wreath keeping males away. He made me *unwantable*. No *wonder* he asked me to wait. The guilt must be killing him. He marked me. He *ruined* me… I refuse to believe it. The bastard. The *bastard*. Tears wet my eyelashes and I start to breathe harder as I stare down at my wrists.

I wheeze, "How can I be marked if we do not have sex?"

Neheyuu chokes. The whispering crowd reels, growing louder and louder. Tatana grabs one of my arms and holds my wrist below his nose. He rubs the break in my tattoo and for just one fleeting instant, one corner of his mouth lifts in what I can only begrudgingly call a smile. I have not seen his smile before and I don't deny that it leaves an impression. A sour one.

"He marked you, but did not breed you?" Tatana says quietly.

I wince at the phrasing, but nod nonetheless. Tatana smiles even more eerily as he turns his gaze to Neheyuu. And he's *still* watching Neheyuu as he lifts his wreath once more — a massive thing, dangling with all kinds of kills and old weapons and riches from battles unknown — and drapes it over my shoulders.

The opening swallows my head whole and I sag a little under its weight, and so does my soul. This moment that I'd been looking so forward to feels *wrong*. Tatana has spoiled it for me — *no, not Tatana, because Neheyuu spoiled it first, solars ago.* I asked him not to have sex with me, and he agreed, but this still feels like a violation. Feelings of frustration and disappointment tickle the backs of my eyes, but I press them back with concentrated force.

Dry-eyed, I look up into Tatana's gaze and say the words that Tri taught me. "I…am honored to receive your wreath. Thank you, Tatana."

Behind me, Neheyuu grunts horribly, an animal gutted.

Speaking over him, Tatana says, "Thank you for saving yourself for me as you said you would, Mian." *What?* "And as I promised, I now offer you my wreath and the promise that I will fight for you on the coming solar to prove that I am the male you should join with." *What promises are these?* "I look forward to completing the sessemara and hope to be your chosen. Should I be so fortunate, I will be happy to remove Neheyuu's marking scent and replace it with one of my own. One that will be permanent."

His eyes glitter and I can't help the way my stomach muscles bunch at the thought. "Thank you, Tatana," I say without much conviction.

He bows to me. Deeply. Honoring me in a way Neheyuu has never and will not. Even if it's wrong. Even if it's forced. He turns and the moment he disappears into the crowd, Neheyuu explodes free of the cage of Mor's arms. He charges me and I might have fallen right over if Chimara hadn't grabbed my arm.

"Easy, First," she says, holding up one hand in warning, but Neheyuu doesn't hear and he doesn't see.

His shoulders lift, his head elongates, his teeth form fangs and he's rattling violently, every bit the snake I know he's capable of. "Is it true?" He says to me.

"Is what true?"

"Is it true!" His voice is a roar that obliterates everything.

I lurch back and feel familiar hands come to rest on my spine. Reffa joins Chimara in supporting me and it seems to take both of them to keep me upright. Reffa already has three wreaths stacked on top of her neck, though none so large as the one I wear now. I feel like collapsing under its weight. I thought it would be lighter, but it feels oppressive. This is *all wrong.*

"Did you promise yourself to him?"

I shake my head, then blink, then narrow my gaze on the deceiving, lying, snake. "What I did with Tatana is not important for you to know."

A blast of energy pulses through Neheyuu — dark, manic energy. It literally pushes out of him like a desert wind, dry and hot. A collective scream rises up and I see the flash of black eyes and the dripping fangs of enormous teeth seconds before the wind throws me — and everyone around me — to the floor. And the last thing I see in the wake of Neheyuu's disappearance is a massive tail covered in scales disappearing through the dolsk leathers.

From our position tangled together on the floor, Reffa, Chimara and I share an uneasy glance. "Everyone alright?" Reffa says.

I nod. Chimara nods.

"Good. But now maybe someone can tell me what the svik that was. That thing that left the tent did not look manerak…"

"Neheyuu," I spit bitterly. "As his snake."

"Snake?"

Chimara just shrugs. "She must mean manerak."

I shake my head, but by then Mor has come to help me onto my feet.

18
Neheyuu

My naxem propels me out of the door before throwing my true form out of its husk. At least, that's what it feels like. A one-two punch. Out into the darkness, out onto my face. I fall flat amidst the tall grasses, naked, head spinning. I have fingers once again. For a moment, I thought I was full naxem. I must have imagined it. Just like I must be imagining Mian's voice calling my name... *Mian...she's coming after us.*

"Neheyuu, sviking Sasorana!" Only it isn't Mian's light, pleasant accent, it's Dandena hard, imposing brogue.

Find Mian. Give her your wreath. Bite Tatana's arms off tomorrow in battle and let him watch you swallow them whole. Tszk. Mian has made her choice. She chose him. She promised him her body when that's not even a promise she would have made me. *Go to Mian. Go find Mian. Give her your wreath. Give her your oath. She is ours. But only because we were hers long before. She is our Xiveri.*

"What the svik are you doing out here? Drunk as a sviking...I don't know what." She has hold of my arm and is lifting me onto my feet. I'm grateful because there's nothing I could do to achieve the same result. I'm not in control of my body. My limbs are being pulled back towards the dolsk, but my true form is fighting.

Tszk. Mian doesn't deserve First. The whore. The akimari sviking whore... *You do not speak of her in this way. You are a disgrace to Sasorana. You are a sightless fool.* My eyes worked well enough to see her take Tatana's wreath. *What do eyes have to do with anything? What do wreaths?*

My left leg jerks backwards, towards the sessemara dolsk, towards her, but I am in control here. *Are you in control?* I start to collapse all over again. Suddenly more hands are under me. I can hear voices flapping in the distance like bird's wings.

"What's wrong with him?"

"He sick?"

"First, can you hear us?"

"First!"

"First!" Dandena says. "The svik is going on?"

The pounding of feet. "Svik, there's chaos in there. What was that about?"

"Neheyuu!" While the last voice sounded kind of like Mor, this definitely sounds like Preena. I open my eyes and see the fury in my Second's expression. It's dark out here, now that so many of the fires from earlier are down to their embers. From far away, I see bodies filtering out of the sessemara dolsk. Those that do, crane their necks this way in an attempt to catch a glimpse of the youngest First — *the disgraced First* — and the mess that I've caused. That is, if I'll even be a First for much longer. Who even cares? Let them take it. Let them take me. *Fool. Coward!*

Preena roars, his pin-straight hair flying behind him like a kite. "What have you done?"

"What did he do?"

As Preena recounts what happened, I feel my head and chest squeeze. My manerak is raging within me, incapable of understanding anything besides what he wants — *to tear Tatana's head off, and then rut Mian into oblivion.* In that order. Give her something for her wreath — *Tatana's head and both his hands and all of his manerak teeth* — only she won't need a wreath because I'll devour everything and shred through everyone to ensure that she's mine and only mine. My naxem is silent. Disappointment and rejection course through my veins as the undertone to my grief. What am I doing? *What are you doing?* A low hiss, a darker tone, *What have you done?*

"We were talking about Mian just now…"

"What?" I snarl, rounding on Dandena as I find my feet.

She frowns at me and though she angles her body to the side, she holds steady, waiting to be attacked, yet without striking. I wish she would strike me. I wish she would strike me *down…* "Yena. Enough members of the tasmaran have approached me, expressing concern that they will lose her as weapons keeper, that I brought together a small group of warriors to determine who will vie for her."

I might pass the svik out. "*Vie for her? She is mine.*"

Dandena starts, looking horrified and aghast before she tosses both arms up into the air. "All you've talked about for the past two turns since you became First is the need to create a union with a stronger tasmaran! Meanwhile, Mian has only ever expressed the desire to be joined with a nice, kind male. Chimara was sure that she would try to find a male at this sessemara and your warriors happen to *like* Mian — we *like* fighting for her.

We don't want to lose her as part of this tasmaran — or have you forgotten about the tasmaran? Do we mean nothing to you anymore?"

"None of you will have Mian," I roar.

"Did you not hear me, Neheyuu?"

"None of you will have her!"

"Then what!" Dandena is screaming at me now. I want to swipe my claws across her throat to quiet her. And to watch her bleed. My manerak wants to kill every single one of them. But none more than me. "We just give her up to the Nevay? Even if that was an option before, do you realize what you've done by disgracing yourself before them now? If we let the Nevay take her, it makes you look weak. It makes all of us look weak! And you *marked* her? For svik's sake! Why did none of you sviking males — *tszk* — why did none of you sviking *morons* tell me?"

Dandena grabs my shoulders and forces me to meet her gaze. "Neheyuu, you have to give her your wreath. If she doesn't choose you, then we've done all we could as a tasmaran, but if she does, then we win our weapons keeper back and you win the female you're clearly smitten with. We'll work out another way to increase our numbers."

Everything she's saying makes sense. It makes sense. Except for the fact that I've given her no reason to choose me — tszk, I've given her every reason *not* to choose me — and I can't survive that kind of rejection. All I've done since I met her is ridicule and reject her and Tatana...he didn't just tend her wounds with his own hands...he saw the treasure he had and made her an offer there and then. Just as I should have done the moment I saw her sitting between those ceramic jugs, waiting for me. A prize to be claimed. *Tszk…a beacon.*

He's stronger than me for it. Maybe just *stronger.* What if I can't even beat him tomorrow during the second solar of the ceremony? Our first battle — the one that brought me this dolsk — was a narrow victory. He could win. And I'm unstable. He could… She could… I could win and she could give him her wreath anyways on the final solar. Mian doesn't care about things like battles. She just wants a male who is *nice.* Tatana was nice to her. I'm not nice. I'm…sviking lost. I just need time. All I asked her for was a little time. Svik her for putting me here in this position…

"Neheyuu!" Dandena screeches. She punches my shoulder.

I lift the wreath off of my neck and throw it. I throw it into the black. And then I curse and I roar as my manerak swallows me whole and I crash into the darkness to meet the horizon, hoping that I reach the fabled edge of Sasor and tumble right off of its jagged edge.

19

Mian

Where is Neheyuu? It's the only question anyone has been asking for the past two solars. He did not appear after his...episode the first solar, and he did not appear the previous one to watch the contests.

I was shocked to have three males vie for me in combat. After Tatana offered me his wreath, I guess it must have piqued the interest of the other males, because I received two other offers. One from a Sessena weapons maker and one from an unranked Hox warrior.

Tatana won the battle against both of them, even with the other two males working together at the beginning of the battle to defeat Tatana first. It was a good strategy, but even with my limited knowledge of fighting, it was clear that Tatana was the superior swordsman.

Following their battle, the three males then offered me their gifts, token tributes. From the weapons maker, I received a modest, yet beautifully crafted dagger. From the warrior, a silver bracelet. From Tatana, a set of robes in a beautiful blue hue.

I wear them now on the third day of the sessemara along with the bracelet. My hair I keep pinned. Not because I've noticed that Neheyuu seems to like it this way. Tszk, of course not… After all, he isn't even here and no one has seen him and it's time for the last portion of the sessemara… The returning of the wreaths. The joining.

The atmosphere is more tense at this ceremony than at the first — at least, until the first wreath is lain. And it's Rita's. Three males I don't know joined Erkan to vie for her, but when his gift was revealed I think it became clear to all that there would be no swaying her. He provided her a crib. One that he carved himself from black wood.

I watch Rita flit about the room, returning the wreaths to the males who fought for her, but lost. They accept their returned wreaths with grace, all of them. "Why do they not seem angry or disappointed?" I ask Chimara beside me. I think of Neheyuu, who only ever seems angry or disappointed.

Feasting on one of her strange yellow fruits, she says, "Gossip is the primary way this whole sessemara thing works. Most males know already if the female they want will accept them. And most males already know the females who will be taken by one of the other males."

"With the marking scent?"

"Sometimes, but remember, not all females who are marked wish to have been. Some who are taken in raids want to get away from the male who marked them as quickly as possible. Other times, like in the case with Rita, they are in love and make it clear. In these cases, other males will still put their wreaths forward for the female, but they don't do it with the intent of joining with her. Instead, they use the opportunity to display their skills in battle, or to simply draw attention to themselves, in order to gain a better position within their own tasmaran or a competing one."

"Clever," I say, meaning it. "But what about females? How do they show their skills?"

Chimara exhales out of the edge of her mouth and shucks the shell of her fruit into a bowl set out for this purpose. "With difficulty. We have to work twice as hard to prove ourselves in battle in order to bolster our wreaths and prove to the other males that we're worth something. The good thing though, is that because there *are* fewer female warriors, we usually have our pick of males. But if we want to join another tasmaran *and* get a ranked position *without* joining with one of their males — that's where it gets tricky."

Clapping spreads like wildfire across the dolsk as Erkan — in a simple wreath made of bright purple fabric — sweeps Rita — in a metal wreath three hands across and studded with kills — up into his arms and runs like a madman towards the leathers of the dolsk, and then through them out into the lunar.

"Looks like it's time for bed," I laugh.

"I don't think they'll be doing much sleeping." Chimara has already returned the three wreaths she received from warriors of other tribes. Now she stands in just her own, looking at me and the large wreaths stacked around my much smaller frame. They are rather awkward and unwieldy. She smirks as I struggle to lift a small piece of battar to my lips around them.

"And what about you? Will you be doing much sleeping this lunar?" She lifts a brow.

The beating of my heart that was excitement for Rita becomes a deep boom of terror. I don't know what to do. I've had all solar to think about it and the one before, but I still don't know who to give my wreath to.

"I like the blacksmith," I say, dropping my tone. "But Reffa, Tri and some of the other females are pressuring me into giving my wreath to Tatana. They think it's a really good offer. He *is* Second...but I don't know that I really like him. And Trehuro, well, he's just...warm."

Tatana's actions, while they haven't been criminal, have been...disconcerting, at best. And something about the way he smiled at Neheyuu's pain struck me as cruel. Is he a cruel male? The fact that I can't answer that question seems like answer enough, and yet, I trust Tri and Reffa.

"It's tough. Second is certainly an allure. But maybe not for you." She eyes me up and down, and I wonder what she sees. "You can always wait. It doesn't decrease your value in the eyes of manerak males. In fact, it may increase it. They will certainly vie for you again in the next ceremony."

That surprises me. It also fills me with a few much-needed droplets of hope. "Do you think? Even with Neheyuu and the mark?"

Chimara makes a face. "I've heard the scent markers can fade with space and time. However, returning with Neheyuu and letting him try to get you back into his dolsk and into his bed could jeopardize that. I don't know," she exhales. "This one's hard. I obviously don't want to see you go — svik, if you go, I might just have to follow you."

That shocks me. *Shocks* me, shocks me. "I...you..." I don't know what my expression looks like, but Chimara laughs. "Don't look so surprised. Like I told you the first moment I met you, I don't come across folks as entertaining as you very often and while that's definitely proved to be true, I also don't come across beings as kind, smart, funny or caring as you either. Good friends are hard to find for a half-breed manerak who can't transform, and for a half-breed human who never lived in any of the villages."

She shrugs and her mouth quirks. "You're my best friend. Now don't do that…" She laughs even harder as she pulls my hands away from my face so she can see the water bubbling in my eyes. "Oh Mian." She pulls me in for a hug and I wrap my arms tightly around her slightly taller frame. Her heart beats through her armor against mine. Just the one of them.

"I've never had a best friend before," I sniff. "I worried you were only hanging out with me because Neheyuu makes you, but you're my best friend too. I hope you know that."

Chimara laughs again and when she finally pries me off of her, I see she's got water in her eyes to match mine. She sniffs quickly and waves me away. "Stop it. You're embarrassing me. Now go tell those males something. I can see them staring from here. Probably wondering if you're reconsidering more than just their wreaths but maybe even your sexuality."

I gawk, and then I giggle. Somehow the decision to wait is so much more easily made. I've never had offers before from males who want me, but I've also never had friends before either. And from the conversations I've had with other humans from other tasmaran about their ways of life, I've come to the conclusion that while none sound quite so chaotic as the Neheyuu tasmaran, they also don't sound like they're as much fun. The Neheyuu tasmaran really feels like family. Like home. And shame on me for thinking he can push me out of it. And shame on Neheyuu too, for trying.

I'm still beaming at Chimara, but before I can say anything more, she spanks me on the ass. Hard. "Now go get 'em, reesa. Whatever you decide, I got your back."

I give her a salute that wins another laugh from her before searching the crowd for the males who did what I secretly hoped Neheyuu would have done — looked at me like a female who would make them proud.

"I'm not ready now, but I am honored to have received your wreath and I hope that I might again have the honor at a future sessemara," I tell the weapons smith, Trehuro, in words well-practiced. I repeat to him the same phrase I told Ipo, the Hox warrior, though with a bit more feeling. Ipo didn't do much for me and I got the sense that he was, perhaps, using the opportunity to give me his wreath as a chance to display himself in the way Chimara mentioned.

Trehuro offers me a bow befitting someone of a much higher rank and I blush when he says, "The honor will be, as it has been, mine."

I offer him a mirrored bow and exhale another breath. My stomach is in knots. Neither Trehuro or Ipo seemed upset that I wanted to wait to join with someone until the next sessemara. Maybe Tatana won't either. I hope.

I meet his gaze from across the dolsk and make my way towards him. He starts towards me at the same time. As I walk, I reach for his wreath, but his expression doesn't change in the slightest. He doesn't look happy to see me coming, but he doesn't look disappointed either. He doesn't seem to be in any way fazed.

As we reach one another somewhere in the middle of the dolsk, I know we're being watched, and when I glance up, I spot Chimara joining a group of familiar faces — Dandena, Mor, Xi, Xena, Rehet, Ofrat, Ock. Whispering as they are between each other, they succeed in jacking my heartrate up, up, up!

"Mian," Tatana says, "You look beautiful in your new robes."

That only makes me feel worse. I *am* wearing his robes. And I'm about to reject him — no, *defer* my decision. The semantics don't help me feel any less sick to my stomach. I bite my bottom lip. "Thank you. I just wanted to tell you that I am deeply honored…"

But he's not listening to me. His gaze has passed over my shoulder and when I twist around to follow it, I don't believe what I'm seeing. I can't. "Neheyuu…" My voice is one-part confusion, two-parts disbelief.

It's Neheyuu, but the version of him that has completely succumbed to insanity. Naked, streaked with dirt and something redder and more viscous, hair matted in chunks that stick up in every direction, he looks like a stark raving lunatic.

Many voices in the dolsk chime his name, but mine is the only one he seems to hear when I say, "Neheyuu, are you hurt?"

His eyes flash black and brown and with a chilling hostility I have not seen before this. "Remove Tatana's wreath, Mian."

I open my mouth to tell him that what I do with the wreaths given to me are none of his business, but then I realize quickly that I don't wish to incite this particular form of Neheyuu any further. Instead, perhaps I should tell him that I was planning on deferring my decision anyways, and returning Tatana's wreath to him on my own, but I'm not given that chance either.

"Neheyuu, I…" And then I scream, because the moment his name leaves my lips, Neheyuu *comes at* me.

I close my eyes against the sudden attack — pain at my throat, a heavy weight lifted — and when I open them, Neheyuu is holding Tatana's wreath. I leap for it, but he blocks me with one arm while using his other to fling said wreath against the far wall. Some of it shatters and crumbles while the rest clatters noisily to the floor, drawing screams from a female nicked by it and a pained curse from someone else caught by its shrapnel.

"Neheyuu," I shout, exasperated and shocked as I stare down the ghost of a male who was sane, and now isn't. "What are you doing?"

"Stopping you from making the biggest decision of your life."

"It is not your decision. Decision is *mine*."

Neheyuu's eyes flash with something lethal, but I'm too angry to be appropriately afraid. "He doesn't like you. He doesn't want you. He only wants to piss me off."

"Because it is not possible for male to want me? Because I am only dirty reed paper?" I accuse.

Neheyuu's eyes slit even more. He towers over me. Behind me, Preena and Tatana are arguing, but I don't hear them. I only hear the lunatic before me and his heavy breath and I only see him and his petulant expression and I only smell him and the blood on his skin and the scent lingering just beneath that, the one that I hate only because it smells like home.

The marking scent? Is it muddling with my mind, convincing me to like this male who is nothing more than rage-colored savagery? He was something else, once. He was something more to me. But his actions over the past solars have changed all that because now I feel myself rising up to meet him with an equal, and foreign, madness.

"You are not dirty reed paper. But we have history…"

"I understand history. But Tatana make me offer when we first meet…met. Before he knows you are… before he knows I am akimari," I stammer, frustrated that I can't get all the words out I want. All the rage.

"And you didn't think to sviking tell me that?"

"Tszk! It is not important for you!" I don't bother telling him that it would have been too embarrassing to live if I *had* told him of Tatana's offer, only for Tatana not to offer it after all.

"The svik it isn't!" Neheyuu advances on me.

"Neheyuu," comes Preena's tight, clipped voice as he tries to shove himself between us. "You need to leave." But then he takes my elbow and tries to pull me back and I know what Neheyuu will do seconds before he does it. I scream as Neheyuu shoves Preena away from me so forcefully it sends Preena *flying*. The male stumbles back half a dozen feet before crashing into a group of females who collapse beneath his weight in a pile of colorful robes and moans.

Neheyuu grabs my hand and presses it to the center of his bare chest. His eyes bore into me. "You are mine. My akimari. My human. *Mine*. You belong to me."

Frustration explodes through the base of my skull. It tastes like metal. I see red. I rip my palm free of his and slap him across the cheek hard enough to leave an imprint. "I am not a slave. Manerak do not have slaves."

Neheyuu roars and the little control he had over his true form snaps like a dead reed. His whole body shifts, becoming snake and manerak before reverting to his own true skin. He has hands again, but they're still tipped in claws. They reach for me and I try to avoid them, but I'm too slow and he's inhumanly quick.

He grabs my upper arms and when I yank backwards, I feel the latent burn across my skin. The sharp, cutting pain of it makes me stumble. I land on my bottom in a heap and glance down to see four parallel slashes on both of my arms just below the shoulder. Shock keeps me from feeling anything for the first moment, and then comes the regret — not that he hurt me, no, I don't care about that. This is the only garment I own that isn't a shift, and in a single rash act, Neheyuu ruined it.

"Ow," I whisper quietly to myself as tears hit my cheeks. I glare up at him, lick my flaming lips and say just as softly, "You ruin everything."

"Guards! Hox!" Tatana's voice rips between us.

A second voice rises up and I notice several males approach. They appear older than Neheyuu and Tatana, yet still look like fierce warriors in their own right. "What is the meaning of this?" The heaviest male says, sweeping his gaze from Tatana to Neheyuu to me, where it lands. "Neheyuu? In *my* sessemara, you dare draw blood from a female?"

But Neheyuu is staring at me like I've sprouted barnacles out of my ears. It's the blood on my arms. He tracks the droplets that stain my sleeves and all at once, lurches towards me, but I wrench back. He freezes.

"Tszk," he whispers, "reesa…"

"Neheyuu!" The older warrior curses and barks a series of orders over his shoulder. Less than a moment later, the sound of stomping feet and jangling metal fills the dolsk. I see a few guards passing weapons out among the warriors gathered — none to the Neheyuu tasmaran though.

"Neheyuu…" I meet Dandena's gaze as she thrusts herself between Tatana, Neheyuu, the older male Firsts, and me. She's breathing hard. Both of her hands are raised. "Neheyuu, let's end this before anybody gets hurt. More hurt," she says in a low, calming tone, but Neheyuu is frozen. He's not looking at her. He's not even looking at me. He's looking *through* me.

"Are you alright?" Tatana drops into a crouch at my side and rips off one of my sleeves to create a tourniquet for the wound there. At the pressure, I make a pained sound. "Guards. Sieze Neheyuu! Hox, give your guards the order."

A moment's pause. Then the order is relayed. But Neheyuu doesn't react. He doesn't even react when the hands of a dozen guards suddenly fall on him. What's strange is that they try to pull him, but he goes nowhere. It's like watching a dozen warriors try to pull an ancient, rooted tree from the ground with their bare hands.

"Too strong in his manerak…" One of them curses.

"He's *not* manerak…this is his true form…"

A similar chorus strikes up before finally one of the warriors releases the hold he has on Neheyuu's shoulder and shouts, "We can't move him."

"More guards," Hox orders, "Preena and Dandena, control your First. Tatana, get the female out of here."

"Don't touch her," Neheyuu says, but his voice is strangled. His eyes close.

Another four guards start to try to lift his feet from the ground — they succeed, but only for the first moment. Because in the next, Tatana pulls me up into his arms. "Are you alright? I will take you to my dolsk and heal you."

Neheyuu lets out an agonized moan and as his head slumps forward, fully defeated, his body seems to go lax. But I still hear him say the words that change everything. Under his breath, so low I doubt many can even decipher it, he whispers, "I need you." A pause. Nothing. Then, "For Mian." And then the world shrinks around him.

Bypassing his manerak state, he morphs directly into his snake form, head extending so high the roof of the dolsk comes up to meet his rounded hood in moments. The guards holding him are forced back by the energy that wicks off of his skin — and so am I. Tatana and I fly apart from one another — him, toppling off of his feet, me, skating over the carpets. Neheyuu continues to grow up and out and around me. Slick scales cover his skin and I hear shouts this time — as expected — but what I don't expect is the lack of fear. No, these cries are of *adulation*.

"Sasorana! He is naxem!" Someone shouts, even as Neheyuu's massive head dives in attack.

"He is a naxem! We tried to tell you!" He rears up and back, a body trapped in his mandible. Tatana's. Could it be anyone else's?

"We knew it!"

"Praise be to Sasorana!"

I scream, "Neheyuu, tszk!"

"Someone control that naxem!"

Either he hears me, or he doesn't, because he flings Tatana's body against one wall and Tatana knocks into a table, taking the whole thing out before disappearing behind it.

"We saw it before…"

"…when he attacked Tatana's roving tasmaran."

"…we saw…"

"Neheyuu!" I shout, and staring up at him, I realize that this snake that I've come to know quite well is utterly unknown to all others. And he's unique. And because of that, no one can stand up to him. Not even me.

Especially not me.

The largest I've seen him since he came to take me from Tatana's dolsk, the circumference of his round body eclipses my height. As such, I can't see over him when he starts to coil his length around me, leaving me curled up, alone in the center of a blood-spattered carpet. The sound of tables falling and people shouting springs up around me. I hear running feet. The tear of fabric.

"Neheyuu…you are…you are naxem…" says Hox from somewhere over the crest of Neheyuu's shape, but Neheyuu doesn't answer him. Instead, those big, black, snake eyes just stare down at me. I stare straight back, angry tears clouding my vision until he blurs.

I ball my hands into fists and pound on the carpet below and when the snake lowers its head, I punch it on the nose. More like bop it. My fist bounces back, nearly smacking me in the head, yet Neheyuu is still the one who rears back. He flinches, as if cut, and even though the packed room is in chaos around us, it feels like we are alone.

And I have never felt more alone.

Neheyuu's giant head, guided by slitted nostrils, edges its way forward. His tongues flick out at the blood on my arm, tasting it, but I slap him away. "I am done." I shake my head violently, sending the pins in my hair springing free.

My hair falls free of its twists and braids while little blue and white flowers spill across my lap, looking like the sad relics of fallen stars. "I'm done!" I beat my fists on the ground again and again. "Go from me," I shriek, voice wretched and not my own. "Go away from me!"

The snake head rears back and up and I hear several different voices saying my name, probably calling to see if I'm even still alive. But the snake just watches me and I just stare up at him and I challenge him with my gaze and in the end, he releases one final, terrible hiss and then like an earthquake in fast forward, he slams towards the open door. Gone, and in his wake, destruction. The whole beautiful space is overturned, left in ruin. Candles are huffed out while torches are toted in to try to create light in the new darkness.

Chimara is calling my name and eventually, I call back. I feel her hands on me a moment later and in the next, Dandena, Ofrat, Xi, Xena, and Rehet have formed a sort of cluster around me. With their help, I manage to escape the stampeding forces going into and out of the dolsk and squeeze out under Sasorana's sky.

Xi and Xena are laughing — well, Xena is laughing — like they just witnessed the most fantastic battle, and are regaling each other with tales of it. In fact, most are, and soon our small group is a fairly large group consisting of those within the dolsk trying to regurgitate what they just saw, while some — Nevay — approach with new stories of their own, from the first time they saw Neheyuu as the creature they call naxem. The first time I saw him, too.

"Has he always been like this?" A random Hox female asks.

Rehet shakes his head. "Tszk, tszk...the Sasorena..."

Eyes turn to me. I hear that word more often as more people crowd the space around me. A random warrior comes close to me and reaches forward like he'll touch me before catching himself.

"Apologies." He glances around as if suspicious of being watched, drops his tone even further and says, "You are Sasorena?"

No. I'm overwhelmed. I shake my head and Chimara steps between us before the male can say anything more while Dandena comes up behind me and places a hand between my shoulder blades reassuringly.

"Clear a space! The Sasorena is injured. We need to get her to a healer."

"I'm not sasor...sasor anything..." I say absently. I'm caught in a dream. This must be one. Or it's a nightmare.

The smell of smoke stings my nostrils. I look up and see that part of the sessemara dolsk is now on fire. People are screaming. Part of our group has peeled off to grab buckets of sand and water to douse the flames, which spiral higher into the lunar, as if trying to touch the sky itself and bring it down on all of our heads.

"Sorry, Mian." Dandena's face manages an expression akin to sympathy. "Come on. Let's get you..."

"Mack is here," Ock, shouts, appearing before us with a female in tow. "She's the Hox's most experienced healer. She's happy to look at the sas...um..."

One look from Chimara shuts him up. "At *Mian*."

"Mian," Ock repeats carefully, as if he's never heard the word before.

"Good," Dandena says, "Let's do this in private. And sorry, Ock, that doesn't include you. Only females. Send Xena to the Neheyuu dolsk. Tell her to make sure it's clear and tell her to bring all the grain alcohol she can find. I think our reesa is going to need it."

In the dolsk, I sit on a poof while the healer works at cleaning the cuts on my arms. Only one requires stitching and I don't feel it as she works. The grain alcohol makes sure of it. My head swims.

"Mian, are you okay?" Chimara's voice snaps me to attention.

"She will have no problem healing from this. With the stitching, she is unlikely to have more than a very faint scar. Hardly noticeable." The female — Mack — gives me a pleasant little pat on the back, but one look at Chimara and I know she isn't talking about my arm.

I shake my head and polish off the rest of my cup. Dandena pours me another. "What did I do to deserve this?" I whisper in human. Manerak words have fled me now.

Chimara translates for me and Dandena answers, "You were born."

I scoff. "Is it Neheyuu's intention to make me wish I hadn't been?"

Chimara frowns and translates, and Xena and Dandena both hiss in unison. "You don't mean that," Xena says, and even though she's right, it doesn't help the ruinous thumping in my chest occupying the place where my heart should be. My heart hole is what's there now. And it hurts being so empty. "It's a blessing, what happened."

"How? Will we not be expelled from the United Manerak Tribes? Will Neheyuu not lose his position? Will we not be all scattered to different tasmaran or absorbed by one?"

Chimara, Xena and Dandena share a look I can't interpret, but surprising me, it's Mack who answers, "Tszk, Sasorena. Neheyuu is *naxem*. If anything, this will strengthen his claim and his tasmaran and all within it. I would think of joining with you all myself if I did not have a family and such strong roots within the Hox, but I am sure that many others who lack such roots will join with you after this lunar. That is, if they are not too frightened away by your First."

Tears wet my eyelashes. I squeeze them away. "So, he gets to behave like a lunatic and then gets rewarded for it?"

"I don't think Neheyuu feels he has been rewarded for anything right now," Dandena says, voice morose. "What Mack has said will hold true, but only if Neheyuu comes back to us. And I don't mean his body. I mean his mind. It seems…shattered. Hopefully Rea will be able to track him and we can find him quickly."

"I hope he doesn't come back."

"Tszk, you don't mean that," Mack says after Chimara translates. At the same time, Chimara mutters, "I don't blame you. What a fucking idiot…"

"How do I get him to leave me alone?" I ask her.

She translates and the females don't seem to breathe for a moment. Then Dandena says, "Has Tri taught you the ancient stories of the naxem yet, Mian?"

I shake my head and listen as she explains a tale of gods and war. Of a love never-ending, one called Xiveri. When she's finished, I shake my head a second time. "And what does this have to do with me?"

She exhales, looking very much like she's bracing for something, but Chimara cuts her off. "Nothing. You only have to worry about yourself and being with the male you want to be with."

Dandena scowls at her and looks like she'll say more, but doesn't. Instead, her head drops back and she stares at the ceiling through closed lids. Muscles in her neck pulse like massive veins. "Chimara is right. You don't have to do anything you don't want to *ever*. We're here to make sure of that."

I squint at her, and switch back to manerak. "Even against Neheyuu?"

She nods. "Even against Neheyuu."

"Then tell me how to make him stop…hurting me," I say, but only because I don't know the word for torment.

Dandena grits her back molars so hard I can hear it. Xena just balks, "Neheyuu is a simple, stupid male. He has a one-track mind. When he was Third within the Nevay, he knew he wanted his own tasmaran. It was all he could think about. Everything he did was for that goal. And even though Tatana had a higher rank than he did, it was Neheyuu who bested him. Neheyuu who was able to branch off and become the United Tribes' newest First."

"You mean that…if he gets goal, he will leave me alone?"

Xena looks confused. "Tszk. Sorry, Mian, but what I meant was that he's not a male I would bet against. He may be simple and stupid but he's also hard-headed and a fighter. He doesn't give up for anything and it's clear he wants *you*. All of you."

I glance at my right wrist. A slim track of blood has wound down my arm and completes the black tattooed band I wear branded into my skin. The red catches the light of the torches mounted in the wall, turning it saccharine and bright. I nod then, stomach pitching even as my mind settles with decisions made and swims with reed alcohol.

"You are right."

"Erm, Mian, I'm a little worried about what you got out of what Xena just said," Chimara huffs.

I shake my head. "No worry. I will not fight."

"Fight?"

"May I have more hibi?" I say, lifting my cup and waiting for Dandena to refill it.

She hesitates, says my name. "Did you hear what I said before? We are here for you."

"Yena, but you are Third and I am only slave."

"You are our weapons keeper," Xena says harshly, "and you are Sasorena."

I shake my head and down my hibi in one swallow. "Against Neheyuu, it is all the same."

20
Neheyuu

"You're a surprisingly difficult male to find." The voice jerks me out of my slumber. Stupor. Whatever the svik it is. Blissful wakelessness.

Everything else is agony of the gut-wrenching sort. The light. Opening my eyes to it. Especially opening my eyes. Because that means I'm here. That I'm real. And so is the pain coursing through my soul. My body can survive it, but the rest, I'm not sure...

"For sviking Sasorana's sake, Neheyuu. I can't... what in the comets did you do? Hunt an entire pack of desert dogs by yourself? Or just let them try to eat you alive?"

"Yena."

"Which was it?"

"Both. It was both..." The sound of scraping and falling numbs my mind, pushing back the pain to a bearable state. My eyelids use the opportunity to open and they see...rocks. Rocks? Yena, rocks. And a lot of them. "Where am I?"

"You don't know?"

I shake my head. Blink the dust from my eyes. Try to move. Fail at it. Grunt.

"Don't sviking move. You're...just...wait." I hear rocks sliding and then a moment later, booted feet appear in my eye-line, small yellow and black stones scattering around them.

I glance up and though sunlight works against me, I still know who it is. "Dandena."

"Yena, Dandena. Or have you been gone so long you forgot?" She stoops down and finds one of the things I'd lost — an arm, one that's still attached to my body though I can't feel it. She slings it over her shoulder and lets out a long, pained "oof" as she hauls me up vertically.

I manage to find my legs after that and shove them underneath me. Sharp rocks dig into the soles of my bare feet, bringing my awareness to them. I glance down and see that I'm naked. My soft cock flops close to Dandena's hip when she repositions her arm around me and starts to use some of the larger rocks jutting into...wherever we are...to drag us both up.

"You better keep that cock to yourself or I'll cut it off."

I laugh, but there's nothing funny about it. "Don't worry. I've got no need for it anymore."

"What in the svik's that supposed to mean?" Dandena says with a grunt, wrenching herself up to the next rocky shelf and then reaching back for me.

I'm a little more alive now. A little less dead. I look up and see that there are three shelves above us, a whole lot of dirt and scree between each one. At the top, there's the gentle sway of tall grass, letting me know I must've fallen into some kind of hole. Some kind of den. A desert dog den. There are bones all around me. Clips of images, memories that aren't mine but *his* revisit me. There was a pack of them and I slaughtered them all.

"What'd you say?" She says, breathing hard above me while she takes my hand. I blink at her, confused as to what she's talking about and let her pull me up beside her. "You said, you *ate* something. Ate what?"

I shake my head and look up to the next shelf. I haul myself onto it and reach back for Dandena's hands. "Not me. Him. He likes hunting desert dogs."

"Svik!" Dandena cries out, and I don't know if it's because of what I've said or because she's slipped. I grab her arm before she falls off of the shelf completely and pull. My heartstrings, more than the muscles in my arms, rip. "You *hunted* desert dogs? By your sviking self?"

"Not me. Him." And now he's gone.

"Who the svik is him?"

Passing the last ledge, she flings herself out of the den and I scrabble after her, rocks slipping past me to pummel the flat, rocky shelves below, and collapse onto the grass. It itches my butt. I wish I had clothes, but there's no shot of that out here. The only thing I've got with me is this thing clenched in my fist. I didn't realize I'd been climbing with it until now. When I was naxem, it slid neatly beneath my scales. Before that, I think I might have had it woven into my hair.

A stone. Mian's stone.

The one I never gave her. The one that belongs to her.

Exactly like my heart.

I suck in a ragged breath as I look down at my body and examine it for wounds. There's a lot of blood, but no openings, no tears. "Svik," Dandena says. She must notice the same thing I do. "How… You went up against an entire pack of desert dogs and came out without a scratch?"

"Guess I did."

Her cheeks fill with air. She huffs it all out. "How many?"

I shrug. "Dunno. A pack. My manerak likes to hunt them."

"Your…your *manerak*? Tszk, tszk, tszk, tszk. You've got to be sviking me. That's no manerak." Her face splits into a huge grin and for a moment, it almost makes her attractive. Too bad she's kin. Too bad I'll never have sex again. "You went *full. sviking. naxem.* You were longer than twenty bodies, bigger around than three linked together. And your head — your hood — was the size of an oeban, your eyes the width of a white wood tree trunk, each one. Do you even remember? Do you know what you looked like? And you just…brought it out, switching into it like it was nothing." She claps her hands together and laughs up to the sky. "It was incredible!"

I don't respond. Just look at my hands, flex them. Look at the way the color strikes Mian's stone in the sun. My insides are hollow. I'm a shell. Tszk. I'm not even a shell. A shell can be filled. I'm just…pieces. Pieces of nothing.

Dandena kicks my shin, intending to hurt me and succeeding. I hiss. "Are you hearing me? You're a *naxem*."

I shake my head, ball the stone in my fist and throw it. I watch it arc through the sky, disappearing far away, some place unattainable, like the one it belongs to. The one who also owns me. My manerak and my naxem offer no council. Since I shed my naxem's form for the last time, they offer only their absence.

"Neheyuu. Don't tell me…don't you sviking tell me that you knew you were a naxem. Don't tell me that what the Nevay warriors said was true," she says, so I don't. I just cross my arms over my bent knees and stare towards the horizon. It's empty. We're far from Hox territory. I wonder where we are. How she found me. But more than that, I wonder where *she* is. I tense. Is she with Tatana now? Did they conclude the sessemara? Do I sviking want to know?

Tszk. I don't. But I want to know that she's safe.

Yena, I do. I want to see her. I want to hold her. I want to watch her face screw up all cute-like when she's ticked with me. But I don't want to see her with water in her eyes and blood on her arm. I never want to see that. My manerak doesn't even have words of condemnation to offer me. Fool. This time, the word is one I call myself and it's never rung so true.

"Neheyuu!"

"Yena!" I roar.

Her face falls. She leans back and shakes her head. "You *knew* you were naxem, but said nothing?" I don't answer. "For how long? Some of the Nevay said that you attacked their camp as a naxem when you went after our females. Was that the first time?"

"Not after our females," I murmur. "After *my* female. And yena, that was the first time I shifted, but it wasn't the first time I felt it. I felt his presence the first time she hit me, on that first raid when we were alone. She agreed to come with me in exchange for letting a group of other humans go free. I did. I didn't…take them with us. There were about twenty of them, maybe more

— I don't remember — but I left them there because that's what she wanted. I didn't know her, but that's what she wanted." I start to rock back and forth. My gaze follows the arc I can still see lingering against the bright pink and blue sky. Why did I throw it? I'm going to have to go get it.

I need it. It belongs to her.

Exactly like my heart.

Dandena grunts and that's all the warning I'm given before her manerak attacks. She comes at me hard, tackling me to the grass and pinning me easily. She swipes her claws across my chest once, twice, a third time before she rolls away from me. I don't even try to dislodge her. The pain feels good. It feels deserved.

"Fight me!" She stands up and starts to circle her weak, wounded prey. Finish it off. Finish me off.

When she doesn't, I roll to my knees and she darts forward again. She moves fast and I manage to evade the first glance of her claws but not the second. This is child's play. It should be anyways. But I just don't have it in me.

"You don't deserve to be First," Dandena snarls.

"You're right." I grimace.

With a grunt, she charges me and I don't bother to brace. I just let her take me down and watch her come up, spitting and writhing as she transforms to her true form, with what looks like difficulty. If I were naxem, I'd be able to help her with that. But I'm not. I'm not anything.

"What is going on? Fight me, Neheyuu!"

"I can't!" I sit up, rip out grass stalks by the root, toss them into the air and watch the way the green strands change to purple depending on the way the light strikes them. "I'm not naxem. I'm not even manerak."

"What?"

"They don't fight for me. They only fight for her! They warned me that they would leave if I didn't claim her, but I didn't listen and now they're gone."

"I don't understand," Dandena pants, still struggling with the effects of her transformation as she settles back into her skin and smooths down her manerak armor, snapping shut a buckle that had yielded to allow for her expansion.

"How can I be more clear? They fight for her. They don't fight for me. She's gone and now so are…"

"Tszk, not that, you sviking arse. I meant your claiming her. Why didn't you give her your wreath? If you even had an *inkling* that she might be our Sasorena and your Xiveri mate, then why didn't you mark her the moment you saw her?"

I snarl, hating the mild way she speaks about Mian, as if Mian were any female to be claimed or marked or even could be. But Mian is only Mian. And only Mian is Mian.

"She did not want to be marked."

"But you marked her anyways."

"Yena. Not on purpose."

"Okay… And the wreath?"

"I wasn't…ready."

"*Svik being ready, Neheyuu*. She's your sviking Sasorena. You belong to her." Yena, I do. But this whole time, I thought she belonged to me.

I curse. "She's human. She has no manerak. She has no tasmaran, no warriors to follow her…I wanted to keep the tasmaran strong. Creyu and Tekevanki were leaving. I needed more warriors, before I..."

Dandena slugs me. I watch it happen, watch her form a fist of manerak proportions, watch that fist career towards my face, feel the sensation of my head snapping to the left, taking my neck and then my shoulders and then my whole body with it. I collapse onto one knee, spots winking in my vision, jaw burning with a starburst-shaped pang.

"Oh. My. Sasorana. May she help you. May she help us all." Dandena is holding onto her hair, like she's worried the unshaved half will fly off her head. "I always knew that your being stupid would be a problem for the tasmaran, but I didn't realize how big of a problem. Or how stupid." She stops and turns to face me fully, planting her hands on the weapons belt at her hips. She fists her sword. I don't react. If she wanted to cut me down, I'd let her.

"Did you even pay attention when we studied the ancient lore as children? Do you even know the story of the naxem?"

"What does it matter..."

"Sasorana was said to have created the naxem out of loneliness," she pushes on, voice carrying over mine. "She grew bored of the stars, which then covered the entire lunar's sky. But when she birthed the naxem, they began to swallow the stars whole. Realizing her mistake, Sasorana banished them to Sasor. She gave them legs and arms to anchor them to the ground. But in their true forms, they couldn't fight or protect themselves from the dangers of this planet. She gave them their manerak forms then, but it had been too long. Most of them started to forget about their origins. They started to forget about *her,* and she grew lonely again.

"So Sasorana gave them a reminder. She gave them the *promise* of naxem. She placed a version of herself in mortal form on Sasor's soil as Saso*rena,* her incarnate. A Sasorena would have the power to unleash naxem, and because she was mortal, would keep the naxem bound to her, bound to the soil. They called it a forever bond, a Xiveri bond. And it meant that he who felt Xiveri for his Sasorena would be so devoted to her that he wouldn't hunger for the stars."

Xiveri... My head jerks up at the word I recognize only from the deepest recesses of my thoughts. That high podium where my naxem lived. That hollow cavern from which he once watched. My naxem knew all along.

Dandena lifts one thin eyebrow and says, "The mortal Sasorena could unlock the naxem of manerak that she deemed worthy. The worthy then had the responsibility to love and worship her as Sasorana herself seeks to be worshipped. The mate of the Sasorena held a position of significance in the stories...but not as her owner, or her master," Dandena sneers, "and certainly not as the one hurting her — as Mian *herself* put it." Her words have all the effect of a fist reaching into my soul, and pulling my skeleton out through my teeth.

My mouth is too dry to swallow. "She said that?" I wheeze.

Dandena nods. "Yena, she did. Meanwhile, the lore states that the mate of the Sasorena is meant to be her *protector*. As a reward, his naxem was said to be strongest of any others created by her life force. He was never First or lord over her. This is just some construct of our own, because we've forgotten. And because we've never seen naxem, and because we've never had a Sasorena. At least the modern tales don't speak of one."

Her tongue ticks the backs of her teeth and I'm pulled from the tale that she's woven across the loom of the sky. "And these are all just stories and all of this might be shit and spittle…"

"They're not. Not from what I've seen," I say glumly, knowing that no matter what the stories might say, they don't matter here in this sviking nightmare I've created for myself.

"Not from what I've seen either."

"Not from what I've felt."

"And now?"

I don't really know what she's asking. But I know what beats in my chest. Nothing. "She doesn't want me…" I shake my head.

"So make her. I will not allow you to cost this tasmaran — this *world* — a Sasorena. The first we've ever known. And I will not allow you to cost us Mian. We like her too much to give her up. We liked her even before."

I rub my hands over my hair and face so roughly I hope it peels the skin clean off. I don't deserve her. I was scared, so I lied to her. And I betrayed her. And I hurt her. And I hurt me. I made her cry and I made her bleed.

The wind is the only one who speaks for a while. It whistles blithely between us. Caring nothing for pain. Mine or Mian's or anyone's.

"Fix it."

I shake my head. A spark of salient hope flares in my chest, but I douse it before it can catch. I cover my eyes with the heels of my hands. "I can't." It's too painful. I'm already beat. If I try and *fail*, I'm not sure what that will do to me.

Dandena's voice is low and slow and dripping with a defeat that's mine by right. "Do you know why I left the Nevay to join your tasmaran?"

It's a rhetorical question, I know that, but I still quip, "Stupidity?"

"Though I didn't realize it at the time." She laughs humorlessly. "Tszk, I joined your tasmaran because I couldn't rank in the Nevay — there were too many warriors and too much competition for that — and your tasmaran was young and inexperienced. With you, I had a chance."

I snort. "Yena, we've already covered that my tasmaran is pathetic and I'm not qualified for the position I have…"

"The second reason," she says, speaking over me for the second time, "and the more important reason, is that *I saw you fight Tatana*. I'd seen you fight before many times, but I'd never seen you fight like that. For something you *really* wanted. You transformed. Your manerak was something to behold. I thought if I could learn from a First like you, I could become a great fighter. And I thought that if you would fight like that for your tasmaran, we could never lose.

"*That* is how you form a strong tasmaran. Forming a union is always a good strategy, but when I saw you transform so *easily* into that naxem, you became an *ancient being.* You became something of stories and shadows. How could a tasmaran be any stronger than being led by a First like that?

"When you were naxem, you flung Tatana across the sessemara dolsk like he was weightless. And if any of what the Nevay says is true, then you single-handedly took on Nevay's entire roving tasmaran with nothing more than your two hands. Or well…your head. Your naxem. Whatever."

She clicks her tongue against the backs of her teeth and stares out at the horizon. "Can you even imagine what it would be like if you weren't fighting for us, or even for you, but fighting for Mian? Sasorena of your tasmaran? How could you *ever* lose?"

Her gaze meets mine and peels the skin right off of me. My blood starts to pump harder, faster… This is dangerous thinking. This is dangerous. Hope. It sparks again. Again, I try to stuff it down, but this time, it reaches kindling.

I lick my lips. Look at my hands. Clench fingers that tremble. I shake my head. "I don't even have a tasmaran anymore. How many solars has it been?"

"Six."

Shock. "I've been gone for six solars?"

"Yena. And yena, your tasmaran still stands, even without you. Shockingly, you still have a couple warriors left — ranked and unranked — who can fill your shoes in such a short absence. After all, your shoes are sand-filled, just like your skull."

I grunt and my expression twists, becoming less painful, becoming easier to carry. "Like you?"

"Like me," she says with a sigh, "though I can't believe I'm still here after all I've heard. Unlike me, Preena had more sense. He left. And so did Creyu. He and Tekevanki took eight warriors with them."

I wince. Preena. That is a loss that will hurt. "Where did they go?"

"Preena is now Sessena's Fourth. Creyu and the charming Tekevanki belong to the Requemi now."

That surprises me. "That's barely a better tribe than mine."

"But it is still better, and Tekevanki is now joined to their First who, unlike ours, is not a *stark raving lunatic,*" Dandena makes air quotes around the insult. "Mian's words."

I grunt, grinning a little. "At least one female got what they wanted out of the sessemara."

"Yena," Dandena sighs, "She calls herself Sasorena already, even though the ranked warriors of the United Manerak Tribes have discussed, and it has been decreed that there will be no more Sasorenas."

"No more Sasorenas?" I shake my head, not understanding. "Then what?"

"No Sasorenas because there is but *one* Sasorena on this planet now. Mian is it. The rest are mates and will be referred to as such."

I smile more fully. "Does she know what she is?"

Dandena shrugs. "Hard to say. Chimara says we aren't allowed to call her that. She doesn't like the title. But it's what we call her when she can't hear us. It's what she is, and I'm telling you now that she *will* remain a part of this tasmaran. I don't care if I have to send every male in our tasmaran to her door, but we will have her joined to this tribe some way or other because if she leaves, you can guarantee that your tasmaran will follow. I will follow."

I nod, understanding that clearly, the tightness in my chest releasing and then clenching all over again. I exhale, "If she leaves, I will follow. I don't care where."

Dandena blinks, looking surprised. I don't know why she would be. I thought it was more than clear by now that I'm in love with the girl. My hearts beat for her *painfully.* She cocks her head. "You really do worship her, don't you?"

I feel the heat in my neck rush down to my abdomen at the thought of just how desperately I'd been worshipping her in the closed confines of my dolsk. I had too few lunars with her. We had too many lunars apart. And it was all because of me. I'm a fool times six.

Quickly, I change the subject. "Do we have warriors on her now? Protecting her? If others think she's Sasorena, they might try to take her."

"I do. Our people left for our tasmaran village three solars ago. They should have long since arrived. Chimara is on her at all times, Xena and Reffa are on her as well, but from a distance. She's not happy, Neheyuu. Not happy at all. And she doesn't like the new attention she's been getting. I've tried to instruct everyone to behave as normally as possible around her, but I still don't trust any of you stupid sviking males. We don't need anyone doing anything stupid to try to unlock their naxem."

I choke. Rage sweeps me and I feel a small, distant tingling in the tips of my fingers and the soles of my feet. I rise.

Dandena scoffs up at me from her position on the ground. "Don't tell me that hadn't occurred to you? How could it not? No one knows exactly how you unlocked your naxem. I guarantee you that someone will try something. That someone will try anything."

"We need to get back." I need to see her. "There aren't enough warriors to watch her." I need to watch her.

Dandena grins and ruffles her hair. "You realize that you only asked me about our losses."

"What?" I grunt impatient.

"You lost eight, but you gained twelve warriors."

"Our tasmaran grew by four?"

"Tszk, we have *twelve* more *warrior* members than we had before. There are *twenty-three* new members total including non-warriors who joined and the families. You gained three kits, a welder from the Sessena — and don't worry, it is *not* the same one who offered Mian his wreath — as well as an apprentice healer from the Eros tribe and a pair of human sisters who cook for the Nevay.

"I should tell you that these sisters specifically told me that they intended to join our tasmaran even before your…outburst. They said it was because they met some of our human females and that they spoke so highly of life within the Neheyuu tasmaran that they wanted to see it for themselves. They mentioned Mian by name, Neheyuu. Without trying — without knowing that she was anything more than a slave — she convinced them. She didn't even like you when she did it," Dandena snorts.

My hearts thump. I start to sweat. My fingers and toes tingle like they're swelling. I need to get back. I need to see her. I reach down and take Dandena's arm as she says, "This isn't a foreign sentiment, Neheyuu. You will need to come to terms with the fact that when we return, the tasmaran no longer belongs to you. Though she does not want it and though she has no idea, the tasmaran is hers."

"Yena. No less than she deserves." I grin and haul Dandena up easily. Her body slams into mine before she quickly pushes me off of her with a disgusted curse. I laugh at the indignation.

"Good. Glad you're finally starting to see reason." My lips quirk. As she brushes some grass off of her own armor, she says, "And since you don't seem to be completely insane as others suspected — including me — I suppose I should tell you that you had *fifty* expressions of interest after the sessemara to join Mian's tasmaran."

Fifty. That's more than any tasmaran has ever seen in one go. The only numbers to even come close to that are the Sessena's, and they are large, seasoned, and successful — in a word, our opposite.

"Don't get too excited," Dandena mutters, "as I mentioned before, that number dropped after the fourth solar you failed to return. When I left, the numbers were at twenty three, but perhaps now there are fewer than that. We will need to see."

"Thank you, Dandena." I meet her gaze and offer her a smile, even if it's a shaky, dangerous thing. One full of hope. Brimming with it. Even if it's what kills me.

I pray to Sasorana it doesn't kill me.

"Whatever," she says and I laugh up to the sky.

My thoughts feel heavy and so do I as I turn towards the horizon. But there are vestiges of life there. Traces of something light, possible to buoy me. If only I can grab hold of them. And if I do, I can't let them go. Not this time.

"Are you ready to run?" I grunt, voice choppy with emotion.

Dandena looks at me and then out at the long, uninterrupted plains rolling out before us. "You want to *run* the solar-journey back to the tasmaran with no manerak? No oeban?"

"Yena."

"You won't be able to keep it up."

"I'll keep up. I've done it before. And besides, my true form deserves the practice." And the punishment. "But first, I lost something we have to pick up."

"What's that?"

"A rock." Mian's rock.

The one that is her slave. The one I'll beg her to take.

Exactly like my heart.

"You've got to be sviking with me, First."

"Just Neheyuu from now on, and tszk, I'm not."

Dandena groans long and loud, but follows me nonetheless. We canvas the tall grasses in search of a stone — Dandena, as manerak, me, just as myself. And completely naked.

21

Neheyuu

"You want *what*?" Rea says. My senior tracker, I don't know whether to be worried or proud that he's staring at me like I've grown two heads. Or just one really, really big one.

I shove my thick, filthy locks over my shoulder and level a look at each of the warriors gathered. I had Dandena bring together the ranked warriors, as well as a select set of others — Erkan, Reffa, Chimara and a few more, manerak and non-manerak. I didn't bathe. I didn't go see her. I know from Chimara that she's safe and working in the weapons dolsk and that, with Chimara here, she has Xi and Xena looking after her.

I lean forward and the hide wrap Dandena tried to get me to cover myself up with slips. I let it and lean forward onto the heavy wooden table, ignoring the way Rea's confused gaze drops to my exposed groin. I grin as he frowns at it.

"I want the entire tasmaran village restructured. The center will be open. We'll continue to use it for bonfires and small, informal gatherings. But closest to the center, I want the largest dolsk. Here, we'll house the females we take on raids and all female helpers.

Opposite the circle from it, I want my dolsk." Though I don't mention that it will only be mine if Mian lets me share it.

"The next ring," I say, drawing an imaginary circle with my finger, "Non-warrior families with kits, and single females living alone or in all-female households. Then I want senior warriors," I say drawing another concentric ring outside of that. "Non-warrior families and males. Then another ring of warriors forms the outer perimeter. A second configuration will abut the housing.

"I want dolsks with our hides near the center, followed by medical supplies, clothing and the rest. I want one dolsk with our most expensive stores in the very center. In this way, any intruders that make it to the center of the dolsk, will be more likely to stay there. I want our weapons as well as our food and drink stores hidden in the middle among the clothing and less valued items, making them harder to find.

"A third configuration will host our weapons dolsk and our training grounds. A fourth, our medical and birthing center. I want this built out. These dolsks should be prepared for an influx in activity. We'll be raiding more. We'll be expanding. Our ad hoc approach to medical care and treatment is not adequate — *my* approach. I've been doing a lot of things wrong," I admit, even though it hurts. I sweep my gaze around those gathered and the chaotically arranged dolsks beyond them. As my tasmaran, this was alright. But as *Mian's* tasmaran, I can do better. "I'm trying to make it right."

"It's a good set up," Erkan says, leaning over the imagined map I've laid out before him. "I'd like to grab a block parchment and map this out properly."

I should have thought of that. "Of course."

"But the middle is still empty. Each of the five rings connect to form a large circle. An enormous one," Rehet says, "But the middle leaves a lot of vacant space. What will we use it for?"

"Part of it is to be left wild. High grasses can remain. Fire pits can be built when needed. However, for the other half, I want grasses removed and braces to be erected. This is where we will form the largest dolsk the United Manerak Tribes have ever seen."

Expressions around the table shift from interest to curiosity to delight. "Fun," Mor says.

"It's not for rutting in," Dandena snaps.

Laughter flutters around the table, mine included. As it dies, Ock asks, "What *will* we use it for?"

"We can use it for anything. Everything. In the rainy seasons, it can be a space for communal eating, it can be a work space for those needing shade in the solars like these where we see all three suns. Tri can move her integration lessons here so that we don't host them on the outskirts of our camp, where they're so exposed." I tip my head to her mate, Gergoro, as I say that. He returns the gesture. "It will also be where we host events."

"Events?" Reffa asks, hefty skepticism on her tongue.

"He means sessemara." Dandena tries to repress a grin and fails. "When?"

"As soon as possible. Right after we make these changes."

"These are a lot of changes," she counters, "And we still need to integrate the new members of the tribe."

"I'll be responsible for that. I'd like to set up a better rotation system for helpers, so they don't remain helpers for so long and find their place. Until I've got a better solution, I plan to meet with each new member individually over the course of the coming solars and determine where they'd like to be, and where they'd best fit."

"Would be a perfect job for a Sasorena…if only we had one." I look up into Chimara's dark eyes. She stands across the heavy wooden table from me, arms crossed over her muscular chest. She's pissed at me. Svik. I get it.

I speak over the light murmuring and jeering that follows. "I thought I better do it myself given that they all think I'm a stark raving lunatic."

"You are!" Someone shouts, eliciting more laughter.

I grin. "I'd like to prove to them that I'm not."

"Maybe consider a bath first," Dandena says.

I shake out my hair in her direction, sending mud chunks flying. One of the female warriors squawks. Mor backs up so quickly, he trips over something and falls onto his ass with muttered curses.

"I've been told recently that I'm a sviking fool."

"You're just now realizing that?" Chimara says.

Laughter, but I raise a hand to quiet it when Erkan returns with a block paper and a stick of charcoal. He begins mapping out all that I've detailed on this solar. "Yena, I'm just realizing it. I'm a fool, remember? I'm not so quick on my feet."

When the laughter subsides, I continue, "I want to hold a sessemara as quickly as we are able. It would be the first time a tasmaran of this size has hosted, so it's important that we do it right. Even more important after I officially established my lunacy at the last one."

"That you did." Dandena rolls her eyes.

"And the need for a sessemara is just part of what all this is about. I know you all are curious about what happened. That rumors are flying that I am naxem and that Mian may be Sasor's first Sasorana incarnate, our Sasorena." A hush falls over the group and I appreciate the collective reverence of it. The moment I confess a truth that I denied myself for so many solars. "I want to reassure you that all of this is true."

A gasp. Something falls. Someone curses. Chimara is the first to speak. "She doesn't know, and she doesn't need to know," she says quickly.

"Tszk. She doesn't. Chimara is right. Mian doesn't share our belief structure. She doesn't know the ancient lore. She doesn't need the hassle of knowing she's awakened something in someone she hates."

"She doesn't hate you," Chimara grumbles. "She doesn't hate anyone. I wish she would, but Mian is incapable of it."

My lips quirk. My pulse thumps. Hope. Dangerous. Too dangerous. "I hope you're right. And I don't…" I bow my head, brace both hands on the edge of the table. As I bear down on it, I hope it holds. "I don't begrudge… any male…for trying…" These words are sviking difficult. "I don't begrudge any male who wishes to try to…win her…now…or during the sessemara."

I look up and feel the blood pumping through my face, about to erupt through all of my pores. I try not to look at any of the males around the table, and instead stare up at the sky, straight into the sun. Blinking quickly, I shake my head. "I can't take any choices away from her. If you think Mian might be happiest with you, then you have a right to offer her that."

"At what cost?" Ock says, half-joking.

I offer him a half-grin. The tingling sensation in my fingertips migrates to my palms. "On the second day of the sessemara, I'll try not to kill you. That's all I can offer." I'm joking, but I don't win any laughter from my warriors. My elite.

Well, maybe I'm not joking.

"You're going to give her your wreath?" Chimara asks, one eyebrow raised. She crosses her arms over her chest and I exhale, grit my teeth.

"Yena. I will. Once I make a new one. And once I… try to win her. But don't tell her. Please. I don't need her any more…"

"Pissed off?" Dandena juts in.

Mor says, "Try *murderous*."

"Confused as svik, if it were me," Reffa adds.

And then Chimara lops the head right off of my shoulders. The cut easy and clean. "She's just disappointed. Sad."

I meet her gaze. Dark and brown. So human. No manerak to be seen. "I know. And she's too important to this tribe — to Sasor — to be wasted on a fool like me. I need you to protect her. You're her last line of defense. Even against me."

Chimara blinks, relaxing a little in her stance. "I can do that. For Mian, it's easy." Her lips quirk a little.

I nod. "Good. Because of the responsibility, I'd also like to offer you a ranked position." Tension threads the group all at once. "We're growing, and I hope to keep growing. Up until now, because of our size, I've kept the rankings to three. But now, I'd like to offer you the position of Fourth."

"But we don't even have a second," Reffa interrupts.

"We have a Second." My gaze flicks to Dandena. Her lips part. "Dandena. And to take her place as Third, Erkan."

Erkan's hand stills over the block parchment. His mouth falls open in the same way Dandena's did. "Third?"

"Yena."

"I...it is an honor."

"It is deserved. When we raided, you saw your female, knew she was yours, marked her, claimed her, wooed her, fought for her, impregnated her and then joined with her. It took you forty solars. Less."

And what was I doing in the meantime? Ruining myself? Running from my Xiveri mate even though my forgotten manerak and naxem were already devoted to her? They're gone now, but I don't need them. I do — but I'll tear apart the other males who vie for her with my teeth if I have to. I'm going to win her back. If it's the last thing I do. And given my lack of manerak, it might very well be the last thing I do...

"I need someone with judgement like that," I finish.

"That you do," Dandena snorts. More laughter, and I couldn't give a svik that it's at my expense.

"Are there objections to these changes? Does anyone issue challenge?" This is where I tense. Chimara is not the most senior warrior here, and she is not the best. She could be taken down in a challenge, but I want her to have the respect and the sway over the others that she needs to best keep Mian safe.

A few tensing shoulders. A few twitching hands. But in the end, the changes are pushed through. I bang my fist on the table. "Good. Then let's get this done."

The orders have been given. The plans have been drawn. They know what they're meant to do. But do I? Tszk. I don't. Because there is no map that can be drawn to direct me to Mian's forgiveness.

But seeing her, maybe explaining myself, taking Dandena's advice and just talking to her — that could be a start.

It's the latter half of the solar now, heading into the lunar. I haven't slept in two, but I'm more awake than ever. A little twitchy, but *alive*. The tingling in my palms is getting more restless, migrating to my wrists, my forearms, my elbows. I know what it is. Or rather, who. I know he's still there, itching to touch her. But I don't care. He can stay dormant for all the sviks I give. I need to touch her too. I need to touch her *more*. I need to drop to my knees and apologize until my voice is hoarse.

I approach the weapons dolsk naked and filthy and determined. A few faces practicing are new ones, and I give them a small tip of the head, but say nothing. Dandena will spread the word that I'll be speaking with them tomorrow. But for now, there's someone else I need to talk to and that need is bordering on something manic and desperate.

"Mian," I say in a rush, but when I step into the weapons dolsk, the body kneeling in its shadowy recesses isn't Mian. He isn't even female.

I frown and quickly head for the dolsk where Tri teaches her manerak lessons, but Mian isn't there either. I cross paths with Chimara on my way out. That's when she tells me something I never in a thousand turns would have expected. She tells me that Mian is already in *my* dolsk. That she's waiting for me there.

I swallow hard. Can't. I feel my pulse in my throat. I can't even breathe past it. My hands clench and unclench. That tingling horror shoots up and down my arms, up and down my spine. I reach the leathers of my dolsk and have to take a few bracing breaths. As I stand there, I realize I have no idea what I'll say.

"Mian, I am a fool." There. That should say it all. Tszk, I can do better.

"Mian, I am a fool and I love you." There. I've got it now.

I hold my breath and slip into my dolsk, speaking in a rush, "Mian, I..." But all the words I'd just perfected flit from my head like a bird.

The dolsk is dark — tszk, not dark, but lit *intimately*. Candles I've never used and didn't know I owned light up the curved edges of my dolsk with several clusters of lit pillars standing on pedestals near the bed. The bed. I'm aware that there are hot tubs of bath water already ready and awaiting me somewhere to my left, but my gaze is held fixed to the bed and the linens and the body lying atop them wearing a delicate robe in the most alluring blue.

For a moment, I hallucinate that this is Tekevanki, coming to exact some sort of strange revenge, but that's not right because my being, more than my body, knows that this is Mian. It's her scent. The way her energy charges the air, radiating with its own current. And me, the lucky bastard, sucked into its whirling, mashing vortex.

"Mian," the word bellows out of me and Mian sits up fully from her reclined position.

She swings her legs over the edge of the bed and comes towards me and I can't help but fixate on the delicate length of her neck. She has her hair pulled up off of it in a beautiful array of gravity-defying ties and knots on top of her head. I love it when she wears her hair like this. I should tell her it looks beautiful. I should sviking say something…

"First." She speaks before I can get any words out and her voice is even. Sweet, even.

My mouth is dry. I can't…I just can't. Reason leaves me.

She tilts her head and then she cuts me down in one stroke. She smiles and speaks to me in her manerak, which sounds more fluent than I remember it — except for the accent, which I hope she always keeps. "I thought you might want a bath. I heard you ran here." She gestures with her long, elegant fingers to the copper tub surrounded by more of these damn candles.

I want to ask her where the svik she got all these candles and what for, but that doesn't seem like the most urgent thing I need to tell her at the moment. Trouble is, I can't figure out what *is.* So I just nod. Fool.

She walks to the far side of the tub and kneels. Her fingertips stroke the water lovingly and, as if hypnotized, I follow her and just…get in. The water is still hot and I feel like asking when she ordered it and from whom and how she knew where I was and when I'd be coming, but I don't say any of these things either.

Instead, I just sit down on my ass and stare at her perfect face, wondering if maybe someone stabbed me on my way into my own dolsk — or svik, maybe I never even made it back from the sessemara — and now I'm dead and in my own personal paradise. I heard from

Gregoro once that that's what the humans believe. We manerak believe that Sasorana takes us back to the stars. That we become them. But maybe the humans were right.

"Mian, I...I need to talk to you about..." I blurt, but Mian lifts one finger and presses it to my lips. The taste of her...oh svik the taste of her...my hips buck in the water and my already-hard cock releases a small jet of pre-cum. She tastes like everything. Like everything... Like Mian.

"You, relax," she says gently. And then Mian produces a large, soft sponge from somewhere — the same place she got all these sviking candles — and dips it into the water. She takes it to my chest in long, firm strokes.

I make a garbled sound as the organs in my body all rearrange themselves. Her willing touch is what does it. Is what rips my true form apart and then stabs my manerak to death. My naxem, somewhere in the recesses of his cave, is salivating. He's also afraid. What is she doing? What is happening?

I feel myself shaking apart as my manerak starts to sizzle and spit, clawing his way forward through my true form, trying to wield it for himself. He wants to grab her. I try to wrangle it into submission, but the trouble is, I want her too badly. I want us to be too badly.

"Svik!" I curse and grab her and pull her entire body with me into the water and hold her there, wanting nothing more than to spear her mouth with my tongues.

But...

There's something wrong. I'm shaking and she's shaking. My eyes are closed. Her breasts are pressed against my bare body, her legs, tangled with my legs.

This feels too sviking much like a dream. *A perfect dream. Take her. She is offering.* But my naxem doesn't agree. My naxem isn't here at all. The voice in my head might not even be my manerak. The voice in my head might be my downfall.

Fingers press on my chest. She whimpers a little, then leans forward and at the same time that her lips find my jawline, her fingertips work their way down… and then down lower. She traces the outline of my cock and I immediately lurch out of the water.

What are you doing? We have her where we want her. Quiet!

I set her down as carefully as I can on the edge of the bed, which isn't really that careful at all. Everything in my body is jumping and pulsing. I sweep a hand through my filthy, wet — now muddy — hair. I let that hand fall. "What the svik are you doing?"

I can't look at her, so I don't read her expression as she answers, "I am helping you with bath…with your bath," she corrects.

I shake my head. "You're doing something else and I don't sviking like it. Why are you…I just…I want to talk to you with your normal clothes on. I want to talk to you with my armor on." Because at least armor will hold back my raging hard on. My cock is swinging back and forth as I pace, like a pendulum. "Turn all these sviking candles off. I want to talk outside. Where there are people."

She doesn't answer for a long moment. So long that I dare a peek. She's dripping wet now. Long coils of her wondrous, eternity hair are plastered to the side of her neck and chest, while the thin material of the robe she wears has completely puckered around her rock hard nipples. The ones begging to be sucked. *And we know how they taste already. Like syrup of the canyon tree. Ready to be drunk.* And then I remember...

"Why?" She says at the same time that I accuse, "Is that the gift that Tatana gave you?" Why the svik did I say that? Why the svik can't I control myself and act like a decent, nice male...for sviking once! I'm going to lose her. *You're going to lose her for all of us.*

But instead of getting angry, like I thought she would, she says, "I can take it off if you like."

"Mian," I growl, and now I'm the one getting angry, "stop."

"Stop what?"

"Whatever this weird...game is. I don't want to play and if you don't tell me what it is you're thinking and doing right now, then I'm gone."

And then it hits me. It *actually* hits me. A shoe or something. I turn around to see what it is, but before I can spot it another one flies at me and tags me in the chin. A leather sandal. At least it wasn't a candle. Her face is all scrunched up tight, in that way that I've come to adore, but right now it's accompanied by the water in her eyes that I hate.

"Of course! Because it is always what you want. Because you are First and I am slave!" She whips her face to the side, like there's something there that she doesn't want me to see. I need to see. I've been doing so little of it lately...

"Mian," I say softly, gently.

"Tszk. I say tszk. You must listen. Now, you do what I say." She shudders and, when I turn towards her, pushes the shoulders of her robes away and lets the entire sheathe fall down around her feet. She has nothing on beneath it. Nothing but the droplets of water on her body and mine separating us. That, and the distance. And my restraint. But there's little left of that now anyways. There was never much to begin with.

"Mian," I say again, but my voice is gravelly and starved.

"Just do it!"

"What?"

"Do what you want and then leave me. When you have it, you will leave. I will find male. I will leave dolsk. I no slave. No akimari."

I still don't understand and shake my head. "What?"

An enraged cry escapes through her clenched teeth before she goes to the bed and throws herself onto it, her legs spread wide. I'm left staring directly between her thighs, dark curls sprinkled across their juncture and below them, glistening brown lips with a bright pink center. The combination makes my brain lurch. What did she ask me for? What are we even talking about? *Sink into her heat. Find the wetness at her brown and pink center.* Oh yena, of course. I'd be happy to…

My steps stutter forward as my manerak sings. He is back. Maybe he never left. Maybe the bastard is just… me.

I freeze. Tszk. What am I doing? If I take her like this, does it make me a monster? *Yena*, comes a dark, distant murmur, *it does*. I close my eyes and take a centering breath. It works, but only a little, because when my eyes open again, I'm still twitchy and tense, manerak jerking forward at the same time that my true form tries to pull me back out of the leather doors. Want. Need. *Need*.

Worship.

I swallow and swallow again. I don't breathe. Every argument I had prepared for her dies on my tongue. *I am a fool. I love you.* Instead, I swallow a third time and nod, just once. "Yena."

She flinches. Her lips part. She releases a breathy gasp and all at once, the room fills with the fresh scent of her arousal, that irreverent musk. It smells like begua blossom and vanthia. Like salt. Like the leaves of that tree that grows only in that illusive canyon. And it smells like me.

I whisper words of encouragement to my cock, about how I'll cut the sviking thing off if it can't control itself, as I approach the bed. I watch her tense and tighten with each step I take. She's worried. Her body may want to be pleasured, but she doesn't want to be taken. Not now and here and like this. But she's determined to break me. She's determined to push me away forever. And if I give into her now, she'll have succeeded, and I refuse to let her.

"You want me to take you now so that I'll leave you alone?"

She hesitates. "Yena." Her fingers clench the sheets beneath her as I make my way to the foot of the bed. Her face is tilted to the side and her eyes stay closed.

Sadness hits me, muting my arousal for the moment. *It should not be like this,* says the dark voice, resurfacing. I know. I know… "You want me to complete your tattoos."

She hesitates again. "Yena." Nods. "You finish taking what you want, then you let me go. To find male. While you find your own female."

I might have laughed if I weren't so sviking angry. Pained. So much has happened in the past few solars, since the sessemara, and she hasn't understood any of it. And I still don't understand any of it. But one thing has changed: Mian will be mine and I will be hers. Whatever it takes.

"We will organize a sessemara in forty solars. Possibly less if we can manage it. It will be the first time this tasmaran hosts a sessemara." I inhale. Exhale. "And I will not stand in your way." I try to focus on her face so it keeps me from looking at her body, but my gaze is disobedient. It strays.

She's gained some weight since she's been with us, and I can't help but feel pride as well as a surge of unbridled lust at the sight of her full, weighted breasts and the cushion to her hips that had not been there before. Her stomach is still very flat and I can still see all of her ribs, but she is eating. She is getting there. She eats from my hand and I want to be the one to feed her until she is a fat old female. My lips twitch at the thought.

Mian still hasn't moved. Her fingers remain curled in the sheets. Her chest continues to rise and fall shallowly. She still doesn't hear me — not what I'm saying, but what I mean to tell her with my gaze. I'll need to get her attention in some way…

I slide one knee onto the bed, ignoring my cock and its angry pressure. It jerks towards her, as if it can control the movement of my body. I guess it can, because I shift between her legs and drop one hand to each of her ankles. I spread her legs wider, drinking in the sight. Gulping it in. She does not want me now, I know that, but she still glistens like precious gems. Her body knows what I have to offer, and if that's all she wants from me now, then that's what she'll get.

"Mian, did you hear me?"

She shudders, but remains there, still. Tense. I lift her right leg and lave the back of her calf with both my tongues, then I repeat the act with her left. Her sweetness doesn't rattle me. I refuse to let it.

"Mian," I say as I nibble and suck, "I will not stand in your way at the sessemara." I move down to her feet, tasting them, before moving back up to her shins, then her knees. I lower her legs and sweep my tongues down the insides of her thighs. Watch her shiver.

With a show of force, I drag myself up the length of the bed, passing the pale brown lips and their molten pink core, one that begs for my twin tongues' entry. "Mian," I exhale against her thatch of damp curls, before dragging my mouth across the skin pulled taut across her hip bone. I bite her there with my blunt teeth. "I will never hurt you again. I should never have hurt you in the first place."

I lick her stomach as I let my shoulders come to cover her hips. I can feel her core's heat against my sternum and I feel my right heart branded by it. "I should never have insulted you." I swirl her belly button with my tongues as I hold fast to her waist. Like it might keep me from flying away. *Too late. We are gone.* "I should never have belittled you."

"Mhmm," she moans. She starts to squirm. Her face twists, like she's fighting. Fighting me. Fighting this. But she's no warrior. She's said so herself many times. And I am First for a reason.

I hold her down. Scrape teeth and tongue and lips across her ribs, counting each one twice before planting a kiss directly between her breasts. A light, tortured moan flutters out of her as I murmur against her flesh, "I should never have made you that offer. I was weak. It was pathetic. I shouldn't have asked you to wait."

I bite the skin of her right breast, hard enough to draw a small cry from her and leave a red mark on her skin, but not hard enough to break it. I glance up at her face. A light sheen of sweat has formed on her forehead and the sides of her neck. Oh how she shimmers. Pure effervescence. "I shouldn't have called you my akimari. I shouldn't have treated you like a slave."

"I *am a* slave. You see my tattoos." I do. I draw myself up eye-level with a small black symbol on her shoulder. A square around another concentric square, though the one in the middle is shaded in and a line passes through both of them.

I press my lips to it. "Then how is it that your skin tastes like freedom?" Like salvation.

That seems to snap something in her, because all at once she pushes against my shoulders. I don't have to move — she's not strong enough for that — but I do, because I will never take choices away from her again. And that is what I tell her.

Water fills her eyes and I hate the sight of it, but whatever words I intended to say to clear them, are second to her barely restrained anger. "Maybe because you mark me without my permission!"

I grimace and sit back on my heels, digging my fingers into my thighs to keep them contained. "I shouldn't have done that either." *Yena, you should have. We should have. And we are proud to have done it.* We? As the thought floats through my mind, I feel a distant, faraway shifting in the recesses of my soul. Someone is watching me. Watching us. Watching her. Waiting for her verdict. His very existence hinges on this moment. And I don't sviking care. Take my manerak, my naxem…take my tasmaran. I just. want. her.

I lick my lips. "But I'm glad I did."

"Why? Why are you doing all of this? What do you want from me?" She bangs on the bed with her fist causing her breasts to jiggle. I nearly lose it, the restraint I have a frayed piece of twine now — it would be too easy to cut my way through it. I shake my head, trying to dislodge such a temptation.

"A chance," I breathe.

"What?" She shakes her head.

"I said I would not stand in your way at the next sessemara. But you should also know that at the next sessemara, every male there will try to vie for you. They believe you to be…"

"I know what they believe. I am not this thing. This Sasorena. Sasorana is the stars. I am no star."

I don't bother to tell her just how wrong she is, but nod, "Doesn't matter. That is what they think, so they will come for you. All of them. I just…I just want a chance to compete…"

She hits me. She hits me and then she flinches, like she does every time. I grin at her and that seems to throw her somewhere else, out of this plane of existence, because her pupils dilate and a surge of arousal pours from her skin like the scent of a blossoming flower. I look down and wish I hadn't. Slick wetness coats the insides of her thighs and makes the curls hiding her core from me glisten. I lick my lips and try to close my eyes. Can't. Stare at her stomach, her tits, her face instead. All at the same time.

"Don't…" She starts to pull back from me, retreating across the bed. She tries to cover herself with an errant linen, but I grab hold of it.

"Mian."

"You only want me now because I am this star."

Rage. I try to quell it. Doesn't sviking work. My hand moves faster than a true form should as I rip the blanket away and snatch up her ankle. "Look into my eyes and tell me that's what you think. That you think I only want you because you're Sasorena. Mian…look at me!"

She jerks and finally lifts her gaze to mine. Her brown eyes are swimming with indecision, but indecision is something I can work with. I slam my claws into it, finding purchase, and climb.

"I did not mark you because I thought you were Sasorena. I did not go back for you when Tatana took you from me because I thought you were Sasorena. I didn't spare those humans on that raid because I thought you were Sasorena. I didn't even know you. I did it, because I liked you. From the moment you hit me in the face, I liked you. And now I sviking worship you. I love you, Mian." Boom. The sound comes from within, but I wonder if she can't still hear it because she's looking at my chest like it just spoke to her out loud.

"How? How can you? You are not kind to me."

I don't waver. I just stare at her straight, wanting her to *know* more than hear, every word I have to say. "I love you more than this tasmaran. I love you more than my manerak and my naxem. I love you more than me. I treated you badly because I thought I couldn't have you and I was sviking scared someone else would take you away. I was a coward and I was a fool."

I spy a small twitch at the corner of her mouth, but no smile. "You are still a fool."

I grin at her. Her pupils dilate a little further. I move up the bed, kneel between her knees, and I don't dare miss the way they flinch, parting just a little for me. Focus. *Focus.* I wheeze, "And I will always be a fool. But I'd like to be something else."

Her lower lip trembles. She sucks in a ragged breath, like she's scared to voice her next question. "What?"

"I'd like to be your mate, too." *Her Xiveri...*

The voice drowns out the sound of my own heart beating with a distant rattling of its own. The longer I stare at her, the louder it gets, the thicker the perfume of my marking scent blooms. Completely involuntary, I have no control over it at all and curse. "I'm sorry. My marking scent. I can't control it right now..."

She doesn't say anything. I take silence for a win. Right now I'll take anything.

I lick my lips and reach forward, touch her cheek. "I won't stand in your way at the sessemara if you choose someone else," I say. I hope it's true, for her sake, but I honestly can't picture what it would look like. Giving her my wreath and then watching her hand it back to me only to give her small string of stones and silk to another male. *We would kill him.* Tszk. *Yena.* Tszk! I will do whatever I have to to make her happy.

I struggle to speak through the surge of emotion in my mouth. The sensation of her smooth skin under my rough fingertips doesn't help. Neither does the glance she gives my angry, straining cock. It's so hard that even the slightest attention from her brings pre-cum to its tip.

I grit my teeth and say, "I just want the chance to compete for your wreath."

"Even if it is only dirty reed paper."

I clench my jaw so hard, spears of pain shoot up into my brain, lancing my thoughts. "*Especially* if it's only dirty reed paper."

She smiles again, albeit weakly. Her glossy eyes glitter. But then she rips the heart out of my chest and the soul off of my bones. "Perhaps I should not."

Pain. Agony. It swirls through me. My manerak and my naxem rebel and retreat and roar. My hand falls from her cheek, but she grabs my wrist and my muscles swell. Hope. It's a dangerous thing. Most dangerous of all.

I look into her face and watch as she drags my hand across her lips. The heat of her tongue brands me as it tastes my longest finger. She pulls it into her mouth and her cheeks suction with pressure as she bobs her head back and forth, pushing and pulling my finger in and out. What is she doing to me?

She bites her bottom lip, tongue peeking out to wet it. The rumbling, rattling growl in my chest is near deafening now. She has to raise her voice above a whisper to be heard, even though we're sitting close enough for me to devour her, and to be devoured.

"But I will." Hope. Sasorana, please don't crush me. "I will not stop you at the sessemara," she finally says.

"Mian," the word rips out of me too tangled to understand as I launch myself at the female, unable to hold myself back. I tackle her down to the bed and press every inch of my nakedness to every inch of hers. I suckle on her lips before trailing my kiss across her jaw and down the side of her neck, where I bite down. A mark for other males to see to know she's mine, even if she won't let my manerak mark her yet completely… I half expect her to be angered by it, but what I don't expect is the force of her moan.

She mewls high and loud, and then she says my name, her warm breath fanning my ear seconds before she bites down onto the serrated edge. She bites hard. Pain flickers through all the places she touches.

"Mian," I hiss.

"Neheyuu." Her hands find my shoulders and neck and then yank on my filthy hair. Damp, muddy water sprinkles over her skin, but she doesn't seem to care. And I definitely don't sviking care.

I take her throat in one hand and press my other to her forehead, angling her head back so I can taste her more fully. Meanwhile, my hips pump in small, restrained movements, trying to svik whatever of hers is nearest — for the moment, her stomach. She's so soft. But I want more. *Need* more. And with her hands sweeping my skin and her thighs hugging my waist and her hips rolling up like she wants…like she wants *me* inside of her…I'm barely holding it together.

"Mian," I say, pushing up from the bed, though my body feels like it's weighted. "Mian, I can't," I choke.

But her thighs just clench tighter around my hips and her hands just pull me closer and her breathing shallows out and her eyes flutter open. I still and let her sweep her fingers up over my chin and across the hollows of my cheeks. She follows the bridge of my nose up to my forehead and strokes the lines of my eyebrows before tickling just the tips of my eyelashes. My heart stutters.

"Mian…" It seems to be the last word left in my vocabulary.

"I do not want to stop."

I hiss out a ragged groan. "Mian, I cannot…my control with you…with them…"

"Them?"

"My naxem. My manerak. They want you and I'm…too sviking weak to fight them. I want you, too. So badly I can't stand it."

She pauses a moment, traces her fingertips over my chest, down to my nipples. She circles them and I bear down onto the bed, twisting my hands into it, gouging holes in it as claws come to tip my fingers. Back! I order them, all of you, down. *Tszk…*

"I want them too," she says, voice husky and low. "I want all of you."

I can't breathe. Hope rears back ten paces. This can't be right. This can't be what I'm hearing. "But I… you will only mate with the male you join with."

"I want to go to sessemara knowing that you are not holding me back. I want to know if we only desire to…" She struggles to find a word, and eventually says, "make joining with one another. If what you say is true and that all males will vie for me, then my tattoos do not matter. But I need to know sex with you."

My mouth is dry. I'm hearing her words but I don't know how to feel about them. On the one hand, having her body even once would be a gift fed to me straight from Sasorana's own hand. On the other hand, having her body only once and then giving her up to another male will kill me. There is not a doubt in my mind about it. If I were a smart male, I'd retract myself from this…

Good thing that I've never been a smart male. And I'm sure as svik not going to change now… *Thank Sasorana.*

I nod, because I can't speak. I could promise her that she's wrong, but I'm not a decent enough male to pull back. Nothing I want to do to her will be decent.

It will be holy.

And I might be damned.

I cup her core, placing one hand directly over her lower lips and then sliding one finger between them to meet her sopping wet heat. My eyes roll back into my skull. She moans.

I grit my teeth. "Mian, you're wet for me."

Her hands grab my hair and pull just hard enough for the pain to feel ravenously good. "Yena."

"Do you get wet like this for other males?" I start to pump my finger in and out of her, my hips following the motion of each thrust in jealous anger.

She licks her lips and shakes her head.

"Say it. Tell me you don't get wet like this for other males."

"I do...not..." But she chokes when I smooth the heel of my hand over her clit, rubbing slow circles against it with each thrust.

"What was that?"

"Tszk. Tszk, I do not. I feel...close...please..."

She pulls harder on my hair but I slow, even though it hurts me probably just as much as it hurts her. Maybe more. "Did you get wet for Tatana?"

"Tszk," she says, panting, her body undulating as it fights for its own release, but she's pinned underneath me, fully subdued. I have her at my compete and total mercy.

"Then why would you give him your wreath?"

Her face twists in confusion. "I did not give him my wreath."

"You were going to."

"Tszk. I was not ready. And even if I had been, I do not give my wreath to Tatana."

Shock. Anger. Confusion. My hand inside of her, stills. "Then who?"

She reaches down between us and grabs my arm. "Please, Neheyuu…"

"Who?"

"Blacksmith."

I release her clit and slap it lightly with my fingers, careful to keep my nails blunted as she cuts a new wound. Letting my head drop forward for a moment, I laugh bitterly. "With any other female, all I'd have to worry about are the other warriors battling for her. I'd know that if I won, you and your wreath would be mine. With you, I have to worry about *everyone*." I pick up speed between her thighs, letting her inner muscles clench and pulse around my fingers. She's there. Close. All she needs is a little…

"Neheyuu," she gasps and as her back arches and her fingernails dig into my skin, I know I want to hear that sound every solar for the rest of my life.

With one last mangled whine, she slinks against the bed. It takes some time for her eyes to open, but when she looks up and sees me and smiles just a little, pleasure in its purest form opens its fist and crushes me inside of it.

"Mian," I say.

"Will you…now?" She moves her fingers down my body, carving paths through the dew there. "We need windows," she whispers, distractedly.

She's right. It's hot in here. Almost no circulation. And I grin ravenously. *She said we.* "Whatever you want."

Her arms come together between our bodies, wedging her breasts up high, making them look fuller than they are. *They will be full when she carries our kit inside.* I swallow hard, trying to shake off the vision, but can't. At least until Mian's fingernails scrape the outside of my cock. She grips it and then lowers it to her sopping wet entrance.

"Whatever I want," she whispers.

I know what she's asking, ordering, culling from my body right now — from my spirit — but I'm scared to give it to her. Too much hinges on this moment. *Coward. Fool.* "There's no coming back from this."

"Yena." She shifts her hips, taking just the engorged tip of my cock into her body.

A growl stutters in my throat and my eyes roll back. I drop forward onto my forearms, bracing them on either side of her head. Her long hair streaks out to either side and I wrap it all up in one fist so I can fully control her. I meet her gaze. "It's going to be fast the first time, but the second time, I'll make it up to you." And the third and the fourth and the fifth…

A little fear flashes in her face, but she nods anyways. "I am ready."

"Good. Because I'm not." And just as the last word leaves my lips, I thrust forward, without giving either of us another chance to think…or change our minds about it.

I push all the way inside of her blazing wet core, seating myself inside of her body up to the hilt. She tenses and tries to push me back, but I use my weight and the hold I have on her hair to keep her still.

Meanwhile, my vision is shot, my heartbeat has exploded through me so I'm just one angry pulse. My manerak…oh my sviking manerak… He and my naxem exalt. Screaming psycho lunatics. They parade around under my skin — tszk, no longer under it, but a part of it. They thread themselves through my bones, weave themselves across my spirit like a thread-forming spindle. Here. They are here and now and they are me and I am hers. We are all hers. Every part of us.

"Mian," I choke. My cock is twitching inside of the tightest, hottest pressure I have ever felt. Lightning fires down the veins in my cock as it twitches, desperate to move, to release and to begin filling her. Not yet. I'm too big for her and she's too small for me, but I'm going to make this good for her. I *have* to make this good for her.

I pull every ounce of concentration I have together and whisper against her cheek, "I'm going to start moving now."

My hazy vision clears enough for me to see that her lips are pressed together and she has dew at the corners of her eyes. Two solitary droplets roll outwards down her cheeks. I stroke one salty bead away with my tongue before dropping my mouth to hers. Her lips are tense and hard, but I lick at their seam, demanding entry. I kiss and peck my way across her jaw and chin gently, finally dropping one small kiss to the tip of her nose.

That wins a reaction. She blinks her eyes open and more tears fall. "It hurts."

"It won't hurt for much longer. I promise. If you relax, it will help. Breathe with me." I inhale and watch her take a shaky breath, then exhale. The next one, she lengthens to match the pace of my own. "Good." I tell her, sweeping the damp strands of hair from her forehead and neck. I trail that hand down the length of her body, reaching her peaked, pert nipple. I gently rub it, and then softly start to rock my hips back and forth.

I use my legs to spread hers a little wider and she clenches at first, but when I grind my hips against her clit, she yelps and slaps her palm down onto my shoulder blade. She pulls me a little closer. "Oh...oh my...svik..." she curses. I don't think I've heard her curse before in our language and laugh.

Her eyelids pop open and she looks like she wants to say something, but when I thrust hard enough to jolt her body up the bed, she can't. She looks dazed. She looks dazzling. I clamp down on every emotion in my body and think of stars and other faraway things. It's all I can do not to release inside of her immediately.

She feels so sviking good. Her walls are milk and honey and the burn feels just as sweet. One moment, she's relaxed fully beneath me, and in the next, she starts to toss her head from side to side. Her body undulates and bucks. Her fingers twine with mine. I hold her beneath me, firm and steady, because I want to look at her as I drive my hips down and grind slow circles over her clit, her own slippery satisfaction acting as the lubricant between us.

"Oh Neheyuu...Neheyuu..." She's an incoherent jumble of words in her language and mine. Her fingers fly over my skin, seeking purchase, finally landing on my neck. She opens her eyes and meets my gaze and the sheer, raw pleasure of watching her lips part and her eyelids flutter as her head cocks back and the delicate muscles stand out in her neck and arms, is what does me in. Well, that and the sudden vice of her pussy around my dick.

Pressure unlike anything I've ever known grips my straining shaft and then massages it, all the way down to its base. I try to hold back — I want this to last, I want it to be the best rut she's ever had, but it won't be because the sound of her screaming my name to the roof of my dolsk whips into me like a lash.

"Oh svik…Sasorana…Sasorena…Mian…reesa!" I bellow her name as my hips piston forwards, trying to get as much of me inside of her as possible — svik, if I could insert my balls in her dripping wet core, I would do that too. But now, they clench up against my body so hard that they sviking hurt. Pain blisters through my back and up the base of my cock as my seed is first notched, like an arrow to a bow, then loosed.

I've never released so hard or so fully. Everything I have, everything I sviking *am* fires out of me and into her. I give it all up. I crush against her, smothering her against the sheets, struggling to keep any weight off of her at all as my vision blacks out and fades in and I float momentarily among the stars. But I'm not finished.

"Mian!" It comes harder, the second wave, pushing at my backside, causing my ass and thighs to harden. My spine arches up, and then comes crashing down. My mouth latches onto the side of her throat, where her neck meets her shoulder. I bite down — my naxem bites down. Mian shudders beneath me and lets out a wild, keening scream.

I hallucinate that I've hurt her for a moment and try to pull back, but her pussy constricts around my cock, like a coiled snake suffocating its prey, her hips buck and she shouts my name. My cock, evidently recognizing the order it's been given, jerks, causing me to thrust forward all over again. I circle her shoulders with my arms and I bite down harder on her neck as a second wave of seed spirals out of me and I fill her belly with it.

"Oh svik," I manage, but her throat is still in my mouth, my tongue lathing all of the places that my teeth have indented her skin. *Not just indented…* My fangs have *broken* her skin and I feel a surge of pain in my gums and teeth, and then a cold liquid surging through them.

Poison. Panic releases within me, but I still cannot move. In the same way I have a hold of her, *he* has a hold of me too. *Thief of life to others,* says the dark, ancient one, *to her, the antidote to death. Now, she lives as long as we do. This is the mark of the naxem…*

She squeals high and sharp and her hips jolt against mine. I feel another bolt of pain spear my abdomen when she climaxes a third time. My body, ever dutiful, responds immediately. I come again, deep inside of her, my senses shot, my mind a jumble of branches, crunching underfoot. The last of the venom releases from my teeth and when my naxem directs me to unlatch from her shoulder and lick away the blood, I do.

My spear-pointed naxem's teeth retract and look down at the four small pinpricks of blood that resurface on her skin. The scent that fills the room comes from these marks in doses that are even more concentrated. My naxem offers no explanation, but I can feel his contentment as my hips spasm one last time, offering up the last dregs of seed it can find within my desiccated sack, and giving them to her.

I groan and she gasps and both of our chests heave and our eyes meet, but we're both blind. I need to kiss her to see. I roll to the side, keeping myself deeply rooted in her body. My cock is still hard, eager to give her more even though there is nothing left. I press my mouth to hers and she surprises me by kissing me back, hungrily. Her lips nip and tear at mine and I deepen the kiss, twirling my two tongues around her shorter, fleshy one. I say her name every time I breathe. She whispers mine back to me.

I don't release her hair and she doesn't release my shoulder and our chests mash together like we are each trying to absorb the other. And then eventually my mind spins, I'm lost to the darkness of her hair where I see stars. I sleep, but first, I throw one thigh across her hips and coil both arms around her like the naxem that I am.

Exhausted, like I've just fought a battle that I both won and lost, I almost miss it when she says, "If you make me an offer to join, I will choose you, Neheyuu." She sighs a satisfied sigh and her breath fans over my face and my toes curl and the skin across my scalp prickles like I've just been hit with a rush of cold air. "I already have."

I squeeze her tight to my chest, but I don't dare hope. I can't. Here, I was terrified of Tatana, when she would have chosen the blacksmith. A lot can change. I can ruin things, still. I can't let myself believe that she's mine. Not until my wreath hangs so heavy around her neck, she can't get away from me. Not until hers hangs around mine, shackling me equally.

"We shall see." I nuzzle her ear through her hair. My tongues duel with her earlobe. She shivers in my grasp and my cock perks up without hesitation. I pull her underneath me and begin a slow, lazy thrust back and forth.

It must shock her, because she grabs my shoulders and gasps, "Neheyuu."

I just keep thrusting, a little harder, a little faster. Because if she's not going to be my female, then I intend to ensure that no matter what happens, she will never forget me.

And because I'm too selfish a male not to spend every solar until the joining ceremony lost in her eyes, her scent, her touch, and her impossible, tight heat.

22
Mian

It's the slapping sound. As his body beats mine into the mattress, the slapping presents a steady metronome that makes me absolutely wild — sviking wild, as Neheyuu would say. Wet and perverse, it fills my whole belly with fire powder and incinerates everything there. I'm a wet, hot explosion.

The chimes in front of our door ring again, but rather than retreat from me, Neheyuu grabs my shoulder to anchor me in place and starts pounding into me even harder. "Reesa, I want you to come for me."

I pull harder on the swatch of his hair clutched in my fist while my lower body bucks, struggling to match his rhythm.

"Say my name, reesa." He growls.

"You're…doing…this…on…purpose…" I gasp for air.

Neheyuu growls and slaps my right breast *hard* — a habit he's gotten fond of, and I have no intention of ever stopping him. "Yena, now scream my name. If you don't, we'll have to start this process all over again and then Chimara and the others will have to hear you beg for mercy because I will punish you through the lunar…"

I scratch my nails down the front of his chest and he groans, head flinging back, hair damp from sweat and slashing across his forehead and neck. His tongues leave his mouth to wet his lips and I feel my lower lips spasm in response. He sucks in a sharp breath through his open mouth, then he slaps my clit. *Hard.*

I yelp and everything below my waist squeezes together. My inner walls massage his massive, punishing length. He's lodged inside of me as deep as he can go, and yet when I shout, "Neheyuu!" to the ceiling — and through the half-open windows — he somehow manages to insert himself deeper. Roughly.

The climax and the pain twine themselves together to create something I never thought I'd like, but that I *adore.* "Say it again," he grinds out, and when my eyelids manage to open for one half-breath, I see his face, a picture of perfection. Strands of gold stick to baked bronze. Sweat glistens along his hairline, making him look like he's wearing a crown. His eyes are fully black and elongated towards his temples. His fangs are fully protracted and they're dripping that special serum he likes to inject me with. Infect me with. And it feels *so sviking good* when he does.

"Please," I beg, riding on the crest of that wave, without falling down. "Please, Neheyuu."

And then in a gravelly snarl that's Neheyuu, yes, but also the snake that lives inside, he moans, "Beg louder. They need to hear."

"I know...why...you..."

"Louder, reesa!" He slams harder, and while one hand grabs a fistful of my hip — which is much fleshier now thanks to his force-feeding me multiple times a solar — his other hand grabs a chunk of my hair. He forces my head back, exposing my neck. "*Tell me what you want from us.*" Us. The first time he used the pronoun, I didn't understand who he was talking about. And I'm still not certain I do, but I know that when I hear the pronoun spoken in that voice I can usually expect a bite to come.

"Bite me," I choke on my own words as my climax bubbles and continues to burst.

"*Tszk,*" he seethes. "*Not bite…*"

"Mark me, Neheyuu," I answer, knowing what he wants and knowing that only he can give me what I want in return.

He dives in like a viper and sinks his teeth into the muscle between my shoulder and my neck. It should hurt, and it does a little, but like a nasty prick from a blood fly followed immediately by a perilous pleasure, I'm left too weak to know I'm wounded. Too weak to stop it. I scream into the dolsk, utter nonsense, really, but who cares when you've reached such a magical place?

The release lasts…and lasts…and lasts…and when all my scattered parts are finally swept up into a bucket and hastily reassembled, I wake to the sight of Neheyuu cursing as he crashes down around me. His fangs stick out of his mouth, their blood-colored tips reaching past his lower lip. A few droplets of venom spill out onto my chest, and erupt in a beautiful, wonderful heat every place they drip.

I moan and Neheyuu responds in kind by massaging the droplets deeper into my skin. Oh *stars* it feels good. I moan like I'm orgasming all over again. Neheyuu is chuckling somewhere above me, laughing glibly at my suffering. I feel hungry all of a sudden.

Starved. I need him again. And again and again and a dozen times more.

He's massaging my breasts now. They fit so much better into his hands than they used to... "Neheyuu, please..."

And then for the first time in thirty-four solars, he tells me, "Tszk."

My eyes pop open as he removes his hands from my body. I'm still hot, like melted butter, and I moan desperately when the full length of him slides out of me. "Tszk," I nearly yelp. "You're still hard! And I still need..."

Neheyuu hisses, but manages to pull his arms out of my hands and stand up off of the bed and onto the floor. He's wobbly, but after a few steps, manages to stand almost straight. He looks back at me where I kneel, crawling after him, likely looking like a mad woman with his shimmery, silver venom on my chest and his thick, gold seed smeared across my stomach and legs. All at once, he lurches towards me, then rears back. He turns to the side and looks down at the carpet purposefully.

I would rejoice in the power I hold over him if I weren't so desperate. "Neheyuu..."

"Tszk. Tszk, reesa...Mian." He clenches his teeth. "Tszk." He looks down at his cock as it does a little dance for me and more seed surfaces on its swollen slit. My tired pussy wants more. I wonder if this is what sex is like for everyone, and already know it isn't. This is something else. And I can't believe I waited so long.

I whimper, but he cuts me off. "Helpers are coming in now with water for your bath. And you should put on your robe because the chimes aren't ringing for me. They're for you. They have a present for you."

Present? The idea distracts me, but not long enough to forget about the heat spreading across my pussy like wildfire. "Neheyuu…I don't want to stay like this. I need you."

Neheyuu buckles, entirely missing his next step and dropping to one knee. He starts to elongate and bend before he snaps back together. "You can't say things like that to me. Not now."

"I know why you're doing this," I accuse as I rise up onto my knees, begging him to just look at me and see me, because once he does, I know he'll come a little closer. When he doesn't, I frown. "You are punishing me because this solar is sessemara."

"Tszk, not punishing you. I'm *reminding* you."

"Reminding me of what?"

"Of what it feels like when my cock is deep inside you. I want you to feel me on your skin when other males approach you this lunar and offer you their wreaths. And I want to remind you that the male you need to satisfy you is me."

His voice gets all quiet at the end and I wonder if… maybe… "Neheyuu, are you nervous?"

He rips a large robe off of the rack and straightens it over his shoulders. "Tszk." His voice comes out butchered, a little broken.

My heart expands. My heart crumbles. "Neheyuu, I tell you…ugh — *told* you," I stammer, frustrated that it's been so many solars and I'm still making mistakes like this. "I told you that I would take your wreath."

I slide off of the bed and try to close the distance between us, but he thrusts a second, much shorter, robe at me before I can touch him. "That was before the sessemara. You will get a lot of offers, Mian. Firsts from at least two other tribes will make you offers."

"I don't care…"

"First from bigger tribes, with more resources."

"You know I don't care about this…"

"Many *nice* males will make you offers. Males who would recognize your worth with eyes wide open and have the courage to take you and claim you for their own immediately. Males *better* than me, Mian."

I finish tying the knot at my belt and clear my throat, willing him to look at me. He does, tentatively, and in his face I see true fear in him for the very first time. I open my mouth, but he says, "Tszk, reesa. Don't give me hope. Hope is for males much braver than I am. I just want *you* and I want to be sure that I have you before I dare…" His voice catches.

He smiles down at the carpet and then abruptly turns to me, takes the sides of my face in each of his oversized hands, and plants a delicious kiss, one wreathed in devotion, to my parted mouth.

"Just step outside with me. I want to be there when you receive your gift."

I bend again, wavering. "But you know your venom affects me…"

He growls out a laugh and tosses one arm snugly over my shoulder as he guides me to the leather entry. The chimes are chiming again by the time we step through it.

Mor and Rehet are the first ones I see waiting on the other side. "Finally! I thought I was going to have to send Mor in there to drag Mian out."

Neheyuu rattles and stretches, his snake shape coming out to tower over us, even if it is a little disconcerting that he still has his arms and legs. I slap him on the arm, and I *don't* jump when the massive head swivels to look at me. I don't flinch at all.

"You know he's teasing."

Neheyuu returns to his true form and when his jaw snaps shut, he levels a glare in Mor's direction. The male shouts, "Don't bite *my* head off! Rehet said it."

"Like Mian said, I'm just joking around," Rehet offers quickly.

"Just give her your gifts and be done with it." Neheyuu makes a sound like an oeban out of one corner of his mouth.

"Yena. I'm ready." *Tszk. Forget presents. I want presents of a different kind…* I scratch my chest and my nipples harden to points, but I deliberately step away from Neheyuu when he tries to snatch at me. He catches only air. I do it on purpose, because I know how much he — *they* — like to stalk me, catch me and claim their prey, but when he starts to lunge for me, Dandena jumps across the small circle that's cleared out before us.

"Comets, First," she says, shoving him back by the shoulders, "We know you're amped, but the Hox are less than a quarter solar out and are expecting a composed, *sane* First to welcome them."

Rehet muses, "Expecting? They're *expecting* the same raging lunatic naxem. What we are *hoping* to show them is the sane, composed Neheyuu we all know and love."

While everyone laughs, Tervond, a new warrior who joined after the Hox sessemara, brightly quips, "I think the lunatic works. It worked for us." He nudges his brother, Eros in the ribs and Xena, standing next to Eros, rolls her eyes. "That's only because you *both* are lunatics…"

Sniggering simmers and when Neheyuu and I finally get some space between us, Mor thrusts his way towards me, elbowing Rehet out of his path and winning himself more laughter.

That laughter only ebbs when Mor stretches his cupped hands towards me and begins to speak. "We like fighting for you. It's umm… I mean, you feel like…aw svik, why are you letting me talk?" He growls at Dandena.

"Tszk," I say gently, "You're doing great. What is it you mean?"

He huffs and a shocking shade of pink blots his brown cheeks. He ruffles his head of half-shaved hair and blurts, "I mean, you make fighting feel fun. We look forward to battle, not because of prizes — I mean, we like the prizes and the chance to find more females and treasures and other svik like that — but also because it's fun to find stones for you. And when you help us with our weapons, or when you find us after training and talk to us, we all want to be the one you talk to. Not because we like you…I mean, we like you, but not like First likes you…well, maybe a little."

Neheyuu grunts somewhere in the distance, but I wave him off, immeasurably touched by this sentiment. Mor continues, "But we like *you* and we wanted you to know that we support whatever decision you make this sessemara, or even if you don't make any decision at all. But just in case, we wanted to leave you with something to remember us. So we got you more stones."

He opens his cupped hands and in their center lies a lovely stone in the palest shade of blue. It's like a crystal. One half is rough and the other, very smooth. I grin and feel tears prick the back of my eyes that I fight away. If these warriors can fight to bring me rocks, the least I can do is not fall to pieces at their display.

"I love it!" I jump up and throw my arms around Mor's shoulders, squeezing him tight. That causes commotion, but I ignore it and take the rock from his palm when offered. "It will be perfect for my wreath."

Mor is gaping at me when I pull back and when I smile up into his face he reddens and jerks. "Erm…yena. We were hoping you would use them. But only the most beautiful ones of course. Mine can be the center stone." He winks at me, regaining some of that Mor-ish confidence and I laugh as the other dozen — two dozen? more? — warriors crowd a little closer.

They each present me their stones and as I take them, it feels like I'm stacking them up inside of my chest, building a rookery to hold my heart and never let it go. They come to me in all dazzling shades that, funny enough, remind me of each of them in some funny little way.

Rehet's, a lovely amethyst, is the same shade as his eyes. Chimara's is a blocky stump of a thing, fighting for its place. Reffa doesn't give me a rock, but what looks like a tooth from a creature I never hope to meet. Dandena also gives me a stone sharpened to a point. Xi's is the one that surprises me the most. His rock dazzles — literally — it shimmers gold, flinging rays of sunshine in every direction.

Mor, seeing it, curses audibly. "Guess you lost your center spot," someone mutters. More laughter.

I just look up into Xi's gaze and grip his stone in my hand and lay it over my chest before depositing it in the soft pouch with the others. "It's beautiful," I tell him. And that may be the first time I see the male smile — just one corner of his mouth ticks up. Though they aren't identical, in that instant, he looks just like Xena.

Before I know it, my bag of stones is too heavy to carry and I have to set it on the ground at my feet. Time is also dwindling down and many of the warriors have gone off to finish tasks or make their wreaths. I should too.

Since the last sessemara, I've amassed quite the cache of fabric scraps. I'm certain if I'd asked Neheyuu for some fuller pieces, he'd have given me access to the entire linens dolsk, but I didn't want to. I like my scraps. Every single piece. Even if they're only dirty reed paper.

Soon Neheyuu approaches with his head bowed. He's the last one left. His clenched fist extends forward, then retreats. He shakes his head then holds his hand out towards me again. "I…"

I shuffle forward and drop my tone so the others can't hear me. "You don't have to give me anything, Neheyuu. You have already given me my reminder. A very…" I want to say *rude*, frustrating, and enraging reminder, but what I say instead is, "not nice reminder." My swollen pussy clenches painfully below the robe I wear.

Neheyuu half-grunts, half-laughs. He ruffles his already tousled hair and exhales through his mouth. "Here. I picked it for you at the last raid. It isn't flashy or fancy or anything. It doesn't shine. But it reminded me of you. How you make me feel. You'll see if you hold it up to the light."

He leans forward and presses his lips to the top of my head for a full breath, maybe three. When he pulls back roughly, he stomps off without looking back. A few helpers stand nearby waiting with water for me to bathe in. I wave them in gratefully, but before I reenter the dolsk, I uncurl my fingers from around Neheyuu's stone.

Simple and brown, it's as smooth as a river rock. And though its exterior betrays little, when I hold it up to the light, its translucent husk reveals a molten core. It beams in shades of brown and orange and yellow, fully iridescent. My heart catches in my chest, way up high as I realize that Neheyuu found this for me on the *last* raid. He knew then. And though it doesn't forgive, it at least helps explains the insanity he showed then. *He really does love me.*

"Need help with that?" Chimara gestures to my bag of stones, taking it from me without waiting for my answer. She heads to my dolsk, Reffa and Xena on her heels.

My brow furrows. "Don't you all need to be getting ready?"

"Yena." Chimara holds up a sack in her other hand. "We have all of our supplies."

"Thought we'd have a cute little crafting circle, we did." Xena's sarcasm does not go unnoticed.

"Neheyuu…" I huff, "He put you up to this, didn't he?"

As Reffa brushes by me to enter the dolsk, she responds with a shrug and a wink.

We spend the next quarter-solar bathing, talking and preparing our wreaths — mostly laughing though. Our energy levels rise as darkness descends. Talking and movement outside of Neheyuu's dolsk grows more boisterous and Xena chides me that she'll miss all the fun if we wait any longer.

She ducks her head out of the dolsk and curses. "The Sessena are here and they are the last to arrive. We should get going before they run out of all of their special malt."

"You should stay away from that stuff," Reffa balks, "It's poison. Terrible for a warrior's body."

Xena levels her with a look. "Bite me."

Reffa waggles her eyebrows in my direction. "If the Sasorena has anything to say about it, maybe I will." She pulls her manerak form forward and makes snapping motions towards Xena with her mouth. That draws Xena back into the dolsk so that she and Reffa can start mock fighting — or maybe real fighting, I'm not sure which — until we hear the gong moments later.

Chimara meets my gaze and laughs when I squeal, "It's time!" I hold up my wreath, happy with the result and start to stand.

"Now, now, now, don't get ahead of yourself. We shouldn't be the first to arrive," Reffa coaches, making no moves to stand herself. Instead, she idly pets her own wreath, a massive thing that hangs high off her chest, studded with metal and tines and wires and bones and all manner of deadly, terrifying things.

"I suppose you're right. The Sasorena *does* need to make an entrance," Reffa agrees.

I start to speak, but Chimara places her forearm across my chest as if to hold me back from attacking the other female. As if I ever *would*. "*Mian* needs to make Neheyuu sweat. We should wait until we're sure that they're all gathered and that the sessemara is underway."

Both of the other females cackle. "Now *that* is a truth if I've ever heard one." Xena claps.

Reffa adds, "Though seeing her like this, I don't think it matters. The second he arrives, he'll do enough sweating. I don't doubt he's sweating as is…"

"Also true. And if he…" But then Xena shuts up, perking to attention like a dog catching scent moments before the chase. She twists to look towards the back of the dolsk. Reffa and Chimara turn to follow her gaze and, late to the party, as I suppose I *should* be, I only register what is happening too late.

The thin tip of a blade slips in through the hide wall of the dolsk. It cuts in a downward stroke, quickly and in near total silence. Six males emerge through the opening, only one of whom I recognize. Tatana sweeps the scene, his gaze settling on me.

I stutter, too shocked to feel fear as I should. Too shocked to run or do anything but drop the wreath dangling from my fingers. "You should not be here…"

I start to stand, but Chimara's grip finds my arm and she jerks me back to the carpets. "Get behind me," she snaps, rising slowly from her position on the floor. The sessemara may be weaponless, but these three females here with me now are armed. *But so are the males…*

I expect some sort of declaration or explanation of what is happening, but the scene evolves around me too quickly for that. Wordlessly, Tatana tips his head forward and all five of his comrades attack.

"Mian, run!" Chimara shouts as she engages one of the males — but these males are manerak, and within instances, all have transformed but Chimara and myself. How can I leave her here?

"Mian, you can't help us," Chimara grunts over her shoulder, as claws catch on the polished leather armor covering her breasts. "Go get help!" She sweeps her staff up and knocks one warrior's head back when she catches the underside of his jaw. Blood spews from his mouth across the floor, soaking spare bits of wreath fabric.

I nod, fueled by purpose, and race to the entrance, but I'm either not fast enough or my moves were anticipated because strong arms come around my waist the moment I reach the leather.

"Neheyuu!" I scream at the top of my lungs even though I know that he can't hear me. Not with the laughter. Not with the drums. Distantly, it occurs to me that Tatana timed this perfectly.

I can feel the male that has me squeeze my ribs even tighter, to the point that I can't get any air. "Xena!" I hear the word in Chimara's voice and feel pain. *Please don't let anything happen to her. Please let them all be okay.* But when I turn my head to see what has happened, I'm pulled in the opposite direction, away from the door, towards the split cloth in the back of the dolsk beyond the bed.

"Mian!" Chimara cries, and then, "Tszk, not a chance!"

A huge weight slams into my jailor, threatening to take him to the ground — and me by consequence. Staggering a few steps away from the dolsk, out into the darkness, he tries to shake the weight loose and my head whips back and forth on my neck. My arms flail, finding nothing to grab hold of to steady myself.

"Tszk!" Tatana's words are punctuated by a series of tuts. "You will damage the Sasorena. Take both females."

I'm dizzy now. All I see are manerak faces and eyes the color of pitch. I start to shout, but the words are ripped away from me as the body beneath mine bolts into motion, away from the dolsk and through the now quiet camp, out among the high grasses, those devouring things.

23
Mian

"I am *not* who you all think I am! I am not the Sasorena! And even if I were, I do not wish to be taken! Tatana. Tatana!" I'm screaming. I've been screaming for some time, but I might as well be screaming in my human tongue for all the effect it's having.

Tatana gives me a passive look, one filled with indifference. "Tut. You are the Sasorena. I have felt it."

The dolsk we are in is slipshod, but the warriors surrounding it aren't. There are at least forty of them. Fifty. Maybe a hundred. I couldn't properly count. They stand in organized, concentric circles around this small dolsk while inside, Tatana begins removing his armor, one piece at a time.

"Don't you dare, Tatana," Chimara shouts as she is wrestled to the ground by two manerak warriors just a few paces away from me. She has blood on her mouth and on one of her legs. Her arms continue to thrash, but something is causing her pain. She keeps fighting.

I meet her gaze, refusing to look at Tatana and what he's doing because the anticipation makes it that much more frightening. "He has completed your wrist markings," Tatana says, low and eerily calm against the chaos, "Is this what turned him naxem?"

Oh svik. I shake my head feverishly, gripping my either wrist to cover the tattoos there. It had been Neheyuu himself who applied them under the direction of a human female called Greta. An intimate affair, the entire time he'd been terrified to hurt me, but after the marks were complete, he'd grinned the entire rest of the solar. He wanted to show everybody, and I'd been proud to let him.

"Tszk," I shout, concealing the completed bands, "Tszk, he turned naxem before. I tell you…told you! I told you at the last sessemara that I had not been tried. I was not lying…"

"But no male has ever marked a female without claiming her. He must have…"

"Tszk! He didn't. I swear it, Tatana! I swear on my wrists."

A pregnant pause, but then Tatana kneels on the bed, his weight settling near my knees as he begins working at something. Chimara's eyes grow wide and I focus on her as if looking at her will remove me from this place.

"Don't you dare! Tatana! *Tatana!*" Her voice is a shriek, spittle flying from her lips. She returns to fighting her attackers, this time with renewed vigor.

A tug on my throat. Wind touches my bare back. The shift I was wearing moments ago is cut or ripped. Big, warm hands come down on my back, stroking me with odd reverence. He pulls away the last bits of the fabric and my body lurches when he wrenches the robe out from underneath me. Oh svik. Oh svik oh svik oh svik. He's naked too. I can feel it when his heat settles on top of mine. Warm breath fans across my cheek.

He whispers, "I will not mark you in the traditional way of the manerak, because you do not want this."

"Tszk, I don't." I start to shiver, shaking with uncontrollable frustration. All I ever wanted was a kind male, a roof over my head, food in my belly and kits someday to love. My hands cover my belly at the thought. I am not this thing that they all seek. I am not this goddess woman. "Please, Tatana. Just let me go…"

He pauses and seems to struggle with what to say. "Neheyuu does not deserve to be naxem. And he cannot — he *will* not — be Sasor's *only* naxem."

I cringe. "You just want to take Neheyuu's tasmaran."

Again, he doesn't answer, at least not right away. "Neheyuu is a disgrace to the United Manerak Tribes and to Sasorana herself. In his current state, it is not possible for me to defeat him. So I will mark you and I will take my naxem for myself and then all of Sasor will be rid of the barbarian who completed your wrist markings…"

"You don't know it will work!" I screech as his chest hits my back and his legs trap mine against the mattress.

"It will." He buries his nose in my hair in a way that is too intimate. "And should you lie still, you will not be harmed. If what you say is true, I do not need to rut you to mark you. I will try it your way first and if it does not work, only then will I rut you."

"You bastard! Tatana, you don't know what you're doing!" Chimara shouts, "Sasorana is not blind! She will not let you do this to the Sasorena without punishment."

Tatana stills, and for just a moment, I wonder if he has heard her. If he realizes what he's about to do, and realizes the injustice of it.

"Tatana!" A male voice breaks through the stillness, my fleeing hope. "Neheyuu comes for her."

"Already?" He snaps.

"Yena. He comes as naxem, but only with a small force. Only a few warriors are with him. For now."

"Hold them back. Give me as long as you can."

"Yena." The fluttering of dolsk leathers, and then Tatana's weight falls against me once more. He brushes the hair off of my face and drags his tongues up the length of my cheek.

"You stink of Neheyuu. At least you should know that this will be as uncomfortable for you as it will be for me." And then he starts to move.

I clench my knees and squeeze everything together as Tatana begins to mark me with his scent. I'm shaking now, arms are clenched tight between my breasts as his hips piston into my back and his broad chest grates my shoulders.

"Mian, look at me," Chimara barks and I meet her gaze. "You're going to be okay. This is going to be okay. Don't retreat from it. You have to fight."

I'm no warrior, I want to tell her, but the expression she wears won't accept that. She stretches her hand towards me, fingers tipped in blood. She fought for me tonight. The least I can do is fight back for myself.

I push against Tatana, wriggling beneath him with force. He holds my shoulder, gripping it as he gags deep in his throat. The scent marker must be potent and the thought makes me grin, just a little. I don't rejoice in others' pain often, but I have to admit that it does bring me some satisfaction. It also makes me think of Neheyuu.

The color of his skin. The shine of his hair. The pressure of his smile and the destruction it causes me. It wrecks everything, because it *is* everything. I knew it when I first saw him towering over me in that shack. Passed around from master to master like a piece of garbage, I looked up into that grin and I recognized it as something different. As something good. And he is.

He is a foolish male, but he is a good male and he is *my* male and Tatana cannot have me. I have thoughts and feelings and a soul. I am not a thing to be owned. A thing to be marked. I am a person. *Not a person. Sasorena…*

I inhale a shaky breath and I open my eyes, feeling how they blaze. Chimara's own eyelids widen and I wonder what she sees. Because as I exhale just a little more, I feel it, for the first time in perfect clarity.

Powerful. Not because I am a warrior. But because I am me.

I jolt forward, reaching for Chimara's hand, and her reaction is instantaneous. Pausing in her war against the males holding her down, she stretches for me, twisting, flailing, until finally, our sweaty fingers catch.

Her palm is sweat-slicked fire and I'm sure mine is too, but I feel her calluses and know that she is kindred to me. And I know that, like Neheyuu, Chimara is something good.

"I'm so sorry, Mian," Chimara says, spittle on her tongue that she works hard to swallow. "I love you, and I failed you."

A balloon fills the center of my chest and I let it. I inhale and I can taste everything in the room all at once.

Chimara's salty fear, her sweat, the lavender oils in her hair. I can taste her thoughts and know her shame. She wishes she were manerak always, but never more than now. She wishes she were anybody else because she thinks that anybody else could have freed me by now. But she's wrong. Because only she can. Because I can taste the canvas of the sky. Because I can touch the stars and I can feel her among them.

I shake my head and squeeze her wrist gently. Her eyes pop open and she stills. "I love you too, Chimara." Her eyes well with water and a single errant tear dribbles down her face and drops off of her chin onto the carpet they're restraining her against.

"You're right. We will be okay." And then the balloon in my chest bursts and my voice is strong as I say, "*Rise*."

Her face twists in confusion and some of the tension bleeds out of her arm, but I hold her firm, nails forming bright white half-moons on her dark brown arms. "Rise for me."

"What are you saying?" Tatana grunts against my cheek. He maneuvers for my mouth, but I draw my lips inside, not wanting to taste him. He smells like sour fruit and burned sugar, two scents I always liked before now.

I do not loosen my hold on Chimara. Instead, I wield an energy I did not know I possessed, and *push.* "Rise, Chimara."

And then her eyes widen and *stretch* becoming diamonds. *Black diamonds.* Her fingers spasm, spreading and bending like gnarled tree roots before disappearing altogether. Her fingers melt into her palms which melt into her wrists. Her chest bucks and a wicked energy pulses out of her that tosses the males holding her off of their feet and Tatana off of the mattress.

He flies from me and I clutch the padding beneath me until the storm Chimara has released finally passes. I turn to Tatana and feel anger in my expression unlike any I have ever known. I meet his stare, feeling bold.

Feeling dangerous.

"I *curse* you, Tatana," I say evenly.

Tatana growls as he makes his way to his feet. He lunges at me, but comes up short. As if punched in the gut by an enemy only he can see and feel and touch, he doubles over, air whooshing out of him and sending him to the floor. He collapses onto the side of the mattress and when he whips his head to look at me, his stiff golden locks fly right off of his skull. He begins shifting.

"You will be naxem," I tell him in a low whisper, "but you will not want to be."

Tatana's mouth opens, as if to reply, but fangs jut out of his mouth and he wastes to the side. He screeches horribly and a challenging screech hisses its reply from somewhere in the distance. *Neheyuu*. The males who once held Chimara are stumbling over one another to reach the tent flaps. They are shouting for help, shouting nonsensical things about manerak and naxem and curses.

I turn around at the abrupt sibilance that echoes at my spine to see Chimara sitting up, face twice its normal size, and then three times, and then ten. She rises to stand — or *not* stand — because her armor has sloughed off and her legs have fused together and her arms are welded to her chest. She has no more neck, but she has a magnificent orange underbelly and skin so dark it appears black. *No, not skin*, scales.

I grin and I move up onto my knees as her diamond eyes meet mine. "Rise."

Her mandible falls open and fangs spear the space where she once had teeth. She screeches and shoots into the air, taking the entire dolsk with her. I cover my face as it whips around my head, pieces of wood scraping the outsides of my arms and my bare belly before finally ripping free on Chimara's elongated hood and flinging into the darkness.

Lowering my arms, I gasp at the world surrounding us. The organized warriors that Tatana brought with him has all but dissolved, like sugar in water. Battles dot the surrounding grasses now, making the lunar look like it's reached full-scale war.

Manerak and non-manerak form fighting circles everywhere the eye can see, but most are concentrated around *him*, the male that's mine. The one who came for me.

"Neheyuu," I breathe and the naxem in the distance rises up from the war raging around him. His eyelids blink from the sides, narrowing, and I tilt my head in his direction, wanting him to know that I'm alright and that he should rather focus on the twin swords careening for his stomach!

I capture my shout with my hand when I see the swords glance off of his body, leaving him without a scratch. The naxem that is Neheyuu seems to grin at me and I stifle a giggle until a rattling draws my attention back.

Cool wind whispers across my cheek and I turn to see the creature that Tatana has become rise up in front of me. He has scales and fangs, yes, but he is *not* naxem. He is a shriveled husk of a naxem. As if he were once a statue in tribute to a naxem and has since been eroded by time. His scales are wispy, flaky things and his fangs are yellow. His eyes are grey and reflect blue when the light strikes them just right and I can sense that he knows that I've done something to him, and I can feel his tangible rage.

He swivels his head and, seeing me, he lunges. I scream, falling back onto the mattress, my chest fully exposed, but in one swift motion, Tatana is batted away and the glittering scales of a magnificent, enormous naxem take his place.

"Chimara," I say with a grin. While Tatana cowers beneath her, she looks back at me, awaiting instruction. "Don't kill him. For now, help Neheyuu. Leave Tatana to me."

24

Neheyuu

My foot is tapping out a beat that I can't control. I've never done this nervous foot-tapping thing, but this is the most important lunar of my life. The most important fight of my life. My hearts beat a staccato that's out of time with my foot thing. My whole body is jangling, what with the extra detail I put into my wreath. I want it to weigh down her neck. I want her to walk sideways wearing it. My lips tick up at the corner. I also want her walking sideways for other reasons. *Maybe after what we did to her earlier this solar, she will…*

I grin around at the crowd. Warriors are watching me from a short distance. They gather around Dandena and Erkan to ask questions about the dolsk, but they don't talk to me. *They better sviking not. Do they know that we will slit all of them from nipple to navel if they approach her with their wreaths?* Tszk, that isn't what we told her. That isn't what we'll do. Now, where is she? *Where is she?*

"Dandena!" I shout, pulling her attention away from the two Hox speaking to her now. "Check on…" Mian. Bring her here! "…the females. Let me know how they're doing."

"And how are you doing? Should I let them know that you're sviking your pants in anticipation?"

I grin. "You can tell her — *them* — whatever you want so long as you bring them here."

Dandena excuses herself from the Hox warriors — both female and manerak and highly desired — and saunters towards the entrance of the vast dolsk. It's bigger than any sessemara has seen and, if I don't manage to bring in enough warriors, will have proven to be an entirely wasteful expense. But I'm not doing this for them. This is for Mian.

She should be here laughing politely with other males, driving me absolutely crazy. Using up every ounce of patience that I have, and then forcing me to derive some more from the fragrant vapors in the air. It's all begua blossom, vanthia seed, palm, canyon tree nut, syrup, and egra leaves. All the scents that remind me of her, and not a single one that doesn't.

"You remind me of me, during the sessemara when I won my mate." I start. Nevay himself stands at my right elbow. I wonder how long he's been there.

I shake my head and try to focus on his face. It's wrinkled across the forehead and around his mouth, but otherwise, very little indicators give away his age. He is a male who has ruled for a long time, and will continue to rule for a long time, if Sasorana has anything to say about it.

"When you won Effreta," I say, acknowledging him with a bow.

He nods and repositions himself, inconveniently blocking sight of the entrance. "Yena. I was tense. Perhaps as nervous as you are now." He chortles good-naturedly. "Well, perhaps not quite so nervous. I did not have so much at stake with Effreta. Though she will always be Sasorena to me, she is not, as we have seen, a true Sasorena. To know that there is only one and that you have slighted her, and that you could lose her to another male must be torture."

I narrow my gaze on the male, suddenly wondering about him and what he's doing here right now speaking to me like this. And it's in looking at his face that it occurs to me…

"Where is Tatana?"

"Do you worry you will lose her to him? I certainly had hoped so, for the sake of my tasmaran. However, he chose not to attend this sessemara."

Something dark prickles up my naked spine. I sit up straighter and scan the crowd. "Several of your warriors appear to be missing."

"Yena." He is the picture of a relaxed male, but something isn't right. "Did you not hear about the Hox raid against my roving tasmaran? They absconded with several females — *humans* — we had taken on a raid, as well as valuable merchandise. I do not wish for any tribes to use the sessemara as an opportunity to abscond with anything precious, so I left Tatana and some of my fiercest warriors behind."

"An attack during a sessemara is a violation of the treaty. So either you fear those warriors might leave you, or you disgrace them by denying their participation."

His jaw ticks. He turns his rugged, brown stare to me and lifts a condescending brow. "It never hurts a First to be overcautious."

"Neheyuu."

I glance up, searching for the one who spoke my name, but there is no one. *There is. Look harder.* Nevay continues to watch me with an odd expression and I continue to struggle to focus on it. "Yena," I grumble half-heartedly. "I have made changes."

"Yena. You have come far. And to be the first First in known history to have uncovered a Sasorena... Well, you may outshine even the oldest tasmaran in Sasor, those of us who are more deserving of it. I still am not sure how you managed to best Tatana to form a tasmaran of your own. You are the last male I would have expected to be able to pull this off. And yet, here you are."

My hackles rise. "Did you come all this way to insult me, or was there another purpose to your visit?" I'm aware that my voice is cracking and remember that I am not here for him or for any of them, but for Mian. What would she think if she saw me rebel against Nevay in anger? *Little. Less than what Nevay thinks of you, that is sure.* I exhale deeply and shake my head. "You are dismissed, Nevay. I have no need of your council in wooing my female."

And then Nevay bites back a brutal grimace — or is it a grin? He says, "I wish you the best of luck."

On the heels of his words, I hear it once again, the stars whispering my name...

"Neheyuu!" Dandena bursts into the dolsk, causing heads to turn and talk to quiet. She has blood on both of her arms and I feel my bones harden while my gut plummets. *Tszk, it cannot be. We would have felt such a loss...* Dandena's gaze falls to Nevay at my side and rage contorts her features, twisting them to manerak.

She stalks forward, growing in size. "You traitor! Nevay has violated the sacred treaty binding our tribes.

His warriors have taken the Sasorena and spilled the blood of our warriors. Nevay, tell us where he took her!"

Nevay takes a step back and holds both of his hands out, palms facing the stars in a sign of concession. "I have no idea what you're talking about. My warriors are all here and accounted for, short of those that remain within the Nevay dolsk to guard it."

"Liar!" Dandena has reached full manerak and her fangs drip with saliva, her claws reach forward and curl.

Any other instance, I'd be right there with her. Quick to anger, quick to murder, quick to svik everything up. But right now, I feel a pressure in my gut demanding something else. A sort of submission. *Let me take over. Give me your body. Let me do what I was placed on Sasor to do.*

I remove my wreath with care and as I rise to stand, the world shrinks away from me, becoming as insignificant as I find all of these beings. As *he* finds them. I blink, the dolsk shifting to grey-green as my naxem's eyes abscond with my own. My tendons snap, my muscles stretch. My bones bend and break. I do not try to fight. I simply *absorb* and let myself be absorbed.

I am yours. Bring her back to me, I tell him. It is a promise, he answers.

"Healers, recover the fallen," I order, my voice remaining cool, chillingly so, while still carrying across the near silent dolsk.

Dandena's manerak eyes widen and she bows, seemingly confused by the action, but I know better. All beasts of Sasor bend to naxem. Including manerak. Danon taught me that.

"They took Mian and Chimara. Reffa is injured and so is Xena." She turns to Xi and orders, "Take the healers and go help her and Reffa." Xi's face transforms, manerak drawing forward as he rushes towards the exit, Verena and Reepal in tow.

"Neheyuu warriors," I breathe, *"Come with me. Any Nevay warriors you see outside of the sessemara dolsk, detain. Any who resist, strike down on sight."*

"You can't do that!" Nevay shouts. He begins to shift into his manerak form, as if it would matter. As if we could not destroy him with a bite.

I turn on him and as I bend and contort and take shape, tail unfurling, arms and legs fusing, head expanding and fangs dripping with a serum that I intend to use to cause immeasurable pain, those in the sessemara dolsk back away. They sense our danger. Nevay attempts to stand tall, but fear glitters in his gaze.

"We will come back for you," I hiss, rising up before turning away, *"Warriors fall behind me. I know where she is. Where he has taken her."*

I rocket forward, knocking Nevay down as I move. I feel, rather than hear, the pounding of feet on the ground as I slither through the dolsk, following the star map in my mind, until I am out of the tasmaran entirely and among the high grasses and lights appear on the horizon.

That's when I feel her heartbeat, as loud as the pounding footsteps. It is surprisingly even. Quick, but unafraid. She must be alright. She must be protected in some way...or perhaps, she knows we're coming. That we will always come for her.

Torches are mounted in the ground at even intervals, and no less than sixty warriors stand between me and the dolsk that they guard, the one carrying her scent. I roar, tail flicking at the air, as I wonder what is happening within the dolsk, and why Mian is not afraid of it. Is he in there with her? And for just a moment, a needle of doubt pricks my body, the tail end. *What if she wants to be in there with him?* And then I remember — she would have chosen the blacksmith.

"Svik!" The voice is Dandena's. She rears up on my right side when I stop. "The treacherous bastards. Sasorana will cast their souls from the stars for this."

I growl my assent as Erkan shows up in her shadow. A sword in hand, he grimaces as his manerak gaze narrows on the horde facing us. "We are twelve now, only six manerak. Ock and Ofrat are rounding up the other warriors. We'll be more soon."

"We cannot wait." I need to see her. Nothing will get in my way. No matter how many bodies there are. No matter if they are human or manerak…or naxem.

The screech comes from within the dolsk and I hiss my own reply. The one that spells doom for whoever or whatever is with Mian inside. *"Split our force and move two halves to the outer flanks. Press in. I will take the center, carving a path through them."* Decimating them. *"Draw them out. Bring them to me. Charge and take the dolsk. Defend Mian."*

Dandena and Erkan relay the orders as more warriors arrive. We are outnumbered five warriors to one, and all of the Nevay present here are manerak. But it doesn't matter. My warriors can take any of these five to one, without shifting, without question. And I can take a hundred. A thousand. As many as I have to.

We move forward as one and the Nevay respond in a coordinated defense. Organized, their troops have anticipated me and they do a better job than I would have liked at holding my naxem back.

They fight with spears that seem to have been specifically built to dislodge my scales, as I learn the hard way when six warriors surround me and two spears find purchase in the gaps between them. One of my scales rips free before I manage to chomp down on the offending manerak's arm and swallow it.

My fangs cleave through armor as heat cleaves through me. Blood of the manerak before me bathes my armored body and I shower in it gleefully. I feel anxious, but I feel no fear, because the pressure in my two hearts that beats with Mian's life force has not faded. If anything, it grows stronger the longer the battle wears.

My hood rips through a crowd of warriors, flinging two of them into the sky and the rest of them off of their feet. As the manerak bodies fly, arms windmilling, I'm left stunned when a huge sheet of hide slams into them, covering them like the sail of some great ship not known to Sasor's shores.

"Neheyuu," I look up and see Mian immediately. She is grinning at me and for the first moment, all I see is the perfect smile strewn across her perfect face.

She's on a bed. She's on a bed and she's *naked* as her nameday and her arms are thrown back and there's a naxem with fangs exposed hurtling towards her. She screams and the sound tears through me and I almost hallucinate the afterlife at the thought that I have just witnessed my Xiveri mate die, and was not there to protect her.

But though I am not there, she is not unprotected.

Behind her stands a second naxem. *How is this possible? What in the stars is going on?* And this naxem carries a familiarity about it that I can't quite place my fangs on…

It switches around Mian's body, moving with an agility that suggests that this is its natural state, and with a quick sweep of its hood, it bats the much smaller naxem away. It hunts for the creature, which looks somehow *sickly,* even from where I rise, paces away, watching the scene unfold. Its scales don't shine like the larger naxem's do, its fangs are blunt and discolored and its cloudy eyes seem to lack focus. It stands no chance against its opponent and I watch with pleasure rolling through my coiled form as the larger beast rears up to strike, surely for the kill. But before it lands, I hear Mian's voice on the breeze, telling it to wait.

She also addresses the snake, calling it by name. *Chimara.*

I inhale and I can't stop inhaling. For a moment, I think I'll rise straight from the grasses and into the sky to rejoin my creator, but I wouldn't even if I could. I'd never abandon her. Even if she does not believe it, she is the star I revolve around. The only star in my entire universe.

"Mian," I whisper. Her face turns to me and I meet her gaze and she offers me a smile, as if she was not just captured, battered and forced to fight. As if, to her, the world is purely good all of the time.

The naxem that is Chimara turns at Mian's request and, seeing me, drops its hood and twists to expose its neck in a sign of submission. I offer it a bow and glance down as the prodding of swords against my scales finally claims my attention.

Batting away my challengers with one sweep, I move forward again, ripping and biting and tearing and mashing my way forward. And as I work, I am aware of the second naxem circling Mian, preventing anyone from coming within ten paces of her, and I am satisfied.

Killing almost becomes a fun thing.

But that fun is cut short. More warriors have arrived — not just of my dolsk, but Hox warriors and Pikora and Wren and Sessena and even some renegade Nevay — and have surrounded the remaining Nevay. The bastards who hurt her guardians, stripped her naked and took her from the place she should have felt safest are on their knees now, palms up and outstretched.

I should let the Nevay be slaughtered, but in some feat of insanity, I recognize that this needless death is not something Mian would want, so rising up as high as I can, until all other bodies are puny beneath me, I hiss, *"Hold. Nevay, drop your weapons if you want to live. The battle is over."*

Wide eyes peer around, seeking out Tatana, but the thing that he is, seems to cower beneath Mian, standing naked on her mattress, staring it down. She holds no weapon and she wears no armor and her hair is a mess and my scent swirls around her, impenetrable and pure and untouched.

The warrior below me stares up, and up and up. I hiss down, narrowing my gaze. He glances at his feet and tosses his sword down between them. It lands with a swish through the grasses, and then a louder thump.

He drops to one knee, like so many of the others have already done. "We were just following orders," he stammers.

"You violated the treaty. You violated the Sasorena. I would dismember each of you with a dull spoon if it were up to me. Be thankful that it is not." I switch forward and

warriors of all tribes bow to me as I move, but I ignore them. I have only eyes for her.

"Mian…" The desperate need to touch her drives me to shed my naxem form and find my true one. Tail finds feet, hood finds head and face and my hands reach for her. I drop down, arriving in time for her to launch herself off of the bed and into my arms.

Her arms circle my neck and her legs circle my waist and I breathe in her egra-flavored hair and I savor the pounding of her heartbeat against my much quicker ones. "I'm so sorry, Mian. I should have expected them to try to take you from me. I didn't think…I never sviking think…"

She pushes back from me just enough to slant her lips over mine. Arousal pours in through my skull, thickening my thoughts. The urge to mount her and apply my mark to her doubles, triples. I can't seem to think past it. I grip her hip in a fist, but a hiss makes the hairs on the back of my arms stand.

I rip my mouth from hers, face already elongating in response to the challenge. *Tatana*. The smaller naxem sits coiled in the darkness where the torchlight does not fully reach. He tries to lunge for me, but he is blocked by a greater force, and I don't have to do a thing.

The beast strikes with its hood, batting Tatana away easily. Chimara rises higher and her tongues loll out of her mouth as she faces off against the creature, and then switches her menace towards the group of three manerak approaching.

"Tszk!" Mian shouts at Dandena, Rehet and Mor. It occurs to me in the next moment, when Mian truly starts to struggle in my arms, that they don't know it's

Chimara. They think she's some evil thing and will act in defense of Mian against her.

"Lower your weapons," I shout, turning on them. Though I'm forced to release Mian's feet to the ground, I don't dare release her hand. I let her pull me forward as she thrusts herself between Chimara and my warriors. *Her* warriors.

"Weapons down!" I roar, hating the sight of their exposed blades trained on my Xiveri mate's chest.

Dandena hesitates, lights from the torches flashing across her face, illuminating her uncertainty. "I don't understand."

Mian shouts, gesturing wildly between them. "This is Chimara! Chimara is naxem."

Rehet and Mor share a glance. Dandena shakes her head, squinting up at the naxem in the dark. "This…is Chimara?"

Mian nods. "Yena."

"But Chimara isn't manerak," she says, and it's the first time since I've known her that she sounds as I do all the time — well and utterly foolish.

"Yena. But Chimara is naxem. She transformed when Tatana tried to mark me."

Rage filters in through my ears, causing my brain to boil. I lurch forward, towards Chimara, towards the *thing* beyond her. "He tried to mark you?" And then it hits me. I round on her, grabbing Mian by both arms. "Are you hurt?"

"Tszk. Not hurt," she says, swallowing hard when my gaze envelops her.

I cup her shoulders and growl low in the back of my throat as my hands draw lines down her arms and then her waist and then her thighs when I drop to my knees before her. I inhale deeply at the juncture of her thighs, feeling relieved when I smell no blood or seed on her.

"Neheyuu, they didn't do *that*!" She bops me on the top of my head, slapping down with the flat of her fist in a way that makes the corners of my mouth twitch.

I murmur against her flesh, "This should never have happened. If Chimara hadn't been there…" I rise to stand and press my forehead to hers. I could have lost her. *We* have *lost her. We failed her in our duties…*

"Tszk." She grins. I can feel it in her cheeks and the fluttering of her eyelashes when they brush my face. "I can take care of myself. I was scared but I brought out Chimara's naxem and I cursed Tatana. He will never hurt me again."

Her voice grows icy and I pull back enough to look at her face and the two naxem — one glowing and golden, the other horrible and disfigured — that she made. "You made them. Intentionally?"

"Yena. I felt it. Here." She takes my hand and places it over her ribs, below her breasts and inhales deeply. "I didn't like that he was trying to mark me, that he was trying to take me away from you. I'm yours."

I blink and feel heat in my face that does nothing to diminish the glory of her words. It sets me alight. I'm overcome with them. "Tszk. I am *yours*, Mian. Your slave. Your worshipper." I bring her hand to my chest. The bandage I wore there earlier in this solar has ripped free, but she's still only looking at my face. "See?"

Her gaze switches down, finds the black ink on my skin and holds. Her lips part and she strokes my skin without understanding. And then with total understanding. Her eyes fill with water and she bites her bottom lip and she beams.

"A star?" She whispers.

"A star." I exhale, glancing down at the tattoo Greta's steady hand branded me with earlier in the solar. A star the size of Mian's fist sits just above my left nipple, right over my left heart.

"Because I am Sasorena?"

"Because you're the only star that exists to me." I lean in close, brush her hair behind her ear. "And because I am naxem, and I want nothing more than to swallow you whole so I can keep you with me forever."

She swallows, her fingers curl over my chest, stroking the outline of my tattoo, it's healing edges. "I will need a tattoo for you then. Maybe a snake."

"Tszk. That's not the way it works, reesa. You are slave to no one. And I will never be master to you. You are Sasorena," I whisper, awed by her, as I am every solar. Every lunar. "You believe it now?"

She hesitates, sweeps my face with her hands, then glances over her shoulder at Chimara who shudders and shakes her great head. Mian doesn't answer my question, but says instead, "I do not think she knows how to come out of her form. Can you help her?"

I glance up at Chimara and jeer, "You tired of being naxem yet?"

Chimara opens her mandible, looking terrifying, and speaks with a voice that is ageless, that is her but not her, that is some great and powerful thing. *"Not until he's dead."*

She's right. "Detain Tatana," I seethe.

I direct my order to Dandena and the cluster of warriors surrounding her only to find that their attentions and their weapons are already trained on the naxem that is Tatana. Meanwhile, the crowd surrounding all of us has grown.

Warriors keep the Nevay traitors pinned to the sands, but behind them, the sessemara dolsk has emptied, and hundreds of bodies now litter the grasses, watching the scene as it unfolds. I notice that Nevay himself is not among them.

My gaze narrows on the false-naxem, huddling in the center of a ring of spears and swords trained for his weak scales and ready to slash through them. "Kill him," I order.

Mian shocks me completely then when she jumps forward, out of my grip. "Tszk!" She roars. "Let him live."

Gasps. One of them has to be mine, because I don't understand. Rage boils my blood, leaving my manerak and naxem feeling unsettled. "For what he did, he deserves to suffer…"

"And he will. Look at him." She points at the thing and he spits in her direction. His head tosses. He rises up, but even at his full height, he is still an unimpressive specimen, hardly larger than a full-blooded manerak. I don't doubt that if she wanted, Dandena could take him all by herself. Likely with ease. So then what *is* he, if not naxem? Not even my own naxem has an answer to this.

And then Mian lifts her sweet, accented voice and speaks to me. To Tatana. To everyone. "A naxem cannot be taken. A naxem can only be given and I did not give Tatana this form. Instead, I cursed him."

The murmuring gets louder, with those who have heard Mian repeating her words to those that haven't. "He is stuck as he is, as a weak, cursed naxem, unable to return to his true form." And then her tone twists savagely, "And I will not release him.

"I want Tatana to live as a warning to anyone who *dares* try to take naxem from me again. I want him to roam the grasslands in this shriveled husk, never able to return to another tasmaran. He will never join with a female. He will know only loneliness and hunger. And that's only if the desert dogs don't get to him. And even after they tear him apart, he will never know Sasorana's embrace. He will never walk among the stars. She works through me, and he is disgraced for he has dishonored us both. Her, among the stars, and me, among you."

She breathes in, and as she breathes out, I feel a chill rush through the air, and sing through my bones. On its wings, her guileless truth is delivered. "I am Sasorena."

I have never heard her angry before and feel my naxem and my manerak both cower behind my true form, terrified to be in her path. And so am I. I swallow. And then swallow again.

Silence reigns in the wake of her commandment. Erkan looks to me. Dandena looks to me. They all look to me. I look at Mian. "You heard your Sasorena. Release him. Let the dogs tear him apart. If he's lucky, a nomadic tasmaran will find him first, chain him up and use him for sport."

"Remind me never to piss Mian off," Mor says with a shudder as he moves in line with Chimara to form an impenetrable wall of warriors between Tatana and the rest of us. Tatana hisses, but does not strike. Instead, he glares at Mian as if terrified of her, or just terrified.

Spears poke and stab in his direction. Chimara lowers her head to strike once, twice, a third time. He jolts out of her path, shrieking as he moves, screeching and recoiling. His defeat hangs like a scent in the air. And in his eyes, there is a blaze of fire, of understanding, of fear and of resignation. He coils up on himself and then shoots towards the starry horizon.

And this is the last I see of him.

I turn to Mian then and take her hand. I offer her a nod and try to pull her back with me towards our dolsk, but she points to Chimara.

"Help her," she says. She commands.

I nod, eager to do her bidding *or else* and step beneath the shadow of Chimara's glorious serpentine shape. She is a beautiful thing. Yellow underbelly a slightly darker color than mine, it glows in the darkness. Though the color of her scales is too difficult to ascertain in this light, I can still see her impossible length, and smile. I press my palm to her hood and stroke downwards.

"Chimara." Her head swivels and I see myself reflected in her eyes. I take Mian's hand and press it to Chimara's center, just below her mandible. "Feel Mian. Feel her breath. Come back to her."

"Mian…" Chimara's naxem rattles, mandible working feverishly. She shakes her head from side to side, as if trying to dislodge something.

"Come back, Chimara. I want to give you a hug. And not like this." Mian sticks out her tongue and the response is immediate.

The snake that is Chimara starts to compress itself and unfurl. It takes many moments, but finally the transformation is complete, her naxem spitting out a human form that has no manerak. That doesn't need manerak.

Naked, Chimara struggles to sit up and catch her breath. The world around us is in an uproar, but I don't give a svik about that. All I can think is that Chimara, my Fourth, the half-human who has no manerak, is now the second true naxem among us. The third most powerful being on Sasor.

Or perhaps the second. I'd be happy to accept rank as Third if this were the case. Though I would, of course, have to fight her for it...

Hugging Mian to my side, I offer Chimara my arm and pull her up to standing. She's panting, disheveled, clearly in pain. Her hand presses over her chest and she makes a face, everything twisting.

"Svik," she curses, and Mian doesn't seem to care that Chimara has met and survived the very definition of agony. She throws both arms around Chimara's neck and the two females press themselves together.

Chimara closes her eyes, then laughs and holds Mian away from her. "As much as I like you," she pants, "I don't know how I feel about a naked hug while your mate is watching."

Mate. She acknowledged us as her mate! My manerak and my naxem are wild beneath my breast. Apparently this is a big deal. Apparently, Chimara matters more than I ever thought possible. *Fool. She matters to Mian, so she is the second most important thing to us.*

Mian laughs. Liquid stars shine in her eyes as she turns them up to me. Her hair is crazy, sitting heavy around her shoulders in all manner of ties and knots and braids. Pins stick up out of it. She has bruises and abrasions on her back and shoulder and yet she looks totally untouched. She is still, as she always was, pure starlight.

I blink many times as a rush of emotion too strong to stand up against comes over me. I sweep her into my arms, press my nose to her cheek and breathe in deep, finding my marking scent and needing to reapply it. Vigorously.

"Svik the sessemara. Svik everything. I'm going to chain you to my leg and walk around with you attached to my body for the rest of my solars. You're never leaving my sight again."

Mian's hands slide against my neck and tilt my face to hers. She plants a kiss softly on my lips, then traces their outline with her small, callused fingers. "That does not seem very practical."

Warriors try to crowd us now, but I bark, "Step aside! Mian is coming through and if anyone tries to stop me from taking her to my dolsk and rutting her into oblivion, they can answer to Chimara."

Chimara blushes, looking bashful as warriors crowd her instead, asking her questions and offering her congratulations. Some ask her about her transformation, how it felt, if she hurts, while males fall over themselves to offer her the wreaths they're still wearing.

"How is this possible? You're just a human!" One female shouts — Egretha's voice if I had to guess.

Chimara points to me — to Mian in my arms. "Mian's just a human too, and yet her dolsk is now the most powerful." Her mouth flares, fangs extending from her mouth for a moment before she catches the shift, physically stumbling back in order to curb the suddenness of her naxem's transformation.

Laughter ensues, including Chimara's. All but Egretha's. Instead, she stares at Chimara, then at me before settling her gaze on Mian.

Her wreath jangles as she moves into a low bow, low enough the weight of her wreath nearly topples her. When she rights herself she says in her strange, warbling pitch. "To join Mian's tasmaran, is there an application process?"

25
Mian

I don't know whose dolsk we occupy, or if they mind the destruction Neheyuu intends to wreak across it. But I don't, because as he whispers every unholy thing he plans to do to me, need is all that I feel.

My mouth is crushed to his as we fall through the tent leathers and onto the low pallet piled high with pillows. It's not even a bed, but I don't mind that either.

His mouth is hot on my skin as he licks the sensation of Tatana covering me away, one kiss at a time. He showers me with them. "I love you, Mian," he growls against my breast before capturing my nipple between his teeth. He pulls and the pain-pleasure makes my left leg shoot out straight. Neheyuu laughs against my chest and a surge of desire thrums through me. A surge of power.

I spear his hair with my fingers and wrench his head up. I curl up and kiss him hard, enjoying the strangled moan he releases. I yank him up the length of my body, loving that he moves under the command of my touch, and with no prelude at all, I reach down the length of his body and position his hot, velvet erection at my entrance.

"I love you too, Neheyuu," I say, and he gasps, like he did not expect me to say the words. Not now. Perhaps not ever.

He grips the side of my face with one hand and blinks many times before bowing his forehead to touch my forehead. He kisses the tip of my nose. Then he licks it. But my light laughter is silenced when he whispers, "Do you forgive me?"

"I do not know what there is to forgive. All I know is that I love you. I have loved you for some time. Since the first time you gave me opikopi."

He barks out a laugh and shakes his head, but refuses to look into my eyes. "If only I'd known grain loaf would be your undoing, I'd have stuffed you full of it."

"You *have* stuffed me full of it. You were successful. I do love you, Neheyuu. Even if I was a slave. Even if you are always foolish." I soften as I stroke the side of his face. I push up on his forehead, hoping to see him, but he's blinking many times, almost like…almost as if…

"Neheyuu," I giggle, "Are you crying?"

"Tszk," he lies. He shakes his head rapidly and sniffles and says, "I am First warrior of my tasmaran. Firsts don't cry."

I laugh hard and loud and from the belly. "You do. But I don't know why."

"Because it's not possible. I don't deserve this happiness. I don't deserve you."

I press my lips to the top of his head, smelling the fire in his hair. Smelling me too. "I say you do, so you do."

He inhales once, abruptly, and looks into my eyes. They are brown this time. And wholly beautiful. His lips quirk. "You are Sasorena, and it is your dolsk. I suppose if you say it, I must believe you."

I grin, shifting my hips up, wishing he would continue what he started. I nod, lifting up to press my mouth to his neck. I taste him and when I hear his breath hitch, I bite. *Hard.* "Yena," I say between my teeth. "You must do what I say. And now, I want you to svik me."

"Whatever you want." Neheyuu thrusts all at once, igniting my whole body in fire as he pierces the wetness between my thighs, finding the heart of my arousal. He pumps into me and out of me ferociously. "It's…always whatever you want…forever."

My back arches involuntarily, my toes curl, the insides of my thighs shiver and shake. He continues to rut me endlessly and at some point, I find myself gazing up through the dolsk's lonely skylight. I grab onto his hair to anchor myself before I float right up through it, up into the sky, and am claimed by the stars.

It doesn't help, because when Neheyuu slows his thrusts and grinds down on my hips, sending sparks of pleasure and pain shooting through my most sensitive nub, the first wave of my orgasm hits me brutally. I'm screaming his name as I resurface moments later to the sensation of his fangs sunk deep into my throat.

My hand palms his chest, finding the space below his left shoulder where he wears the mark drawn for me, and me alone. Tears are in my eyes. Something huge pulls at my chest. I feel sunken into it and I feel lifted by it in equal measure.

"Say it again," he grunts as he continues to piston his hips, thrusts becoming more frantic.

My legs are spread wide, heels digging into the pillows, struggling to find purchase. I grab hold of anything I can, clawing his back, but everything slips away from me. The stars, pain, my past, reality. Until there's only pleasure. There's only us.

"What?" I say, struggling to hang on to words. Who needs them anyways?

"What you said before," he whispers against my neck, soothing the bites he just made with his tongues. "About how you feel...about me."

I moan as a wave of pleasure rushes over me. I slap his skin, loving the sound. Slipping deeper into it. "I love you, Neheyuu."

He groans. "Again."

"I love you..."

"Again...svik," he shouts.

"I love...love...umph...ah!" I scream as I spiral into another direction, into another universe, right out of that skylight, to Sasor's farthest moon. The pretty blue one.

Neheyuu roars above me, but manages to pull back enough to see my face, to look into my eyes. He holds me there, pinning me fully as he stiffens, grits his teeth, and empties into me in the way he knows I like.

He grinds down on my clit as his seed fires into my body, warming me from the inside. It lasts forever. For eons. And even after he relaxes more of his weight onto me and his head drops forward onto the pillow above my shoulder, the cock inside of my body still seems to stir and its heat doesn't fade.

"Neheyuu?" I whisper.

"Yena, reesa?" His head lifts and he rapidly searches my face with his gaze, fully concerned.

I smile and gently comb his hair behind his ears, seeking to calm him. "I just wanted to tell you that I'm pregnant. Verena confirmed it two solars ago, but I wanted to wait until after the sessemara to tell you. I'm only forty solars along or so, but Verena says that things look very promising. I've reached a healthy weight to be able to carry our kit to term…Neheyuu?"

His eyes are closed and he bows his head quickly, holding his forehead to my chin.

"Neheyuu? Neheyuu?" I start to panic, until he goes totally weightless and lets me look at him. I start to laugh anew.

He shakes his head and clenches his eyelids together as tears drip from his long lashes onto my face. He kisses me. He *smothers* me in sloppy wet kisses.

"Neheyuu," I say, laughing.

He mumbles something that sounds like, "I love you…don't deserve you…" before my big, bad naxem breaks down fully then.

I pet his hair as he plants worshipping kisses across my stomach, muttering more nonsense to the tiny bean inside, and as he does, I smile up through the skylight. The world is full of stars, and something shoots across the darkness. It could be anything. A comet. An asteroid. A star making a break for it. More humans on a satellite bound for some other world…

And though I don't know what wrong turn we made to bring us humans to Sasor, all I can do is spend the rest of my solars thanking the universe.

Two solars later…

26

Neheyuu

I sit nervously on the fluffy pillow of the bank, tapping my foot again. This time, there are no jangles around my neck because my wreath hangs around Mian's and jangles there. She is talking to Ofrat, doing her best to turn my anxiety into despair. And she's succeeding.

She looks beautiful this lunar. *She always looks beautiful, fool.*

Fool, whispers the darker brogue.

But this solar, she is carrying my kit. *Our kit. And she has been carrying it for many solars, fool.* I don't have an answer to that, but I grit my teeth and force my cock to control itself. Just the thought of my kit in her belly makes me want to rut her just to ensure that it's there, maybe plant another one. At least, try. Can we have two at once? More? *I don't know. But we should attempt this also.*

But right now another male from the Sessena tribe is coming to speak to her. He's their Third. Their Third and their Second offered her wreaths and she wears them both around her neck now, stacked so high, she has to tilt forward and look up to be able to see. Four Firsts offered her their wreaths. Four. My wreath isn't even the biggest among them. Does that matter? *You know it does not.* But Mian wants a nice male. *She will choose us. She loves us. She carries our kit. Be patient.* How can I?

Dandena is laughing at my side. Her wreath jangles as well, but she only wears the one — the one of the male she has selected. The Second from the Hox tribe has chosen her and she, him. But rather than her joining his tasmaran, he will join ours. I try to remember to smile since this male will now be our Fifth, but I don't hear the questions he asked me and when he makes jokes, I laugh at all the wrong moments.

It is a huge coup for us, his joining. Not the only one won this sessemara. Most importantly, Reffa and Xena both survived and are recuperating with Verena, Reepal and Doro looking after them. Doro acts with Verena now as lead healer, and is formerly of the Nevay.

After Nevay himself was outcast from the United Manerak Tribes for conspiring with Tatana to steal Mian, his tasmaran was disbanded. Many joined the Sessena, but most joined with us. Mian's tasmaran. We're now the second largest by my count — after the Sessena — and the sessemara hasn't even ended. Mian's tasmaran will likely be the largest if she chooses a male from within it…if she chooses me…

My eyes remain pinned to the wreath in Mian's hands — Wren's wreath. Another First. And he's nice. Is he nice? I think so. But before I have a chance to determine just how nice he is and if he'd make my naxem a nice chew toy, she hands his wreath back to him. I exhale. A little.

A very little.

"Are you sweating yet?" Dandena says from somewhere to my right.

"Yena. I've been sweating for solars. I haven't stopped sweating."

My vision flashes between a grey-green haze to full color as I track her, stalk her, hunt her as she works her way across the floor, handing wreaths to all of the males that offered them to her, until there are just three remaining. Mine, the blacksmith's, and her own.

I hold my breath as she approaches him, the male called Trehuro. He has a small dolsk within the Sessena and is apparently very good at his craft. He fought like svik, but I refused to allow myself to smash him on the battle pitch the previous solar, opting instead to help him stand when he fell. Stupid, sviking female. Stupid sviking me. The things I'd do for her *and* our unborn kit... *You mean, anything?*

"I wish I could chisel a portrait of you right now. I'd keep this bust on my mantel and remind you of it every time you start behaving like an oeban."

"That is an insult to oebans," her male says somewhere to her right.

She laughs. I don't. "Sviking shush," I order.

"You know she will choose you," Dandena says. "We've heard the rumors of little feet stomping around the tasmaran."

"You mean Mor's?"

She laughs. "Yena. Those, among others. Now stop sweating otherwise you'll start to stink."

"Good," I growl, gouging deep grooves into the armor plating above my knee. "Better to mark her with."

"Gross."

"You're one to speak. You stink too."

Dandena grunts. "Yena. I couldn't wait. Watching Elrik fight in the arena was an art."

"Thank you," he says.

I groan outwardly. "Shush. The both of you." My sweaty palms grip my knees. She's taken the blacksmith's wreath around her neck…and then she hands it back to him.

I exhale, shoulders sagging forward. I clench my jaw so hard I wonder if it's possible to break it. *Tszk, it's not.* Every damn wreath feels like a fresh battle. Because even though he was a nice male and she didn't choose him, she could still choose someone else. She could choose *not* me. *She won't. Our souls were carved as one by Sasorana. She is ours and so is the kit she carries.* Shush! If all that's true, there's only one soul on this planet, I want to hear it from…

Mian is searching the crowd as if she isn't painfully attuned to my every movement, as I am to hers. Her fingers toy with some of the stones woven into her wreath, and some of the bones woven into mine. Hers and mine are the last two wreaths she wears.

Chimara stands next to her, wearing only her own wreath as she already returned the dozens that had been stacked around her throat — choking her, as she so aptly put it. Even though she's limping slightly from her injuries, she doesn't leave Mian's side. But she points. To me.

Mian turns and when she sees me, her gaze has all the power of a spear thrown at twenty paces. It plunges in deep, nearly toppling me. I sit up straight. Everything else falls away. Svik, I *am* sweating. *Calm the svik down!* Some otherworldly voice screams at me.

"Should we give them some privacy?" Elrik asks.

"Tszk. Are you sviking crazy? I'm not missing this." Dandena shushes him when he tries to say something else and for a brief moment, I could kiss the female. In the quiet now, Mian skips through the crowd, not seeming to notice how it parts for her. Low talking and laughing still add to the background of this moment, but I can tell that we have stolen more than our fair share of focus. Let them watch. It will either be my ascension to the stars, or my ruin.

She arrives in front of me, so close that my knees bump her stomach through her pale green robe. It matches her skin somehow. Makes her appear more bronzed by the sun, more radiant. Her hair is done up again in twists and knots and I imagine myself taking the time to undo each one. Or maybe just rip all the pins out at once, throw her down and…

"Neheyuu," she says in a bright, tight breath.

"Mian," I croak, wishing I sounded more gallant than this.

Her fingers caress the fabric of her robe over her stomach as she glances down at the seat beneath me. Immediately I jolt out of it. "Sorry, I didn't even realize…" I grumble, offering it to her. "Should you even be up and walking? Don't you need to rest? Verena says…"

"Shh," she says abruptly, so I shh and swallow and wait.

She just smiles. As if this weren't the worst moment of my life. I could throw up from the tension. "Thank you for giving me your wreath." Is this it? Is this the beginning of the let down? Is this where she tells me she thought about it, but she'd rather start her family somewhere else? That she'd rather wait for the next sessemara before choosing another male and leaving me? That I'm a fool for even thinking we're in the same league? Because we aren't. Svik, I just hope she hasn't realized it…

Her lips part. I hang on every word. Every breath. She says, "And thank you for giving me your heart. You know you already have mine."

Tightness. Pressure. I don't breathe. I haven't been breathing. I just nod. *Fool.*

Fool…

Mian squints at me. "Are you alright? Is your tattoo hurting you? They can be painful, if you aren't used to it."

What is she talking about? I glance down at the large star on my chest and then back up. She's teasing me. I glare, then shuffle from side-to-side, trying to be calm and kind. At the very least, civil.

Mian smiles wider. "Ah. You are worried?" Her fingers dance around the collar around her neck. My wreath. When I don't answer, she shakes her head. "I told you already, I would choose you. How could I not?" She says, stroking her belly lovingly.

"So do it already!" I want to scream. "Okay," I say instead, rather dumbly.

So slowly time seems to stand still, she lifts my wreath off of her head…and then her fingers touch her own. She lifts that off too and it's like she's lifting the weight of a fallen asteroid off of my body, off of my soul. She slips my wreath back over her hair, letting it settle once more on her shoulders. With two hands, she grips her own wreath, then rises onto her tip toes.

"You have to bend down a little." There's a pink in her cheeks that wasn't there before and I wonder fleetingly if she's even a little bit as nervous as I am in this moment. I lower my head, feel the brush of fabric rustling by my ears. "There," she whispers finally. "I'm yours. Officially, that is."

I blink and glance down and my chest heaves as I take in the wreath dangling around my neck. Little swatches of different colored fabrics fold around a single loop from which stones dangle in all of Sasor's many colors. My stone hangs right between Mor's and Xi's on the string in the very middle.

I look up into her eyes and watch them sparkle. I can barely speak. I can barely think. "How long have you known that you won't join with any other male?"

"Perhaps only in this moment." She places one hand on my shoulder and uses it to pull herself up. She kiss my right cheek. Then the other. Fire incinerates my flesh every place she touches. "Perhaps I have always known."

"You exist to torture me, don't you?" I drop my tone into a growl and grip the sides of her waist. I wrench her against me. "I am capable of my own tortures, Sasorena. You should know that I am a dangerous male when it comes to you."

Mian laughs and I melt into the sound, into her touch. "Oh, I am well aware." She kisses my lips softly. Dangerously so.

I growl and as our lips part, chase the connection. I hook one hand around her elbow and draw her in close. "I'll begin by taking you back to my tent and ensuring that you feel my mark all the way down to your toes."

She clasps her hands around the back of my neck and leans into me, her breasts pressing against my chest, our wreaths twining together. "And I look forward to marking you, too."

"Females can't mark males."

"Haven't you heard? I am no ordinary female. I am Sasorena now and for the good of our people I think it's my duty to try. Many, many times."

I crush her mouth with mine, tasting her flavor, worshipping it. I'm panting as I pull back and so is she and around us there is clapping and laughter and riotous cheering. Talk of bets won and bets lost open up the room, enabling me to breathe again, though even that effort is shaky. Let them all laugh. I'll laugh with them too when I regain control of my other senses. For now, there is only her touch. Only Mian. My reesa.

My naxem and my manerak rejoice under my skin, letting me savor this moment without rebelling. The three of us are one now, just as I am one with my Sasorena.

"I love you, Mian," I whisper to her lips.

"I love you, Neheyuu. All of you." She smiles. "But I am getting a little tired of wearing this wreath. I think I could use your assistance in getting it off. Along with everything else I'm wearing…"

My groin tightens, straining against my armor. I snag her around the waist and snatch her up so that her feet dangle over the carpets. "Whatever you wish…"

"Don't call me Sasorena," she says, covering my mouth with one of her small hands. It's no less callused than it was when I first met her. And she is no less radiant than she was then.

I snatch one of her fingers between my lips and suck it deep into my mouth. When I pull it free, it releases with a wet, popping sound. Mian's pupils dilate. The scent of her arousal washes over us.

"I wasn't. I was going to call you reesa."

And then I dash off with her into the lunar, tripping over some stupid carpet in my haste to be free of the sessemara dolsk and nearly plowing through a massive sviking candle. Laughter lights up the lunar, but we leave it behind as I make plans…so many plans…to worship her in my dolsk just as I plan to worship her for the rest of my life. With every piece of me.

No matter how foolish.

Thanks so much for joining Mian and Neheyuu on Sasor! I hope you enjoyed their story! Reviews, even the one-liners, are very much appreciated on Amazon or Goodreads.

To get access to future books filled with hot, possessive alphas and the resilient, warrior women they worship _first_, not to mention freebies, exclusive previews and more, sign up to my mailing list at www.booksbyelizabeth.com/contact.

Until the next time,
Stay wild ¤°´´˜°¤,,,ø*

Elizabeth

Continue the journey and be…

Taken to Heimo

Krisxox hates humans, but is determined to keep this one alive. Even if Svera worships a god he's never heard of, wants peace between her people and his, and is being hunted by space pirates.

Taken to Heimo: A SciFi Alien Romance
Xiveri Mates Book 4 (Svera and Krisxox)

Available in paperback anywhere online books are sold or on Amazon in ebook or hardback

1

Krisxox

"Svera!" I shout.

Her body is trembling, covered in slick, glistening red — *it's blood, human blood,* her *human blood* — but at the sound of my voice, she looks at me and comes to life. *Good girl.* She makes it to her knees. The walls of this ancient C-class transporter shimmer. They shake. Svera falls.

"You're xoking slow! Get *up*, human!"

She hates when I order her. Hates when I curse. Hates when I call her *human.*

A frown disrupts the irritating kindness that is her stupid, human face and that's fine, because it distracts her from her fear.

"That's it. Don't be afraid. I'm not going to let him hurt you."

But I'm lying.

I can't move. I can't feel my own body. I can't feel anything except for the heat of the C-class engines releasing energy in great clouds of steam. This ancient beast comes from another time. So old, I'd never seen one with my own eyes until I climbed aboard with every intention of saving the female that I hate most in this universe.

"I need you to come towards me," I say, trying to be gentle even though I'm never gentle. I don't know how to be. And I'm not going to change for *her*. *Then what is this, if not trying?*

"Svera, *please*."

The crinkles in her forehead smooth when I beg her. I never beg *except* to her and increasingly more often. Right now I'd give her both my legs if it meant she'd walk any xoking faster!

"Move!"

She takes one wobbly step, and then another. I tense and growl and grunt and wince with each move she makes. These human females are so disgustingly fragile. The tiniest little movement and they fall the xok apart.

"Come on…" She moves so xoking slow… *"Come on!"*

Svera's too wet gaze meets mine. I see pain shining in their green depths. As green as the leaves of the baby werro trees, those bright, brave little saplings.

Meanwhile, the blood on her face shines in the most alarming, visceral shade of red, a color not often seen in nature. But worse than that color is the sound the engines make. Somewhere in the recesses of this transporter, they're screaming the same word over and over.

Failure.

"Krisxox," she whispers.

Everything is a blur. The black and grey against the aquamarine of the floor-length covering she wears…the pale brown of her skin with its haunting, yellow undertones…the small wisps of her hair that have escaped the covering she fixes to them…and then the silver shadow that falls over her body.

The Niahhorru attacks.

"Svera!" I roar as the pirate falls on top of her, taking her to the slated, metal ground.

Bloodthirsty beasts, the Niahhorru pirates ascribe to no quadrant, have no honor, no laws, no treaties with anyone and are led by a king obsessed with finding the location to the human colony so he can steal and breed the human females to repopulate his species' dying numbers.

I'm going to tear him apart for taking her from me, starting with all four of his arms…

These beasts are born fighters, killers and thieves and Svera is a weak, pathetic human *with skin as soft as Qath's sands, unblemished by the suns or their winds, untouched by time.*

She doesn't stand a chance.

Xok me! Xok her. *Don't. Please, don't.*

I struggle. I don't know what has me, but its hold is stronger than iron ion and heavier than stalyx. I've never been caged. Never been rendered weak. I am Voraxia's Krisxox — its strongest fighter and battle strategist. I wage war and I have never known defeat. *Until now…*

Now, I'm left to watch the Niahhorru bring one clawed hand down and rip away Svera's head scarf, revealing her hair to the light. With his next swipe, he tears through the front of her shift, baring her body.

"Get the xok off of her!" I shout, but even my voice is weak and ineffective, growing fainter and fainter.

He holds her down easily and positions himself between her legs. His bare backside gleams up at me. He's going to violate her. Can she even take him? Will he kill her?

"Svera. Nox…please…" I say, and this is the first time I've despaired. This is the first time I've felt a fear heavy enough to bring me to my knees.

The full power of the Xanaxana that binds me to Svera explodes through my bones. I roast alive, heating, sweating, burning, shaking, *dying…*

And then I wake and the dream fades just as it did last lunar and the lunar before and the lunar before…

2
Svera

I'm lying in the dark, wide awake even though my eyes are closed. My whole body is tightly coiled against the sheets. Or well, not sheets. The Voraxians use furs and animal skins to line their curved nests.

The edges are so high I can't see over them and I fall into the center. Just a little ball, trying to hide from my nightmares. But there's nowhere to hide. They sweep in like the wind through the trees outside of my window — with blistering force.

"Kiy gadol yawveh mikol ha'elohim," I remind myself. "Allah alakbar." I pray to the Tri-God to chase away the visions.

Visions of being chased, of being caught, of being hurt. I picture the horrible four-armed, spiked male that tried to...do more. *Nondah. The pirate's name was Nondah.* I remember holding a little dagger and trying to cut at him in order to protect myself. I'm not a fighter. Hurting him had hurt me. I don't want to have to do it again. I don't get any pleasure out of it. I'm not a warrior. I'm not like...

The door to my room opens with a nearly silent *whoosh*. I freeze. My heart is in my mouth. *Allah al akbar.*

Sh'ma Yisrael Adonai Eloheinu Adonai Eḥad. Tri-God help me. It's him. Nondah. The name of the pirate who tried to…

And then I hear a familiar grunt and the same angry stomping that I heard last lunar and the lunar before and every lunar since the two of us have returned to Qath. Since I was taken onto that pirate ship, knocked out when it exploded, and woke up to the sight of Krisxox's angry red face. He'd been holding me.

And here he is rescuing me again even if it's only from my bleak and brutal thoughts. *Thank the Lord and thank the stars.*

I exhale my first easy breath of the lunar as he stomps to the plush seat in the corner and takes it. He unfurls the blanket I left out for him and, for a while, I listen to his agitated breathing until it eventually deepens and I know he's asleep.

I know because I'm familiar with this sound by now — the sound of him stomping in angrily every lunar, and stomping out at solarbreak just as angrily. Then he'll go down the hall and start to prepare first meal *loudly.* And eventually, I'll get up and fold the blanket he'd been using and wonder the same thing I do each solar — if he knows that I know that he comes to my room, or if he even cares. At the very least, he must have realized that the blanket he uses doesn't fold itself.

But he never says anything and I never say anything and like this, we both keep pretending.

I sigh contentedly and my muscles loosen and the darkness ceases to feel quite so cold. I close my eyes, still wondering about Krisxox and his brutish silliness and his pretending to be clandestine and my pretending to be asleep until, with alarming quickness, I'm not pretending anymore.

I sleep dreamlessly.

3

Krisxox

She could sleep through a Muxung Boar attack.

No matter how the summer winds wail, every solar I wake up, she's out cold. Her little body sprawled wildly over her nest, the delicately woven vervu-fiber blanket tangled around her legs, the heavy fur splashed haphazardly over her body.

She keeps her hair covered even when she sleeps. A light-colored silk encases it, but there are still small strands of gold and ashy brown that escape near her face and curl near her cheeks.

I follow the long line of her neck with my gaze. It's so thin and delicate. She shouldn't even be alive. None of them should be. And this one *definitely* shouldn't be here sleeping the solar away in my city in my home in my nest.

But she is.

And I don't wake her. I can't. I need to be careful. I don't need her knowing that I spend each lunar in her room. I don't need her knowing that I dream of her. That failing her gives me nightmares. *I don't need her knowing about the pressure in my chest. The fire that spreads across it. The heat that's so vociferous it makes me stark-raving mad.*

The colors that sometimes…flare…oh xok…xok! I can feel those colors now rising within me like a sickness, a disease that festers and corrupts.

I'm staring down at her ankles, exposed up to the shin. Her skin is a flawless light brown. The bottom of her feet, very pale and strange by contrast. It's disgusting. *It's beautiful.* I remember what it had looked like to see her full body bared. To hold it in my arms. To hold her. Her. *My Xiv* — nox. Never.

I swallow hard and turn from her, but the weight in my chest is enough to slow me down. I stagger once, but make it to the door. I wave it open and move down the hall. The farther from her I move, the more the pressure releases. The weight is almost totally lifted by the time I reach the cooking pit.

Only a few steps down and I'm in my lair. Everything is right here. My head clears. After the training flats, it's the place I feel most stable. I pull out a host of ingredients from baskets below the red werro-wood cooking surfaces. I light the fusion fire cooking trays and I forget that I have an *alien* living in my house. It's sickening and so is she. Not she. *It.* The alien. *What would my sires say if they saw me living with it?*

I wince as the fusion knife cuts into the edge of my longest finger. The blade is sharper than any I've used before. It's one of the new Rakukanna's designs. *What would my sires say if they saw me using it now?*

"Hefenena, Krisxox," Svera — *it* — greets me in the Drakesh language. Though distinct from Voraxian, she's somehow managed to master both languages in the short time she's been among my kind and speaks them fluently now with only the slightest *most charming* hint of an accent. Nox. Not charming. Despicable. That's right. *Despicable*.

I do nothing to acknowledge her. Setting the blade aside, I pull out a flat, stalyx knife and continue cutting into the tough roots spread across the wooden surface in front of me. *It feels so dull by contrast.* I shake away the thought and dump the roots into the fusion tray. Steam rises from them and with a quick flick at the controls, they brown beautifully. I spice them and then I pull out a second tray and toss in a few strips of meat. Svera, she… doesn't eat this meat. So if I want to feed her, then I have to cook the meat separately.

And I do.

Every solar.

Her heat reaches me before her scent as she steps up beside me. She smells like darkness, a danger not yet known. My hand flinches like it's going to reach out and touch her without my consent…pull her against my chest, brush my mouth over those soft, pink things she calls lips…Nox!

"Mmmm," she says. She says the same thing every solar. That small sound of satisfaction. My xora stirs and my hearts beat harder knowing that she is pleased with what I cook for her.

I tilt my head from side-to-side and it cracks loudly. "It smells delicious in here. What do you call that root? The purple one?"

She points to a block of gum root as big as her head, and that's only half. I hand it to her and grumble, "Viron."

"Ouch, prickly, aren't we?" I can't decide if she means me or the xoking root. I grunt again, scoop roots out of the tray with a spoon and dump them on a plate that I shove her way.

"Thank you, Krisxox," she tells me in her human tongue, for this gratitude is something they express more easily than we do.

She takes her plate to the low island behind me and pulls out a string of herbs I know she likes. She chops them using the smallest stalyx knife I have. It's still way too big for her, and I glance at her periodically, hating that I'm impressed by the way she wields it. There's a disturbing fluidity in her movements. I train warriors to have such grace. *Most don't come close to Svera.* I growl aloud. *To it.* To it.

I eat at the island standing across from her and I accept the herbs she's chopped for me. Does she know I don't care for the taste? How could she? I eat them every time she offers them. I like the idea that she wishes to feed me.

"You're welcome," she says, when I don't say anything at all.

It's tradition for us, at this point.

She has a small cushion she sits on every morning to eat, pressed right up against one of the walls. The one with the largest window. She didn't like all the windows at first, until she realized that the sleeping quarters are insulated and that even if they weren't, there's no one up here with us.

All of the homes sit elevated among the trees and among the clouds when they drop low. The village where I train the xcleranx is a short journey away, but the next village is a half span from that. Qath's many markets are chaotic, but here in my home, Qath almost seems like a quiet place. It's why I like it. Even if it's no longer quite so quiet.

She starts to hum. A melody so delicate and beautiful it hurts. Like sunshine through Qath's dense canopy of leaves, it touches me gently, in a way that makes me want to tilt my face up to the light.

My stomach twists. The flavors that were bursting in my mouth a moment ago turn to ash all at once. *Nox. Nox nox nox.* The *pressure*. It rushes up from my stomach and presses down from my throat. *Nox.* I scrape my wooden spoon across my plate loudly and choke down whatever's left. *Who gives a xok?* Just so long as the pressure…just…just *dies!* I've had enough.

I return to my room, pull on my training armor and attach a fusion ion gun and stalyx sword to my belt. I ordinarily would never walk through Qath armed, but these solars, things are different. I don't know why. *I do know why. Now, I have more to protect.* But only because I agreed to keep the filthy human alive. If it were not that vow I made to the Raku, I wouldn't care at all.

Right. I would have just let Nondah…

I stagger into the living area. *It* has moved into the cooking pit and is washing up both her own dishes and the ones I used. I've told her she doesn't need to do this many times, but the fool doesn't listen.

I open my mouth to tell her as much, but that's when it occurs to me. Where is her incessant chatter? Her relentless questions about all things Voraxian and Drakesh? Her pointing at things and asking me how to say them in Voraxian? Constantly asking for my help to improve her accent?

I step up to the edge of the pit, but don't take the few stairs to descend into it. I just watch her with my arms crossed, my jaw ticking, wanting desperately to know what in the xok is wrong with her, but wanting equally to just keep going and accept her silence as a win. I hate when she talks to me. I hate it when she doesn't.

"What's wrong with you?" I blurt out. *Xok me.*

Svera turns. In her long, graceful fingers, she dries a plate. Setting it down in a stack with the others, she smiles. "Don't you know?"

Xok. If I'd known I wouldn't have started this xoking conversation. I shake my head.

"We leave today."

We do? I don't acknowledge her, but my hand twitches towards my life drive. Perhaps there was some important directive I'd missed.

Svera rolls her eyes just a little and I panic when they twinkle. *It's pretty.* "She's giving birth in two solars. We leave this lunar to Voraxia. I'm going to the market one last time before we board our transporter. I'd like to get Miari…" Her eyes widen and she shakes her head quickly.

No matter how much time she, or any of the humans, spend with us, they all falter over our use of titles. They find it strange when one title is transferred to another, when titles change depending on the planet, when titles stack, when xub titles are taken… They always slip into the habit of calling one another by their slave names — the ones we each receive from our sires. These names matter so little, I sometimes forget I ever had one, but other times…other times, I wonder what it would sound like for her to call me by mine…

"I mean I'd like to get the *Rakukanna* a few gifts from the market and some other things I promised her. I've asked Tur'Roth to take me. He'll be here any moment. He'll bring me to the training grounds afterwards and you and I can go home together to pack our things. Does that sound acceptable?"

Nox. Nox, nox, nox. None of it does.

She is going to the market. She is coming to the training grounds. She is going with *him*. She calls this place home. She says us. And yet, I can't. say. anything.

I told her that she could have a protector in my absence even though *protector* is a generous term. Tur'Roth is barely a xoking warrior. So weak.

He's a Voraxian and though he's not Drakesh he's still pureblood. The way *he pursues her*. A pureblood Voraxian pursues one of these…alien things. He disgusts me. And since she disgusts me equally, it should be fine that he follows her around like a pup to a teat. But that she *likes* that he follows her… I don't like them together.

I don't nod. I don't even move. I just watch her smile and put away the dishes she and I both used. I hate that she cleans up after me like a servant while wearing a petulant little smile.

"I'm going to get ready now. I need to gather some supplies. I have things I specifically want included in my gift to the Rakukanna. Are there any things you'd like for the Raku?"

"What for?" I snap.

She gives me that look again — the one that says that everything is obvious and that I'm a xoking fool —

then says slowly, "They are having a baby. And they are having the first hybrid human-Voraxian baby born in this new era. Post-Hunt. It's an exciting thing. A beautiful one. Mashallah."

She makes a four-pointed figure across her chest, one gesture at either shoulder, one to her forehead, then one to her belly button. I don't understand it, but I've learned that it's a symbol of her Tri-God. *So many strange things she gives to him...and I'm jealous of them all.*

I grunt and watch her finish cleaning up, tracking her wherever she moves. I wish I didn't, but even when my life drive beeps with messages, all I want to do is watch her.

"Perfect timing," she says abruptly. "He's here. I'll see you at the setting of the first sun?"

I look away from her and nod.

"See you later, Krisxox. Have a beautiful solar."

She waves at me. I don't give in to the urge to respond and too soon, the door to my home slides open and shut and she leaves and the pressure in my chest swells like a wave, urging me to rush after her and drown her in my monsoon *and perhaps slay Tur'Roth in the process.*

I nearly rip the door off of the frame as I watch her go. Watch her cross the rope bridge. Watch the disgusting xcleranx Tur'Roth cross to meet her on an adjacent one. He bows and extends his hand. Svera grins. I can see it from here. She bows and offers him her delicate fingers. They touch.

I hallucinate a thousand ways to butcher him.

He has no right to touch her. She's *mine. Nox. She's too disgusting to be mine. I'm pure Drakesh and from an ancient line. What would my sires think seeing me with an animal like her?*

So, I don't stop her. And I don't slaughter him. I stand there and flay myself alive as I watch them exchange words. He says something to make her laugh and that sound xoking *wrecks* me. And when they finally take the rope bridge leading to the market square suspended among the xribar treetops and disappear among the foliage I feel…nothing.

The swirling, churning rage and fury and disgust and revulsion and bitter, tormented happiness I feel whenever she's near me is gone. Hollowness numbs out into an even greater hollowness.

My ridges betray a multitude of colors I can see reflected against the walls of my home. They're darker than they should be, filled with an urgency to follow her that I can will away in my body and mind, but not in the dark, lost chasm of my soul.

4

Svera

My bags are full and weighted with the gifts I've prepared for Miari. I can't believe the day has finally come! I can't remember *ever* being so excited. No Christmas celebration with my family and the other worshippers of the Tri-God on the human moon colony, no Yom Kippur, no Eid or Iftar has ever left me with such anticipation.

I find myself bouncing on the balls of my feet with every step, the rope bridges swaying a little more precariously than usual as I do. I just want to board *now*, get on that transporter and return to the human colony on Cxrian's moon.

I'm a little nervous to return, too, after so much time has passed. Now that I've taken on so much more responsibility as not just Miari's advisor, but Voraxia's advisor on *all* things human, it's left me feeling a little strange about my relationship with the humans and especially, the Antikythera Council that leads them. It'll be good to communicate with Mathilda and the other Council members face-to-face to hopefully alleviate some of the tension.

To prepare, but also to help distract me, Tur'Roth joins me as we weave through the labyrinthine markets of Qath.

Stalls bearing beautiful, colorful blocks of fabric followed by vibrant spices in a dozen different shades unfurl before me. We eventually pass the foods and deserts — all of which I've tried, for better and certainly for the worse — and then end in clothing and technology. Each of these stalls is suspended among the trees. Rope bridges connect all of them.

I look over the wooden railings as often as I can. The world here is beautiful. The sturdy trunks and branches of the green-leafed xribar trees allow for the world of Qath to thrive despite the dangers lurking on the planet's surface.

Rope bridges connect tree-based structures that house all manner of trading stall, restaurants, manufacturing units, and homes. Occasionally, the bridges do break and those that fall to the ground are rescued as quickly as possible... Other times, beings fall from the rope bridges and go unnoticed... Then, they have to fight.

The creatures of Qath are large, scary, and remind me of the stories Miari and Kiki told of the eight-armed beasts who live on our moon colony. I'm grateful for the attention of Tur'Roth. As one of Voraxia's principal warriors — a xcleranx — following me around should be beneath his rank, but he seems happy to do it. And I'm happy to have him.

"Do you need help carrying anything?" He asks.

He blinks his large, black eyes and I smile, again having to guess at his emotions by the muted colors of his ridges. They are a pale blue at the moment. Blue is typical of contentment.

"Nox. Thank you though, Tur'Roth."

He nods again and looks forward, helping me navigate a path among the many rope bridges and landings until we eventually arrive at Qath's training grounds. One of the few places that touches Qath's soil, the training grounds span a considerable portion of land. Here, the earth is dense and packed and the trees form a protective perimeter around the vast space, at least a thousand paces long.

I climb down the ladder, lower my packages with the surprisingly simple pulley system, and turn to face the open square with Tur'Roth by my side. My breath shortens, as it does every time.

The warriors of Qath are an impressive thing to behold. Spread out in a grid formation, each warrior is exactly the same distance from the warriors surrounding him — or her, though there are quite a few more males here than females. This lack is another thing I mean to speak with Krisxox about, though I'm certain he won't change his admittance policy on my account. Or even consider it. In fact, I think with a frown, my intervention could make the situation *worse* for the female warriors looking to be trained by him. I will just need to find more inventive means of tricking him into doing it. Maybe, I could suggest that there are *too many* females training under him. *Surely, he'd admit a dozen more immediately if I did that,* I think and laugh under my breath.

More than sixty warriors train under Krisxox's tutelage at a time. Each of them currently holds a large, bow-shaped weapon with outward-facing spikes. *Like*

Niahhorru spines… I shudder at the memories, and subtly make the sign of the Tri-God across my chest before forcing all thoughts of the Niahhorru back to the depths where they have no life.

"What is this weapon called?" I ask Tur'Roth in Voraxian as we approach the arena-style bench seats that span the full length of the training ground. They are often full and this solar is no exception.

From where we sit, Krisxox's back is to us while his trainees face us. They mimic his motions as he makes them, though none come close to his brutal elegance.

I've seen Krisxox fight many times now and it's a mesmerizing thing, belying an endurance, a calm, and a stoicism that his attitude towards me does not.

"That is an erdpremor."

"Erdpremor," I repeat, tilting my head. "A star sling?"

Tur'Roth laughs lightly and leans in towards me conspiratorially. His scent is like fresh straw and a deeper, heartier musk. It's attractive and so is he, with his jet black hair in tribute to his proud, Voraxian heritage, and his pure purple eyes, which are without pupil or iris.

"A star *saw*," he corrects and I warm.

"Ah. That does make more sense," I say quickly. I wrinkle my nose.

"You don't need to be embarrassed."

His dark grey-blue lips quirk. He has undoubtedly spent enough time around me to recognize my blush and its meaning, which naturally only makes me blush harder.

"Your Voraxian is very good."

"Thank you. And thank you for helping me learn."

I grip the glossy, dark wooden bench beneath me to keep myself from leaning back when Tur'Roth leans in even closer. *I hate it when he does this…*

"I'm happy to help you with anything you need."

He strokes the backs of his fingers down my cheek and, so subtly as to almost seem unintentional, over my bottom lip.

With a forced smile, I take his wrist and place his hand back in his lap where I give it a gentle squeeze.

"Tur'Roth, we've talked about this. Whatever feud exists between the two of you, you don't constantly need to exacerbate it."

He at least has the decency to look contrite. "Apologies. I just don't think it's fair that I should be denied the right to touch you simply because it pisses him off. Though you have to admit, it is fun pissing him off a little bit, isn't it?" He winks at me and I can't help but choke back a grin of my own.

"While that may be true…" And it is, though I'd never openly admit to it… "It is highly disruptive and with the Rakukanna and Raku so preoccupied, I don't need this devolving into an excuse for Krisxox to strike you." Which he has already, more than once.

"I don't mind being struck if it's for such a worthwhile cause," he says and my belly tightens or flutters or churns. I'm never really sure which, when he says these things to me. Part of me adores the attention. The other part of me worries that his attentions are bestowed for all the wrong reasons.

"I'd rather not see it."

He takes my hand in a gentle, platonic grip. "I'm sorry. I forget you are a sensitive female."

My lips quirk at that. Sensitive, or weak? I don't like that in the Voraxian culture, there doesn't seem to be much of a difference. I know how Krisxox sees me.

I nod and force a smile, returning my gaze to the training ground as Krisxox's tone picks up along with the pace of the warriors' next movements.

He stands elevated from the others, positioned in a spotlight. At least, that's how it looks with the way the sunlight filters down, illuminating the dark orange-red of his skin. It contrasts violently against the bright white of his hair. He has it tied up in a bun on the top of his head, but strands still break free of the knot and stick to his skin in sweat.

I swallow as I watch him move. If Tur'Roth is an attractive male, then Krisxox is a *very* attractive male. He is almost all muscle, yet he moves with the sinewy silence of a snake. Elegance. Grace. Words I would never have though to describe him, once. Now, I can't think of anything else.

He lowers into a crouch and his hide pants stretch taut around his rear. I quickly divert my gaze, only for it to land on the muscles swimming across his back. I admire the way they catch the light when they shift and swell. A single droplet of sweat claims my attention next, winding slowly down his spine, catching the sunlight. *So impossibly slow…*until he moves.

He's here and there and then he's not. He's remarkably fast. The other warriors attempt to match his speed, but it almost seems as if time has two different tempos — one where the rest of the warriors and I live, and a second where Krisxox moves alone.

A moment of stillness and then he thrusts his weapon forward like he might a spear before ripping it down. The motion draws my attention to the scars winding across his body. He's covered in light, silvery ribbons, like xamxin rivers winding their way across a crowded map, but no scar stands out so prominently as the one Tur'Roth gave him.

My breath formed steaming clouds as I struggled to control my anger. I felt filled with fire, like a dragon of ancient Earth's lore. Then came the charged whip. The way it sang when it met Krisxox's bare flesh. I was angry with him yes, but I didn't think he deserved that.

Tur'Roth raised his weapon to deliver Krisxox another blow — this one unsanctioned — and I will never forget it. Frozen in my thoughts, as the world was frozen around me on Nobu's icy fields, it was the first moment I saw Tur'Roth as... someone else. And the way Krisxox bore the first stroke of the flail and then, despite having heard it, patiently waited for the next... I was angry, yes, but I found that there was also something noble in that.

I suck in a breath as I watch Krisxox repeat the same motion, drilling it into his recruits over and over. And I can't help the warmth that spreads through my belly as I do. Okay, *lower* than my belly. I press my knees together and squirm as I try and relax the tensing muscles high in my thighs, because squeezing them only makes the pressure *there* worse.

While I have no experience with males short of a few chaste kisses with human boys, I have always been...easy to excite. For many rotations, I was ashamed of my thoughts — far too ashamed to touch myself in the darkness of the lunar — but after openly confiding in my mother about my body and its treacherous ways, she convinced me otherwise.

Your body is a pure, natural vessel of the Tri-God. He would not have created you this way, if it was not his intent.

After that, I stopped feeling so self-conscious and I learned how to alleviate the pressure myself, but... among the Voraxians and Drakesh, some of that old shame has resurfaced because the aliens...they can smell it.

"Svera," Tur'Roth grunts. His teeth are clenched and the ridges along his brow are a fluttering jumble of blues and purples. *Lust. Purple is lust. The darker, the more demanding.*

"I'm so-sorry," I stutter, smoothing down my skirts and breaking his gaze.

His hand reaches out and touches my thigh, just above the knee. I jerk up to stand. "I will just go down to speak with..." I glance around frantically. "...the Evras below."

"Do you want me to come..."

"Nox." I laugh nervously. "Nox, it's alright. I'll just be a moment."

Tur'Roth gives me a conciliatory bow before pulling back and allowing me to slip past him. I don't look back at him as I descend the arena-style seats. I don't look up at Krisxox either.

My name is said by many of the Voraxians gathered. I greet them in return and doing so helps my head clear and the heat knotted in my belly. I know these beings all by name — or occupation, rather — and I know their families, their hobbies, what they like and even their hopes for Voraxia.

Taking a seat nestled among the Evras — those responsible for managing the food stores, including everything from harvest to import — I listen to them talk, enrapt, as I continue to keep my gaze focused and away from Krisxox as he lowers his star sling — star *saw* — and repeats new motions without a weapon.

Tel'Evra is in the middle of describing a new type of bean the Evras are trying to source from Quadrant Three when my life drive buzzes.

I glance down at the holographic image floating across my skin, like a constantly changing tattoo scribbled in letters that are as blocky as they are green. The message is from Lemoria. My heart stills. I flick open the holoscreen and view the full contents of her communication.

I leap out of my seat and have to catch myself on Tel'Evra's outstretched hand to stop myself from tumbling down onto the next bench as I shout, "The Rakukanna has gone into early labor!"

Natural labor. Her labor was meant to be induced on the coming solar from the safety of the moon colony's new medical facility, but something must have happened. *I hope it is a blessing. Not a miserable repeat of what happened to so many females who came before who lost their young ones, or even their lives.*

"Verax," Tel'Evra says, his lashless eyelids fluttering rapidly.

The younger male continues to grip my hand firmly as I stand up on the wooden bench beneath me and look up at the faces of so many Voraxians and Drakesh.

I find that most are already looking at me — the novelty of having a human among them has yet to fade for most, even after the half-rotation we have already shared together — and it does not take long to catch the attention of the rest.

With all eyes on me in swirling shades of purple and blue and black and orange and grey, I shout as loud as I can, "The Rakukanna has gone into labor! Voraxia will have it's Ra or Rakuka soon!"

A chorus of shocked murmurs gives way to cheers. Tur'Roth is clapping encouragingly and when I meet his gaze, he winks. My heart sings. I quickly hop down, stumbling a little in my long shift, but a heavy hand slides under my elbow and keeps me from falling onto my rear.

"Thank you," I say reflexively. Instinct leads me to believe it's Krisxox, but the scent is all wrong. Drakesh coloring and a warrior's uniform are all these two males have in common.

I start to retract my arm, but the male tightens his hold. He's smiling, but a flicker of black crosses his ridges that makes me tense.

"You must be thrilled that another bastard *oud* is going to be born into the world, just like your *Miari*," he sneers her name, meaning it as an insult. Though I don't share in this tradition of guarding names, I still hate that he knows it. "I hope she and the baby both drown in blood."

The chatter and chaos rise around us, but I still pitch my voice low and even and say, "You would do well to release my arm, warrior. Both the xcleranx

Tur'Roth and Krisxox himself are tasked with my care…"

But he only grips me tighter and pulls me further under the umbrella of his heat. I grunt and my heart throws out bolts of lightning as I remember being handled much more roughly than this on board that ancient Niahhorru ship. My lashes flutter. I see the dark carcass of a Niahhorru pirate with each blink.

"Krisxox is the best of us. If he doesn't kill you outright it's only because he's doing his duty, but he won't stand in our way. And that spineless Voraxian, Tur'Roth?" The horrible male balks, "He's hardly going to be enough."

I rip my arm down, but he's already let me go. The momentum sends me stumbling backwards, straight into Tel'Evra.

"Are you alright?" He says, then immediately, "That is such wonderful news! I cannot wait to meet the little one when our Raku and Rakukanna are able to tour. You will have to send us images before then. Will you promise?"

It takes me a moment to remember where I am and what words I need to say and in which tongue. In the time it takes for my mind to catch up to me, I glance back to where the male had been, but he's gone, replaced by congregating bodies that are laughing and smiling.

"Advisor Svera?" Tel'Evra says.

I start. "Oh um…"

"Do you promise?"

"Images. Images of the baby. Of course. I'll send through as many as I am able. Under the directives of the Raku and Rakukanna, of course."

"Oh! Of course. Of course," he repeats, bowing to me again and again. "Did you hear that, Er'Evra? Advisor Svera will send us the first holo images of the new kit…"

He's already turning away from me when I'm pulled around by more voices. The next, Tur'Roth's.

"I saw Vendra speaking to you. Are you alright?"

He caresses my cheek intimately as he scans my face and body. It's touching, his care…*but it doesn't make my pulse quicken or the breath in my lungs catch. It doesn't make me heat between the thighs. It doesn't make me wet.*

"Thank you," I say, feeling stupid as that's not an answer to the question I was asked. "I mean, I'm alright." Physically, anyway. But that threat. There was something wholly sinister about it and, while I've gotten my fair share of glares and grimaces, none have been so bold as to threaten me like that. Not with such *hatred*.

"Good, I…" Tur'Roth's gaze pans past me and his expression falls. His shoulders square and his hands drop to form six-fingered fists. The surrounding talk quiets and the fuzzies on the back of my neck stand on end. And even if the cumulation of these things was not enough for me to know that we've been interrupted, it would be given away by his scent.

He smells like citrus fruit. Tangy and acidic with just enough sweetness to make it bearable. It's a smell I find myself thinking of late in the lunar and even a scent that I sometimes, daringly, touch myself to…

It affects me more than it should. More than I appreciate in this moment. The clenching of my stomach has become a sharp pang, the ringing of a gong whose ripples feel almost as powerful as the first touch.

"Krisxox," I say, voice too high to be mine.

I clear my throat and look away from his face, which is wreathed in an anger that most Voraxians are well-schooled not to show. Unfortunately, that leaves me eye-level with his ribs, or rather, the plates that are layered like rough cuts of wood on top of them and protect his vital organs.

He's still dripping sweat. Well, glistening really. And the smell of it…citrus and burnt sugar…I inhale a little deeper. I never thought that male sweat could smell so clean or so oddly sweet.

A small thimble of sharp, hot pressure spears my clitoris, like it's been flicked roughly with a callused thumb.

I straighten and meet his gaze and try not to breathe as I blurt, "Did you hear the news?"

"Everyone in xoking Qath heard the news. What were you thinking, announcing it like that?"

Tender wisps of white hair cling to his cheeks. They're hollow, framed by a stern jawline and high cheek bones. His dark vermillion lips are full. He's staring down at me with his enormous screa eyes. His nostrils are flaring. He looks ready to devour and in that moment, I feel ready to be devoured…

And then I register his words.

I spit, "I was thinking that it would be an excellent occasion for the people of Qath to celebrate their federation's newest member. What is happening now is the most significant event in the history of Voraxia since the dissolution of Cxrian's empire and the Drakesh absorption into the Voraxian federation. If you cannot see that, then you're blind."

"I can see it, human." He growls and ducks his head, patronizing me in that way he knows I hate. He crosses his arms and licks his dark red lips. "But it's not a moment worth celebrating."

I tense. I wish I didn't let him rile me like this, but he is either intentionally trying to hurt my feelings or he genuinely believes what he just said. The latter is a worse scenario than the former, but both hurt.

I decide then that Krisxox must have been placed in my path by the Tri-God's own hand in order to test my faith. Not in the Tri-God, of course, but in myself. In me. Can I endure him?

I close my eyes and exhale through my mouth. I count to three. *One. The weight of the sun pressing down on me from through the canopy. Two. The sound of the faraway rope bridges swinging as vendors and shoppers swarm the rowdy market. Three. Cold citrus drink on a hot sunny solar. The smell of Krisxox's skin.* I open my eyes. *Release.*

"I am very disappointed that you feel this way."

A muscle in his neck spasms and his whole head twitches. I'm under his skin, just as he's under mine. This is a battle between us, our every interaction. I lose often, but not as often as he does.

The Tri-God does not place rivers before us too wide to cross.

"You're disrupting my xoking training. Look at this. It's chaos." He isn't wrong.

Only about half of his warriors are in their original grid formation. Perhaps less. I don't care though. This isn't a day for training. This is a day for celebration, inshallah, and I refuse to let him ruin that.

"It's perfect timing to leave, then. Wouldn't you agree? Training looks like it's over."

"Why the xok would I leave now?"

"I thought you said you heard me, Krisxox. The Rakukanna has gone into labor. We need to travel *now*, not this lunar as originally planned."

"We leave when I say we leave and I'm not letting some filthy hybrid ruin this training session or any other. You need to sit back down and shut up and wait until I tell you otherwise."

The insults I could stomach — at least that's what I tell myself — but the callous, listless way he speaks about Miari and the Raku's baby?

I want to scratch and claw and bite. I want to enter his arena and wage a war I know I'm unlikely to win… but that I *might*.

Words rile within me and I spit out the first ones that come, without thinking. "You are a foul, ruined thing and I *hate* you," I snarl and in this moment I mean it even though I've never hated anything.

He freezes. Even the strands of his hair, once caught in a breeze, seem to still. He narrows his gaze and red rolls across his ridges.

"Krisxox, settle down," Tur'Roth grits out at my back.

Krisxox is breathing hard now, shoulders lifting and sagging with each breath. Ignoring Tur'Roth, he leans even closer to me and that scent…that cruel scent. It plays tricks with my body that my mind is too weak to fight. I break. Wetness surges past my underwear and drips down the seam of my clenched thighs.

Krisxox's mouth opens. His hands flinch for me and he seems to be fighting a losing battle, too, because he brings himself even closer. My chest is one deep inhalation away from brushing his. I stare straight up at him. Purple flashes in his brow and he chokes and the sound is not full of malice, as I'd hoped, but thick with male desperation.

I quickly turn away from it. Krisxox *cannot* think that the arousal pooling in my core is for him. He *cannot* be rewarded for his degrading and demeaning behavior. I have to get myself out of this because if he comes any closer, I might *give in*...so, I do the first and only thing I can think to do.

I turn around, reach for Tur'Roth, raise myself up on my tiptoes and brush a kiss across his cheek. At least, that was my intention. But Tur'Roth turns and captures my mouth with his.

Continue reading in ebook or hardback on Amazon and in paperback anywhere online books are sold

All Books by Elizabeth

Xiveri Mates: SciFi Alien and Shifter Romance
Taken to Voraxia, Book 1 (Miari and Raku)
Taken to Nobu, Book 2 (Kiki and Va'Raku)
Taken to Sasor, Book 3 (Mian and Neheyuu) *standalone
Taken to Heimo, Book 4 (Svera and Krisxox)
Taken to Kor, Book 5 (Deena and Rhork)
Taken to Lemora, Book 6 (Essmira and Raingar)
Taken by the Pikosa Warlord, Book 7 (Halima and Ero) *standalone
Taken to Evernor, Book 8 (Nalia and Herannathon)
Taken to Sky, Book 9 (Ashmara and Jerrock)
Taken to Revatu, A Xiveri Mates Novella (Jewel and Gorak)

Population: Post-Apocalyptic SciFi Romance
Population, Book 1 (Abel and Kane)
Saltlands, Book 2 (Abel and Kane)
Generation One, Book 3 (Diego and Pia)
Brianna, Book 4 (Lahve and Candy)
more to come!

Brothers: Interracial Dark Mafia Romantic Suspense
The Hunting Town, Book 1 (Knox and Mer, Dixon and Sara)
The Hunted Rise, Book 2 (Aiden and Alina, Gavriil and Ify)
The Hunt, Book 3 (Anatoly and Candy, Charlie and Molly)

Made in the USA
Columbia, SC
30 December 2021

53053427R00245